THE MUSEUM AT THE END OF THE WORLD

THE MUSEUM AT THE END OF THE WORLD

John Metcalf

BIBLIOASIS
windsor, ontario

FIRST EDITION

Library and Archives Canada Cataloguing in Publication

Metcalf, John, 1938-, author
The museum at the end of the world / John Metcalf.

Short Stories
Issued in print and electronic formats.
ISBN 978-1-77196-162-2 (bound)
ISBN 978-1-77196-107-3 (paperback).--ISBN 978-1-77196-108-0 (ebook)

I. Title.

PS8576.E83M88 2016 C813'.54 C2016-901846-6
C2016-901847-4

Edited by Daniel Wells
Copy-edited by Emily Donaldson
Typeset by Chris Andrechek
Cover design by David Drummond

Published with the generous assistance of the Canada Council for the Arts and the Ontario Arts Council. Biblioasis also acknowledges the support of the Government of Canada through the Canada Book Fund and the Government of Ontario through the Ontario Book Publishing Tax Credit.

PRINTED AND BOUND IN CANADA

Myrna's

Who would have thought my shrivelled heart
Could have recovered greenness? It was gone
Quite underground; as flowers depart
To see their mother-root, when they have blown;
Where they together
All the hard weather,
Dead to the world, keep house unknown.

...

And now in age I bud again;
After so many deaths I live and write;
I once more smell the dew and rain,
And relish versing. Oh, my only light,
It cannot be
That I am he
On whom thy tempests fell all night.

(Stanzas from "The Flower."
George Herbert, 1633.)

MEDALS AND PRIZES

Where the Yazoo Cross the Yellow Dog

Jimbo Palmer and Rob Forde were both fourteen, with Jimbo some months older than Rob. Jimbo's mother was warm and friendly but ineffectual. She remonstrated by saying in a trailing-off voice, *Now, James*... or *Really, James*... She made nice sandwiches. Jimbo was quite fond of her but said that he'd only give it two or three more years before they carted her off to the loony bin. She washed things a lot in the washing machine and her blonde hair clung darkened to her face but she was still elegant and she often smelled of TCP and her high cheekbones gave her a gaunt beauty, and, though mad, had, Rob thought, distinct sexual possibilities. Had it not been for, being realistic about it, had it not been for her evangelical fervour, the spirit moving in her to request casual callers, the grocer's boy, the postman with a parcel, to kneel with her in prayer.

Jimbo's stepfather, a retired army officer, was older than Jimbo's mother, a bristly, abrupt, bark-y man, uncommunicative, wrapped in a silence that spread uncomfortableness around him. He had a smudge moustache and kept a Webley revolver and a box of bullets in his socks-and-underwear drawer. When not wearing a regimental tie, he affected a foulard.

The Major's breakfast never varied, a three-and-three-quarter minute boiled egg served in a brightly coloured egg cup shaped like a cockerel, a slice of Hovis toast with unsalted butter accompanied by a small cut-glass dish of jam he sometimes called "preserve" and sometimes *confiture*. The cut-glass dish sat on a miniature silver salver-thing on which also lay a special silver spoon, smaller than a teaspoon, for spooning up a dollop of jam onto the Major's plate but why he couldn't just—

"I view hot toast," he said, in one of his rare communications, pointing to the solitary Hovis slice lodged cold in the silver toast-rack, "as offensively American".

He had once lowered the pink barricade of the *Financial Times* and tapped his wristwatch's leather strap and said, "Camel."

After breakfast, he and his attaché case departed for the City.

Jimbo referred to him as Double-U or Dub, short for Wind-Up Man. In their flights of invention, their badinage, their cherished embroideries, the Key in the centre of the Major's back had a milled shaft…

…No, no, not *milled,* you total ape…

…baboon's arse…

it's knurled, smegma, *knurled*…

They shared their pleasures in his peculiarities while in his presence by rubbing thumb over forefinger in a gesture of watch-winding. Both boys thought of him as an escapee from *The Goon Show,* an avatar of Major Bloodnock. *No more curried eggs for me!* they cried, *Quick, Nurse!* they called, *The screens!*

Jimbo had worked out from the hallmarks—he had a handbook of them—that the toast-rack had been made in London in 1921; he was interested in such things and his interest was expanding into Sheffield Plate, pewter, and Britannia Metal. He had found a loupe in a junk shop.

"*You* say, 'I wonder when it dates from?' and *I'll* say, 'Pass me my loupe.'"

The Major had had Jimbo sent away when he was twelve, before he and Rob had met, to a military-flavoured boarding school to cure what he called Jimbo's softness; Jimbo had overheard "mummy's boy" and "lack of manliness" and the weeping. He had been expelled after the first term and said only that the letter had described him as "a malign influence." What he had been expected to learn was uninteresting and the people had been utterly preposterous.

"Utterly," he repeated.

"But what did you *do* that was malignant?"

They loved the word.

"I committed infractions," said Jimbo, "and showed no remorse."

"What infractions?"

"Mainly, I fomented."

"What's that mean?"

"O.E.D." said Jimbo, tapping his finger three times on the table. "The S.O.E.D. old chap, old boy, old sport, old fellow-my-lad. What? What?"

The Major's decanters were kept on the sideboard in the dining room in a mahogany-and-brass cage-thing. The decanters, visible inside the spindles, had silver chains round their necks from which hung little oval silver plaques: Whisky, Sherry, Brandy, Gin.

"It prevents theft by the servants," the Major had once remarked as he was unlocking it.

"We haven't got any servants," said Jimbo.

"What?" said the Major. "What?"

Which was his usual response to any reply short of complete agreement or grovelling.

"I said," said Jimbo, "we haven't got—"

"Don't say 'haven't got,'" said the Major. "It is both redundant and ill-bred. 'Haven't' will suffice."

"Righto," said Jimbo.

Rather dangerously, Rob thought.

"This is Victorian. A valuable antique," said the Major, putting the little brass key back in his pocket.

"Called?"

He stared enquiry at them.

"Mmmm?"

Rob and Jimbo looked at each other.

"No?" said the Major.

Jimbo shrugged.

"A tantalus. Called a tantalus."

His eyes began to wander as if seeking a way out of this unwonted intimacy.

"Remember that," he repeated. "Tantalus."

Did the raspy-thing with his thumbnail against his moustache.

"It will stand you in good stead."

*

In that summer of their fourteenth year, Jimbo was hankering after a languorous smoking jacket; it was the contrasting lapels that so seduced him. He realized that he was too young to wear one but vowed that when he had escaped to Oxford it would be one of the first things he would acquire after he had secured a print by John Piper he'd long desired, a print, in reds and black, of the edge of a church façade and tombstones, some aslant.

Rob dreamed and luxuriated in the fantasy of an amiable father taking him to a Paris *maison de passe,* red plush, divans, mirrors, gilt, where the *madame* put him in the hands of a lissome... but glum thought his *real* father, remote in his black dickie with its white attached clerical collar, the Sunday Geneva bands, the dickie looking in certain lights as if it were turning dull green with age.

He was reading Huysman's *A Rebours* and not at all sure what to make of it. Though he particularly liked the tortoise.

In that summer of their fourteenth year, they rootled in junk shops for amber cigarette holders and cigarette cases for their cigarillos and cheroots. Jimbo insisted that kitchen matches were simply classier than Ronson lighters. "*Swan Vestas.* The *feel* of wooden matches," he said. "*Inhale* that sulphur!"

They stockpiled *Skira* art books—Klee, Mondrian, Picasso, Toulouse-Lautrec, Miro. Touching the *Skira* covers with his fingertips, "buckram" whispered Jimbo, "buckram." They devoured *Faber and Faber* monographs on Paul Nash, Ivon Hitchens, Stanley Spencer, and Walter Sickert. Rob found a book of George Grosz drawings called *Ecce Homo* to which he returned again and again without knowing quite why.

In that summer of their fourteenth year, when Jimbo's mother and stepfather had gone away for two days to visit "Maid" Marian, his stepfather's vinegary, spinster sister, "barren" Jimbo said, her house astringent with furniture polish and ammonia, "every surface *frothing* with crinoline figurines," they shot the rear wall of the wooden toolshed at the bottom of the long garden six times with the Major's Webley and rubbed over the startling scars with mud.

In that summer of their fourteenth year they encountered Theresa.

Theresa was Carol's penfriend from Yugoslavia. Carol worked at the record shop on Saturdays and Theresa came over that summer for a holiday. She was quite beautiful and her English was beautifully broken. Both Rob and Jimbo were attracted. They bumped into the two girls one day in the High Street and Theresa was wearing a singlet-thing that sometimes revealed her armpits. In these armpits were tufts of brown hair. Rob was both attracted by these glimpses and not attracted; he had never seen such a thing before; it made him uneasy. Jimbo said that he'd like to put his mouth to her armpit, enclose all the hair, and suck it slowly, sweat and all. It was this decisive and shining imagination in Jimbo that Rob adored.

But Jimbo's most lasting gift to Rob was jazz.

It all started, rather ridiculously, with a chance record by a cheerful, foot-tappy band called Bob Crosby and the Bobcats. It was the first jazz record they had heard. In later years, Rob was unable to remember how the record had come to Jimbo. Possibly through Carol. Nor could he remember what two tunes it played. This was a 78 rpm acetate record in a plain brown paper sleeve. He seemed vaguely to remember up-tempo vulgarity, trombone rasps, circus noise, *Tiger Rag* possibly? And what company pressed it? *Brunswick? London? Victor? Decca? Vocalion?* All he really remembered in later years was that the label at the record's centre was black, the printing gold.

Being the boys they were, but wished to become, they were soon swept up into the traditional jazz revival.

Jimbo had said one day, "The art school people at the record shop, they're always talking about people we don't know about."

The art school students were that much older so the boys couldn't talk to them and the girls were haughty but the boys admired them from a distance. The students were a connection of a sort to a world the boys longed to enter, the *Skira* world, the world of the *Faber* monographs, worlds far distant from the world of privet hedges and mown lawns. The boys sat near the students in the café two doors down from the record shop, the café with an espresso machine that was crowned by an eagle in gold. They took note of the titles of books the students dumped on tables: *The Outsider, The Theory of the Leisure Class, Slan* by A.E. Van Vogt, *Foundation* by Isaac Asimov, *The Fountainhead.*

They agreed that they *sort of* liked Amos Tutuola's *The Palm-Wine Drinkard.*

The new young woman at the Public Library procured these titles for them; she was friendly and chatted with them and had, Rob thought, distinct sexual possibilities.

"You know," whispered Jimbo, "this," covert gesture towards the table of students, "might just be *it.*"

"What? What might be what?"

"What they're talking about."

They eavesdropped.

Their heads soon began to fill with dreamed-of destinations, Chicago, New York, St. Louis, New Orleans, cities inhabited by fabulous personages, Kids, Earls, Dukes, Counts, and Kings.

They overheard the students talking: Buddy Bolden, Freddie Keppard and the Olympia Band, King Oliver's Creole Jazz Band, Kid Ory, the New Orleans Rhythm Kings ...

They overheard: Louis Armstrong's Hot Five, Louis Armstrong's Hot Seven, Jelly Roll Morton's Red Hot Peppers ...

They overheard: Chicago: the Royal Garden Café, Earl Hines, the Lincoln Gardens Dance Hall, Bessie Smith, Zutty Singleton, Baby Dodds, Ma Rainey, Oran "Hot lips" Page ...

They overheard: Savoy Ballroom Five, Bertha "Chippie" Hill, Sidney Bechet, Jack Teagarden, George Mitchell, Bubber Miley, Ward Pinkett, Bunk Johnson …

And then they found the music.

And were ravished.

The school terms ground on, a ludicrous background to their new passion. History unreeled: the Tudors, the Stuarts, the Hanoverians, Sir Robert Walpole, Farmer George, the loss of the Colonies, Whig, Tory, the Spinning Jenny, Manchester, rotten boroughs, the French Revolution, Nelson, Napoleon, the Tolpuddle Martyrs. Rob's history teacher had a single false upper incisor on a plate, which he jiggled out with his tongue and extruded onto his lower lip; it sat there while he listened to halting recapitulations.

They listened to Freddie Keppard playing *Stock Yards Strut* and *Salty Dog*. They were enraptured by the King Oliver recordings for *Gennett* in April 1923, *Canal Street Blues, Snake Rag,* Oliver's famous three-chorus solo on *Dippermouth Blues,* Louis Armstrong's playing on second cornet in *Chimes Blues,* Armstrong's plaintive, subtle phrasing behind the majesty of Bessie Smith.

They read and reread the few works of jazz hagiography that existed—*Shining Trumpets* by Rudi Blesh, *Mr. Jelly Roll* by Alan Lomax, whatever scraps of information were provided by the *Melody Maker.*

They absorbed arcane knowledge.

That Kid Ory was born in La Place, Louisiana.

That Bessie Smith's husband's name was Jack Gee.

That Bunk Johnson was re-discovered in the Parish of New Iberia, Lousiana.

The American language ravished them, *bills, ten-spots, nickels and dimes, grits and collard greens, reefers, vipers* … That Bunk Johnson made his comeback when two young musicologists, Fred Ramsay and Bill Russell, procured him "store-bought teeth."

Store-bought!

That Jelly Roll Morton was named, in early documents, Ferdinand La Menthe; that the family name was La Mothe; that he was baptized Lemott but took the name Morton from a stepfather whose name was actually Mouton.

That Morton's *nom de guerre* meant "womaniser."

jelly roll n. (US Black) [late 19c. +] a lover. [Standard Am. Eng., a doughnut, which has a hole at its centre.]

School offered them the Rhine, the Rhone, the Pripyat Marshes, steppe and taiga, loess, seas various: Caspian, Baltic, Beaufort, Azov, Dead, while in their heads and hearts sang Armstrong's revolutionary stop-time choruses in *Potato Head Blues,* the dramatic descents of *Gully Low Blues,* the cascading phrasing on *West End Blues, Hotter than That,* and *Big Butter and Egg Man;* in their heads and hearts sang what Jelly Roll called "the Spanish tinge," tango and Latin rhythms in *New Orleans Joys, The Crave, Mamamanita.* They took joy in what Morton called, in the Red Hot Pepper recordings, "the breaks," those two-bar suspensions of the beat in the *Victor* recordings of 1926-28, *Dead Man Blues, Black Bottom Stomp, The Pearls;* took reverential joy in the intense, almost unbearable beauty of *Smokehouse Blues* in the middle of which a jubilant, exultant Morton arrests his delicate solo and cries into the magical silence:

Oh!
Mister Jelly!

*

School ground onward. The approach of the Ordinary Level Examinations was causing hysteria in both households.

Study, they were urged, study. Rob's mother bought him Glucose Tablets from Boots the Chemist for energy. Jimbo discovered the word "frottage." Rob's French teacher was from Aberystwyth and both boys amused themselves by simple exchanges in a French inflected with the singsong rhythms of Welsh English. At the 10:15 a.m. recess, school milk was distributed and currant buns were available for purchase. Reading Victorian pornography, Rob discovered the word "gamahuche." Study, they were urged, study. Rob was beginning to tire of Jimbo's Oscar Wilde quotations. *Work,* Jimbo said, *is the curse of the drinking classes.*

For lack of conclusive evidence, the allegations against Jimbo in the matter of the conflagration in the metalwork shop were allowed to lapse; he maintained a posture of baffled silence; his Headmaster was brought to concede that we lived in an imperfect world in which certainty … certainty beyond even a shadow of doubt … the Major paid to replace the other boy's blazer and stricter standards of supervision in the annealing of copper were instituted.

"I turned," said Jimbo, "to answer a question while holding the roaring-thing and flame inadvertently played upon him."

Rob thought this deadpan explanation verged deliciously on dumb insolence.

All authority, said Jimbo, *is quite degrading. It degrades those who exercise it, and degrades those over whom it is exercised.*

Mr. Fontane, Rob's English teacher that year, was widely believed to be shellshocked; he wore a toupee and tortoiseshell glasses and sometimes forgot to remove his bicycle clips. One memorable morning he had jammed his foot into the metal wastepaper basket and stumped up and down the front of the classroom clanging and clanking in the silence and growling through clenched teeth and distorted jaw, *Well, sir! Well?*

He conducted daily exercises in dictation, speaking slowly and distinctly to the window pane, his breath fogging it; enunciating: *comma, colon,* blah blah, *semi-colon,* blah, blah, *exclamation mark, paragraph, period.* After the passage of dictation was concluded, the boys exchanged papers and compared the copies in front of them with the distributed copies of the mimeographed text. The sum of mistakes was then calculated: minus 1 for errors in punctuation, minus 2 for omissions, minus 3 for errors in spelling. This figure was subtracted from 20 and the total circled beneath the pupil's name and the papers again traded. The papers were then handed forward until they all reached the boys in the front desks and were then all gathered up by Mr. Fontane and secured under a spring clip in an immense binder. This activity took up nearly half the lesson's allotted time.

Dictation was followed by silent study of the mimeographed passage for précis, the actual writing of which was set daily for homework. When the bell rang and as the boys stood, gathered books, and began to file out, Mr. Fontane offered final nuggets, crying out almost gaily:

Non-restrictive clauses are our quarry!

On Friday evenings or Saturdays, the boys, pleading mental exhaustion and the need for restoration, started getting the train up to Victoria to lose themselves in the hot pleasures of the jam-packed club at 100 Oxford Street, home base of Humphrey Lyttleton and his band, though from time to time other bands took the stage: Mick Mulligan and his Magnolia Jazz Band with George Melly, Mike Daniels' Delta Band, Alex Welsh, Ken Colyer, Chris Barber with Ottilie Patterson.

Sometimes they went to *The Six Bells* in Chelsea to hear Alex Welsh, sometimes to *Pizza Express* in Dean Street. In sundry afternoon cafés with loud espresso machines and tired cheese rolls under plastic domes on the counter, the pale yellow rat-trap cheese sweating under wilted lettuce, they listened condescendingly to Lonnie Donegan's mongrel skiffle.

"Christ!" said Rob. "Thimbles! Washboards and *thimbles!*"

Art, said Jimbo, *should never try to be popular; the public should try to make itself artistic.*

"What do you think?" said Rob indicating the two girls on the banquette, girls pretending to ignore them, girls to whom Rob was too shy to speak but who had, he thought, distinct sexual possibilities.

"Non-évoluées," said Jimbo.

"Cuddly, though," said Rob.

Jimbo looked at him and then looked away.

The Rock Island line is the road to ride, said Rob.

Pointing to the sandwich domes on the counter, Jimbo said, *When I ask for a watercress sandwich, I do not mean a loaf with a field in the middle of it.*

*

The last train from Victoria rolled on through the night. Rob's carriage was empty except for the girl and a blue serge porter, his leather bag in the aisle, a red flag and a green flag on wooden handles lodged under the bag's flap. In the creaking silences, Rob pretended to study the diagram of the train's station stops while sneaking glances at the girl's reflection in the night window.

She was wearing a blue skirt and a white blouse, suede desert boots, an undone duffle coat, a ponytail held by an imitation red flower the size of a fist, he didn't know the name of them, autumn borders sort of thing, *dahlia* was the word in his mind.

The railway man settled his peaked cap on his lard-pale pate and got up to get out, nudging his flag bag along against his knee.

BRIXTON

A rush of cold air into the carriage.

On his way out of the club, Rob had picked up a crumpled *Melody Maker*. As he was flipping pages, glancing at the doings of the big dance bands, Jack Payne, Nat Gonella, Ray Noble, Jack Hylton, Lew Stone, photos of flossy-hair vocalists sheathed in sequins, the latest caterwaulers from Tin Pan Alley, Pops Parade, the crowning of Miss Musical Manchester, the girl said, "Were you at Uncle's?"

He looked up.

Said to the girl's reflection, "Pardon?"

Then turned towards her.

"Were you at Uncle Humphrey's?"

"Oh," he said. "Oh, yes. When you say 'Uncle', is he—"

"No," said the girl, "but he's uncle-*ish*. Bonhomous. Gives you a fiver when he visits, slips you a drink in the kitchen, looks down your blouse. He's always the same. You know what you're going to get."

"Well, he *does* wear brothel creepers," said Rob.

"Bonhomie," she said. "It makes me think of a man with a big gut and one of those watch-chains stretched over it."

"Old Humph?" He smiled. *"The Old Grey Mare—"*

"She Ain't What She Used To Be," said the girl and with finger and thumb shot him in approbation.

Then patted the seat beside her.

"Robert Forde," he said, "but usually it's Rob."

"My surname is Marks," she said, "and you can call me… Helena."

"Are you at school?"

"Yes," she said, "and, well, no. Sort of. And you? At school?"

"Sixth form," he said. "And you're…?"

"A-Levels. Sat three. Passed Religious Knowledge."

"What did you mean, yes and no?"

"Suspended at the moment," she said, "but shortly to be expelled."

She laughed and patted her head and rubbed her stomach simultaneously.

"Can you do that?"

Rob shook his head.

"My father's fighting it but I've got so far up Miss Henny-Penny's nose she hasn't much choice."

She laughed again.

"Dried-up old twat."

"But why do you want—" said Rob.

"Right to her face," said Helena with relish. "She's *got* to expel me. I called her dessicated to her face."

"Yes, but—"

"*Because*," said Helena, "I. Am. Going. To. New. York."

Shuffling noise underneath the carriage, in the wheels.

LOUGHBOROUGH JUNCTION

?

"New York," repeated Rob. "Doing what? I mean, if your father—"

"He doesn't know yet."

Rob looked at her.

"He adores me," she said, "I'm his little princess."

"Hmmm," said Rob, his mind made mushy by the warmth of her thigh.

"I've been accepted at Goldsmith's," she said.

"Goldsmith's? Sorry?"

"Ha!" she said. "Only *the* art school. Only the best in London."

"Oh," said Rob.

"Yes," she said, "and the Slade and Holborn—the Central School—they've seen my portfolio and I'm invited to apply for next term. Just to show him. Just to show him I can go anywhere. At the Central I could have Victor Passmore or Keith Vaughan."

Not having heard of either, Rob inclined his head doing a judicious, impressed face.

"And I expect I could get into the Beaux Arts in Paris. But you know what?"

"What?"

She blew a farty noise.

"Who *cares* about the Beaux Arts and the fucking Slade!"

She gripped his wrist and shook it.

"Henry Tonks is *dead!* Or hasn't anyone heard!"

She rolled the *Melody Maker* into a loud-hailer and shouted through it into the empty carriage

HENRY TONKS IS DEAD

HENRY TONKS IS DEAD

"The train left *that* station years ago. This," she dismissed the carriage, the train, the night's reflections in the windows, "this isn't the world. You know where the world is? The world isn't here. The world's not Paris. The world, Robert Forde, the world's New York. And that's where I'm going."

She batted the sheets of the *Melody Maker* with the back of her hand.

"Uncle Humphrey's just to fill in time until I can get there. And when I do, Robert Forde, when I do, it's Bird and Diz."

People, he presumed, this Bird and Diz, he had no idea what she was talking about, this dead Tonks, New York people he supposed, made note to find out, but feeling excitedly captive to the passion in her voice and eyes.

The train shuffling into a slow curve.

SYDENHAM HILL

He peered out at sodium lights.

"So," he said, to fill the little silence, "what kind of painting do you do?"

"I'm an Abstract Expressionist," she said.

"Oh," he said.

She turned in her seat and stared at him full-on.

"Oh, don't tell me!" she said. "Robert Forde! Don't tell me!"

So she told him.

She told him about Arshile Gorky, the *sound* of charcoal, goose bumps, the featherlight charcoal stick jumping to the paper's grain, the living rasp. She told him about Hans Hofmann, Willem de Kooning, Franz Kline...

Her hands wove shapes.

She talked on and on, dealers and galleries, jazz clubs, Washington Square, this rather mysterious-sounding "The Village," flapping her hand at his expression—lower Manhattan, for God's sake, *The Village, The Village,* an incantation of words that washed over him as he watched her face and pretended to be unaware, as she gestured, of the play of the cloth of her blouse.

Spinning out this Village spell, 52nd Street, The Village Vanguard, Minton's, The Five Spot, The Blue Note, lofts, studios, storage racks, stretchers and shims, and in The Village she'd have her first show, magazines she'd seen, a dealer called Benevento she rather fancied, but when she was launched her sights were on one she had a feeling was the coming man, Leo Castelli, and she'd get a studio loft in one of the old textile buildings or dry-goods factories, somewhere still cheap, on the edge of The Village proper, Houston and Lafayette, she imagined, somewhere around there, a building with freight elevators big enough to take the canvases she'd paint…

"It sounds wonderful," he said. "Have you *been* there?"

She focussed on him again.

"No," she said, "I've *dreamed* there."

"Was that WEST—"

"DULWICH," she said.

The stopped train, doors slam-slamming, *whistle,* the lights flickering, the train sliding on into the night.

Adolphe Gottliebe
Jackson Pollock
PENGE WEST

As she scooped up her bag and a chiffon scarf and stood and as they made their way to the door she was talking rapturously about Mark Rothko and Robert Motherwell, Rothko, *God!* the colour! and elegies, something about elegies…

And then the train's dwindling tail lights and then they were standing on the cold, silent platform.

She suddenly said, "Do you live here? In Penge?"

"Next one," he said, "Beckenham."

"Why did you get off then?"

"Well," said Rob, "we were talking, it was so interesting, I, um, well, I don't know…"

She seemed to consider him.

"If you like," she said, "you can walk me home."

They walked along the High Street and turned up a long hill. Helena was spreading her arms talking, getting in front of him and walking backwards talking, bubbly with excitement, irritably brushing aside the dead buddleia spears overhanging low front-garden walls, talking about space and size and scale and Franz Kline, a chap she'd mentioned earlier he vaguely recalled, a chap who used a paperhanger's brush, no WRIST painting, no piddly three camel hairs and easel but great *swaths* of black, Helena said, ARM painting, spreading hers wide to demonstrate the inevitable body logic of GESTURE.

The house looked huge, and to one side of it, and seemingly part of its grounds, there was part of a wall he could see, a black coppice. The drive was loud to walk on. Crushed white shells.

Her key in the lock, she turned and put her hand on his arm.

Stared into his eyes.

"Do what thou wilt…" she said.

The intensity of her gaze made him feel uncomfortable.

He stared back at her.

"…shall be the whole of the Law."

"Pardon?"

"Aleister Crowley," she said.

"Sorry?"

He felt that his not knowing this person had somehow let her down.

"Don't keep saying 'Pardon.'" she said. "Say 'What.'"

She put her finger to her lips and eased the door.

"And take your shoes off."

The entrance hall seemed enormous, squares of black and white marble, a blazing chandelier, staircases curving on each side of the hall summoning a vision of Fred Astaire. It was the sort of chandelier, the size of it, like those in palaces or the State Rooms of country seats, though the glass pendant things, the "peardrops," as Jimbo called them, were chunky rectangles of differing lengths, light shimmering up and down.

She opened the pair of doors facing them.

White carpet stretching everywhere. Furniture. Another pair of doors at the far side. On either side of the fireplace, long low bookcases, white, painted an olive green inside, vases and things on top, paperweights. Books and inch-thick shiny magazines. Above the slate mantelshelf, a big slabs-of-colour sort of painting, orange, yellow, umber, white, squares and rectangles, which slowly resolved themselves into stooped figures with machetes cutting—what would it be—sugar cane?

"Yours?" he whispered.

She gave him a narrow glance and snorted.

"They bought it in the West Indies," she said. "On a Sunshine Cruise."

She knelt and slid back the panel door of a cupboard in the line of bookcases. Twelve-inch LPs. She flipped along them until she pulled out what she was looking for and handed it up to him. Then she got up and stood beside him.

"Oh, wow!" whispered Rob. "*Good Time Jazz.* I've heard of this label. You can't get it here."

"It's American," she whispered. "My father brings these home for me, art magazines, records, stuff like that when he goes over there. When he does operations and lectures."

"So this," said Rob, turning the record over, "is a reissue of 1946. George Lewis with Bunk."

He tapped the photograph.

"Alcide 'Slow Drag' Pavageau on bass."

He smiled at her.

"'Slow Drag!'"

"Shsss!"

"And here it is *again,*" said Rob. "That clarinet solo on *Just a Closer Walk with Thee,* they *all* say the accompaniment—there's no drums or bass—they all say it's guitar, but look at the photo! What's Lawrence Marrero holding? A *banjo!*"

"Shsss!"

"And you'd have to be cloth-eared not to hear it anyway."

"Stop *reading,*" she whispered.

She was standing close to him, her arm against his.

"Take the record out."

He pushed the edge of the record sleeve against his chest, bowing it, and drew the record out, thumb and forefinger, by its rim.

"It's *red!*" he said in astonishment.

"And bendy," she said. "See? And you can see through it!"

She stood close beside him as he held the record up to the light. The room turned raspberry with the settee and chairs and television and coffee-table darker shapes, blurry, brownish in the red.

"Let me see again, too," she said.

He angled the record closer to her.

"If you twist it," she said, "you can make new shapes. Do that chair."

He could feel wisps of her hair against his cheek. He could feel his heart, he could feel his breath shallow. He could feel her breast against his arm.

"You can have it," she said. "It's a present."

"But it's so, so..."

I've heard it," she said. "It's a present."

"Helena—" he said.

"I *want* you to have it. I *want* you to."

She put her hands either side of his waist and gave him a little push.

"I'll put the TV on," she whispered, "so they'll know I'm home. Then they won't come down."

She paused.

"Probably."

She switched it on and said, "But you'd better lie down behind the couch just in case."

He edged himself in between the back of the settee and the window curtains. Then he knelt. Then he put his arms down and stretched his legs out behind him as if he were going to do push-ups. His shoes dropped onto his back. Then he lowered himself until he was lying face-down, then squirmed over onto his back and lay staring up at the ceiling.

He heard running footsteps, shouting, bursts of gunfire, cars accelerating.

"*Helena?*" he whispered.

Cars crashing.

All the lighting was coming from somewhere just below the ceiling, "cove lighting" he believed it was called. He had never seen such a thing before in a house. He lay looking up towards it. It reminded him, the light flooding from the top, of one of Jimbo's currently favoured words for windows, "clerestory." Odd thumps his heart was giving.

He heard a faint noise somewhere distant that might have been a lavatory flushing.

Loud footsteps. Keys. Commanding voices. Straining, he thought he heard the word "Buster." Cell door clanging. Keys.

"*Helena?*" he whispered.

After what seemed minutes, her voice said,

"*Take your trousers off!*"

He stared at the back of the settee.

"*Pardon?*"

Further fraught silence.

Into that silence he said, sibilant, "*What did you say?*"

He lay feeling his heart's turmoil, every now and then its rogue pumping performing finales in his throat.

"*Helena?*"

He decided that he would take off his socks. There was something about doing, well, *it*, in socks, something essentially plebeian. *Non-évolué*, Jimbo would have said. He'd got one off and with contorted squirming, drawing up the other knee, was working on the other, fearful he might bring down the heavy curtains onto himself, when a beagle stuck its head round the end of the settee. It clambered over his ankles, tail *thunk-thunking* against the taut fabric of the settee's back. It gave a peculiar impression of smiling.

"*Shoo!*" he whispered. "*Go! Bad* dog!"

It squirmed its way up onto his chest and sat there, tilted, its behind half-on. He pushed it away. Risking his hand being seen on the top edge of the settee, he gave the dog a powerful shove. At the other end, it started to lick his bared foot. Then it backed further out, dropped into a play-fight posture, front legs flat on the carpet, bum in the air, and got hold of the other, drooping-off-his-foot sock, and, against his frantic kicking, worried it free, and disappeared, sock in mouth.

He heard the small sound of a door closing.

He waited for what felt like hammering minutes.

"*Helena?*"

She suddenly appeared at the far end of the settee. She had taken down her ponytail. She placed her bare feet carefully, straddling his legs, moving up him until she stood astride his chest. Then she caught up the hem of her blue skirt and began slowly to bunch it upwards.

He gazed.

A thatch of hair.

Holding the bunched skirt against herself with an elbow, she spread with her thumbs what Rob, from the study of diagrams, supposed must be the *labia majora*.

The pile of the carpet was forcing its way under his fingernails.

She pulled the bunched material of her skirt closer to her stomach and held it clamped flat with her fist and, with the thumb and forefinger of her other hand still holding the *labia* open, bent forward regarding herself.

sinking closer

breathy whisper

Rosebud

He made a sound, an involuntary sound, a râle, a sound he heard as if it had been made by someone else.

tat-tat-tat

metallic

Behind the curtain, on the window, sounding inches from his head.

A panic seized him.

"*What is it?*"

She straightened and let her skirt fall.

"It's Joshua," she said.

"Who's Joshua?"

"He's unpredictable when he's drunk so I'll try to draw him off but you stay hidden."

She backed down his length and disappeared and then the TV went silent.

Then she was back kneeling on the settee and looking down at him.

"If it's on," she said, "he'll come in here and sit in front of it and stare through his drunken knees at this shoes. Handmade," she added, "Italian. It could take minutes, could take hours."

"Who *is* it?"

"My brother. He's a houseman at Guy's. Very *distingué*. If I were you," she said, "I'd draw my knees up and move tight in against the back here. Just to make sure you're out of his sightline."

As he shuffled himself tighter in, she sighed and said, "*Quel dommage!*"

The knocking, now duller, sounded to be on wood.

"Won't he wake them?"

She placed an actressy back of her hand against her brow and said, *"Je suis désolé."*

"Won't the noise—"

"To think," she said, hanging over the back of the settee, "You were nearly, on the very brink,—*sur le bord* of being diddled."

She gave a theatrical sigh.

"Quel dommage!"

He rolled his head and shoulder out to watch as she crossed the hall and knelt at the front door, raising the large brass flap of the letter box.

"Who is it?"

"Becca, let me in."

"Please identify yourself."

"Becca, it's *raining.*"

"You'll have to do better than that," she said. "State your name and the purpose of your visit."

An outbreak of hammering on the door and indistinct imprecations.

"If this *is* Joshua, then you're drunk again, drunk like a goy, a *shiker* who brings *tzures* upon our father."

"Open the fucking door, Rebecca. I'm warning you."

His voice through the letter box sounded distorted, sounded like the voice of a character in a cartoon.

"How *rude!*" she said.

The outer brass flap clanged and there was silence.

Rob lay clenched, sure that the raised voices would bring down her parents.

The *whinge* of the outer brass flap being raised.

Helena raised hers.

A bush burst through, a branch, a thrash of leaves.

Helena reared back.

The bush withdrew.

"I'm afraid," said Helena, "it's the garden shed."

"Let me in, Rebecca, you vicious little cunt."

"I'm afraid it's the garden shed for Joshua," she said, "on those greasy grass clippings with earwigs on him."

There was silence.

He started kicking the door.

She flipped the catch and ran. He saw a flash of her blue skirt near the staircase. Then the door began to open and he hugged himself tight in, pushing his body and face into the settee's fabric.

He heard nothing and then the far doors opening.

Then nothing.

Then a stumbling noise.

"*...fucking dog...*"

Further obscure noise. Bottles rattling. A door closing.

Then no sound. Was he crossing the white carpet? Then—was that shoes in the hall? He lay there for long minutes in the silence then rolled over onto his back. He looked at his watch, deciding to wait for fifteen minutes. After fifteen long minutes, he emerged on hands and knees and peered around the end of the settee. The chandelier still blazed in the hall. The far doors stood open into the deepening darkness of a passageway. He got up and stood wondering what to do.

He edged into the passage. An open door, the shape of a long table, chair backs, a dining room. Beyond that, another door. He stood in front of it breathing through his mouth, straining for sounds. He put his fingertip to the door. It opened a crack onto darkness. What he had heard earlier, the stumbling noise, footsteps in the hall, must have been the brother on his way upstairs. He felt about on the wall for a switch and the kitchen lights stuttered on and swelled and settled into a humming. Faucet, stainless-steel bowls, copper pans, blue tiled backsplash, cupboard doors matte-plastic inset with strips of steel, it was a glossy kitchen, magazine and Mondrian.

The wicker dog basket the brother had stumbled over sat in the middle of the floor where he'd kicked it. Rob looked all around it and in it for his sock, lifting a bunched-up old quilt panelled in roses. Looked underneath the basket. Underneath the table. Allowed light to wash along the passage. The dog, too, must have gone upstairs. He looked about at the ends of the settee, looked at the bottom few steps of both staircases, scanned the black squares in the hall. Then, resigned, sat on the settee to put his shoes on.

He stood in the silent hall under the blaze of the chandelier. He felt fearful the parents would appear. Hopeful that Helena would. Nervous that the unpredictable brother might. He felt like a guest, rudely abandoned. He felt like a burglar. There seemed to be no understandable shape to the evening's events, no dénouement. There was nothing but this brightly lit silence. He looked at the twigs and stripped leaves scattered near the door.

He began to suspect that the hanging rectangles of the chandelier were made of some sort of plastic, there was... he wondered what he meant... a *thickness* about them as though each piece had a skin, not alive like glass, a *rind*, a nearly invisible rind.

He eased the door ajar. Miserable drizzle.

To one side of the door stood a tall vase-thing they used as an umbrella stand. Perhaps *made* to be an umbrella stand. Porcelain, he thought. Decorated with a profusion of flowers and foliage. Japanese export-ware, Jimbo had instructed him. *Imari*, was that the word? Garish *he* thought, but fetching a pretty penny, Jimbo said, in the sales rooms.

He drew from it a slight green umbrella.

He wondered if he ought to turn off the lights.

Eased open the front door, eased it inch by inch closed behind him. He crunched down the drive and began to walk the long miles home under the ridiculous parasol, under the persistent rain, his sockless shoe rubbing, blisters rising, rubbing. His mind kept repeating, against the rain, against the weariness of walking, an incantation, a rune, a couple of lines from an early Mississippi blues he'd caught late one night on a Hamburg radio station, no idea of the song's title, or the singer, just a fretwork of notes leading into the two lines he'd heard before the FM signal wandered. He was ridden by this fragment, a blues of loss and longing, the singer searching…

Lord, I've been to the Nation
An' roun' the Territo…

He did not know what the words meant.

In his right hand, the frail parasol, and clamped to his body by his left arm, under his sheltering jacket, the red and magic record.

*

Jimbo won a scholarship to St. Edmund Hall in Oxford. Rob, awarded a State Scholarship, but much smitten by a girl from Beckenham called Cecilia, trailed after her to Bristol University, which held the additional lure of a critic with a fabled reputation in Shakespearian studies. Disappointment awaited him on both fronts.

The tedium of Anglo-Saxon was mandatory but Cecilia compounded this mindless affront to his free time by electing to also embrace Old Norse, a move on her part that Rob felt was—while at the same time feeling himself ridiculous for feeling it—was, somehow, a betrayal.

She had been named, she had once told him, after a Christian martyr who in the second century had taken a vow of celibacy, a baptism and naming by which, he was coming to believe, she had been unduly influenced. During their amatory grapplings, rather lukewarm engagements on her part, Rob increasingly thought, she trotted out that they must not get carried away when being carried away was Rob's precise desire.

She was soon lost in a prickly thicket of thorns and wens, lost letters representing the voiced and voiceless dental fricatives ð and þ and the runic letter later replaced by w; she thought the kennings of skaldic recitation were the essence of poetry whereas Rob thought that 'whale road' and 'oar-steed' meaning 'sea' and 'ship' were but heroic boilerplate.

Upon graduation, Cecilia was awarded the University's Walter William Skeat Medal in Etymology.

The famed Shakespearian scholar was also a disappointment. He was both lank and stoop-shouldered. His leg-crossed suit trousers revealed shins of riveting whiteness. For some unfathomable reason, he put Rob in mind of a potted hyacinth, the flowers grown so heavy that the fleshy stem bowed to meet the peat and potting soil. A dry, pretend-cough, guarded by the back of his hand and dangling fingers raised to his lips, heralded each practiced witticism. What could be seen of his tie above the grey pullover sported tiny devices or emblems, a club, college, or regimental tie, Rob thought, until he put himself near enough one day to make out they were horseshoes. During the seminars, while seeming to listen to their comments and discussions, *And what has Miss Mayberry to contribute to this... ah...?* he nibbled mixed nuts from a crinkly cellophane packet and sometimes celery.

Rob soon abandoned the university, going in only for the tutorials in Anglo-Saxon as he knew he needed external discipline to learn the language and vocabulary and read such scraps of verse as survived. He found Middle English—Chaucer aside—to be equally arid; he felt that life was too valuable to expend deserts of time upon the much-admired alliterative masterpiece *Awntyrs of Arthure at the Tern Wathelyn.*

His life fell into a pattern that pleased him. He read most of the night, getting up at noon or thereabouts for breakfast, usually some variety of Madras curry and a pint of George's Glucose Stout. He spent the afternoons pottering in the zoo, the dreary city museum and art gallery, used bookstores, and in nearby Bath at the Baynton bindery and the art school where William Scott taught. On some afternoons, he took the bus out to Berkeley Castle and walked in the water meadows or to Chipping Sodbury to browse the antique shops. Post-Cecilia, though, more and more of his afternoons were filled with dalliance. Post-Cecilia, his world, surprisingly, seemed filled with girls.

He and Jimbo had been drifting apart before they entered university simply because the demands of their sixth form years had left them little spare time; both had realised that scholarships were the passports to lives they were beginning to imagine. Both made light to each other of their deepening interest in what they were studying. Cecilia, too, had come between them. Jimbo at first dismissed her as a passing *coup de foudre* but as the liason continued—*twin sets*—did not bother—a *charm* bracelet—to disguise his hostility—for Christ's sake, Rob, she plays a *recorder*—nor his physical aversion.

He wrote three letters to Jimbo at St. Edmund Hall but received no reply.

Weeks later a telegram arrived.

Rob associated telegrams with glad tidings or news of a death.

He opened it to read:

Imperative read Robert Byron.

He usually went to The Green Bush at opening time, drank with old local men and flashy, secretive Jamaicans and played darts seriously. Usually, before Time was called, he walked back to his room in a house of students in Redland and settled to reading; it added little to his life, he felt, to know that Redland had nothing to do with redness but derived from "thrid," land that had been cleared, rid of trees.

His squalid room, his bed with its increasingly unappetizing sheets, the purple eiderdown, the huge sentinel wardrobe with the silvering of its mirror decaying into black patches and freckles, all formed a haven. Books were piled on his table and stood about the bed in stacks. A gas fire with a meter had been installed inside the Victorian cast-iron fireplace, the floral motifs of its surround blurred by successive layers of black paint but on cold nights, lacking shillings, he wrapped himself, in lieu of pyjamas, in his undergraduate gown.

In his first weeks he had filled in gaps in early novels reading Defoe: *Captain Singleton, Colonel Jack, Moll Flanders*; Smollet *The Adventures of Roderick Random, The Adventures of Peregrine Pickle, The Expedition of Humphrey Clinker*; Fielding: *An Apology for the Life of Mrs. Shamela Andrews, Amelia*; Richardson's *Clarissa*; then on to the Gothic: *Melmouth the Wanderer, The Mysteries of Udolpho, The Monk, Vathek*; then on to the tedious attractions of Thomas Love Peacock: *Gryll Grange, Crotchet Castle, Headlong Hall*; then to the book to which he kept returning: *Don Quixote*, in the 1620 translation by Thomas Shelton. Its language filled him with a purring pleasure as he spoke aloud its rhythms in his silent room under the unshaded bulb.

At the same time as loading in this necessary ballast he had discovered Joyce Cary's first trilogy: *Herself Surprised, The Horse's Mouth*, and *To Be a Pilgrim*. He was also reading, with large surprise, Samuel Beckett's *Murphy, Watt, Molloy,* and *Malone Dies*.

Certain strange books he acquired on sight. It felt as if he recognized them. He scoffed them off the shelves of used-book stores as greedily as a lover of caramel picked out the square shapes in a box of *Black Magic*.

Robert Burton's *The Anatomy of Melancholy*, Newman's *Apologia pro Vita Sua* and *The Idea of a University Defined and Illustrated*, John Speke's *Journal of the Discovery of the Source of the Nile,* Bernard Berenson's *Italian Painters of the Renaissance*, Mayhew's *London Labour and the London Poor,* the 1587 version of Holinshed's *Chronicles*, Sir Richard Burton's *Personal Narrative of a Pilgrimage to El-Medinah and Meccah.*

And there were, of course, poems, not the bulk oeuvre, not Selecteds and Collecteds, but individual poems and fragments he held in something like reverence. Lines that chimed. He copied them out into a ledger, leather back-strip and marbled endpapers. Hopkins, Edward Thomas, John Crowe Ransome, Louis MacNeice, Auden, Dylan Thomas... He read through the ledger daily attempting to commit another to memory.

John Crowe Ransome

"Bells for John Whiteside's Daughter"

He closed the ledger and tried; tried to visualize the page. Shut his eyes.

...The lazy geese, like a snow cloud
Dripping their snow on the green grass,
Tricking and stopping, sleepy and proud,
Who cried in goose, alas...

Sometimes, starting at the other end of the ledger, he worked sentences and paragraphs, descriptions of things seen, purple willow herb waving tall in the roofline gutters of Redland's once-proud houses; carved on the front panel of a Jacobean chest he'd seen in an antiques shop in Chipping Sodbury, two facing whales spouting from their blowholes, the ginger-and-white cat sat on the pavement outside the butcher's, so fat its tongue stuck out.

He turned a page in the ledger.

Dylan Thomas
"Fern Hill"

He recited "sky blue" for "blue sky," his mind mechanically transposing.

He checked himself and returned.

And nothing I cared, at my blue sky trades, that time allows
In all his tuneful turning so few and such morning songs
Before the children green and golden
Follow him out of grace.

The night

starless and bible black

giving way to the false dawn at the edges of the blind and the hum of the milkman's electric cart, the milk bottles rattling in their metal crates, he reluctantly closed Sir Austen Henry Layard's *Nineveh and its Remains* and set it on the upended box that served as a night table. Knuckled the soreness in his eyes. Still on the carpet where he'd dropped it in irritation, *The White Goddess,* Robert Graves' dotty, stillborn vapourings.

Deaths

he dared to think

and Entrances.

*

After enquiring of passers-by, Rob found the sequestered street, one of the few that had escaped the German bombing of the docks and city centre. It was a short street of ancient higgledy-piggledy houses, the ground floors converted, obviously many years earlier, to cubbyhole shops, Shoe Repair and KEYS CUT, Modelling Supplies, Costume Rentals, CONSULTATIONS, a chemist's with a window of sun-faded packets, dead bluebottles on their backs, and a KODAK advertisement, a life-size cut-out of woman in an unalluring bathing suit, smiling and holding out a camera, behind her, palm fronds, beach, sea, all leached out to a dull purple.

CLOSED read the sign on the door but Rob could see the barber sitting in the barber chair peering into a tabloid. In answer to the rapping, he levered himself up and unlocked the door, turning CLOSED to OPEN. His white jacket was grubby and the cuffs greasy.

"Good morning," said Rob. "I was told—"

The barber nodded and stood back to allow him in, but was suddenly bent into a bout of red-faced, mucous, phlegm-pulpy hawking. Rob politely looked away. At the hair on the floor. The strop hanging from the chairback. Combs standing in a jar of green disinfectant. An industrial-size bottle of Bay Rum. Beside the scissors, a tin-lid heaped with ash and dog-ends.

A purple plastic sign:

DUREX

...and will there be anything for the weekend, Sir?

When it had all subsided, the barber, glasses off and mopping, Rob said, "I was told you could direct me to an office called The Second Line." The barber pointed to an ordinary wooden door at the end of the room and said, "He's at the top of the stairs. There's a light switch as you go in there. And mind your step. The lino's lifting."

The stairs and landing groaned.

The door to the The Second Line opened.

"Good morning," said Rob, "I have some records—"

"Indeed?" said the man.

"And I was told—"

"Told what and by whom?"

"Charlie Denton. And he said—"

"Ah! The redoubtable Mr. Denton! A veritable confrère. You are most welcome, I am Christopher Mawson and you are Mr.…?"

He held out his hand saying "God, I do find myself boring!" He was tall, long floppy hair, a drooping moustache. Wearing a peculiar sort of coat, a frock coat made of suede and a white shirt open at the neck, a blue silk scarf with a huge knot askew at his throat. The coat was what Americans called, Rob thought, a tailcoat, and it had reminded him instantly of a treasured Wild West picture book he'd owned as a child, a book he'd won at a ring-throwing fairground booth, glossy boards, wonderfully garish colours, Wild Bill Hickok, Doc Holliday, and Wyatt Earp on the front board and a Colt *Peacemaker* on the rear.

"Edge your way in, Rob. And let us not stand upon the order of our going, as it were. Do call me Chris. As you can see, I'm rather cramped. Not," he said "that I expect the rozzers to burst in brandishing truncheons and shouting *'ello, 'ello, what 'ave we 'ere then?* But *legally* speaking, as, perhaps, Charlie intimated…"

Rob had got talking to Charlie Denton at The Bristol Nails, a dingy bar, home to the Avon City Jazz Band. Charlie was in his thirties and lived with his mother and an extensive record collection.

" …so if you wouldn't mind parking yourself on this crate."

Rob handed across the five records Charlie had lent him.

"And Charlie *lent* you these? You've listened to them?"

"Well, only at his place. He said my record player would destroy them."

"But *still!* You *must* be favoured!"

Rob smiled and shrugged.

"Let's have a dekko, then."

There was a workbench under the window and a sink, pegboard hung with tools, two or three record players, wires everywhere, a shelf above with glass and plastic spray bottles, other electrical-looking things. He wondered how old Christopher was. Forty, he guessed. His fingers were yellow with nicotine. The rather mournful moustache a little yellow-stained too. He kept tucking his hair back behind his ears.

"So. Charlie Patton, Kokomo Arnold, yes, ah! Sleepy John. Two of the 1929 sides. Now where did friend Denton get *that*. Son House, yes. And Sonny Boy Williamson. The very first side he cut was "Good Morning Schoolgirl." Know it? Sold like hotcakes. He was murdered, you know. Like Trotsky. An ice pick."

He paused.

"You know... I've never *seen* an ice pick. Of course, on the other hand, we don't have ice."

He paused again.

"Charlie Patton. You've read about that? It was in *Jazz Journal*, I think."

Rob shook his head.

"Well, he first recorded in 1929 and then again in 1934, and one of those tiresome, spotty, World Authorities on The Blues—they live typically in frowzy bedsits in Slough or Swindon—he wrote quite seriously that Patton's delivery of the 1934 sides was weaker 'probably because his throat had been cut in 1933 in a juke-joint brawl.' I did treasure 'probably'"

Rob grinned at him.

"Swindon!" said Chris.

Shaking his head.

"And you do understand I can only cut 78s. Not 45s or anything sophisticated. They're *pressed*, you see, from a machine like, oh, a die, *stamped*, whereas I *cut* acetate blanks employing a..."

He had stood while talking, staring down out of the window.

He scuffed aside sheets of the *Western Daily News* on the workbench, and his hand reappeared holding a small revolver.

"Even the words 'cottage industry'..."

Opened a drawer beneath the bench and took out a box of cartridges.

"...would dignify my level of production..."

Pushed the revolver's chamber out and loaded.

"...and the sophistication of what I —"

Rob released his breath as he saw the cartridges were crimped .22 blanks.

Catching Rob's expression, Chris said, "What? It's just a starting pistol. Ease up the window on your side and I'll get..."

The sway-backed roof some three or four feet below seethed with pigeons.

Crack! Crack!

"Die, you fuckers, die!"

Crack!

The pigeons clattered up, wheeled into a flock over the chimney pots, beat strongly into the sky.

"Sorry," said Chris, "sorry. I loathe pigeons. Those raw pink feet. I have a horror of them. One got in here once. Banging off the walls, smashing against the window. I killed it with a tennis racket. We were both hysterical. And those *eyes*—they have a, what is it, a membrane or something, it drops down over the eye and they suddenly look opaque, deformed, they remind me of my ex-wife. And those pink feet. I associate them with psoriasis."

He paused.

"Now where were we?"

"You were saying," said Rob, "something about employing equipment…"

"'Employing' did I say…? Ah! And then, of course, there's avian psittacosis. But, yes. Gotcha! *Employing* a pair of Pye *Black Boxes*. Or, as we in the trade say, *Les Boîtes Noires*. Do you want more technical…?"

Rob smiled, shaking his head.

"So," said Chris, turning on a swan-neck lamp on the bench and tilting the discs, scanning the playing surfaces, "Twenty-five bob a piece, OK?"

"Yes. OK."

"That's both sides, of course."

"Fine. Good."

Chris performed his mysteries, an orange Ilford Antistaticum cloth, one of the spray bottles, knobs, wires, what he called 'the cutting carriage,' and started the Charlie Patton record.

"I can turn the sound on if you…"

Rob shook his head.

"Quite right," said Chris. "Better to listen in silence and alone."

The room was filling with the pungent smell of acetate, sharp in the throat. After each face was finished, Chris brushed detritus from the grooves with a bushy paintbrush and sprayed the surface with another pump bottle. Put on headphones and listened to a snatch. Nodded to Rob that all was well. The acetate smell was strange, something like, Rob thought, a mixture of hot vinegar and the rotten sweetness of diarrhea.

"When you think about it," said Chris, his tan half-boots up on the bench, "it's not unlike human congress."

"What isn't?"

"He's puffing himself up, neck feathers iridescent mauve, green, ruffing himself up. He parades about her in circles, strutting and bobbing. *She,* meanwhile, ignores this technicolour production, obvious resigned irritation, pitpats away to escape his amorous intent, resumes a desultory peck here, peck there, seed, husk, crust. Ridiculous in his desire, swollen, puffed up with self-importance like Malvolio, he corners her. Covers her. The briefest of flutters. The deed is done. Without pause, she's back to a *flick* of the head, peck, orange peel, peck, dog-end, *flick*.

"And there *he* is, solitary, subsiding.

"Just like women, when you think about it. They lie there staring indifferently the while, staring up at the pelmet, costing new curtains, tracing the crack in the ceiling she's always thought looks like the top edge of Australia."

He got up to turn the Kokomo Arnold record.

As he brushed out the curlicue wisps of acetate, he said, "What you've brought in interests me. It's a pleasing change, young Robert, from the mainstay of my business—cutting disc after disc of the Yerba Buena Jazz Band and such. A little jolliness goes a long way. Or the George Formby or Vera Lynn fanatics."

Hands clasped loosely against bosom, he intoned:

We'll meet again
Don't know where
Don't know when
But I know we'll meet again some sunny day...

He made a snorty noise and turned back to bend over the turntable.

"Six months," he said, "that's what I'd give it. *Had* she met him again some sunny day, I'd have given it six months before she'd have been staring at the pelmet."

"Sir!" said Rob. "You sully the name of 'The Forces' Sweetheart'!"

"And who shall blame him?" said Chris.

"Who's 'him'?"

"Me," said Chris. "But enough of this Pat and Mike stuff. How would you describe," pointing to the records on the bench, "what it is you're after?"

"After?" said Rob.

"Yes. 'After.' Don't prevaricate."

"I want..."

"Mmmm?"

"I want the passion of it, that's what I want to get at."

Saying it, he felt hot embarrassment, felt self-conscious, exposed.

"Good," said Chris, tucking his hair behind his ears, "good."

"When it's raw," said Rob. "When the words aren't important, it's the voice, the timbre, the *sound*. When the voice is singing to the guitar, when it's all, you know, one instrument."

Chris was nodding.

"I have to come at this," he said, "in a roundabout way, 'circuitously' as we say in the trade."

"Come at what?"

"Plantations."

Rob regarded him.

"I expect you think of plantations as a big house, white columns, Spanish moss, all the trimmings and a few big cotton fields—that sort of picture. But they weren't like that at all. They were *huge*. Dozens of little farms, small-holdings, sharecroppers… they all rendered up tribute, of course, but the plantations were communities. It was the feudal system, more or less. They were like manor houses or great houses here. The big houses supported by surrounding tenant farms. In some places, entire villages or even more than one—thousands of acres.

"You should read up on these plantations—Stovall's, say, or the Dockery Plantation.

"Why should you?

"Because these plantations were more or less self-sufficient worlds. They were—how would you say?—time capsules. They preserved the slave life in a modified form. And—*our* interest—they preserved the music from an earlier period. And what gave rise to the music wasn't *that* much modified. Slavery was over but the social structure hadn't changed at all.

"Most of these plantations had jukes, bars, little dance halls—safety valves for the estate—and blues singers travelled widely. Charlie Patton, for example, travelled with Son House from plantation to small town to plantation. Son House was a big influence on Robert Johnson and Muddy Waters. Big Bill Broonzy learned guitar from Lonnie Johnson and Blind Blake.

"They were *expressing* that community. We're talking about a time when there actually was 'a folk.' Most of these men recorded in the late twenties or early thirties—that was a matter of race, of course, and of technology—but they'd been singing for many years *before* that so we can hear music that has strong links back towards slavery. Prisons did the same thing. The work songs in there, the blues, locked away decade after decade, untouched by change. Listen to

Lomax. It'll open your ears. More African than you'd believe possible. Parchman Farm was the Harvard of the blues.

"Did I just say that?

"How brilliant!

"What you want, Rob, is what *they,*" he made an encompassing gesture, "*them, that* lot, call 'primitive.'

"You can feel it in the music of other communities too, in flamenco, *cante jondo*, *fado*, even the cantor at my mother-in-law's funeral. Raises the small hairs.

"There's a word for this feeling, this effect, a Spanish word, *duende*, and Lorca... have you read Lorca? Lorca said that *duende* was beyond the limits of intelligence. He said, 'All that has black sound has *duende.*' *Duende* means emotional darkness, blood, suffering, death, sorrow. It speaks beyond the rational. Those who had *duende* weren't so much exercising a skill, Lorca said, as expressing a power. *Duende* possessed them. The audience fed them, became part of the playing and singing. Lorca saw it, the night in the juke, in the bar, as a *rite*—secular, but a rite. Something very far from a 'show.' Hemingway presented the *corrida* more or less the same way, as ritual, as *duende*. *Death in the Afternoon.* You've read that? and Lorca? No?

"Ah! His poem for Ignacio Mejias. *A las cinco de la tarde.* Killed in the ring. A close friend of Lorca's.

> *A boy brought the white sheet*
> at five in the afternoon.
> *A frail of lime already prepared*
> *at five in the afternoon.*
> *The rest was death and death alone*
> *at five in the afternoon.*"

Chris suddenly stopped talking.

He was silent for a few moments then said, "It is the tolling of bells."

Then, making an exaggerated mime of consulting his watch, he said, "Fancy a drop of Mother's Ruin?"

"Lovely," said Rob.

Chris took out a large bottle of gin. Set the kettle on the tiny gas stove.

"Away with tonic, lemon, and other pollutants," he said. "Take a tip from the dears you see every night in the snug listening to *The Archers.* A drop of hot water releases the botanicals."

He gestured at the stove.

"Sometimes," he said, "I eat baked beans."

He opened a cupboard underneath the sink and, taking out two glasses, held them up to the light.

Tut-tutted.

"I really *must* speak severely," he said, "to my housekeeper."

Catching Rob's eye, he said, "Oh, she's not a real one. Unfortunately. I made her up to comfort myself—and who shall blame him? I call her Fiona Macpherson. But always 'Mrs.,' of course. She's widowed. Very Scottish and reserved and severe. Wears tweed skirts below the knee and high-necked blouses. Breakfast is either porridge with salt on it or Arbroath Smokies, though where she gets them in Bristol I have *no* idea. She refers to me as Master Christopher and cuts the crusts off my sandwiches."

"Sounds very satisfactory," said Rob.

Gin fumes mingled up his nose with acetate.

"And when you follow up that plantation idea, look up a character called Lester Melrose. He was a talent scout for *Victor*, other labels too. He found much of the talent in the plantations. Follow who he turned up. Get Charlie Denton to play you Ishman Bracey. And Skip James. You've never heard Delta picking till you've heard

Skip James. Get Charlie to play you 'I'm So Glad.' Sings falsetto. Ungodly. And see if he's got the other two sides Sleepy John Estes cut in Memphis in 1929. They're on *Victor*. I'll cut them for you. You'll thank me. Twenty-five bob a time."

"Where would I find out about Melrose, Chris?"

Chris paused.

"Mmm. I can't remember where. I read rather a lot. It might have been a book about record companies... Well, I'll just have to *tell* you when you come back. I'll get Fiona to make us a packed lunch. Sandwiches. Oh, what a way she has with sandwiches! What would you say to cold scrambled egg and smoked salmon, one of her yummier..."

The second gin warm inside him, Rob put the records into the carrier bag, walked along the gloomy landing.

"The greatest of them all," called Chris from the lighted doorway, "the very apotheosis of what you seek, Bukka White. Released from Parchman in 1940—shot someone—he recorded just twelve sides for *Victor*. The *apogee.* All we have is just six 78-rpm records."

"White?"

"Ask our Mr. Denton."

"Say the first name again."

"Bukka."

Chris waved.

"Bukka White."

Treading down the lino traps on the stairs, *how pleasing the morning had been...*

Chris' voice again.

"Pardon?" Rob called back up. "What?"

I'll get Fiona to cut the crusts off.

the street, the ancient, ramshackle houses,

how pleasing the morning had been

the disgusting barber, the pigeons and the revolver, gin and hot water and the botanicals, Chris' pronouncements and improvisations and the bounteous flow of his knowledge, his frock coat, all this, Rob thought, all this, trying out in his mind this new word *duende*, all this mildly louche kind of life was where he was intended to be; all this, he thought, all this was home.

*

"Mr. Palmer is awaiting you, sir," said the waiter, "at his usual table."

The menu under his arm had a yellow tassel at the end of its cord. More a goodish tuft than tassel and Rob followed it, scarcely taking in starched napery, the blur of diners braying, gilt frames, walls of salvaged brick.

The waiter halted and ushered.

"Jimbo!"

Jimbo stood and tossed his crumpled napkin onto the table.

They embraced briefly.

"Jimbo! It's been so long!"

"It's 'James' these days, Rob."

"What?"

"'James.'"

"You're kidding!"

"'Fraid not."

"And that suit! Posh! Anyone'd think Savile Row."

"And anyone would rightly think so," said Jimbo, shooting his cuffs, flashing links of silver and jet, "for that is what it is."

He composed a Varnished Portrait Face.

"Bespoke," he said, "from the Henry Poole atelier."

"And the shirt, Jermyn Street?"

"Guilty," said Jimbo, "if you're accusing."

"Admiring," said Rob.

They sat looking at each other.

"Drink?"

"Absolutely," said Rob. "One of those'll be fine."

Jimbo caught the waiter's eye, pointed down, twiddled his finger round.

"So," said Rob, "why 'James'?"

"Jimbo was another person."

Rob nodded slowly.

"Actually," said James, "the suit is necessary. It's a uniform, if you like. A badge of rank, as it were. I am, what shouldn't say so myself, squire, personable. And as such, tend to get despatched to hotel suites to charm and chivvy along certain clients into this course or that."

Rob nodded.

"Surely you must see that the House of Oldfield cannot be represented by a 'Jim.'"

"So tell me," said Rob, "how you got this Oldfield job. The degree business—being sent down—that didn't count against you?"

"No, no," said James, "not at all."

"What *did* happen at St. Edmunds? I heard something from my mother via your mother but you can imagine the vagueness... it was, according to her, well,... the *gist* of it seemed to involve a Memorial Window and a bayonet..."

"Poor soul," murmured James.

"I have taken the liberty," said the materializing waiter, "of bringing a little jug of non-carbonated spring water."

James nodded dismissal.

"So come on, Jim—*sorry*—James, GIVE.'

"Well," said James setting down the glass of Pernod, "have you ever heard of a tome called *Select Charters* by one

Stubbs? William Stubbs. Expired 1901. This Oxford chap actually expected us to read it and based all his lectures—Oh, God! I never could. And it weighed on one so, the non-reading of it, I mean, it was like carrying around a paving slab. That, I suppose, was the start of it. But the essence of the matter was that I was supremely bored. I don't think I was temperamentally cut out to be *in statu pupillari*."

He shrugged.

"I realized I was much happier in the Ashmolean and the Pitt-Rivers where I spent most mornings recovering."

"So was there an exam or anything to get into Oldfields? I had the idea these houses were besieged by women waving degrees in art history, debutantes and heiresses from America. No? And grim graduates from whatname down there off the Strand, No?"

James made a *pshaw* noise.

"Anyone," he said, "can learn that stuff. Simple factual *stuff*. Those Courtauld people can tell you *to the hour* when some quattrocento artisan farted, but what they can't tell you is whether it's a good fart or a bad fart or even a fart fake.

"Oldfield asks only two questions—they *assume* knowledge. The questions are 'Do you have the makings of an eye?' and 'Do you go after properties like a barracuda?' The Courtaulds are rather, well, righteous, whereas Oldfield's—you'd have to dig pretty deep to find anything Quakerish in Oldfield. The dominant ethos is..."

He picked up his fork.

Regarded the tines.

"...more piratical."

He raised an eyebrow.

"So two of us were plucked from humble circs and raised to the purple. Money was advanced for gents' suiting and Annabel got a couple of posh—what? suits? no, well, *outfits*. I don't pay as much attention to feminine matters as I probably should."

While the waiter hovered, James said, "I could recommend the sole unreservedly and do you know a Loire white called Sancerre?"

Both nodded to the waiter.

Tapping his forehead, James said, "Couture. Make mental note. But enough about me. Bristol sits well? Are you still consorting with, mmm..."

"Cecilia," said Rob. "No. We found we lacked..."

He felt himself suddenly not at ease, constrained in talking to James about what then had been his ruling desire and Cecilia's reluctance. Odd, he thought, this sudden reserve, given their boundry-less boyhood. When he thought now of Cecilia, the thought was often accompanied by a remembered line in an Evelyn Waugh novel: "she made him free of her narrow loins." Cecilia had not made him free of her loins but *had* she done so, he thought now, he would have found them juiceless, joyless, stingy.

Loins doled out.

And him left feeling like Christopher's pigeon.

"...what shall I say, we lacked a commonality of interest."

"Thank God," said James. "That wicker basket."

"*What!*"

"On her bicycle. Emblematic. Indeed, the very bicycle *idea*. Ankle socks, stalwart calves. She was so obviously destined to embrace a future," said James, shaking his head sorrowfully, "decorating the Parish Church for Harvest Festival with enormous marrows. So what do you *do* there? Bristol?"

"I'm reading a lot. Taking what appeals, what I can use."

"Use for what?"

"I'm not sure really. I'm just..." he shrugged. "I don't know, just looking at things. Poking around. After those sixth-form classes, it's all a bit like a rest home. I'm feeling my way around. Paintings. Bristol Old Vic, Music, some. Some days I go up to Clifton, to the zoo, to visit a very ancient gorilla called Albert. But you. You're really happy at Oldfield?"

"Rob," said James, "I can hardly wait to get there every day. Love it. Love it. And the actual auctions. If you like the Bristol Old Vic, you'd *love* an Oldfield evening auction. The tension in the room. Heat rising. Bids duelling. Coming off the wall. The phone. The white flashes of paddles being raised or quavering down in indecision. It has an utterly gripping rhythm, the quiet chant of it, the auctioneer driving it, setting the pace, the conductor at the podium, Old Mr. Vine on the rostrum."

James lowered his chin into his neck and mimed an ancient peering over spectacles.

"I have twenty thousand in the room. It's not with you, sir. Nor with you, madam. And it's not with Magda on the telephone. It's in the room, with Mr. Curtis, at twenty thousand. Do I have twenty-one? Twenty-one? Fair warning now. All done? In the room, in the room,"

—his gavel raised, poised, his eyes travelling the room like an ancient tortoise.

CRACK

"with Mr. Curtis in the room at twenty thousand."

Rob grinned at James and mimed clapping.

"But," he said, "you haven't told me the *how* of it."

Lifting a lapel, James said, "You mean…?"

Rob nodded.

"Ah!" said James. "The situation was this. I'd applied to Oldfield's for a job as a porter—as in 'one who carries'—and I was assigned to British and European Painting. The lowliest of gofers, you understand. So for four months I lugged paintings about, dusted things, washed frames in warm water and mild soap. You have *no idea* of the chaos and squalor of behind-the-scenes. Made up packages. Helped getting the lots lined up in order in the corridor and storage behind the auction room. Picked up Francesca's dry cleaning. Flowers for wives or boyfriends.

But a slow change began. I was asked to help one of the probationers in deciphering the handwriting on ancient labels on the back of frames. I was loaned to Prints to collate a couple of disbound Redouté flower books. Small changes, small changes. But straws in the wind. And if British and European was in portering doldrums, I hung about other departments and asked questions and borrowed books and monographs and asked if I might touch things. Made note that Mr. Bedale loves Extra Strong mints and made sure I always had a little bag of them when I visited his storeroom. Whatever their bark, they just can't resist teaching the ardent and attractive young. I, of course, being the attractive forementioned."

Looked up at the waiter.

"Capers?" he echoed.

"Chef suggested, sir, hearing it was for you, that against the richness of the butter, they assert a pleasing piquancy."

"Did he, by gum!" said James. "Well, yes, give it a go, then."

"Blimey!" said Rob as the waiter withdrew.

"'Shimmered,'" said James. "Remember how we used to laugh at Jeeves 'shimmering' in? Anyway, after work one day there was a group of us, me—the lowly porter—and the others were probationers, we were 'volunteered' to get the lots marshalled into catalogue order, and supervision that evening had fallen to Oriental Ceramics—Freddie Godwin, very jolly, very avuncular, and he said how about playing a game before we started and the winner gets dinner free. So he proposed a sort of Kim's Game.

"Remember?

"Those unbearable Christmastide festivities where one's parents invited in to the Christian jollity of our homes forgotten aunts with ricochet hearing aids and the most colourfully afflicted in the congregation, and after excruciatingly tense pig-trough dinners, after the mince pies, before the carols, Kim's Game was attempted.

"Difficult to say anything in the Major's favour, but he did put his foot down following incontinence on the couch.

"Where was I?

Wine?"

"Kim's Game," said Rob.

"Right."

James sipped.

"But in *this* game you didn't have to remember the items, you had to guess what they were. So Freddie gathered up fifteen things from the stockroom and laid them out on the table and I actually scored twelve. One of the things we had to identify was the material covering the copper sheath and handle of a dagger—and let into the material there were Arabic characters in silver. The material actually looked rather nasty—like heavily pebbled plastic. Freddie went round the table, various ridiculous leathers were proposed, embossed hide, rubber—Saudi Arabia, Yemen, Turkey, Ottoman area generally, and I said, very off-hand,

"'It's shagreen.'"

"Sorry?" said Rob.

"Shark skin.

"And by this time, Edged Weapons—Charles Burchill—and Drawings and Watercolours had wandered in asking what we were doing. The noise we were making, I thought.

So anyway, I went on to say that I didn't think it came from the Middle East at all, but from India. And that the silver letter groupings were pseudo-Arabic, the craftsmen not being Arabic speakers. It just didn't look right. Just a feeling. Like pseudo-Kufic script on Abbasid-dynasty pottery.

"And Tribal Art had appeared, moody bugger, leaning against the door frame with those rank *Gauloises*.

"And it just happened the next thing up was a copper horseshoe-shaped thing with the ends flattened from the round and flared outwards at a small angle—the whole thing seven or eight centimetres across. A nice chunky thing. Bracelet, anklet, bangle, pendant, part of a primitive machine, a sort of handcuff-thing? Some sort of weapon-thing, brass-knuckly-thing, perhaps? and with creepy humility I said that my guess—and it *was* only a guess—was that it was a *manilla*, a sort of coinage—cowries, beads, that sort of idea—made in Britain for trading with the West African tribes. And if that was indeed what it was, then it had probably been made in the early-nineteenth century in Wales—near Swansea—where local ore and local furnace coal for smelting and a seaport combine to—oh, I was *sickening*.

"And I ended up being even more insufferable about a Cotman watercolour. Annabel had identified it as such and I said she was absolutely right, it *was* Cotman, and, with certainty, a Cotman prior to 1831, after which date he employed watercolour mixed with rice-paste producing thereby an impasto rather vulgar when compared with the almost ethereal delicacy…

"And this innocuous 'game' was, of course, the 'entrance exam.'

"The devious buggers!

"So now Annabel and I are being groomed.

"Couture, yes," he said tapping his head, "mental note."

"How," said Rob, "did you know all that stuff?"

"Well, that's it, isn't it?" said James, laid his hands flat on the table. "'Stuff' is what it is. What does it signify? Where's its depth? It's a magpie talent."

"Oh! come on!" said Rob.

"No," said James, "no. Fluent bollocks, really," he said. "Entirely accurate, of course, as far as it went. But underneath the sheen, and I'd be the first to admit it…

…well, admit it to *you*…

…maybe glib's what I'm good at."

He fell silent.

Sat looking away from the table, looking out across the restaurant, looking into some bleakness.

Rob had the sense not to say anything.

He felt the silence as deeply uncomfortable.

James gave a sigh and turned back to the table.

"Do you remember, Rob," he said suddenly, an animation relaxing and filling his face, "when we were kids, mmm? And I'd get you to pretend to ask me about a hallmark—remember that?—so I could say to you,

"'Pass me my loupe.'"

*

"Rents," said James, "are, of course, near impossible, but Charlie Burchill secured me the attic where he lives, Chelsea, very handy. He charmed the owner, who's the relict—delicious word, 'relict'—of a man who was something impossibly grand in the army. She wears what Charlie describes as 'heather' clothing and goes for walkies with her collie every day, thumping along with a cut-down shepherd's crook. Charlie and I have been designated her 'young men,' though Charlie must be at least *fifty*, and our principal duties are to deal with the dustbin men, who are disrespectful, and to prosecute her *Daily Telegraph* feud with Mr. Patel at the newsagents. And one or other of us brings the flowers.

"Perfect, in a way. The number 14 takes you from Fulham Road and Old Church Street to Old Bond Street or the 22 takes you there from King's Road. Then I just stroll up through the Burlington Arcade and I'm more or less outside the front door.

"I've painted everything in the attic a stark white and there's nothing there except a bed and a table and chair. *But*—and here's what I was setting out to tell you, we're allowed—encouraged—to log out antiques and to live with them for a while so that—and I do deeply believe this—so that a kind of, well..."

His fingers clenched into fists.

"...well, an understanding far deeper than... a kind of *aesthetic osmosis* takes place."

"Yes," said Rob, nodding.

"So my otherwise stark little abode is enhanced by displays of—do you think we need another cognac?"

"I would say so."

"In fact," continued James, reaching down for his briefcase, "here are a couple of things..."

He reappeared with a tiny black-velvet purse, tipped out of it onto Rob's palm a thick, silver coin. The obverse was the head of a warrior wearing a helmet with what looked like a snake rearing up from it, while the reverse was of a half-naked man holding a club, his musculature sculpted in—Rob didn't know quite how to express it, but sculpted in, well, blobs. He'd seen horses beautifully depicted in that way, too. Sort of Bronze Age-ish. In his mind was the White Horse at Uffington. The coin was heavy, chunky, pleasing to hold.

"It's a Tetradrachma of Demetrios I," said James.

"Who was *he*?" said Rob. "I like that figure on the reverse. Very powerful."

"He certainly was," said James. "That's Hercules."

"And who's this Demetrios character?"

"Ah!" said James. "He was the first Greek king after Alexander the Great to rule Bactria and northern India."

"Why the snake on the helmet?"

"No, no, it's not. It's an elephant's raised trunk—you know, curled back. That side piece—look—is a tusk. Alexander used to wear just such a helmet to proclaim his conquests in India in 326 B.C., so what Demetrios was signalling was that he was Alexander come again. So much history in your little hand. Gives me the shivers. Or more precisely, it gives me that Tamburlaine feeling, that *is it not passing brave to be a king, and ride in triumph through Persepolis* feeling."

He moved brandy glasses and coffee cups to one side and brushed away crumbs with the edge of his hand, clearing and cleaning a space between them.

"But what I really wanted to show you," he said, bending down again and then reappearing, "was this."

He placed on the table between them a black box.

Rob touched it with his fingertip, following its lines. It was about ten inches long and five or six inches high. Its four corner uprights were in the form of pilasters with Ionic scroll capitals.

"How very elegant!" said Rob.

"What it is," said James, "is a lead box, lined with untreated birch and covered with very superior black-dyed goatskin. The actual casket is lead, to preserve the faint odour of musk they give off."

"What give off?"

"We get boxes and mounts and settings made for us by an old chap not long retired from Asprey's—just down the street. They were granted the Royal Warrant by Queen Victoria and have held it under every monarch since."

"What's in it?"

James eased up the lid and turned the box around to reveal two brown balls.

They once had been gilded and the gilt was now time-worn, thinned, the brownness showing through. One ball was nearly the size of a golf ball, the other slightly smaller. The freckly gold-brown reminded Rob of truffles dusted with cocoa powder.

"Can I touch?"

James nodded.

"What are they? Stones?"

James made a snorty-giggly noise.

"Well stones they are," he said, "but stone they're not."

"So what are they?"

Rob waited.

"Those examples," said James, "are huge."

"So tell me what they are."

"Quite possibly the largest examples known."

"Stop fucking about, Jimbo!"

"Stop fucking about, *James,*" said James.

Rob made a gesture with his right hand of concession.

"They're Bezoars," said James, "and Bezoars are gall-stones of the Bezoar goat."

"Gallstones," repeated Rob.

"Of *Caprus aegagrus,*" said James.

Rob eyed the stones.

"And *do* they smell?"

James made a help-yourself gesture and Rob lifted the heavy box. 'Musk,' James had said. He breathed in the slightest smell, very faintly marshy, boggy, but it might just have been the birch lining. And he was a bit pissed anyway.

"What do you think?" said James.

"Gallstones as in, like, kidney stones?"

James nodded.

Rob shrugged.

"Rob, Rob, you have no idea of how highly valued these were. That our examples are gilded suggests their preciousness. They've been prized for centuries as an antidote to poisons. The writings of the Alchemists, the Hermetic literature is full of references to them, the various Arabic treatises, the Al Bituni texts, even our own Roger Bacon in the thirteenth century makes reference to them in his *Opuses.*

"As to *these,* we have some rather tantalizing provenance connecting them to Ranjit Singh, 'Lion of the Punjab,' or at the very least to his court. He was the Amritsar chap. Gilded the Golden Temple. Nothing we could actually assert but... tantalizing. Some of this sort of material began to appear on the market in England following Sir Francis Younghusband's punitive expedition into Tibet in 1903. Caravans of loot—*caravans*—were strung along the trails leading back into India. The slaughter and looting were so widespread it raised a popular outcry. And the looting was not merely inside Tibet itself. We do have some indirect documentation linking these Bezoars to Lord Curzon, he, of course, being the Viceroy and the actual instigator of the Tibet incursion, family letters, at some remove, from Younghusband relatives to Curzon himself. Nothing involving Ranjit Singh, of course—he was early nineteenth century—but in a period of turmoil precious artifacts tend to travel. Nothing specific *enough* though. You can, however, see the richness of the history swirling *around* Bezoars.

"And here's yet *another* tidbit. Years ago now, I've seen the catalogue—Christie's I believe it was—Doctor Dee's silver bracelet came up for auction. You know of the good Doctor?"

"Just the name," said Rob, "and that he was an alchemist."

"Doctor Dee *was* an alchemist," said James, "and also a quite genuine experimental scientist, though at the same time he was an astrologer, practiced crystallomancy, staged plays and masques, translated, amassed a magnificent library—volumes still around in the market—but all in all he was a fraud, a flamboyant fraud, a favourite for a time at Elizabeth's court. You can see his pink glass *speculum* in the British Museum, came to them from Walpole's Strawberry Hill collection."

James stopped and looked blank for a second or two.

"His bracelet," prompted Rob.

"Right!" said James. "His bracelet had all kinds of hocus-pocus charms dangling from it and one of them—guess what? In a tiny, silver cage, a Bezoar."

"Well," said Rob, "I can see they're interesting if one knows everything you've been telling me, but I still wouldn't want to sit *looking* at them. And I can't see how looking at them could, you know, what you were saying earlier about osmosis."

"Believe me," said James, "I've—"

"I believe that's true, that osmosis idea, of something *made*," interrupted Rob, "something that's been crafted with artistic intention—dish, bowl, dagger—but these are just, well, *curios*, aren't they? Like a pretty shell, an ammonite or—remember we saw an armadillo once in a junk shop? Curled up with its tail in its mouth to make a handle and lined with satin to make a lady's sewing basket? Remember that?

"So what's the point? What does Oldfield's see in these Bezoars? Who'd want to buy gallstones? They're just two stone balls. They might just as well be—what?—two stone cannon balls. And I wouldn't want to commune with them either."

"Well, for a start," said James, "they're incredibly rare. But that aside, there's absolutely no call to use the word 'commune' in that sarcastic manner."

"But nothing gets us away from the fact," said Rob, "that we're just dealing with the accidental product of a diseased goat."

"You're being insultingly *prosaic*, Robert."

"No insult intended—come on! It's just that, in this instance, I think prosaic's what's called for."

"In *my* world, Robert, prosaic is rarely called for."

Those two "Roberts" signalled, he realized, one of Jimbo's familiar mercurial changes of mood, but in the heat of the matter he said, "How about copralites?"

"I *beg* your pardon?"

"I *said*—"

James gave an indrawn *ttt* of exasperation.

"Even if they were gilded," said Rob, in turn annoyed, "would you ascribe value to two balls of coprolitic shit rolled up by a dung beetle?"

"*Why,*" said James, "*why—exactly*—are you attempting to provoke me?"

Rob heard the familiar setting-in of frost, the hauteur.

"Oh, come off it, Jimbo! We're not thirteen and arguing in your bedroom still."

"I can interpret your manner," said James, "in no other way than as an attempt to belittle me."

Rob shook his head.

"An ineffectual attempt."

James closed the casket lid, pressing with his thumbs on the front corners. He lifted up his briefcase and set it on the table, Scraping back his chair, he stood and eased the casket into its baize bag and settled the bag into the briefcase.

He glanced at his watch ostentatiously.

"Oh, don't take umbrage, Jimbo. Please."

"'James,'" said James. "'James.'"

Still sitting, Rob watched him start away.

"The cost of your wining and dining," James threw back over his shoulder, "has been defrayed by The Old Curiosity Shop."

*

His night reflection in the window.

Perhaps a third of the seats were occupied, businessmen mostly, blue or black suits, City men by the look of them, bowler hats and *Evening Standards*, black shoes glinty.

He watched the man on the seat across the aisle struggling to undo, from its cardboard-and-cellophane containment, a triangle-packaged sandwich. After picking with his fingers, he had tried with his teeth, and was presently addressing it with his nail-clippers.

Rob kept coming back to

Jimbo

James

He did not know quite what to make of the evening's sad collapse. He was used to Jimbo's moods and rages and oratorical performances, but the evening had surprised perhaps both of them in its eruption. It was an eruption startling to him as it was happening, yet now—

The sandwich man had got half of it out but had ruptured it in the extraction. Through the railway, smell of hot dust and hot oil mingled with what he very privately thought of as the smell of electricity, salmon on the air—

—yet now, in the gentle rocking and creak of the railway carriage, the clash was beginning to feel far less surprising, was beginning to feel as if he had been released, as if at last he had unburdened himself.

He kept returning to the nag of *why* he'd been unwilling to share with Jimbo the real gen about Cecilia, *why* he'd felt the need not to leave himself vulnerable when for so long they'd shared everything.

Phrases, odds and sods of James' conversation, were playing in his mind.

...the ardent and attractive young.

I, of course, being the attractive forementioned.

I am, what shouldn't say so myself, squire, personable...

...despatched to hotel suites to charm certain clients...

Wondered if it was these remarks that had made him wary. Wondered what, if anything, had been implied in "certain clients," wondered what might have distinguished such clients, other than, say, indecision, made them *certain* clients. Wondered, as he'd been wondering all evening, and unable to quite make up his mind, if Jimbo was wearing on his eyelids a subtle trace of blue eyeshadow.

Though really, he knew.

Had Jimbo felt Cecilia as a wedge into their friendship? Almost certainly so. He'd made his hostility no secret. In the time they'd been more and more apart, though—pressure of schoolwork, his preoccupation with Cecilia, Oxford—Bristol—he'd slowly come to realise that Jimbo's hostility towards Cecilia wasn't so much about Cecilia herself or Cecilia as girl. Cecilia could have been anyone. Jimbo's designs upon the world were far too grand and monstrous for him to have been provoked by Cecilia as girl or Cecilia as person, a sixth-form girl with, as Jimbo had once remarked, "fat lips."

ankle socks
stalwart calves

Jimbo's hostility towards Cecilia was towards Cecilia as interloper undermining his expectation of...

expectation of... the word *fealty* suggested itself.

not *exactly* the right word...

He'd felt constraint and wariness because any intimacies about sex with Cecilia, or, more to the point, perhaps any talk of sex itself, would have admitted into the conversation something dangerous.

What did "dangerous" mean?

Though really he knew.

The sandwich man had finished wiping mayonnaise from his fingertips and was looking about him in a helpless manner for somewhere to deposit the paper serviette. Rob watched covertly, quite fascinated by what he would do.

Rob preferred Jimbo to James. He felt that James was perhaps betraying Jimbo. Not in a calculated way. There was too much of the old Jimbo in the way, but...

He could see that Jimbo probably couldn't resist the lure of antique beauty, the piratical—what had he said?—*barracuda*—the hunt, the chase, the acquisition of the quarry. Probably couldn't resist the seduction of being, in his world, among the elect.

He could imagine Jimbo, or James, rather, in his white room's austerity, communing with bronze, gouache, Roman glass iridescent in its slow decay.

Rob felt for all this.

Conceded without quibble.

How could he not?

But he wanted no part of flummery. Bezoars. He mistrusted a world that could so easily and imperceptibly steer one towards the shallows of interior decoration, a world where caskets worked to flatter contents.

Gilded goat gallstones

Whatever the history, the provenance, it seemed to Rob that a gallstone, whatever properties it was believed in earlier centuries to have possessed, and whether gussied up in gold, bronze, or chrome with knobs on, was nothing more than a brown stone-like ball dug out of a goat's insides.

In my world, Robert, prosaic is rarely called for.

But it *was* in his.

It was precisely the prosaic, he was beginning to understand, that he wanted to grasp.

Clattering suddenly across rails, the train heeling into a slow curve.

LOUGHBOROUGH JUNCTION

The shuffle of the train, the slow creaking of the carriage in that odd silence trains seemed to impose, the journey's suspended time, there swam into his mind's eye the cat, the butcher's cat.

Captured in a sentence whose sounds and rhythm he stubbornly stood by

The ginger-and-white cat sat on the pavement outside the butcher's so fat its tongue stuck out.

*

Rob and Charlie Denton and Peter Villiers, a pub acquaintance who played darts at the Green Bush and who was apprenticed to a joiner and carpenter, stood together on the pavement in sight of the judas door of the massive gate of Bristol's Horfield Prison.

At a minute or two past six, the door opened and Stanley Shakespeare stepped over the iron-bound ledge.

Handshakes and hugs and Pete passed round his silver hip flask and they drank ceremonial whisky.

Stan was another Green Bush acquaintance, a Jamaican who had come to Bristol as a child. His improbable name had caused him lifelong trouble. His father, Royston Shakespeare, had been a cook and deckhand on one of the West Indies boats but had disappeared when Stan was small. He was... Rob had more than once tried to sum him up but Stan was difficult to define. Usually affable, he could become dangerously violent if he felt insulted. He sometimes seemed a little simple but wasn't. Sometimes he was flush and generous, sometimes on the dole. He called himself a handyman, painted things, dug gardens, carted junk, worked from time to time for a moving company, lived with his mother, squired preposterous tarts.

From week to week he also offered, at bargain prices, sets of steak knives, Le Creuset pots and casseroles, Black & Decker power tools, Stanley chisels.

Stanley chisels said one Green Bush wag, get it?

There was much discussion in the bar about what the word "fence" really meant and the general consensus was that Stanley wasn't your *real* fence so much as what you might call a *sub*-fence.

If The Green Bush was in deep discussion—Cyprus, say, and Makarios, or whether it really was, as rumour had it, Lord Bolton, starkers except for a maid's apron, serving them other Cabinet Ministers at the orgy—Stan would sit listening, looking from face to face. Sometimes he surprised Rob. Odd things were lodged in his mind. One St. Patrick's Day he had put green vegetable dye and Rose's Lime Juice in his beer. What you doing that for? Not exactly Irish, are you, mate?

Saint Patrick, he'd explained, was a slave but he'd excaped.

Rob looked this up later and was surprised.

The Green Bush consensus was that Stanley was no criminal mastermind, a bit bent but nothing egregious or really untoward, his little activities more peccadillo than what you'd call criminal. *And* he played useful darts.

That morning he had finished serving three months for assault.

I was riding my bike late, late and this copper stops me and he says what's your name and I said Shakespeare an' he slap my head so I took exception, din' I?

The incident and the sentence had not been reported in the *Western Daily News*, so at the bar of The Green Bush what the actual charge had been was much discussed. Various legal tags were bandied about: Assault, Battery, Affray, Grievous Bodily Harm, Aggravated Assault…

What! Grievous Bodily Harm with a bicycle pump?

Well, it was more Stan that was aggravated, wasn't it?

Doesn't matter—not if it was a copper. Not even with a feather, not if it was a copper.

Charlie, Rob, and Peter took him for a *proper* breakfast at the Adora Grill—eggs, bacon, fried Gammon steak, fried bread, fried potatoes, and grilled tomatoes.

fuck porridge!

They outlined the plans for this special day. After he'd seen his mum, they'd come round to his place at about ten o'clock and *then*—they revealed that that night Count Basie and his band—

"The New Testament Band, they call it," interrupted Charlie—they were playing at the Colston Hall and they'd got tickets for all of them—"and there's Eddie 'Lockjaw' Davis," said Pete—

and they had to honour the Count so they were going to John's Hatters in the Centre to buy fedoras—they *had* money, don't worry about it—and white shirts and did he have a tie and it was at eight o'clock.

They drank beer in the afternoon and felt self-conscious in their hats.

What?

I was just thinking.

What?

What he's doing with that Charlotte bird.

*

As the house lights went down and the stage lights swelled, the band began to file onto the stage, first Sonny Payne seating himself behind the drums on risers slightly higher than the piano and starting to mark a steady rhythm with brushes, shimmering hints on the high-hat, Eddie Jones beside him, raising up his bass, Freddie Green starting to play chords across the beat, a slow blues emerging. Then the trombones in the back row—Charlie Denton, who had the band recordings on *Verve* and *Capitol*, whispering their names—Henry Coker, Al Grey, Benny Powell. Then the trumpets filed on and sat behind their stands also in the back row, Snooky Young, Wendell Culley, Thad Jones, *that one, that one, that's Joe Newman.* Then the reeds behind the front-row stands—Bill Graham and Marshall Royal on alto sax, Charlie Fowlkes on baritone, Frank Wess on tenor and flute, and also on tenor, Eddie "Lockjaw" Davis.

The soft blues ended.

The audience broke into applause.

Basie appeared in a spotlight.

Slipped onto the piano bench.

Nodded *three/four* and the band blasted into his signature *The Kid from Red Bank.* Then into the quiet following the band's initial statement, buoyed by the driving guitar and bass, Basie's right hand pinking single percussive notes, space round the notes, blue space, jabbing notes that were the distillation, the spare essence of the stride tradition from which he'd grown, each note carrying all the weight of all the notes he wasn't playing. Then the horns and reeds smashing in ShowTimeTime'sSquareVegasCasino, an assault of sound, glitter-wave-upon-wave.

They were stunned by the sound, the precision.

Stunned, too, by Basie's piano revealing itself in dots, spots, dabs and jabs of sound, bright and sharp, driving the band relentlessly and then rising from the reed section, Eddie "Lockjaw" Davis ripping into improvised solos raw, savage.

"The charts," Charlie Denton whispered, "they're all Neal Hefti and Jimmy Mundy."

"Shss!" hissed Stanley.

Flight of Foo Birds, Splanky, Lil' Darlin', Moonlight Becomes You, In the Evening, Whirly Bird, Corner Pocket, Shiny Stockings, Double-O, the slow, slow blues *After Supper, Midnite Blue, The Late, Late Show, Alright, Okay You Win…*

Rob was beginning to feel he could absorb no more.

He could feel he was sweating.

He couldn't draw deep breath.

Stan, with shut eyes, had clasped his arms about himself.

The band ended with a rocking version of *April in Paris.*

In the last notes, Basie stood, inclined his head as applause started, then turned to the band and shouted,

"One more, once!"

and the current switched on again, and like a shining steel machine the band slid into a reprise of the final choruses, driving, swinging mightily, Sonny Payne high above the band laughing at Eddie Jones and bouncing sticks off the skin and catching them out of the air, the band swinging into the crowd's hubbub, Basie standing then again, small smile, stretching out his hand towards the band, head travelling the theatre stalls and gods, inviting pandemonium, stomping, whistles, cheers, the clapping steady, programmes fluttering up white into the rising house lights.

In the Bristol Nails, no band playing that night, they sat lowering beer, not talking, Charlie his usual pineapple juice and soda water.

Rob felt drained.

"Fuck me," said Pete into their reflective silence.

They nodded. It somehow seemed to sum the evening up.

"I mean," said Pete, "a *flute*."

"So?" said Rob. "What do you think, Stan?"

Stan had had nothing much to say. He sipped beer and smiled, somewhere separate. He looked about him now as if waking. Then looked into their faces in turn.

"They..."

Then broke off and started running his finger round the crown of the fedora hanging off his knee.

Shook his head.

"*The Atomic Mr. Basie*," said Charlie, "was a reissue, in part, of an earlier album called $E=mc^2$ and—"

"For Christ's sake, Charlie!"

"Stan?"

Stan set down his pint.

Spoke at his hat.

"Man," he said, "*they does be my dream*."

Bar sounds, the cash-register, a bottle clack back on a glass shelf, a woman's voice, a voice suddenly quite distinct, saying... *made of pears*.

A loud group came in.

A voice coming towards them.

"*Stanley!* Stanley, you old wanker!"

A girl, Molly, an acquaintance from jazz evenings at the Nails.

"I thought you were in prison! When did they let *you* out!"

"This morning," said Stanley.

"Really, really? Well, I'll have to buy you a drink to celebrate. Three scotch and a pineapple, right?" she said.

"Won the pools or something?" said Pete.

"Sort of," she said.

She hefted up onto her shoulder again a huge bag that looked as if it was made of carpet, a big rose on the side of it in sort of raffia stuff and rope handles.

"What the hell's in that?" said Rob. "The kitchen sink?"

"Just about," she said.

They all quite liked Molly, a bit fluff-brained, keener on dancing than listening, but jolly and easy to be with. She ran a poky little Sub-Post Office, a counter in a booth behind a grill in a corner of a chemist's shop.

She brought the drinks over on a tray.

"Doubles!" said Pete. "Christ!"

"Here's to Stanley," she said, "getting out of clink."

She downed the scotch in two gulps, *brrr* shuddered, and her eyes started to water.

"Bloody hell!" said Charlie.

"Drink your pineapple," she said, "and mind your own beeswax."

"Hoity-toity," said Charlie.

"Hoity bollocks, Charlie Denton! Drink your little, little bottle."

"Children, children," said Rob.

"Really though," said Pete, "come into an inheritance?"

"You at Basie?" said Rob.

"Wow!" she said, "wow! Jesus! wow! What?"

"That rather ably sums it up," said Charlie.

Difficult to tell if he was being snarky, difficult to tell with Charlie.

"I'll get some more Scotch," she said, squawking her chair back, "and a tiny-tots pineapple" patting Charlie's cheek, "no, no, really, it's all right, I've got lots."

They watched her behind as she walked past the dark platform stage to the bar.

"Wonder what's up with *her*," said Pete.

When she came back, they touched glasses, sipped.

"Funny," she said. "Stanley's just got out and I'll be going in, Monday, I suspect."

"In where?"

"In the clink."

"What are you talking about?"

She bent down fiddling with the carpet bag, pulled the sides apart.

Rob leaned over and looked down.

The bag held a considerable number of rubber-banded packages of bank notes.

Rob stared then looked up into her flushed face.

"Molly!" he said. "Molly. What did you *do*?"

"It's from the Post Office," she said. "I just didn't put it in the safe."

Pete sat back down again.

Charlie looked stricken.

"Fee-fi-fo-fum," said Stanley.

Pete stared at Stanley then at Molly.

"Can you put it back?" said Rob.

Molly shook her head.

"Why not?"

"I gave a wad of it to Susan, she's my cousin, I don't think you've met her—"

"*Molly!*"

"And I've bought me mum things. And I gave our Brian some towards a bike."

She looked at their faces.

"And I buried some for later near the rhubarb in a Huntley's tin. Royal Assortment."

"Oh, god!" said Charlie.

"*Well?*" she said.

"We're just thinking…" said Rob.

"Well," she said, "I'm just tired of it all. I mean, I'm not married or anything and it's all just selling stamps and stamping savings books and being nice to biddies and old geezers, can I borrow your sticky tape, will it hold together without string, how long does a letter take to get there? but what if it's going to Glasgow? and what exactly *is* a custom's label? I'm not going abroad, you know, oh, but I can't write what's in it on a label because it's for my grandson's birthday and if I wrote on the label what's in it, it wouldn't be a surprise, would it? And he'd miss the excitement of *wondering* what it might be… so I don't think I should fill in a label, though it was kind of you to ask, but, no I think…

"*Well!*

"What if I'd be doing that when I'm thirty, forty even? What if I was going bald? So I thought, pardon my French, *fuck it*, I thought. And speaking of that and such," she said, leaning over the table, staring at him, "I really ought to shag you, Stanley. In the circumstances. Always did fancy you more than a bit."

Stanley smiled at her.

"Fo-fum," he said.

The publican clanging his bloody brass bell.

Time, please.

Time gentlemen, please.

"In elementary school," said Molly, "all in white, funny the things you think about, all in white clothes, I was a Snowflake."

*

She was house-sitting for her sister and brother-in-law, who lived up towards Clifton and who were on holiday in Malaga. She'd parked his car somewhere near the Colston Hall. She walked ahead of them arm-in-arm with Stanley.

"We can't let her drive," said Charlie.

"No, you."

"You've got to admire his stamina," said Pete.

"What?"

"Well, this afternoon. Charlotte."

"It's red," Molly called back. "Look for a red one on a bit of a hill."

Charlie moved the seat back, adjusted the rear-view mirror. Molly delved into the carpet bag and came up with a bottle of Dimple Haig, swigged, passed it round.

"We really ought to address the problem in hand," said Rob.

"Oh, shut up!" said Molly.

Nearing Clifton, she insisted they drive onto the Clifton Suspension Bridge.

"Engineered," said Charlie, "by Isambard Kingdom Brunel."

"Stop talking cobblers," said Molly, "and stop *here* so we can look down."

Lights from the bridge speared and rippled over the river's expanse. A tugboat-looking thing, lit by just its running lights, travelling fast downriver towards the sea. The breeze off the water was blowing Molly's hair onto her face. They watched the tug.

"Where's he going?" shouted Molly.

"New York," said Pete.

"Patagonia," said Charley.

"Cardiff," said Rob.

Molly took another swig of Dimple and reached down again into the bag and worked the rubber band off a block of notes, riffled, loosening then, riffled again, then ungainly hurled them into the air, a fluttering lifting, falling, a swirl, blowing away into the dark.

Stanley started laughing.

He picked up another block, riffled, splayed, shouted,

One more, Once!

Consigned them to the wind.

Another.

One more, Once!

Intermezzo

Before going through the arch into the yelling surges of the asphalt quadrangle, they paused, looking back down over the extensive lawns towards the distant Custodian's Lodge and the high surrounding brick walls topped by angled barbed wire.

"I'm very partial to this view," said Uncle Arthur, "very nice it is, very pastoral."

Far below them, a figure trudged the lawns, stabbing up litter and scraping it off his spike into a yellow sack.

"He's working late," said Rob.

"It's more like a what-you-call-it, a ritual," said Uncle Arthur. "Part of his routine, you might say, and routine saves lives, as the Service *quickly* teaches. Litter, for the Old Man, it's like a glass of warm milk, as it might be, at bedtime."

The figure passed out of sight into a clump of rhododendrons.

"You mean," said Rob, and paused, "do you mean that that's the Old Man?"

"You haven't phoned him, have you?" said Uncle Arthur. "Announced your presence? In any way?"

"No. Should I have? Just the Lodge."

"Chain of command," said Uncle Arthur, "Any communication with the Old Man—it proceeds through me. I most earnestly advise you, Mr. Forde. I could not answer for the consequences else."

"Oh, OK," said Rob.

"Better, *wiser,* if you follow my drift, to wait for morning."

"Right," said Rob. "*Mid*-morning," added Uncle Arthur.

He tapped his finger against the side of his nose.

"A nod's as good as a wink," he said.

"Oh, absolutely," agreed Rob, who was baffled entirely by Uncle Arthur's enigmatic conversation, its feints and sallies, this tubby little man in a frayed sweater pullover who was, apparently, Senior House Father, "right," added Rob, "got you."

"The ravelled sleeve of care," added Uncle Arthur.

"Yes, quite," said Rob, "absolutely."

"The best induction into our communal procedures, into what I think of—call me fanciful, Mr. Forde, call me fanciful, but what I think of as the Eastmill Family—the wife and I were not blessed with issue, Mr. Forde, so every last lad in Eastmill we think of as *our* lad."

Rob nodded.

Vigorously.

"So if you'll accompany me, Mr. Forde, on Evening Rounds, your task will be to observe, to observe and, as the Good Book says, *inwardly digest*. But before we start we'll just pop into Churchill here and I'll show you the whereabouts of the Staff Room."

He followed Uncle Arthur along disinfectant-and-polish-smelling corridors, door after door unlocked and relocked with keys on Uncle Arthur's bunched ring. Uncle Arthur in ceaseless flow, coffee laid on in the mornings, tea, the redoubtable Doris, elevenses, comestibles, condiments, the Mug Policy, Mr. Austyn's administration of the Biscuit Fund, oh yes, many a convivial evening, up a sounding steel staircase *pong-pong-pong* and here we are, presenting with mock-flourish, a door, our Home Away From Home, our Refuge, as we might say, our Haven from Life's Storms.

Six shabby Parker-Knoll armchairs, a big central table, two coffee tables, a rack of pigeon-holes on one wall spewing papers and a sock. In one of the armchairs a bald head, and feet stretched out towards the electric fire, woolly tartan slippers. By the chair, a wooden crate of beer.

"Mr. Grendle," said Uncle Arthur, "our metal-work teacher. Our new English teacher, Mr. Forde."

Mr. Grendle remained motionless and did not reply.

The yellowing muslin curtains stirred in the breeze.

Portrait of the Queen.

"Well..." said Uncle Arthur.

Mr. Grendle belched.

"Coffee," said Uncle Arthur, "tea," pointing to an electric kettle beside the sink and some unwashed mugs.

Mr. Grendle tapped out his pipe on the arm of the chair, swept the ask and dottle onto the floor, wiped his palm on his cardigan.

"A *scriber!*" he said, staring into the imitation coals, "A scriber is the back. Or battered with a ball-peen hammer. That's how I'll end."

Back out along the polished corridor, halting for locks, *slam*, locks, Uncle Arthur saying, "Yes, gets a bit low, sometimes, does Henry. Following the accident."

"Accident?"

"That's right," said Uncle Arthur.

Pallid faces, cropped hair, army boots. Rob was the centre of much obvious speculation. He kept close to Uncle Arthur and tried to look bored, nodding casually at the faces that stared most openly. He followed Uncle Arthur up the steps of the North Building. Uncle Arthur blew a long blast on his whistle and all motion froze. His glance darted about the silent playground.

"Nothing like a routine," he murmured, "to settle a lad down."

Two blasts: four boys ran to stand beneath them, spacing themselves about ten feet apart.

"House captains," murmured Uncle Arthur.

Three blasts: the motionless boys churned into a mob and then shuffled themselves into four lines. He allowed a few seconds to pass as they dressed ranks and then blew one long blast.

Silence was rigid.

As each boy, House by House, called out *Present, Uncle Arthur!* in response to his surname, Uncle Arthur ticked the mimeographed sheet. When numbers were tallied and initialled, Churchill House and Windsor moved off first to the showers.

"Never initial anything," said Uncle Arthur, "until you've double-checked personally. Best advice I can give you. I learned that in the Service and it's stood me in good stead ever since."

He bumped Rob with his shoulder and added, "No names, no pack drill."

"Exactly," said Rob, ever more mystified.

Stripped of their grey overalls, the boys looked even more horribly anonymous, buttocks, pubic hair, feet. Rob glanced down the line of naked bodies trying not to show embarrassment and distaste. He looked down at Uncle Arthur's mauve socks in the brown, open-work sandals.

At the further end of the line, a mutter of conversation was rising.

Uncle Arthur's whistle burbled, a sound almost meditative.

"Careful you don't lose your pea, Uncle Arthur," said one of the taller boys.

All the boys laughed.

"It won't be me, son," said Uncle Arthur, nodding slowly, ponderous work with his eyebrows, "It won't be *me* as'll be losing my pea."

Rob recognized this as ritual joke.

The laughter grew wilder, ragged at the edges.

Order was restored by a single blast.

Uncle Arthur advanced to a position facing the middle of the line.

Into the silence, he said:

"Cleanliness, Mr. Forde, as the Good Book says, is next to Godliness. So at Eastmill here it's three showers a day, *every* day. We get lads in here that come from home conditions you wouldn't credit. Never had contact with soap and water, some of them. Last time some of this lot touched water was when they was christened. *If* they was christened. Sewed into their underclothes, some of them are. And dental decay? 'Orrible! Turns the stomach, Mr. Forde. Athlete's foot. Lice. Scabies and scales. Crabs of all variety. Crabs, Mr. Forde, of every stripe and hue."

He surveyed the silent line.

"Start with the little things, you see, Mr. Forde, because little things lead to big things. That's something that in the Service you *quickly* learn. And talking of *little things,*" he bellowed suddenly, his face empurpled, "what are *you* trying to hide? Stand up STRAIGHT!"

Half-turning to Rob, he said from the side of his mouth,

"A rotten apple if ever I saw one. Attempted rape, got off with interference."

In spite of all the showering, there was a close smell of sweat, feet, sourness.

Uncle Arthur's keys clinked in the awful silence. He selected one and the Captain of Churchill stepped out of line to receive it. The boy unlocked a metal cupboard and took out a square ten-pound tin and an aluminium dessert spoon.

Upon command, the boys began to file past holding out a cupped hand and Uncle Arthur spooned into it grey tooth-powder.

"Better than paste," he confided. "What's paste but powder with the water added?"

The boys were crowding round the racks of tagged toothbrushes, bunching round the six long sinks, dribbling water onto the powder, working it up with the brushes to make paste in their palms.

"What about the others?" Rob said. "The other boys?"

"They'll be at their healthy exercises in the yard with Mr. Austyn. Stuart House and Lancaster tonight. Anyone who goes on report, any infraction, you see, the whole House suffers. Gingers them *all* up. Doesn't make the offenders popular, that of course being the point. Discourages them as likes to think of themselves as hard cases."

A scuffle was starting around the last sink. The sounds of hawking, gargling, gobbing, were becoming melodramatic.

"Right! Let's have you!" bellowed Uncle Arthur. "Lather yourselves all over, paying special attention to all crevices—and no skylarking!"

He turned on the showers and the dank concrete cavern filled with steam. The pale figures slowly became ghostly, indistinct. Conversation was impossible against the roar of the water.

When the showers were turned off, the boys dried themselves, fixed the soggy, threadbare towels round their waists, gathered up their clothes, and formed a single line facing the far door. Uncle Arthur unlocked it and the line shuffled closer together. The first boy stopped in front of them, stuck his head forward, contorted his features into a mocking grimace. Rob stared at him in amazement, fearing for him. Uncle Arthur inspected the exposed teeth and nodded. Face after snarling face, eyes narrowed or staring, flesh-stretched masks, until the last white towel was starting up the stairs.

"Here's a tip for you just in passing," said Uncle Arthur as he double-locked the door and they followed them up, "a wrinkle, as you might say, that they wouldn't have taught you at the university. Tomorrow, in morning showers, keep your eyes skinned for any lad as has a tattoo. Right? Then you have a read of his file. Right? Files? Where? Just touch up Doc Aubrey. So any young offender, as they're now called, any young offender 'as as got a tattoo, you be on the *qui vive* because sure as the sun shines you've got trouble on your hands. Right?"

Rob nodded.

"Most particularly," said Uncle Arthur, stopped, puffed by the stairs, "if it says 'Mum' or 'Mother.'"

There were forty beds in the dormitory, twenty on each side of the room. On each bed was a single grey blanket. Hanging from the end of each iron-frame bed was a grey cloth drawstring bag. Some of the beds were empty. The boys, now in grey pyjamas, stood at attention at the foot of the beds.

Uncle Arthur surveyed the two silent rows, walked down the lines as if inspecting an honour guard.

Eventually nodded.

The boys opened the cloth bags, taking out rolled bundles of *Beano* and *Dandy*, *Hotspur*, *Champion*, and *The Wizard*.

"Providing there's no undue noise," said Uncle Arthur, "comics till nine."

*

Rob's own room was featureless. His suitcase had been delivered from the Lodge and stood beside the iron-frame bed.

On the bed were two grey blankets. A red printed notice on the inside of the door said: *Keep This Door Locked At All Times*. Green floral-printed curtains, lilacs, covered the window. He drew one of the curtains aside to look out but there wasn't a window there at all, just the ochre painted wall.

He hung up his clothes in the varnished plywood wardrobe, put shirts onto jangling metal hangers. He stacked underwear and socks in the chest of drawers. Set his travelling alarm-clock for six-thirty and put it on the floor near the door so that he would be forced to get up to turn if off. Stowed the suitcase under the bed.

He found himself wondering if the serials he'd read as a child were still running in the comics, the adventures of Rockfist Rogan, the exploits of Wilson the Amazing Athlete. Was it *Hotspur* or *The Wizard?* He could feel their coarse paper, smell the wonderful smell of the print. He found himself wondering if the Wolf of Kabul, with his lethal cricket bat bound in brass wire, was still haunting the Frontier.

Standing in the fluorescent light of the bathroom, insane-asylum light, the light in the white basement where they conducted the experiments, he stared at himself in the mirror.

The Wolf of Kabul—it was flooding suddenly back—the Wolf had called the cricket bat *clickee-baa*.

The toilet paper was in a box, stacked harsh sheets, each sheet printed with the Broad Arrow and across it diagonally the words:

Not For Retail Distribution.

*

When he entered the Staff Dining Room in the morning with his tray, one of the two men at the end of the central refectory table called,

"Do come and join us! Austyn. With a 'Y.' Sports and Geography."

He was tall and boyish, dressed in a white shirt and cricket flannels.

"My name's Forde," said Rob, shaking the outstretched hand, "and I'm supposed to be teaching English."

"And my surly colleague," said Mr. Austyn, "is Mr. Brotherton. Woodwork. Not an early bird, Mr. Brotherton."

Rob nodded.

"You're a university man, I understand?" said Mr. Austyn as Rob unloaded his tray. Something of a *rara avis* in Approved School circles."

"Just a novice," said Rob.

"I, myself," said Mr. Austyn, "attended Training College. Dewhurst. In Surrey."

Mr. Brotherton raised one ham off his chair and farted.

"Well, look," said Mr. Austyn, rising, draining his cup, consulting his watch in military manner, "time marches on. I'd better be getting my lads organized. I'll look forward to talking later. Actually," he added, "we'll need to foregather for an info session because, as you may have been informed, I administer, for my sins, the Biscuit Fund."

Rob watched as he walked out. He was wearing plimsolls of a dazzling whiteness. He walked on his toes and seemed almost to bounce.

Mr. Brotherton explored his nostrils for long, introspective seconds and then started to split a matchstick with his horny thumbnail.

Rob drank Nescafé. Mr. Brotherton picked his teeth with the matchstick.

"'I *attended* Training College'!" he said.

"Pardon?"

"I've 'attended' a symphony concert at the Albert Hall," said Mr. Brotherton, "but it doesn't mean I played first fucking fiddle."

"Quite," said Rob.

"You wouldn't likely think it," he said, getting to his feet and dropping the crumpled paper serviette on the table, "but I was once a cabinetmaker."

*

The classroom was less than a quarter the size of a normal classroom and the twenty-three boys were jammed along the benches. There was somewhere, Uncle Arthur believed, a set of readers. Rob issued each boy with a sheet of paper and pencil, and, as he had been instructed by Uncle Arthur, wrote on the blackboard:

When I grow up, I want to—

These papers were to be read by Dr. Aubrey, described by Uncle Arthur with a wink and a finger tap to the side of his nose as "the old trick cyclist."

Rob watched the boys writing, watched the way the pencils were gripped or clasped. He curbed the use of the wall-mounted pencil sharpener after a couple of boys had reduced new pencils to one-inch stubs. He denied nine requests to go to the lavatory. At the end of the allotted time, he collected and counted the pencils and glanced through what Uncle Arthur had called the "Completions."

They were brief, written in large, wayward scripts, and violent in spelling. Some of the papers were scored almost though.

*

Files in his arms, with an elbow Rob depressed the Staff Room door handle and backed in.

"'Evening," he said, "I'm—"

"Arson!" said the man in an armchair, feet up on the coffee table. He closed the ring-binder and chucked it on the floor. "A little show of spirit, don't you think? A certain assertion in the face of..."

His languid hand took in the unwashed mugs, the ochre walls, the Portrait of the Queen, the sock.

"I'm Robert—"

"Forde," said the man. "I've read your file. Timothy Audrey," he said, not getting up. "As we're cellmates, banged-up together, as it were, shall we be Bob and Tim?"

"So you're the Doc! I was about to read some of your files."

"You'd be better employed," he said in a deliberate and weary tone, "pulling your pud."

To mask his surprise, Rob dumped the files and the Completions on the coffee table and straightened them.

"Actually," he said, "most people call me Rob."

"Arson," said Tim again. "Cheers me up, a spot of arson...as would almost any sign of initiative..."

Timothy Aubrey looked, Rob thought, like one of those schoolboy cricket heroes depicted on the covers of boys' books from the twenties and thirties—tall, lean, mop of fair hair, blue eyes, his stance at the crease expressing an elegant but manly power, the sort of boy who grew into being debonair.

Rollwright of the Upper Sixth

"Are you actually a Doc? If you don't mind my saying so, you look a little young—"

"I have a B.A. in psychology," said Tim, "from Hull. One of our more dispiriting seats of learning."

"Uncle Arthur," said Rob, "refers to you as 'the old trick cyclist.'"

Tim shrugged.

"The point *is,* whatever his jocularities, he's still uneasy, a bit leery, unsettled. He hasn't decided yet what his move'll be. It's because of the files."

"These?"

"No. The personnel files."

"What do you mean 'leery'?"

"I suspect," said Tim, "he thinks I might be a spy."

"Sorry?"

"This Reception Centre," said Tim, "doesn't answer to the Local Education Authority like an ordinary school. Right? We're not open to inspection or regulation. You can't just drop in. No visitors without written consent. No parents popping in. No nosy journalists. Nothing gets past the Custodian's Lodge—not even tradespeople—without Uncle Arthur's say-so. We're like the prisons. We're under the aegis of the Home Office. For example, when I applied for this job, I was interviewed in London and *assigned* here. What about you?"

"Bristol. In an office in the Labour Exchange place. He did have pinstripe trousers, though."

"Right. But do you see the point? You weren't interviewed by *these* people, Eastmill people, were you? We're part of a deliberate new policy, you see, to feed more university graduates into the system. Same thing goes for the army, the police, and prison services—we're probably flagged for fast promotion. And why? Because eventually those so marked will hold top positions and they'll be slightly more civilized than the present norm and more fit for public consumption than the Old Man and Uncle Arthur.

"But because we're favoured from on high, we're resented everywhere else. They're paranoid about us. They think we've been planted to uncover their deficiencies. There's a strong feeling *we're not of them.*"

"I hadn't thought about any of that," said Rob.

"And in my case, old cock, they're exquisitely fucking right. I am *not* of them."

"At breakfast this morning," said Rob, "Mr. Austyn said that someone in Approved Schools with a degree was a *rara avis.*"

Tim nodded.

"Know what the inmates call him? *Browner* Austyn."

"But I suppose," said Rob, "resenting us, you can see their point of view."

"Fatal," said Tim, wagging a finger, "the seeing of other points of view."

"So," said Rob, "how long have—"

"My seventh month coming up. Feels like eons. Saving up the shekels. And when I've filled my poke with nuggets, I'm going to the States and I'm going to drive around in an automobile the size of a landing craft and fuck coeds. Pompom girls. The ones in the little white skirts. What about you?"

"It was the only job in the area I could find advertised. Because I wanted to stay around here because my girlfriend's in town, you see, and—"

"And do you intend teaching," said Tim, "for ever?"

"I was quite happy reading," said Rob, "and Madras chicken curry for breakfast at noon but the grant ended…"

"You were on a State scholarship?"

Rob nodded.

"Woe and alack," said Tim, "and so you were forced onto the streets to hawk your dubious wares. But this service to humanity, this saving of souls, say you don't envisage a lifetime of this."

"I don't envisage a lifetime of anything."

He paused.

"Tim…? About Uncle Arthur…"

"Be warned," said Tim. "More there than meets the eye."

"When I arrived the other night…"

"Have you seen *Mrs.* Arthur?"

Rob shook his head.

"No reason. Just asking. Just curious. Sightings," he added, "are blessedly rare."

Rob recounted Uncle Arthur's incomprehensible nods, winks, nudges, the *mid*-morning business, the chain of command, the implied threats, and the seeming assertion that the solitary figure spiking up litter was the Headmaster.

Tim nodded through this recital.

"The old NCO thing," he said, "bullshit baffles brains. This litter business is simply a reversion to that less stressful time when he had a job he could actually understand and perform."

"So you mean it *was* the Headmaster?"

"Oh, yes," said Tim. "Before he was headmaster he was employed by Eastmill as a municipal gardener. Not, you understand, as anything fancy, a landscaper, say, no, a day-labourer. So how did he get *this* job? Coached boys' soccer, cronyism, old army contacts, who knows? It was all murky years ago. Labour Party stalwart? It happened long before university graduates were even dreamed of. It was all a part of the prison system being a working-class structure. Just as the police pretty much are.

"As to Uncle Arthur's *mid*-morning warnings, what was being conveyed to you—or not conveyed—take your pick—is that the Headmaster is brutally drunk every evening by seven.

"Picking up litter, that's the only connection he has left to a world he can still vaguely grasp. Humble, bumbling, lovable old Uncle Arthur keeps him sodden—it's delivered in an unmarked van every Friday—and Uncle has increasingly undermined him on all fronts and is now the *de facto* power."

Rob nodded and nodded during this recital.

"Some mornings," said Tim, "the Headmaster actually manages to appear at Morning Roll Call and Assembly. He's always purple, snaky veins in his temples pulsing, and his face patched with bits of blood-dotted lavatory paper. His inspirational addresses are..."

Tim slowly shook his head.

"...memorable," he said, "memorable."

He paused, smiling, seemingly in gratifying recollection.

"He picks up litter, you see, because by doing that he feels he is still doing his job, *doing the right thing*."

Tim paused.

"Enough to bring a tear to the eye, isn't it?"

"It all sounds like a film, a Cagney," said Rob, "or a Graham Greene novel."

"Interesting," said Tim. "Interesting you'd mention Greene. He wrote it."

"Wrote what?"

"*The Third Man*. Orson Welles. The zither film? Penicillin. You saw it?"

"Harry Lime," said Rob, nodding.

"Because," said Tim, "I suspect that Uncle Arthur actually *was* in the Army of Occupation in Germany. In the stores. I see him as a sergeant. And he would have compromised a Quartermaster and then corrupted him entirely—booze, boys' bums—and there they were flogging food, cigarettes, nylons, drugs... same pattern, you see..."

"Strewth!" said Rob making a mock-astonished face. "What *have* I got myself into!"

"Learn to live *in* the world, old son."

Tim bent himself over the arm of the chair and picked up the ring binder.

"Arson!" he exclaimed again. "The little bugger burned down three derelict row houses. Shows a certain level of something or other, wouldn't you say? The social-working mind explains this as the expression of anger at childhood deprivation or abuse, or as a deformed sexual imperative, but the social-working mind seems not to grasp that theft, arson, mayhem in general are exciting, enjoyable, that they're *good fun.*"

"Well," said Rob, "maybe so, but being practical, what do you *do* with such a boy?"

"Hardly my concern."

There fell a small silence.

"Oh! By the way," said Rob, "I was supposed to put these in your pigeonhole."

"I can't *abide* missionaries. What the fuck is this?"

Rob shrugged.

"Uncle Arthur had me doing them this morning. He called them Completions."

"*Completions?*"

Tim took them.

When I grow up, I want to

be plesman
have big musls
get tatu
go home

Tim clanged the wad of papers into the metal waste bin.

"So, what you said earlier," said Rob, "your files, you were suggesting they weren't…"

"My files," said Tim, "are entirely useless but in good order. They will pass muster. They contain anecdotal reports, teachers, parents, social workers, police, vicars—that sort of thing—and some numbers that purport to be the results of the usual voodoo tests, the Wechsler-Bellevue, Stanford and Binet, Terman and Merrill, the Multiphasal..."

He flapped a dismissive hand.

"When you say 'purport,' do you mean..."

They're *numbers*. They purport to show I ran tests, was conscientious in the execution of my duties."

"But they're not accurate?"

"Accurate! I assume you've seen such tests? How could they even be administered to *them*," he said, pointing to the Completions in the bin.

He raised his arms as if in surrender and then locked his hands behind his head and seemed to be staring at the Portrait of the Queen.

"Even under optimum circumstances," he said, "these tests are like... Blind Man's Buff or Pin The Tail On The Donkey."

Still staring up, he tapped his fingers on the arm of the chair.

"*Although*—"

He got up and gathered the Completions out of the bin.

"*Although*... Is this a pawn opening?"

Rob shrugged.

"Rejection of assistance by duly constituted Authority. Might he be playing that one?"

"Well, whatever he's doing," said Rob, "you probably shouldn't let him see them in the waste."

"Of course," said Tim walking over to the door. "Yes, of course. Thank you. I shall file these," waving the wad, "with promptitude, promptissimo. I think, Rob, I think we might just have countered a probe, an opening move."

*

Rob soon lost his nervousness of these boys under his charge. As the days passed, he stopped seeing them as exponents of theft, rape, breaking and entering, aggravated vandalism, arson, and affray, and saw them for what they were—working-class boys of low-average intelligence or mildly retarded. With, as Tim described them, an occasional "dull normal."

They laboured on with phonics, handwriting, spelling, reading.

Of all the boys, Rob was most drawn to Dennis. He looked a waiflike ten but was actually sixteen. He was much like all the rest but unfailingly cheerful and co-operative. Dennis could chant the alphabet from A to Z without faltering, but he had to start at A. His mind was active, but the connections it made were singular.

If Rob wrote CAT, he would stare at the word with a troubled frown. When Rob sounded out C-A-T, he would say indignantly: Well, it's *cat*, innit? We had a cat, old Tomcat, he was. Furry knackers, he had, and if you stroked 'em…

F-I-S-H brought to mind the chip shop up his street and his mum what wouldn't never touch rock salmon because it wasn't nothing but a fancy name for conger-eel.

C-O-W evoked his Auntie Fran—right old scrubber *she* was, having it away for the price of a pint…

Such remarks would spill over into general debate on the ethics of white women having it off with spades and pakis, they was heathen, wasn't they? Said their prayers to gods and that, didn't they? *Didn't* they? Well, there you are then. *And* their houses stank of curry and that. You couldn't deny it. Not if you knew what you was talking about.

These lunatic discussions were often resolved by Paul, Dennis' friend, who commanded the respect of all the boys because he was serving a second term and had a tattoo of a dagger on his left wrist and a red-and-green hummingbird on his right shoulder. He would make pronouncement.

I'm not saying that they are and I'm not saying that they're not but what I *am* saying is...

Then would follow some statement so bizarre or so richly irrelevant that it imposed uncomprehending silence.

He would then re-comb the remnants of a pompadour.

Into the silence, Rob would say,

"Right. Let's get back to work, then. Who can remember what a vowel is?"

Dennis' hand.

"It's what me Dad, 'ad."

"*What!*"

"It's yer insides."

"What is?"

"Cancer of the vowel."

*

The long summer days settled into endless routine. The violent strangeness of everything became familiar chore. Uncle Arthur left Rob more and more entirely on his own. Showers and the Inspection of Teeth, Meal Supervision, Sports and Gardening, Dormitory Duty, Evening Rounds.

The occasional morning appearances of the Headmaster were predictably unpredictable. The Lord's Prayer was interspersed with outbursts about what would happen if boys did not pull their weight, and did those feet in ancient times walk upon England's mountains green? the excessive use of toilet paper, incoherent homilies concerning the bravery of The Few, the flotillas of small craft which had effected the strategic withdrawal of the British Army from Dunkirk, all with promptings in the aphasic pauses by a *sotto voce* Uncle Arthur.

What was that, Arthur?

Every afternoon was given over to Sports and Activities.

Cricket alternated, by Houses, with gardening. Gardening was worse than cricket. The garden extended for nearly one-and-a-half acres. On one day, forty boys attacked the earth with hoes. The next day forty boys smoothed the work of the hoes with rakes. On the day following, the hoes attacked again.

A few petunias were once planted but died.

The evening meals in the Staff Dining Room, served from huge aluminium utensils, were exactly like the school dinners of Rob's childhood, unsavoury stew with glutinous dumplings, salads with wafers of cold roast beef with bits of string embedded, jam tarts or tinned mandarin-orange segments accompanied by an aluminium jug of lukewarm custard topped by a thickening skin.

Uncle Arthur ate in his apartment with Mrs. Arthur but always appeared in time for coffee to inquire if what he called "the comestibles" had met with satisfaction.

Browner Austyn always said:

May I trouble you for the condiments?

Between the main course and dessert, Mr. Brotherton, usually boisterously drunk, beat time on the table with his spoon, singing, much to the distress of Mr. Austyn:

Auntie Mary
Had a canary
Up the leg of her drawers

And:

You can tell old Joe
I'm off the Dole,
He can stick 'is Red Flag
Up 'is 'ole

Every two days, Mrs. Chert—Doris—appeared to receive plaudits and requests.

Lancashire Hot Pot!
Boiled Onions in White Stuff!
Fish Cakes!

"Now, gentlemen," cried Mrs. Chert. "You're getting me all flustered."

Haunches, Doris!
bellowed Mr. Brotherton
Haunches!

Mr. Grendle drizzled on about recidivists and the inevitability of his being dispatched in the metal-work shop. Mr. Hemmings, who drove an MG, explained the internal combustion engine. Mr. Austyn praised the give and take of sporting activity, the lessons of co-operation and joint endeavour, the Duke of Edinburgh's Awards, Outward Bound, the beneficial *moral* results of pushing oneself to the limits of *physical* endurance.

But conversation always reverted to pay scales, overtime rates, the necessity of making an example of this boy or that, of sorting out, gingering up, knocking the stuffing out of etc. this or that young lout who was trying it on, pushing his luck, just begging for it etc.

The days seemed to be growing longer and hotter; clouds loomed sometimes in the electric evenings, promising the relief of rain, but no rain fell. The garden had turned to grey dust; cricket balls rose viciously from patches of bald earth. Someone stole tobacco; there was a fight in the South Building dormitory. Comprehension declined; pencils broke. Showerings and the cleaning of teeth measured out each day.

*

"Tim? How about this?"

"Have you cut the bit about being in the vanguard of the—what was it?"

"The Church Militant," said Rob.

"Fucking *ridiculous*," said Tim.

"OK. OK. So how about this?

TO WHOM IT MAY CONCERN:

Robert Forde, Rob to all our boys and girls in the Sunday School, has been one of my parishioners at St. Michael's for all his years at Bristol University. He is a young man of the utmost probity and has been a vibrant presence at our Thursday evening Bible Study Group. I am entirely confident that as a teacher he will be a tower of strength within the school community and a source of inspiration to those committed to his care.

Rev. Ernest Fildes, M.A.

St. Michael and All Souls

Tim nodding approval. "Nauseating," he said. "But shouldn't it be '*The* Rev'?"

Rob shrugged.

"But did you like 'All Souls'?"

"That Sunday School stuff's a bit queasy, too."

Lounging about every week with the Sunday papers, they read the advertisements for jobs, trainee tea-plantation manager in Assam, rubber plantations in Malaya, House Master in private schools in Trinidad, Nigeria, and Goa (Oxford and Cambridge Syndicate Examinations, generous emolument, two weeks' paid Home Leave *per annum*), the Hong Kong Police Force, Singapore, Significant Careers in H.M. Customs…

One week they had noticed that representatives of The Protestant School Board of Greater Montreal were interviewing graduate teachers for positions in all subjects and that Bristol was one of the cities they would visit.

"Do you think that's a misprint?" Rob had said, leaning down across Tim's shoulder and tapping the Salary Range.

"Christ!" said Tim.

"How much is that in pounds?"

Tim lowered the paper.

Stared at the wall.

Rob watched his blank face.

"It's..."

"What?"

"A lot."

"Should we?" Rob had said.

"It is impossible," Tim had said, "for Montreal to be worse than being locked up with one hundred and three smelly boys."

The interview, in a suite in the Avon Hotel, was little more than a formality. Beyond furnishing degree certificates, the only complications were a letter attesting to general sobriety and good moral character from a Vicar, Priest, or Equivalent Figure and a negative result from a Wassermann Test.

What the fuck's an Equivalent Figure?

Do stop being so tiresomely literal, *Rob.*

But we don't know *any vicars.*

We shall become *vicars.*

*

The VD Clinic was in the bowels of the General Hospital and was referred to as The Annex. The waiting room offered six plastic chairs. At the end of the room, a further room, frosted glass, two figure-shapes inside. Two of the chairs were occupied by West Indian men, the whites of their eyes in one case yellowish, in the other bloodshot. Neither one looked affable. Rob sat beside a scruff wearing a leather jacket and clunky motorbike boots.

The door in the frosted room opened and a man with hair bleached yellow and wearing a white coat called, "Has everyone filled in the questionnaire? Ooh, no! You're new, aren't you?"

"I'm here because I'm emigrating," said Rob.

"Don't be embarrassed, dear. We've heard every story known to man."

He collected clipboards and papers from the other three, gave a set to Rob, went back into the frosted-glass room.

While Rob was filling in the form—*Discharge—Contacts*—the man beside him started talking. He was so Welsh Rob had to concentrate to follow what he was saying. The account rambled, mumbled.

"It was just the once, see. In the park. The trees all flashy green in the street light after the rain."

His hands conjured the night.

"She said she was a virgin, like. Hadn't done anything like this before. Quiet, it was. I'd spread my jacket on the bench, see. Quiet. Stars. 'No cause to be frightened, my lovely,' I said to her."

He gave a profound sigh.

"She was tight as a mouse's yearole."

Rob turned to him full-on.

"As a…? Oh! *earhole.*"

Shaking his head, the Welshman gestured at his crotch.

More Welsh-inflected mumbling through which Rob thought he caught the word "weeping."

He patted the man's knee in a gesture of sympathy.

"The cure's pretty simple these days, you know. And I know it must be hard, but really, is she worth weeping over?"

"No, no," said the Welshman, turning to him. "I didn't say—"

"You'll be sure to meet another girl—"

"No—"

Cutting him off again, Rob said, "Oh, I'm *sure* you will."

"I didn't say *I'm* weepin'," said the Welshman. "I said *it's* weepin.'"

The frosted glass door opened.

"Blood serum?" called the man with the bleached hair. "Who's for syph?"

Just a Closer Walk with Thee

After the horror of their first winter in Canada, hacking and scraping morning ice off the windshield, ice chips up one's sleeve, breath hanging in the car's interior, frozen vinyl seats unyielding, the fear, daily, of piles, they were heading south for New Orleans.

Or, as Rob thought of it:

South.

On the road, he thought. They were on the road.

Though actually they had not yet left Montreal, the car jammed in traffic on the Champlain Bridge.

Tim's car was a red barge of a thing, a used Pontiac *Laurentian* with white vinyl interior and whitewall tires. Rob thought it vulgar.

"*Precisely!*" Tim had said.

Unable to contain his pleasure in the day, Rob said, "'Than longen folk to goon on pilgrimages.'"

"What?"

Tim's thumb was tapping on the steering wheel; it put Rob in mind of the thrash of a displeased cat's tail.

"Chaucer," said Rob.

"I hadn't supposed it was Little Richard."

They gained another yard.

"'Than longen folk…' well, it *is* a pilgrimage," he said, "sort of…"

"Good Golly," said Tim, staring steely ahead, "Miss Molly."

One of *those* mornings.

After a few heavily silent minutes, Rob said, "I was reading… Sharkey Bonano's got a regular band, his own place on Bourbon Street."

"Hmmm."

"A lounge, they called it."

"Hmmm."

"*The Dream Room.*"

*

For much of the journey south there was little really to see because Tim was driving on Interstates. Rob had never learned to drive so felt he had little say in how they got to New Orleans. They had planned the journey south a scrimping one because their reservation at the Hotel Monteleone on Royal Street in the French Quarter was very expensive. Rob had tentatively proposed it as it had, at one time or another, housed Faulkner, Hemingway, and Truman Capote; Tim had merely shrugged saying, "Bring on the the fleshpots."

They slept in the car fitfully. When they woke, usually at first light, the car smelled. They washed and shaved in gas-station washrooms. Tim always emerged looking spruce and elegant; Rob shambled out.

They turned off the Interstates for meals.

Tim fulminated about small-town eateries where the only cheese was bendy.

Rob was amazed to discover that chicken fried steak wasn't chicken.

In a shirt-pocket notebook, he noted things that caught his attention, advertisements, the names of stores, ads on the radio offering a dozen day-old chicks with a bonus photo of Jesus.

VENETIAN BLINDS & GUNS

Bread was another disappointment.

"On the plus side," said Rob, as Tim pointed at the dingy thumbprint on his white sandwich, "you've got perfect proof of who did it."

The frigid lagers, the only beer available, Millers, Coors, and Bud, prompted another of Tim's diatribes that began with the temperature and alcohol content of this insipid piss and moved on to hops... some way into it, de Tocqueville was involved...

On eatery TVs they caught footage of the civil rights uproar, desegregation, voter registration, police in riot gear, the marches, churches burning...

Tim liked the driving and liked the radio on so that, hour after hour, the commercials, the songs and singers, the newscasts, the holy rollers, the yatter and blather, became numbing noise, a noise in some odd way like deep silence, Rob's mind drifting into erotic remembrance of Jenny so vivid he had to cover tormenting erections with the unfolded road map, drifting into imaginary conversations, into remembered conversations with Jenny, awkward, sad, sometimes recriminating, all regretted, her attic room in the shared house, her canvases standing along the walls, she, Jenny, the mess of it all.

A peculiar painting of hers strong in his memory, a night painting, a passageway along the side of a building, a wooden door painted green, a section of brick wall, a bulb in a wire cage casting a partial yellow light. She'd been taught in Bath by William Scott so there was an obvious abstract quality about the painting—but the construction of it, the shapes and feel of it had reminded him, he didn't know quite why, of Walter Sickert.

When Jenny had first met Tim—dinners out in Bristol, away from the pen, as Tim put it, the three of them, films together—she'd said of him that she thought he was 'very public school' though saved from being entirely that by Basil Seal tendencies; 'very elegant' she'd said "ruthless," "world-weary," and "wonderfully snotty." She'd wondered if he might be… just a thought…

"Indefatigable," Rob had said, "in the opposite direction."

The public school he'd attended was a minor one with a number of scholarships endowed specifically for the sons of RAF pilots. Tim's father had died in a Spitfire over Kent in 1940. His mother lived in Surrey with a succession of "pals," imbibed gin, smoked cigarettes in a cigarette-holder, and emulated, in style, film stars of the thirties and forties, studio portraits, eyes soulfully uplifted to the left top corner, black and white, pearls.

Tim did not talk about her much but Rob did remember his saying, "She lives in a world she prefers to imagine exists."

Tim's imagination revolved around arranging life about him to command money and power. On their arrival in Montreal, he had promptly enrolled at McGill to study for an MA in matters Educational while Rob had failed to pass a teacher-certification exam because he could not, would not, bear the tedium of reading the prescribed handbook, the mindless detail of register-keeping, the number of seats permissible in a classroom.

"The obvious move," Tim had said, "is out of teaching and into administration."

"But I quite like teaching."

Tim had shrugged.

"Goodbye," he had said, "Mr. Chips."

His larger vision was the acquiring of a PhD and then working to supplant, suppress, subjugate, all the Guidance Counsellors under the Board's jurisdiction—
riff-raff, dear boy, pathetic, qualified by virtue of summer camp experience, by St. John's Ambulance Certificates in First Aid and Water Safety and in a few appalling cases by Ordination in the lower reaches of evangelical Protestantism—and becoming the Board's Consultant,

the obeah Top Hat man of Psychology

...answerable to no one, the *fons et origo.*

"I shall come down upon them," he had said, "like the wolf on the fold."

Then, credentials established, translation to the States to some warm land-grant college languorous with faculty wives desirous of fulfillment, and perky with pom-pom girls in little white skirts.

West Virginia gave way to Kentucky.

The road seemed endless.

Kentucky gave way to Tennessee.

They wandered about in Knoxville for a while but it struck them as a leftover, washed-up place, a place time had left high and dry.

In Nashville, described in the free tourist brochure as *The Athens of the South,* they went to look at the full-scale replica of the Parthenon. It amazed them. In a liquor store, they were also amazed to see Scotch from the UK *in gallon jugs.* They wondered who drank such prodigious Scotch, wondered who had dreamed up the idea of building a full-scale Parthenon in poured concrete. The brochure informed them that the Parthenon now functioned as the Nashville Art Gallery permanently exhibiting its entire holdings, the sixty-three paintings donated by James M. Cowan.

Memphis seemed more promising. On Beale Street, Rob wanted to look round a famous record store. The recording studio of the Sun Record Company was also on Beale or Main, the company defunct but the studio apparently much visited by Elvis Presley devotees. The label's founder, Sam Phillips, had discovered and promoted Presley, Johnny Cash, Jerry Lee Lewis, Roy Orbison, and suchlike rockabilly tosh but, of much greater interest, had recorded the beginnings of B.B. King, Sonny Boy Williamson, Sleepy John Estes, Little Walter, and Howlin' Wolf.

They started to wander along Beale Street looking for the record shop called *Home of the Blues*. The area was seedy, automotive workshops, LOANS, clang-clang of trams.

Rob stopped to read a handbill in the window of a delicatessen. Crady's Bar and Grill. A blurry photograph and, beneath, the call letters of what Rob guessed were radio stations, WMSL, WREC. Advertising that week the dynamic blues artist Frog Legs Henry.

A crawling police car behind them.

"Is it us?" said Rob.

"Don't look round like that," said Tim.

The car surged ahead of them, slewed in, a nightmare policeman emerging, dark glasses, paunch, gun, and baton. He stood leaning against his car as they came abreast. He pointed down at the sidewalk in front of him.

"What you boys lookin' fo'?"

"A record shop," said Tim.

Eyebrows rose above the gilt rims of the dark glasses.

"What you *in fact* lookin' fo'?"

The dark glasses looking them up and down.

The jaws chewed.

"A record store," said Rob.

"Huntin' cooze?"

"Pardon?"

"Ah know a cooze-hound when ah see one," said the policeman.

They stared at him.

"Y'all chasin' black pussy?"

Tim, his tone getting frosty, said, "We are 'chasin' a record shop called *Home of the Blues.*"

Hurriedly, Rob said, "In search of a..."

Further chewing and cogitation and mirrored examination.

"In search of, huh?"

The policeman gave this further thought and then heaved his bulk off the car and pointed back the way they had come.

In the store, Rob bought a record by Arthur "Big Boy" Crudup. It had on it the track Charlie Denton had raved about, "That's All Right."

They climbed the loud, wooden stairs to Crady's Bar and Grill, Tim fuming still... cartoon sociopath, morbidly obese *animal*, Brownshirt, Thing from the Swamp...

At the top of the stairs, a pair of swing doors. Inside, conversation and shouts, the background sound of a radio. Rob followed Tim through the swing door.

The room was smoky, loud with the hubbub, separate round tables and chairs, bar facing them along the far wall. As people noticed them, the conversations died down, men turning around to stare. As people deeper into the room became aware of something happening, *What?* turning, staring, *Say?* the silence deepening. The radio seemed very loud.

Every face was black.

Rob touched Tim's arm.

The bat-doors *thunk-thunk*, the gunslinger walking to the bar, spurs *jink-jink*, but he and Tim weren't slinging, the thought flashed, but rather, about to be slung.

"Tim..."

But Rob followed him through the room to the bar.

"I can hep you with somethin'?"

"Two beers, please," said Tim. "Make it, oh, I don't know, not that it matters much... let us say, *Millers*."

The bartender stared at them.

"I cain't serve you."

"Pardon?"

A man wearing a white shirt and black bow tie and crimson arm bands who'd been leaning against the bar in conversation—Tim nodded to him—picked up his shot and beer and edged down the length of the bar stopping at a bowl of peanuts.

"I got to be about my work," said the bartender.

He half-turned and busied himself with a cloth and glass.

Tim cleared his throat.

"*Millers*" he said.

The bartender made head-down mumble.

"Pardon?"

"You not welcome here."

"Nonsense, my good man!"

The bartender set down the shining glass.

Chair-scraping noises. Rob could sense people behind him.

The bartender said,

"Where you *from!*"

Rob understood this as neither question nor geographic enquiry. Tim, however, said, "Not that I see it as germane, but we are presently resident in Quebec, Canada, though essentially we are from England. Surely you would not be—?"

What he sayin'?

I ain't real sure.

"—so churlish as to turn from your door..."

"England?" said the bow-tie man.

He bore back his shot and beer.

"Aubrey. Timothy Aubrey."

"Jordan. Isaiah Jordan."

Gesturing, he said,

"Pay no mind to these low-rents."

A cheerful afternoon ensued. Isaiah Jordan turned out to be a concierge at the Metropolitan Hotel. Rob was given lessons on how to pronounce New Orleans. His "New" didn't even figure. *Noo Orleens* caused cackles. *Noowawlins* secured sort-of approval. And "French Quarter" seemed to be pronounced something like *Quotah*.

A New Orleans beer called *Dixie* was commended by those who had travelled.

No one had heard of Arthur "Big Boy" Crudup. Rob's record was examined. The "Crudup" amused some. "Big Boy" provoked considerable prurient and bawdy back-and-forth, much of which Rob was unable to follow.

Tim was asked to say more things in English.

It was confirmed that London was blanketed in fog.

Frog Legs Henry would not be appearing as, earlier in the week, he had been taken to Tennessee State Prison for some jackanapery with a pistol.

Tim and Rob were taught to say:

Gimme a double Beam and a back of Dixie.

Tennessee gave way to Mississippi.

In Mississippi, the countryside changing, Rob saw statuette egrets for the first time, a blaze of whiteness against green and swamp.

In Decatur, they saw a blind blues singer being led about by a boy, the old man's outstretched hand on the boy's shoulder.

Near Vicksburg, they saw a chain gang cleaning roadside ditches, the line of them not actually in chains, but overseen by a gunbull on a stallion, pearl Stetson, boots gleaming, the butt of a double-barrel twelve-gauge resting on his thigh.

This was the South Rob had been waiting for, the South he'd read about, imagined.

Take this hammer
Carry to the Captain
Tell him I'm gone
You can tell him I'm gone...

Somewhere south of Vicksburg—they'd stopped to look around, besieged in 1863 by the Union forces under General Grant, the last Confederate holdout on the Mississippi—they decided to stop and sleep. Dusk was fast deepening into night and they started looking for a place to park for the night where the car would not draw the attention of the police. Where they were driving seemed to be along the edge of a park of some sort.

Tim saw an opening off the road and drove very slowly into a bare-earth area behind the roadside trees and dense bush, a sort of lay-by. After Tim turned of the ignition, silence began to fill the car like rising water. They wound down the windows and that silence filled quickly with an unending drone of sound, insects, frogs, tree-frogs and bull-frogs. Sudden piercing night cries. It was like a movie soundtrack, on patrol in hostile jungle.

Another car sat some distance away.

Moon behind cloud glinted occasionally off the windshield.

A black car.

Their eyes were adjusting to the darkness.

A dark figure was crouched beside the car's rear wheel.

"What's that bloke doing?" said Rob.

"Changing a wheel, looks like," said Tim.

The car's trunk lid stood up.

"Why don't we put our headlights on where he's working?"

Tim turned the car and crawled across the potholes towards the black car.

He called out of his window, "I'll put the lights on so you can see what you're doing."

The crouched figure called, "No, no."

Put his palm up flat, pink, as if to ward them off.

"It's no trouble," called Tim.

Their headlights sprang on like floods filling a movie set. The hubcap upside down, inside it three nuts, the crouched man, his forearm raised above his eyes, the whites of his eyes, white in the blackness of his face, a tire iron on the ground, the grip end of it painted red.

He shifted himself around.

Was forcing down on a wrench.

Behind the dazzle on the windshield, they could make out a woman holding a baby.

The noise that had fallen in volume when they'd switched on the lights was rising again, the croaking, *urge, urge, urge*, a throb as steady as blood pulsing, blood felt under a pressure-cuff.

The man was wrestling off the wheel.

Skinned his knuckles, licked the rawness.

Rob felt captured in this scene, bound, as if all the world had contracted to this plot of bare earth, the man's back, the streaming asylum light as from a film projector, a spray of leaves caught in the light's fringe, glint of steel, frogs pulsing, a scene intense, incandescent, searing on and on and on.

And then, suddenly, the scene released him, the film resumed running through the sprockets at what seemed silent-film speed, out of the trunk, lifting the spare, trundling round, bending, pushing, wrench, clank of the jack collapsing, hubcap snapping into clamps.

He was wearing a long, brown overcoat.

How strange in such heat.

"All O.K?" called Tim.

The man turned towards them and lifted his forearm above his eyes again. He might have nodded. The fingers of his raised hand spread in what might have been a farewell gesture.

Tim tucked their car tight in against the brush so it wouldn't be readily visible from the road.

"Humph," said Tim, "rather rude, wouldn't you think."

"I think," said Rob, "that he was terrified."

"What?" said Tim. "*Us?*"

"I think," said Rob, as if he were discovering what he was saying as he spoke, "I think he thought we were going to kill him."

*

Rob and Tim sat under the awning of the Café du Monde, looking out over Jackson Square onto the Cathedral Garden in front of St. Louis Cathedral. The early-morning sprinklers were shpritzing into the Garden, regular and soothing as the spray climbed, sounding up the low fence.

Breakfast was something they'd read about, *beignets* and coffee, the coffee heavy and black and blended with chicory.

"Essentially," said Tim, "doughnuts."

They both felt slack and luxurious, restored yet weakened by showers and by sleeping in beds.

The sound of mules clip-clopping, drawing carriages of tourists.

They gestured for more coffee.

Rob didn't much like the look of the Cathedral, its monotonously severe and rigid lines, ruler and thick lead pencil, looking like the creation of a literal child.

Rob imagined—the magical street names, Burgundy, Bourbon, Canal, Perdido, South Rampart Street—the parades and funeral processions there once had been when men traditionally belonged to one or more fraternal clubs, mainly clubs like the Odd Fellows, the Masons, and the Knights of Pythias, but also to clubs that grew out of the mutual-aid societies that mushroomed with the influx of immigrants from the plantations, the Zulu Aid and Pleasure Club, the Tammany Social Aid and Pleasure Club, the Jolly Boys, the Original Swells, the Autocrats, the Charcoal Schooners. Even the pimps had a club.

Membership dues were as low as fifteen cents a month. Club members took the afternoon off to march in the processions for their departed brethren; fines were levied for non-attendance. The best bands then for the societies to hire had been the Tuxedo, the Onward, and the Eureka.

The funeral procession gathers at the Club Hall or meeting place and the club members fall in behind the band that starts to play slow renditions of *Sing On, Just a Closer Walk with Thee, Just a Little While to Stay Here.* The colourful buttons the members wear on their coats are reversed to show the side that's flatly black. The Grand Marshall with his baton, mace, or furled umbrella has also turned his wide silk sash of office that crosses his chest and hangs at his side nearly to the ground to its flat black side, hiding its flamboyance.

The Second Line has been gathering—friends, neighbourhood women, children, following the band on the sidewalk. When the procession reaches the house or church where the body is resting, the Club members go in to pay their respects. If there is a church service, the band disperses into nearby saloons; a child is sent to fetch them when the service is over.

The child, Rob imagines, a boy of nine or ten, could have been Louis Armstrong, still, at that age, wild on the streets before his incarceration in The Home for Colored Waifs.

The coffin is carried out and placed in a horse-drawn hearse sheeted in black shrouds. Bass drum and snare drum start playing. As the parade assembles, the band is playing *Free as a Bird.*

Voices in the Second Line are singing.

Two women, holding up decorative umbrellas, are breaking into slow dance steps and drinking Jax from bottles.

The Grand Marshal blows a whistle and hoists his furled umbrella to signal the start to the cemetery. The hymn is *Nearer My God to Thee.* When the band rests, the snare drummer continues a stark beat, the drum muffled by a handkerchief between the skin and the wires of the snare to mimic the military sound of a kettle drum. The pace is ritually slow. Crowds stand along the sidewalks in silence. Men doff their hats and hold them to their hearts.

At the cemetery, the band slows the pace even more and begins to play a dirge, usually *What a Friend We Have in Jesus.* The cornet is playing the lead melody straight with little embellishment while the clarinet weaves an obbligato counterpoint high and sweet.

The preacher pronounces the words and he or the widow throws a symbolic handful of earth onto the coffin, a final gesture, Armstrong once said, that *turns the body loose.*

After a respectful pause—

ashes to ashes

—the Grand Marshal flips his wide silk sash over from its black side to its blazing yellow and the club members do the same with their buttons. The snare drummer removes the muffling handkerchief and, *razz* restored, with a loud roll, calls the band into position.

They break into *Oh Didn't He Ramble*.

As they swing out into the street, the Second Line swells, jostling, skipping to the beat, singing, dancing a shuffling, pelvic-thrusting dance, women with their skirts raised. Children race with and through the Second Line. Some of the boys study the especially fancy dance steps of the Grand Marshal as he marks time wheeling the band and the procession round corners, dancing the steps that are the exhibition of his authority, his signature style.

When the band rests, a favoured boy is allowed to carry a bandsman's instrument.

Rob imagined the child Armstrong carrying the cornet for one of the famous men of the day, Freddie Keppard, say, or Bunk Johnson, though both had been dance-band leaders rather than marching men.

Over the clip-clopping mules, the click and spritz of the spray on the fence, the surrounding conversation, crockery, Rob could hear the forthright tones of Freddie Keppard's cornet, remembered with immediacy from an obscure record lent by Charlie Denton, and Kepard's rough voice:

Let me be your Salty Dog
Or I won't be your man at all
Honey let me be you Salty dog...

He watched the play of sun and shadow, the arcs of spray fading into the Garden's myrtle and banana-tree leaves in a rainbow mist.

Jackson Square was beginning to fill with people setting up small tables to sell jewellery, cookies, to display tarot cards. One of the tarot-card readers was a man wearing an embroidered vest over his bare chest, thick clumps of armpit hair, a lavender chiffon scarf at his throat, every finger bedizened with clunky turquoise rings. As he turned, the cards pattering his spiel, the woman's husband took photo after photo.

Psychics in Sikh-like turbans sat behind crystal balls; fortune-tellers hung the fronts and sides of their tables with zodiacal charts and diagrammatic representations of the human skull phrenologically divided by heavy black lines, reminding Rob of diagrams of cows similarly divided to illustrate the various joints of beef; artists daubed; jugglers juggled; tap dancers danced; I-Ching initiates in straw coolie hats cast yarrow stalks.

A girl in a leotardish-thing, bare feet, tambourine, red hair tangling down her back, squinty in one eye, said:

"A traditional tribal dance?"

She looked vaguely insane.

They smiled at her and strolled on.

What tradition? thought Rob, What tribe?

As they wandered out of the Square, they were accosted by an urchin of nine or ten. He was one of a quartet. The other three little boys drummed on the surface of a three-legged stool, a bongo drum, and a large can with a label still on it picturing a huge strawberry.

"Betcha I can tell ya where ya got them shoes!"

"Oh, yeah?"

"Betcha dollar."

"O.K. You're on."

The little boy started to dance. He'd strapped onto the bottoms of his sneakers the halves of a tin can hammered flat and *clackety-click-clack*, with stamps, scrapes, slides, and slurs, singing to the accompaniment of his three drummers:

Betcha I can tell ya
Where ya
Got them shoe, shooes,

Betcha dollar,
Betcha dollar
Where ya
Got them shoe, shooes.

Got your shoes on ya feet
Got your feet on the street,
Betcha, betcha, betcha
An' the street's in Noo
Awlins, Loo—
Eeez-ee-ANNA

They wandered on, Rob stopping to scrawl in his notebook.

MANICURE & MARTINI
$5.00

A shoeshine man performing upon the shoes of those seated, throne-like, above him, juggling tins and brushes high into the air, clacking the wooden brush-backs *clack-clock-clack*, pirouetting, dancing back in again, stooping to spray, burnishing *slip-strap-strop* with a cloth strip.

THE CONSECRATED CHURCH OF CHRIST

Sordid serial bars on Bourbon Street, strip joints, meat markets; they could not find Sharkey Bonano's Dream Room.

MARIE LAVEAU'S VOODOO RENDEZVOUS

gris-gris, fetish dolls, mojos, love potions, amulets, John the Conqueroo.

RITUALS BY ARRANGEMENT
(SMALL GROUPS)

"Well, I don't know," said Tim. "If you want to peer into the future, cockerel's blood's probably as accurate as a Stanford Binet."

REAL FOOD
DONE REAL GOOD

A sign that got them started again on lunch, on dishes they wanted to taste, on restaurants. Rob wanted gumbo again; he'd never tasted okra before and had been an instant convert. Tim urged *boudin*. They'd talked about food interminably. Oysters at Felix's or the Acme, crawfish étouffée, shrimp rémoulade, turtle soup. They would definitely dine at Galatoire's and Commander's Palace. Though chicken Rosmarino at Irene's, garlic and rosemary, also lured; they'd smelled the aroma in the street.

A malodorous strip joint, its morning doors propped open, mop and bucket. A servitor with a stiff-bristled yard brush was driving spattered vomit towards the gutter. From the joint's dark and cavernous interior a stench of bleach.

One of its signs prompted Rob to recall for Tim an anecdote he'd read in a travel book about the South, an anecdote concerning the heir of an old and wealthy New Orleans family who fell in love with a stripper. The heir assured his parents that the girl was not at all as they imagined and urged them to come to the club to meet her. They sat and talked and it was immediately obvious that the girl was well-educated and ladylike. More, she was charming. She quite won them over. After they'd been chatting for some time, the girl got up and said, "Excuse me for a minute, y'all, I've got to go show 'em my monkey."

Rob, eyed suspiciously by the yard-brush man, copied the sign into his notebook. He remembered that carrying a concealed weapon was perfectly legal in New Orleans.

WASH THE GIRL OF YOUR CHOICE

He was disappointed they would not be seeing the Lafayette Cemetery No. 1, with its above-ground tombs and extravagant, decaying family vaults, but the concierge had warned vehemently about the thugs and hoodlums from the nearby projects, the robberies, savage beatings, murders.

ST. PAUL SPIRITUAL CHURCH OF GOD IN CHRIST

Overall, he was beginning to feel that the city was split by poverty, overwhelmed by tourism, was becoming a freak show, the remaining local population reduced by service to servitude. But he continued to take pleasure in small things, the smell on the morning air of plums and strawberries in punnets and slatted crates delivered and waiting on the sidewalk to be taken in by corner stores.

The look of okra.

Of crawfish.

And courtyards.

He'd always liked courtyards, the *idea* of courtyards, a life lived inwards, elegant oases hidden behind high walls and blank, locked gates, but here and there as they walked, water sounds, a glimpse, the rill and *ribble* of a fountain, the smell of wet stone and ferns.

*

There was a line-up on St. Peter Street outside Preservation Hall. Tim and Rob coasted up and stood behind two German students who were talking to, and, Rob assumed, trying to chat up the two girls ahead of them.

The house band was George Lewis' with Lewis on clarinet, Jim Robinson on trombone, Kid Howard on trumpet, Manuel Sayles on banjo, Alcide "Slow Drag" Pavageau on bass, Isaac "Snookum" Russell on piano, and Joe Watkins on drums. Largely the same personnel Rob had heard on records.

The *Times-Picayune* had advertised *And Guests!*

"George Lewis," said one of the German students, "is not actually George Lewis. His birth name is Joseph Louis François Zenon."

"So why does he call himself George Lewis?"

"That I do not know. Though he is descended from Senegalese slaves."

"Though?" said Rob to Tim.

"Oh," said the girl. "Really?"

"Oh, yes," said the student.

"Oh," said the girl.

Rob had drunk most of a bottle of wine at dinner and was finding the conversation of this German chap tortuous.

"The Pavageau Family tomb," he was saying, "is in Cemetery Number Two. It is beside the tomb of Marie Laveau, the dangerous Voodoo Queen. Alcide Pavageau is her nephew. Some writers say, writers of repute, that Alcide Pavageau can claim descent from the kings of France, through the Hernandez line. The Valois kings, that is, not, of course, the Bourbons. His grandmother being Theresa-Olympia Hernandez."

"The Hernandez line?" said the girl.

"Quite so."

"You're joking!" she said. "Kings of France?"

"No. I am not," he said. "Though some say this claim is not so. There is disputation. But it *is* so that Alcide was often called 'Prince Alcide.' So this question is still to be resolved."

"But," said the girl, "isn't he…well… black?"

"Aha!" said the student. "But so, in part, was the Russian aristocrat Pushkin!"

"Oh," said the girl.

"Whose maternal grandmother was *also* a slave."

"Well," said Rob, "I'd say that about clinches it."

"From Cameroon," concluded the student before launching into an exploration into the meaning of the word "tailgate" in describing the trombone style of Jim

Robinson, an exploration involving tails, carts, the tails of carts, parades, not "carts" but—

His friend interjected, "Floats!"

Ja, Ja, *floats!*"

"Sorry?" said the girl.

"The trombone—because of the long—" he mimed a slide extending "so not to discommode his band, over the tailgate of his float he extends."

Rob said, "Fuck my Aunty Ann."

The seating was wooden benches uncomfortable and uncomfortably close together. The band was sitting on wooden chairs on a low platform. In the rear of the front line, Watkins, behind a bass drum with the words Jazz Band painted on it, and "Slow Drag" Pavageau drooped onto the double bass. His hair was a frizzy white cap like a lawyer's wig.

"He looks so *old*," said Rob.

Leaning forward from the row behind, his breath hot on Rob's ear, the German student said, "Born 1888."

The band was dressed variously, a couple in white shirts, others with a suit waistcoat over a shirt. The room was humming with quiet conversation and expectation. The space was so small that the band did not need microphones.

George Lewis pointed into the front row and a tubby white man stepped onto the low platform. He bent and fiddled with a black box, then stood with a hand mike.

Pavageau hoisted the double bass upright.

"Good evening ladies and gentlemen, good evening y'all. Welcome to the home of New Orleans jazz. I'm Johnny Moreau of Radio Station WDSU, where for years I've hosted…"

Points.

"...the Living Legend... the Soul of New Orleans... Mr. George Lewis!"

Who rose and then sat.

Applause tumultuous.

He tapped his foot *three/four* and the band launched into *Savoy Blues*. *Savoy Blues* was followed by *Perdido Street* and *Too Tight.*

To Rob's ear the group sounded a little ragged, not as crisp as they'd sounded on record. Kid Howard was playing a lead punchy enough but lacking flair, lacking fire. Jim Robinson added slurs and rasps and sounded... Rob was reminded of the coarse *Tiger Rag* record they'd listened to in Jimbo's bedroom.

Too Tight was followed by *Sweet Lorraine* and *Just A Closer Walk with Thee.*

A group in the audience called out *"Ice Cream! Ice Cream!"* and Jim Robinson raised and shook his trombone above his head in acknowledgement—"Born in 1892," whispered the student hot behind Rob's ear—and got to his feet and clowned into what had become his party piece.

Applause was long and fervent.

As applause died down, Johnny Moreau stepped up again and switched on his hand mike. The band settled instruments into rests, except for Manuel Sayles, who moved to stand behind George Lewis with his banjo.

"Ladies and gentlemen, over the years George Lewis has perfected his expression of the soul of the blues in his intricate solo performance of the now-world-famous *Burgundy Street Blues*. He has written the words to accompany this lyrical masterwork, which I will have the honour of reading as he improvises around them. He is accompanied by Manuel Sayles."

Sayles started to strum.

This was the moment Rob had been dreading.

Lewis came in, limpid.

The notes wreathed, entwined, putting Rob in mind of *art nouveau* decoration, foliage and flowers.

Sayles' strumming was simply percussive.

The silence in the room was devotional.

Johnny Moreau began to intone.

> *Blues were born in New Orleans*
> *They're in the heart of each one that you meet.*
> *Yes, the Blues were born in New Orleans*
> *they're in the heart of each one that you meet.*
> *Why, they make you laugh and sing, and you'll cry*
> *all the way down Burgundy Street.*
>
> *You know, on Toulouse and Burgundy*
> *things may seem to you just a little bit wild*
> *just a little bit wild*
> *That's on Toulouse and Burgundy*
> *where, to you, things may seem,*
> *just a little wild.*
> *But each and every one is having their fun*
> *like it should be done, even down to the smallest child.*

There were four more plangent verses.

Tim's face was drawn.

He said, "I hold you accountable for this."

Rob turned his palms up and shrugged in apology.

The sides of Tim's nose had turned pale, a sign usually of irritation or anger.

"This," he said, "was *even worse* than Billie Holiday singing *Strange Fruit.*"

Through the wild applause, the band was moving their chairs to one side of the stage.

Johnny Moreau said, "Ladies and gentlemen! We happen to have with us tonight in the audience honoured guests—if they could stand—

'Sweet' Emma Barret!

Kid Thomas!

Louis Nelson!

and

Billie and Dee-Dee Pierce!"

Dee-Dee Pierce seemed to be blind.

"And *now*, needing no introduction, the world-famous Peg-Leg Bates!"

"Oh, God!" said Rob, the words wrung from him. "Isn't that the chap who was with the Louis Armstrong All Stars show in London? Did you see that? When *was* that? Christ! What a circus!"

"Forgive me," said the student, "for not precisely knowing, but I believe it to have been 1955 or 1956."

"He *what?*" said Tim.

"He's got a wooden leg and he tap-dances."

Which he did.

Interminably.

The platform was boomy.

He tap-danced to *Everybody Loves My Baby, Summertime,* and *After You've Gone.*

Then the band reassembled in a facing line.

They played *Weary Blues, Careless Love, Trouble in Mind,* then *High Society* featuring Lewis, again reproducing the famous Alphonse Picou clarinet solo.

"Paraphrased by Picou," whispered the student, "from the original piccolo solo in the marching-band part of 1901."

This was followed by a sugary *I know What It Means to Miss New Orleans.* Then, in what was obviously to be the evening's finale, Joe Watkins started rolls on the snare drum, paradiddles, bass bombs, rim shots, as a parade preliminary to *Oh Didn't He Ramble.*

The band stood.

The audience clapped to the beat.

Pavageau slapped his bass

Jim Robinson essayed dance steps.

Manuel Sayles stepped out and sang.

Oh, didn't he ramble... he rambled
Rambled all around... in and out of town

Kid Howard signalled with a sideways swerve of his horn that he was leading into the final chorus.

Oh, didn't he ramble... he rambled
He rambled till the butcher cut him down.

*

The beaten-earth pathway soon petered out onto bare rock. They had driven from New Orleans into Texas, up to Fort Worth, Witchita Falls, Amarillo, heading towards the Sangra de Cristo Mountains and Colorado Springs. Tim had said that he wanted to be able to say that he'd climbed in the Rockies.

They soon had to start picking their way upward, careful on surface-shattered stone. Granite and gneiss, Tim had informed him.

Rob had paid little attention to the endless miles, his mind stewing in impressions, pictures, anxieties, groping through this confusion towards some understanding of what he was being made to feel.

The squinty-eyed girl in Jackson Square, bare feet and tambourine, red hair tangling down her back.

"A tradition tribal dance?"

What tradition?

What tribe?

He thought of the George Lewis band and the *ordinariness* of the music, winced mentally at the crudeness of Jim Robinson, realized that he'd been giving assent to the *idea* of a music, that the tradition was played out, that the music was of its time and context, that it had ended when its context changed—the red lights of Storyville extinguished, the storied brothels with their piano "professors" bulldozed, replaced by now-decaying Projects. It had ended when it ended.

He pictured Johnny Moreau of WDSU on the platform stage of Preservation Hall, stooping to press buttons on the black case.

Gotcha! Employing a pair of Pye Black Boxes. *Or as we in the trade say,* Les Boîtes Noires. *Do you want more technical...?*

Chris Mawson would have found in that evening's performance nothing of *duende.*

The evening had been... *he rambled till the butcher cut him down*... and the butcher had cut down in him, too, something shining.

Yet... *was that true?*

Out of it all, only three mountains stood from the plain—Louis Armstrong, Jack Teagarden, Jelly Roll Morton.

All the rest of it—brutal truth he was having to acknowledge—was antiquarianism, the epithet "moldy fig" justified. From that first awful record in Jimbo's bedroom, Bob Crosby and the Bobcats, Jimbo and he had been like arid scholars poring over fragments of Miracle Plays and *Gammer Gurton's Needle,* claiming their essential links to Shakespeare.

He even wondered if it had been about music at all, wondered if he had been chasing a will-o'-the-wisp, wondered if it all had been as tediously commonplace and *ordinary* as adolescent rebellion, an escape from the confines and complacencies of middle-class existence, plump armchairs and sugar-tongs.

At the opposite pole, underlining all this, burning at the forefront, horrible to have it so constantly revisiting one, the crouching black man in the lay-by south of Vicksburg caught in the incandescent light, the night pulsing with the noise of frogs, pierced by the screams of night creatures.

He was also heavy with sexual tension.

The tension informed his anxiety.

He was thinking often about Jenny, picturing her, feeling guilty, desiring her.

His muddied thoughts, feelings, picturings, carried through to no conclusions.

The lacy ironwork in the French Quarter kept intruding, the feeling that it was somehow Spanish rather than French—though why the matter kept recurring he had no idea—its Spanishness having something to do with a head-and-shoulders portrait of a woman staring out of the canvas at him with huge, dark eyes—who *was* it? Degas? Velazquez? Goya? Manet?—a woman wearing over her hair a mantilla, black openwork lace.

The decision to leave, leaving Jenny behind, was easy, the leaving painful. He hated himself for causing pain. Jenny's father was an admiral and was referred to by Jenny and her mother as The Admiral; that was connected in some small way with his decision to leave; the depth of Jenny's talent was another cause for concern; he feared she was insufficiently devoted to it, feared she would abandon what he loved in her, feared that as she grew older she would revert, the traditions of the Quarterdeck reasserting themselves, and that he would end up all shipshape and Bristol fashion in a life that involved lawnmowers.

Involved in this stew of thoughts and feelings, the heretofore unacknowledged decision that he intended to escape from teaching; register-keeping, the number of seats permissible in a classroom, he realized that he had no intention of ever becoming Certified; what he would do next he did not know; time was pressing on him…

Jenny.

What he would do, whatever the shape of it, when it was accomplished years hence, might make him feel less culpable, might, even in his own mind, exonerate him.

While Tim clambered and scrambled up ahead, Rob shouted after him that he was going to rest where he was and would wait there for him.

Small stones and scree rattled down for a minute and then silence settled again. Rob rested under an overhang of rock that shielded him from view above. The land spread out below him. The sky was vast. The black shapes of turkey buzzards circled on the thermals.

Heavy with anxiety and the need for sexual release, he was already tumescent. He ejaculated in spasm after spasm, pumping his seed onto cool Precambrian rock where it lay, glistening.

Medals and Prizes

There was a young man of Devizes
Whose balls were of different sizes
One was so small
It was no good at all
With the other he won medals and prizes

Forde lined up at the Canada Post counter in the Quickie Convenience Store in the mini-mall near Alex's place. Many postal outlets, he now found, were staffed by families from India. This one, however, he could hear was French Canadian. Forde was particular about stamps. He wanted sober stamps. He did not want Signs of the Zodiac stamps, the Stompin' Tom Connors Memorial stamp, Batman or Mickey Mouse stamps, Canadian Mammals stamps, Emily bloody Carr stamps, the Mary Pratt Meticulous Dead Fish on Saran Wrap stamps, Colville stamps, bloody Bateman stamps, stamps featuring the marquetry of the feeble interior decorator Klimpt, nor did he want Extra Large Stamps of gap-toothed Hockey Players, nor those celebrating the Chinese Year of the Snake, Pig, or Goat.

He would have been embarrassed to send such stamps to anyone, but especially to correspondents in England or the USA.

He wanted decorous stamps bearing simply the Sovereign's head.

"Have you any with the Queen on?"

The youth tapped his long fingernail on the flat display case on the counter that contained a single booklet of ten.

"She's all gone, her."

"Then what do you have?"

The youth indicated the booklet.

Three groundhogs sat up in a row on the earth mound excavated from their burrow, peering towards possible danger.

"You're sure?"

The youth again tapped the showcase.

"All we 'ave," he said, "are rodents."

*

Suzy Hughes opened the door and said, "Where's your medal?"

"It was heavy," said Forde, "ruined the way my lapel sits."

"Nice suit, though," said Suzy, "new?"

"Sheila took it home with her. It's not new. It's pressed. She's getting her hair cut or whatever for tonight."

"Lunch?" said Suzy.

The floor was marked out every two feet or so with strips of white tape.

"No, no thanks, Sheila and I stopped in at the Chateau Laurier on the way home and raised a couple of brandies and some peanuts."

Walking ahead down the passage into the kitchen, Suzy said "I should damn well think so! Do you think my behind's getting too big?"

"Too big for what?"

"Cheeky!"

"Well," said Forde, "it's a *bit* cheeky."

"Oh, Forde!" she said. "Oh, Rob!"

He gathered her to him and they stood in the kitchen holding each other.

Through her hair, he said, "What are those stripes for?"

"What?"

"On the floor."

"Oh," she said. "Well, you've heard of this Parkinson's shuffle, that feeling they have that their feet won't move, so this is what his doctor told us to do. It gives him something to aim for, something that shows him where his feet should go."

"This is sudden, isn't it, Suzy? Worse, I mean. Suddenly."

She nodded.

"Yes, this last month."

They pulled out stools and sat at the counter.

"Coffee?"

Forde nodded, watched her getting a package of beans and the grinder out of a cupboard.

"Christ!" he said.

Something to aim for!

"But I had a good idea a couple of weeks ago!" said Suzy. "He's been hiding in the house more and more lately, but I know he likes to go out with me grocery shopping—God! How pathetic that sounds! But even that's begun exhausting him and so I hurry and that just makes him more tired and more stressed and anxious, ohh…"

She sighed.

"I have to have a bag in the car with a complete change of clothes in case he has an accident."

Forde shook his head.

"Which we've had."

She sighed.

"Anyway, he likes to watch people—of *course* he does—and lots of immigrants go there to buy produce they're used to—I don't know—papayas, Ugli fruit, Lebanese cabbage, curry leaves… he likes to look at the colours, peppers, and celery, apples, mushrooms, fresh mint, and watercress… and you have to *drag* him away from the fish counter *look at the mackerel,* he'll say, *the markings, the dark bars, that black-green with a glint of gold.* He always did have that kind of eye, didn't he? He used to write like that.

One week, after the groceries, it was a bad day, the drugs fading out, he couldn't speak more than a whisper and I couldn't understand what he was trying to say, so he wrote over and over on a scrap of paper, but the handwriting's so tiny now you can't really read it—hand muscles..."

Suzy's eyes shone with unshed tears.

"This was the man who wrote novels and short stories. He wrote this one word over and over until I could make it out—he wanted me to know how much he liked seeing the fruit and vegetables.

Variegated, he wrote."

She turned her back squarely.

Fussed over the cone of filter paper.

Reached down mugs from the cupboard.

Busied herself.

"So this idea?" said Forde. "This good idea you had?"

"Ah!" she said. "Yes. Well, the shopping tired him and the stress of walking and the fear of 'freezing'—do you...?"

Forde nodded.

"Go on."

"So I thought of getting him a shopping cart and putting a couple of heavy cases, you know, soft drinks, on the platform underneath as ballast and he could lean on that like a big walker. Then give the cases back to the cashier—changed my mind—and *it's working.*

She sat and raised her mug.

"Cheers," she said, "and congratulations."

He smiled and hummphed her congratulations away.

"I was thinking the other day," she said, "about when you and Sheila and yours and our kids—driving up to our cottage. And when you got up into the Rideau Lakes area there were estate agent For Sale signs everywhere, that company called Bowes & Cocks. Remember? And Alex used to call out to the kids,

'Bows & Cocks! Keep your eyes skinned, hombres! We're entering Mohawk territory.'"

"*I* remember," said Forde, "coming back from one of these jaunts, when he started in Brockville putting forward the proposition that concrete was among mankind's most useful inventions. Useful *and* beautiful. It went on from Brockville until he pulled up in the drive here."

"In all the years of my marriage," she said, "I've never lacked for conversation."

"What do you mean, 'the drugs fading out'?"

"Well, he has to take them every four hours, and by about the end of hour three, the symptoms get stronger, the tremors come back, the rigidity... Everything slows down again and he gets more anxious and he's slower to answer a question or understand what I'm saying to him."

"Does the doctor know? Give him something stronger?"

"There's nothing more they can do. It's dopamine replacement—two drugs every day. *Sinemet* it's called. *Sinemet* and *Stalevo*. Diminishing returns, that's the story. It's the best they can do."

A silence fell between them.

"So," said Forde, "do you know what it is he wants to tell me?"

"Yes," said Suzy. "But I wanted to warn you. What his life's about now is dignity. He insists on showers every day even though the struggle of it is awful. This bloody thing makes you sweat heavily and it makes your skin oily. So that involved drilling through tile and grab bars and a sort of walker structure in the shower that stands on rubber mats.

Oh, Forde! I sit on the floor outside that bathroom every day waiting for the sound of his fall.

Most days I help him get dressed—which he doesn't like—he can't do buttons because they're too fiddly now. And shoe laces he can't do because they're fiddly too, and if he tries to bend over, he falls. I tried to get him to wear shoes with a Velcro strap but he said they were for children and he won't wear pull-on shirts like, oh, I don't know, polo shirts or rugby shirts, anything *without* buttons. And his razor—I bought an electric one, but he said it didn't shave properly, it was dirty. And when he has a not-getting-dressed day—dressing can take more than an hour—he wears pyjamas and a dressing gown but he wears polished dress shoes on his bare feet. Get the picture?"

Forde nodded.

"So don't be 'understanding' or pity him."

Forde nodded.

"He feels humiliated he can't use a knife and fork and cutting up food for him is worse—rubs in the child thing—so everything I make has to be things he can eat with just a fork in his good hand."

"Talk about 'blessed among women,'" said Forde.

"And then there's the constipation. Chronic. But let's not get into *that*."

"Is that drugs or part of the beast?"

"The beast. And *odd* things happen, things they didn't warn us about. There was a while there he couldn't seem to grasp if a glass was upright or upside down, and he'd pour orange juice onto it not into it, so I had to teach him to feel the glass first to see if he could put a finger inside it."

She shook her head slowly.

"Can you see that? One of the finest literary minds in the country standing in his pyjamas, frowning at a tumbler."

"Oh, God!" said Forde.

"The kids have been good, though. One or the other usually comes round and polishes a couple of pairs of shoes. Danny bought a shoehorn and spliced it onto a broom handle so he wouldn't have to bend. Part of trying to get him to accept loafers so he won't have to fiddle with laces. Which him being him, he's always trying to do."

She fell silent again.

"Which him," she said, "*still* being him."

Smiled at him suddenly.

"You with that pack of kids trailing you, going around old manure heaps with a pitchfork catching milk snakes for them."

"Long time ago."

She squeezed his hand.

"Not forgotten."

"So…" he said.

"Oh," she said, "I've got to tell you this. This is exactly up your alley. We were at the hospital for an X-ray and the girl technician said he'd have to take off his *button-up*. His *what?* he said. Your *button-up*, she said. *This?* he said, plucking up a fold of his shirt.

And I had to unbutton it because he couldn't and he was terribly embarrassed even though she was scarcely more than a child. Poor little creature, one side of her face *ravaged* by acne. Marked for life. Anyway, on good days when his voice was strong he kept returning to this, saying she had to be quasi-literate to be a technician, high school, a college course, but she didn't seem to know the word 'shirt.' To her, it was 'a thing with buttons on,' *a button-up*.

Do you see what this means? he'd say. *Where we're headed? It's a glimpse into the abyss. Terrifying.*

Actually, of course, he was very pleased."

She fell silent and then said, "What was I talking about?"

"Dignity."

"Those mealy-mouthed bastards at the university," she burst out, "he's worked there for thirty years—*thirty years*—and they voted to deny him emeritus status because they said novels and short stories and essays weren't academic achievements. *Sick* petty, but it hurt him."

"Ah, baubles, Suzy. Like this morning. Baubles."

"What was it like this morning? What was *she* like, the Governor General?"

"I'd have to admit, charming. Gave a surprising, unsugary speech. I was surprised, *pleased*. I'd been fully prepared to dislike her. I hadn't expected such seriousness from an ex-media thingy. But there were forty-some people getting the damn things, knee-deep in philanthropists, entrepreneurs, donors to this and that, NGO people fertilizing the desert wastes, ancient nuns—I was *awash* in do-goodery. *Not* my usual scene. And tonight it's the formal dinner. God! *Absolutely* not my scene.

And the funny thing *is*, Suzy, I have *no* idea who proposed me for the bloody thing. I just can't imagine the Chief Justice of the Supreme Court of Canada giving me the old *Nihil Obstat*. Worries me, actually, being acceptable. Tokenism. Makes me think I've lost my edge. Their literary exhibit. Won't bite. Toothless."

"Not you, you boozy old sod!"

"Now, now. 'Suzy, play nicely!'," chided Forde.

She put one hand over the other under her chin and did contrite little girl.

"But the best part for me, midst all this what passes in Canada for pomp and circumstance, was Sheila, we were looking round the more public rooms in Rideau Hall afterwards and I'd drifted on and I was looking at a nice little landscapey abstraction by Ulysses Comtois and I heard Sheila's voice calling me.

I turned round and she was standing about ten feet away.

She looked me up and down, suit, damn great snowflake, and she said,

'Not bad Forde.'

Made my heart turn over."

"Well, of *course* it did," said Suzy. "She *adores* you."

Forde nodded slowly.

"So..." said Suzy. "What Alex wants."

"Go on."

"Well, contracts, paperback reprints, all that rights stuff, he wants you to handle it. He feels he's been too long on the sidelines. He wants to get his best work into print again. *Really* what he wants—he wants you to save what his life's been about."

Forde nodded.

"Of course," he said, "Of course, I'll try my hardest but I have to be blunt, Suzy. Of course I'll do everything that can be done, but Alex's reputation is in decline. Mine, too. We're what are called 'midlist' writers—if we're even that. 'Midlist' means that in the eyes of conglomerates we're failures. The judgement's financial, of course. Good equals large number sold. *We* know the exact opposite's true.

We're at the mercy of 'the media.' People talk about it as if it exists as an abstract force, but what is 'the media'? Simply the sum of hacks and flacks who are individually unfit to polish Alex's shoes.

The populist tide rises!

The world's persuaded itself that easy's the new great.

Once it was glory, Suzy. Now it's mayflies dead in a day.

The cachet Alex and I once had... *comic books*, Suzy."

Arseholes are cheap today!

sang Forde

Cheaper than yesterday!

"Are you sure you only had two brandies?"

"Alex and I are in the same boat, Suzy. And it's sinking."

"But you'll try."

"Oh, yes," said Forde, getting to his feet, "oh, yes. Yes, indeed."

Then, turning back to her, he said, "And it can't be cured or, you know, the drugs can't hold it at bay?"

Suzy shook her head.

"Parkinsons usually live out a normal lifespan, but with everything just getting worse and worse, more pronounced, the symptoms, I mean. The drugs apparently become less and less effective."

"It's like a fucking Beckett play."

"And some way off yet there's incontinence."

Forde kissed the silent tears from her cheeks.

"They often do die, though, from pneumonia. Food particles going down the wrong way into the lungs. Then bacteria. I can't, in my faith, wish for it, Rob, but I do sometimes. For him, I mean."

"So," he said.

Then he said, "Well, I'll go and see the boss and get my marching orders."

"He drools, sometimes," she said, "you know, the swallowing, it's difficult, but there's a box of Kleenex and—"

"Stop it, Suzy. Stop fussing."

He went up the stairs and along the landing.

Tapped on Alex's door.

He heard Alex's voice and went in.

Alex was standing gripping the top edges of a chest of drawers.

"So, Alexander, old cock!" said Forde, coming around him to hold his left arm, his hand travelling down the length of the arm to free Alex's left hand from its grip on the chest.

a gentling hand down the length of the horse's leg before lifting its hoof

Moved them over to the couch.

"You've been talking to Suzy."

The voice near normal but the face rather expressionless, as Suzy had warned.

"I was getting worried."

"A bit delayed. I'm sorry, Alex. It was Rideau Hall all morning."

"Your investiture."

"Not as grand as that sounds."

Alex nodded slowly.

"Are you working?"

"I'm still working on *Medals.*"

Alex said,

One was so small

It was no good at all

Forde said,

With the other he won medals and prizes.

"It's a good title," said Forde, "for the emotional—you know."

Alex needed no explanation.

"*But,*" said Forde, "it's nowhere *near* as good as yours."

Alex put his left hand, flat on his knee, then moved his right hand across, placing it over his left hand, covering it to quell the tremors.

"What one?"

"That title you were always threatening to write."

Unsmiling, Alex said,

Fecal Matter

*

The more Sheila nattered, the more darkly uncommunicative Forde felt himself becoming. The looming evening could not have come at a worse time. The afternoon visit to Alex had left him scraped, bleak. Talking with Alex, the medal an elephant in the room, had left him feeling shabby.

This bloody day, just at this time when he wanted life undisturbing, uneventful, because a story was coming into focus, the insistent images beginning to cohere, the slow forming filling his mind: a Jewish wedding, the young couple under the tent-thing, the canopy whatsit, the—what was it Sheila had given him—the *chuppah!* the whole thing moving closer and closer, defining itself enough for him to have given it a title

If I Forget Thee, O Jerusalem

The old man lying on the dance floor felled by a heart attack, the grouped figures around him suggesting a painting of the Italian renaissance, possibly a Deposition, the Klezmer band playing *If I Were A Rich Man*, playing on and on *dabba-dabba-do*, on and on through the confusion, the old wife kneeling, the old man's stricken white hand climbing her arm.

If I Forget Thee, O Jerusalem, let my right
hand forget its cunning.

Alex had never wavered, never forgotten, but his trembling hand was cunning no longer.

He would never write again.

His destination had always been Jerusalem, Zion his constant dream; he stood now staring in perplexity at a tumbler.

By the rivers of Babylon...
we wept when we remembered Zion.

The instructional bumph from the Chancellery of Honours had detailed a Reception in the Tent Room followed by Dinner in the Ballroom. Each inductee was permitted a Spouse/Companion and one Guest. Inductee and Spouse/Companion had been assigned seating at separate tables so that both could benefit from "mingling and sharing the richness of their life experience."

life scrotums, thought Forde, *life bollocks.*

Sheila had said that their guest must be Joshua or Ben, as she wanted one of them to witness this honouring of their father. Josh was her choice as being the elder and as having no visible tattoos.

Forde was wearing the suit he'd worn in the morning as he had no other and was recalcitrant about putting on a fresh shirt. He had squabbled with Sheila about fixing into his lapel one of the miniatures that had been handed out prior to the morning ceremony, before the bestowing of the medal proper; she had been adamant.

"Just—" she said. "On this Day of days, could you just once spare me all your *piffle.*"

The bed was draped with discarded choices: dresses, blouses, pantsuits.

"Beautiful," he said.

"Lovely," he said.

"Most becoming," he said.

"Don't be fucking ridiculous," he said, "Of *course* I'm not going to shave again."

*

Forde tasted the flute of champagne lifted from a passing waiter—*not* champagne, a cheapish prosecco or cava. He downed it with a slight shudder.

From another circulating salver, he plucked a smear of something brown on a saltine.

"Bison pâté," said the girl.

And you are?

The man had bounced out of a knot of people like a steel ball bearing binking in a new direction on a bagatelle board into a new pocket of nails.

"Robert Forde."

Denis Markle. I'm the Miramichi Herald. *And in what field of endeavour...?*

"Services to literature."

"My, my! Charming, charming. Actually, I'm in search of Saguenay and Athabaska... we Heralds...

He smiled vaguely, White Rabbitish, and pottered off into the heating throng.

Forde acquired a large scotch from the bartender, who dispensed with the precision and impassivity of a croupier.

Sterling fellow, thought Forde, deserving himself of a medal.

Services to Humanity

Josh, he saw, chatting to a young woman with a layered haircut and very large, purple-framed glasses; doubtless, just chatting; sadly, not chatting her *up*. A world of wasted possibilities.

Josh approached holding a flute.

He eyed the glass in Forde's hand.

"Liquor," he said.

In stage-Irish, a *Juno and the Paycock* accent, his Joxer Daly accent, Forde said,

"And a blessing it is, a blessing."

Then,

"Where's your mother?"

"Listening to that woman in a sari."

A strange creature who, despite the sari, was stoutly, lumpishly un-Indian. Blonde brillo-pad hair, a sparkly thing in her nose. The over-the-shoulder wrap of the sari exposed the left side of her waist bulging out in rolls. Her bared left arm was festooned nearly to the elbow with metal bangles and sparkly glass bangles, the sort of bangles sold in cheap Indian Import shops that smelled of sandalwood incense and patchouli.

She jangled as she gesticulated.

"Who the hell is *she*? said Forde.

"She's the CEO of an NGO called CICA."

Forde eyed him.

Joshua worked in the Civil Service as an AS-5 in Supply and Services. Forde had little idea of what AS-5 meant—he'd heard Sheila say it and hadn't been interested in inquiring further—nor had he any idea of what Josh actually did beyond, he assumed, supplying things and servicing them. Though he made efforts to deny it to himself, he found Joshua stultifying. His haircuts cost about half of what Forde was paid for a short story or article in the literary magazines.

"'Seeka,' people seem to say it," said Josh. "An acronym of *Canada India Child Adoption.*"

"Hmmm," said Forde, turning back to the barman.

"I hope," said Joshua, "and pray, that you're not going to—"

"Mere anaesthesia," said Forde.

"Because you know how much it hurts her when you get—"

"Thank you—" said Forde "—Joshua."

When the throng was herded into the Ballroom for Dinner, Forde was seated beside Joshua on one side and a large, fattish man on the other. The combined, confluent chattering was so dense, it left Forde straining, watching lips, teeth, eyebrows, eyes, words and occasional sentences drifting his way. Sheila, his lifeline, hopeless tables away.

He became aware, white cuff, black-clad arm, of a hand reaching across his place setting, picking up his name-card.

The man then grunted and dropped it.

Rumbled.

"Don't recall your citation at the ceremony. Your award was for...?"

"Services, so it said," said Forde, "to literature."

"Publishing company?"

"Nothing so exciting."

"Well?"

"Writer."

"Would I have heard of you?"

Forde more squarely turned to look at him, took in the embonpoint, the black glass studs in his starched shirt front, the acreage of rubicund face, was instantly visited by Gore Vidal's description of Senator Edward Kennedy as *three hundred pounds of condemned veal*. Putting both hands flat on the table, he said, "Well..."

Joshua, who'd been leaning anxiously, said, "Don't! *Please!*"

Smiling beatifically, Forde said, "Well, it depends, of course, on your reading habits, but most probably not."

He paused.

"Though it gives one something to aim for."

Waiters and waitresses were circulating with bottles of wine from British Columbia. Forde endured Joshua's reproachful eyes as he quaffed the rather nasty acidic red.

...we wept when we remembered Zion...

The woman's painful voice was cutting through the babble of lesser voices.

"Oi," said Forde: "Think of waking up to *that*. What's SAP?"

"SSAP," said Joshua. "It stands for Sahel Sahara Acacia Project. They plant acacia trees to stem the southern advance of the sands."

...though headquartered in Ouagadougou...

Query was heard around the table.

"*What* did she say?"

"It *sounded* like 'Ouagadougou.'"

"Good heavens!"

"It's the capital."

"What of?"

"Burkino Faso."

"Burkino *what*?"

"What *was* Upper Volta."

"Always *changing* things."

"Funny. We've got an acacia tree in the backyard."

"That'll be a False Alcacia."

"Nothing false about it, I can assure you, pretty white flowers, and these long, black, dangling—"

...so we called the compound 'Dar Es Salaam,' Arabic for 'House of Peace' or 'Haven'...

"*We* were there on a cruise. It's a port."

"A family of thorny, leguminous..."

"She's talking about a *compound*. In Burkino Faso."

"We were advised not to disembark."

"Yes, it's in Tanganyika."

"Tanzania, you'll find, now."

"Always *changing* things."

...something of a setback when most of our male volunteers were massacred by Tuareg marauders and the young women...

"Not to be argumentative, but I distinctly remember that this port, Dar Es Salaam, was the capital."

"The capital now, I think you'll find, is Dodama."

...not to put too fine a point upon it, the young women were handed about among the Tuareg and then sold on into slavery in northern Mali...

"Despoiled?"

...and avoidable, but no security-vetted army officer could be found who spoke Tamasheq to carry out negotiations... perfectly possible to have traded our girls for four-wheel drive vehicles the Tuareg prize for the tobacco smuggling...

Forde studied the printed menu.

"See that, Josh?" he said.

"'All food items sourced in Canada'

Croquettes (Prince Edward Island)

Fiddlehead Greens (New Brunswick)

Caille/Quail (The celebrated Game Bird from Alberta)"

Game of any kind, feathered or furred, summoned instantly *Vile Bodies*, a book precious to him, a lodestar in his life.

Waugh describing a game pie.

...full of beaks and shot and inexplicable vertebrae...

Forde moved his wine glass to the side, giving the waiter easier access.

Joshua watched.

A loud-talking woman at the other side of the table was apparently CEO of an NGO called GAM.

Forde indicated her with a slight movement of his head and raised his eyebrows.

Josh said, "Goats for African Mothers."

Forde pieced together that her organization collected money to buy goats that they gave to village women. The goats seemed to thrive on even the sparsest and unpromising vegetation. It did not take long before a flock was established; milk, meat, leather for the production of handicrafts, wallets, for example, sold internationally in One World shops. A simple, practical solution to poverty.

Then the piercing-voice woman moved into high gear again.

SSAP—GAM

GAM—SSAP

It was like listening to bloody ping-pong.

...the other major setback, a devastation of the acacia plantings by an extraordinary and entirely unforeseen explosion in the native goat population...

"Wine, sir?"

"*Absolutely,*" said Forde.

Picking up the charged glass, glancing left to Fatso, right to Joshua, he proffered it in toast proclaiming,

"Jerusalem!"

Touched to his lips British Columbia's acidic bounty.

Joshua made a business of sighing.

Fatso frowned.

Puzzled.

"Enough?" repeated Forde.

He got to his feet *with*, his mind supplied, *lissome grace*, placing his chair neatly back under the tabletop.

To Fatso, he said,

"Sitting too long. Plays the dickens with the old wound!"

Placing the flat of his hand on the crown of Joshua's haircut, he said,

"Remember the ref's last words before he ducks under and out."

He stooped and whispered,

Protect yourself at all times.

*

Of the intricacies of prose in English, he thought it more likely than not that the Chief Justice of the Supreme Court of Canada and his/her buddies knew *bubkess*.

The pleasures of the medal, well... it possibly offered him some slight protection from the more rabid of his critics, but as he'd said to Suzy, it was frippery, like the emeritus status denied to Alex, a bauble.

During the grinding ennui of the Reception, a man had materialized beside him at the makeshift bar and, touching his lapel miniature, had blurted out, "I feel that this, well, for me, it validates a lifetime of work."

He had requested Ginger Ale.

As he walked on into the evening, there played in Forde's head one of his fantastic monologues, his farragos, his habitual fanfaronades...

I, sir, am unable to share your feelings in that I think continually of those who were truly great, of those who left the vivid air signed with their honour.

A dry-clean-y smell about the man, a carbon tetrachloride miasma.

Rented, probably.

Full formal rented fig except for, stubbornly, Forde felt, coarse grey Walmart work socks in sandals.

Possibly a Quaker.

After the noise and heat and pomposities of the mansion, after the *ping* of SSAP and *pong* of GAM, after Joshua's reproaches and Joshua's condescension, the cool of the evening was a pleasure, few cars passing, the trees becoming still shapes, eldritch cries of nighthawks stitching invisibly through insects above the banks of light left on in government edifices.

Dark emotions swarmed him

He felt heartsick at his failing contact with Joshua.

Anger.

But it was Alex he was ridden by.

Certainly he would call in markers, do what could be done, but it would be a rearguard action, the delay of defeat.

White strips on the carpet.

Something to aim for

The path below the Parliament buildings and the Supreme Court, the path alongside the river was dark and quiet. Only small river sounds, but a sense of the weight of the water coming down.

He slowed to a stroll, needing to absorb the silence.

Some distance ahead of him, he saw a patch of light and, as he drew closer, saw a man, a man fishing. Closer, and he saw at the man's feet a small Coleman lamp, a folding canvas stool, a canvas bag. The lamp was dancing light out over the river's currents. As Forde drew level, the man was raising the rod with his left hand, lifting the line out of the water, the line swinging in and caught in his right hand, light glinting on the brass rig, off the brass stem, three brass arms, from which hung short, baited lines.

There was a word for such a rig—he'd used one himself as a boy, sea-fishing—his mind chasing the word… but it was gone.

"Evening," said Forde. "Any luck?"

The man nodded and stirred the sodden newspapers with his foot.

"Couple," he said.

"Carp?" said Forde.

The man nodded.

Forde propped himself on one of the boulders that sat either side of the small spit, boulders placed there, presumably, to keep vehicles away from the crumbling bank. Stones, broken concrete blocks, rubble. Rushes at the tip of it.

"Do you mind if I sit for a bit? Such a soft night."

The man was intent on threading worms.

"They had themselves a free feed," he said.

"Where are they?" asked Forde. "I mean, what does this little breakwater do?"

"Moves the current out just a bit in a curve, see? and that makes a small, slower-moving backwater—can you see there? Where the water's moving with less surface on it?"

"Right," said Forde. "So that's where they're lying."

"That's it," said the man. "Where they don't have to fight water as much."

As he bent back over the rig, the left side of his face was lit in the naphtha glare and Forde saw that the flesh was tight, immobile, shiny. As so often, Hemingway flashed into him mind, one of those imaginative feats that now crammed his mind, Hemingway's description of the *mutilés de guerre* ...

...an almost iridescent cast about the considerably reconstructed faces, rather like that of a well-packed ski run... crammed brilliances that shone, fragments that earlier in his life had opened up verbal possibilities, sudden vistas of verbal splendour.

"I don't mean to be rude," he said, "but I couldn't help noticing—"

"My face, is it?"

"A fire?" said Forde.

"Sort of."

"I'm sorry if I—"

The man shrugged.

"Years ago," he said.

"What happened?"

"Well, the long and short of it, I was making fries for my boy, Donny—in the rushes there—and the chip pan, the fat caught fire, to this day, I don't know how *that* happened, it was on a gas burner but still—anyway I got in a panic, there was flame up the wall, and I opened the kitchen window over the sink to chuck it out—there was a walk alongside the house up to the back door—well, most of it went out but the pot hit the window frame and some splashed back on me but what went out hit my wife. As fate would have it, she'd been coming up the side path with a bag of groceries.

"Christ!" said Forde. "How awful!"

"She died, Mary did, the burns, but the shock as well, the doctors said. Her heart gave out. They had her on morphine and she didn't last long, thank God!"

"I am so sorry," said Forde.

"You learn to live with it."

He cast out again.

"Easy casting," he said, "with this weight of lead on it. Strip off a few lengths of line and it's just lobbing it into place. The lead keeps it on the bottom where they're feeding."

He wound the reel until the line was taut and propped the rod against the stool.

"We do alright though, me and Donny. He's a bit..." the man nodding meaningfully. "Good-hearted, though. I'm on the pension but we do odd jobs here and there helps us out. I had a proper business before. Painting. Donny does the roller but I still do the cutting. I can't do a full day now because my arm got some of it and I was wearing an old workshirt—nylon or rayon or whatever, you know, flammable, and some of it must have melted into the burn and it was infected and they had to cut some muscle away... but we do alright, Donny and me. Has something of Mary's looks, Donny has.

I don't sleep so well so we come down here most nights, soon as the ice goes out."

"Pain?"

"No, not now. Just, well, thinking about things. I can't sleep for thinking about things. One minute you're just jogging along, everything's like it always is, and the next the whole world's changed. What must you make of that?"

"It must be very hard."

"But what are *you* doing in a suit and tie? Down here sitting on my rock?"

"I was at a fancy dinner but I got bored and I had a row with one of my sons."

They sat and watched the river.

"That's a beautiful old reel you're using," said Forde, "Years since I've seen a wooden one. They call them 'fixed spool' reels now but I can remember when they were the only reels there were. I had one just like that when I was a kid. For sea-fishing, that was. Imagine! They sell reels like that in antique shops now."

"Are you from England?"

"Yes, years ago."

"I thought I could hear it, that accent."

"A long time now," said Forde.

"I've never been over there. Nottingham's where my dad was from."

He ran his fingertip along the edge of the reel.

"This was me dad's. About the only thing of his I have left. Someone—I don't think it was him—someone had painted it with marine varnish, like on yachts, but it had gone scabby so I sanded it down and treated it with linseed oil and brought it back up and it came up beautiful, the grain. And a drop of machine oil under the spool..."

"And the beauty of them, too," said Forde, "is there's nothing to go wrong or break."

"I never was sure," said Ken, "what wood it was. What do you think?"

Ford squatted.

"Oak?"

"The grain's not right for oak. Oak's big, isn't it? The patterns of it, I mean."

"And it's not a foreign hardwood," said Forde, "not like mahogany or teak, say. Could it be elm? That's a hard one."

"You know what I'm thinking," said Ken. "I don't know why it's in my head but I think it's maybe boxwood. Could he have said that? Or else why's it there? And 'heartwood,' that's in my mind. *I* wouldn't have said that, but he might have."

"Ah?" said Forde. "Could well be because that's got a tight grain, hasn't it? Very hard. They use it for carvings and making prints."

"That's my guess, anyway," said Ken.

"And you're not using nylon line."

"No, real old-fashioned, I am."

"Lovely to see a reel like that," said Forde.

A companionable silence fell.

The wooden reel moved memories in him.

He saw himself as a boy of nine or ten.

He fished religiously. Most evenings he rode down to the river Stour. Heart-pounding evenings poaching in a private fishing club's waters for roach and bream. Endless, timeless summer evenings. An evening when all the boys went mad as a big pike was spotted from the bridge, boys running, shouting, pointing, getting rods into the water, irritating mothers calling bedtime and boys' names in the hot, deepening dark.

Sometimes he cycled for miles to watch lampreys gathered under the bridge over the stream that ran through the grounds behind Christchurch Cathedral. Sometimes at low tide, he'd jump, mud-spattered, from tussock to tussock across the Christchurch saltings to reach Mudeford and the Black House and watch salmon fishermen laying nets at the estuary's narrow mouth, watch them sometimes hauling in a fury of roiling silver.

And sea fishing.

He saw himself as a boy of nine or ten scrunching along the pebbles, scavenging along the tideline of sea-wrack, the tangles of kelp and bladderwrack. He always left his bike at the cliff top and walked miles past the promenade and the beach huts, walking towards a ruined old jetty that was fringed with weed. At its end, where once a beacon stood, beds of kelp sloshed and swayed. Cormorants voided white on the crumbling concrete.

He liked going out in subsiding storms, a solitary little figure exulting in the wildness of the booming wind, the immense roaring, waves smashing, spray and spume driving inland to the very base of the cliffs.

Scattered above and below the wandering line of seawrack lay seashells—limpet, mussel, periwinkle, whelk and cockle, painted top and paddock. Razor shells. The white shields of cuttlefish, whelks' egg cases like coarse sponge, mermaid's purses.

He once had found in the flotsam a torso, nippleless breasts, broken thighs, a manikin.

Sometimes among the tarred rope and grey driftwood branches that looked to him like ancient antlers, among the broken crates, a Brasso tin, the cracked crab shells and hollowed bodies of birds, great baulks of timber lined with grey-blue goose barnacles stinking in the sun.

This would have been in the year before his father had moved to a new church, a new circuit, as he was supposed to do every five or six years. This would have been then, yes, when he was nine, the year before they'd moved to Beckenham, where he was destined to meet Jimbo.

Sometimes on the trudge over sliding pebbles, he'd sit and attack stones with the hammer he carried along with his rod and knapsack of tackle. He chose larger pebbles, especially those with yellowish areas of discolouration; they broke more easily and sometimes harboured the perfect fossils of sea urchins. The cliffs themselves sometimes yielded ammonites.

He would sit for hours on the broken jetty, casting out over and beyond the kelp beds. He was never bored. He watched his rod-tip, watched waves chasing, watched the sea's shifting planes, the flight of gulls and cormorants.

Often he would hold the taut line between delicate thumb and forefinger feeling its tensions and its easings, its vibrations, feeling a *frisson* of anticipation from the living line's minutest quivering, feeling its connection to that world beneath the water where the lugworms he had dug were being touched, nosed, nudged by whatever he would raise from the depths into the struggling air—wrasse, sea bass, flounder, soles…

The invisible Donny shouting.

Pebbles sliding, crunching, commotion in the rushes.

"I've got one on!"

"I hear you," called Ken.

A rachet clacking.

Then Donny's voice, *"aaaah!"*

"What?"

"It's only a *little* fucker."

"Well," called Ken, "you're only a little fucker yourself."

*

Down river, below the bridge, a boat was approaching, a blaze of lights, sounds of music.

One of the tourist boats, thought Forde, that were advertised aggressively on the stretch of sidewalk above the locks beside the Chateau Laurier, sandwich boards, brochures pushed onto passers-by by youths in nautical, peaked caps.

Romantic River Cruise

Free Champagne

Dance to the Music of the Bytown All-Stars

As the boat drew closer, Forde began to hear that the All-Stars were a Dixie outfit.

He could imagine the music being played by men now growing old, men who'd brought the Trad Revival to Canada from England in the late fifties and early sixties, men who were part of the large influx of immigrants, the professionals and skilled trades who'd been needed then by such enterprises as Canadair in Montreal. He'd heard such a band in his first months in Canada, a band with an expatriate following.

It was not, he thought, inconceivable that the Bytown All-Stars were their *sons*.

The boat forged nearer, cresting the current.

The All-Stars launched into *Darktown Strutters Ball.*

Forde thought suddenly of the oleaginous Hoagy Carmichael.

> I'll be there to catch you in a taxi, honey
> Better be ready 'bout half past eight
> Now baby, don't be late
> I wanna be there when the band starts playing
>
> Remember when we get there, honey
> Two-step, I'm gonna have them all
> Gonna dance out of both my shoes
> When they play the 'Jelly Roll Blues'
> Tomorrow night at the Darktown Strutters Ball.

Christ!

As the boat churned in towards its mooring, the band tackled *Tiger Rag,* the tune's only distinction being that it was the first or second recording in the history of jazz, five young white men from New Orleans, *The Original Dixieland Jazz Band*, recorded in New York by *Victor* in 1917. The personnel clicked through Forde's memory: Nick LaRocca (trumpet), Larry Shields (clarinet), Ed Edwards (trombone), Henry Ragas (piano), Tony Sbarbaro (drums).

A frenzy had seized the Bytown drummer—highhat, cymbals, wood blocks, rim shots, Chinese gongs, bong-bells, bass drum bombs, heralding, Forde hoped, a conclusion. The crew had cut the boat's lights leaving the deck lit only by the tiny multi-coloured fairy lights strung along its lines.

Jiggling, gyrating, the dark mass heaved.

So many years ago, thought Forde, gazing across the river, so many years ago, in the innocence of Jimbo's bedroom, listening to *Tiger Rag*, the first jazz record they'd ever heard, a version of the bloody thing by the long-forgotten Bob Crosby and the Bob Cats, a 78-rpm disc of acetate that had started him on a convoluted path that seemed now to have set him bemedaled on a boulder.

CEAZER SALAD

The review of *Chamber Music* had appeared in the Saturday edition of the *Calgary Clarion*, which arrived in Ottawa at Magazines International on Wednesday. The tone of the review was hostile and oddly aggrieved. The reviewer—"a Calgary writer"—suggested that Albertans, commonsensical and down-to-earth as they were, would only be repelled by the book's so-called sophistication, a sophistication which might be lauded by Brahmins in the East but which was elitist and effete. "Tony" had been one of the reviewer's words. He went on to attack Forde's contempt for his readers, as evidenced in his pretentious use of the word "ziggurat," and the book's alleged humour which he, Calgarian, found brittle if not epicene.

Forde rattled the pages of the *Clarion*.

"'Picasso COMMA the famous Spanish painter COMMA.' Well, I suppose you can't go far wrong assuming ignorance in Albertans."

He smacked the sheets with the back of his hand.

"Christ! Here's an amazing one. 'Napoleon COMMA the Emperor of the French COMMA.'"

The sections, Sports, Classified, Wheels, Entertainment, fluttered down the wall to the floor.

"'Brahmins,'" said Forde. "'*Brahmins!*'"

Sheila, who was taking a day off, pulled the lapels of her bathrobe closed and, dipping the brush into the varnish, concentrated on the spread fingers of her left hand. Whenever she took what she called mental health days she sat around in her old terrycloth robe and painted her fingernails and toenails and turned the radio on. She did not listen to the radio. She knew what anguish its bland bonhomie caused him and he was convinced that she turned it on not only to assert her presence but to persecute him.

"One wonders," he said, "why they didn't feel compelled to go on and on and ON. 'Emperor of the French COMMA who lived in olden times COMMA and died in exile on St. Helena COMMA a small island in the South Atlantic Ocean.'"

Sheila tapped the lid of the marmalade jar with a knuckle.

"Please," she said.

"'Unlikely,'" said Forde, "'to be of interest to Western readers.'"

"Do you think this'll still be good, Rob?"

"Hah!" he said. "What," he demanded, "*would* be of interest to Western readers? Eh?"

"It's turned very dark," said Sheila, "almost black."

"Think of the headline that *would* engage the inhabitants of Buttfuck, Alberta..."

"*Can* it go bad? Do you think? With all the sugar?"

"ANOTHER COW," said Forde, "FOUND DEAD."

"Mmmm..." said Sheila.

"What a sad sad dump. I *hate* Alberta. The whole bloody landscape littered with fun-loving Mennonites and oil pumps on the nod. Bulging, my Lovely, bulging with huge Ukrainians internationally wanted for Nazi war crimes. People dressed up in silly cowboy hats. And boots everywhere that look like skin disease."

"*What?*"

"*Boots.* Lizard-skin boots. Or ostrich or snake or some fucking thing. Nasty *pimply* boots. Remember Ed Lacey? He was teaching in Edmonton and in a letter—now *here's* a turn of phrase—he called Alberta 'that bleak latrine.'"

The acid peardrop smell of the nail polish suddenly brought to him the balsa-wood aeroplane kits of his childhood. Spitfires, RAF roundels. Messerschmitts, swastikas. The clear glue smelled of peardrops and had always been called "aeroplane dope."

Dope! thought Forde.

He watched Sheila fanning her nails with an envelope.

"Did you know—this is absolutely true—there's a town in Alberta called Dog Pound?"

"*Home,* he sang, *home on the range…*

"And home to the Aryan Nation and the Northern Guard and home, my winsome marrow, my Dunmow Flitch…"

"Who he?" said Sheila.

"What? Where was I? Home to Jim Keegstra and the whatnames, you know, the Heritage Front, and to sturdy Survivalists standing on guard against the encroachment of turban and curry. Yes, my old fruit, when you think about it, it's not very surprising they've got a Eugenics Board. And a Sexual Sterilization Act. And as to the daily round," he said with a wide gesture of his arms, "the amenities, life's little pleasures and refinements—well, there's hardly anything, just to take one example, hardly anything you'd recognize as a restaurant. There were, as I recall, muffins."

He paused.

"Crullers."

Paused again.

"The occasional perogi. But precious little of the old *haute cuisine.* The supermarkets there sell packets of stuff called

Tuna-Extender. And when they're not eating Tuna-Extender they eat steaks. They all have barbeques, propane barbeques with dials and switches like airplane cockpits. And they take their gobbets of Alberta Grade A marbled beef and incinerate them on their propane barbeques which is the cause of the yellow dome that sits pudding-shaped over Calgary and which is visible from as far away as Drumheller."

Forde raised a finger.

"Steaks rare would not be requested *saignant* or *bleu*—or even 'rare.' They would be ordered in the Steakaramas, if at all, by those witty rascals in the cowboy hats with, 'Honey, just saw off its horns and wipe its ass.' And to accompany these burnt offerings—do you know what they eat? They eat iceberg lettuce slathered with a concoction called Creamy Cucumber Ranch.

"You think I'm inventing this?

"*Nobody,* my peardrop-smelling inamorata, nobody could invent this.

"And they drink wine that comes in one-and-a-half litre bottles. It is called *Mediterranean Warmth*. That's the carriage trade. The unwashed drink poisonous rye called *Golden Wedding.*"

Forde uttered a kind of groan.

"In Alberta," he said, "there is nothing old. The buildings are brutal. The streets merely numbered. Bottle-openers are screwed to the headboards of hotel beds."

He stirred the pages of the *Clarion* with his toe cap.

"There's a drear museum in Calgary that about sums it all up," he said. "Looks like a mothballed factory. Full—are you listening, my fruit of the loom?—full not of the glory that was Greece and the grandeur that was Rome. No, sir! No, siree! Not in Alberta. But furnished with fascinating old scythes and billhooks, patent medicine bottles, Louis Riel's suspenders, pioneer buckets..."

Forde paused.

"Christ!" he whispered, as if broken. "Christ! The balls-withering boredom of it all."

*

Forde ran his forefinger over the polyurethane on his desktop, hating it. He wished that he could afford an eighteenth-century desk or table. He thought it probable that if he had a beautiful desk it would induce a greater elegance in his writing. He did not necessarily want a piece from the workshop of Robert Adam or Chippendale or Gillow or Hepplewhite. He would have settled for a country piece in applewood or beech, a piece alive with the patina of years.

Pogo clicked along the hall and padded in and subsided across Forde's feet with a sigh, and, following the sigh, arising from the seeping beast, the silent stench of Chunky *God!* Alpo.

And a Turcoman rug would warm the room, a Beshir or a Royal Bokhara. Or a small Persian tribal—his mind drifted on—Baluch or Heriz. He remembered being in London after the overthrow of the Shah when every carpet dealer in town seemed to have shoeboxes of Luristan bronzes for sale, horse bits, adzes, votive axe-heads, finials, harness bells. There had been rumours of sacked museums.

Museums; he thought of the one in Calgary he'd described to Sheila. He'd stayed at a hotel close to that museum. The Palliser. He'd been doing something at the university, what he couldn't now remember, but *did* remember standing on the front steps of the Palliser, the evening sun low, almost blinding, and a barefoot woman came running out of the sun, crossing the road to the sidewalk a yard in front of him. Her blouse had been completely open and her grimy breasts flopped. She ran past and disappeared into a nearby alley. He had stood there waiting, waiting for a pursuer, waiting for a sequel, a motive, a meaning.

And in Edmonton he'd once booked into a hotel near the municipal airport. It was late at night, he remembered. Some disruption of travel plans, Vancouver, fog. The plane had been diverted. The desk clerk gave him a key. As he opened the door a man who was sitting in an armchair watching television turned an astonished head. He was naked except for a dove-grey Stetson and mauve ankle socks.

But it was the foyer of the hotel that had stayed in his mind. There had been a small rectangular pool in the foyer all set about with tubs of ficus trees. A spattering of vomit rode the surface of the pool. In the elevator an empty beer bottle was rolling about on the floor.

A sordid place. He had lain awake half the night, a revolving searchlight washing the ceiling.

Forde wrote on his pad of yellow paper.

"In the elevator an empty beer bottle rolled about on the floor."

Obviously it would be empty. He crossed the word out. The words "about on the floor" were stupidly redundant.

Then he wrote:

"In the elevator a beer bottle rolled."

Ending with "rolled" was pleasing, a strong ending you could *hear*.

"Beer."

"Beer?"

He sat staring at the paper, mouthing the words; considered striking out "beer."

When he had been thinking about the pool in the foyer and the ficus trees in tubs, the words "all set about with ficus trees" had been in his mind, yes, "all set about with." He could see the book's shiny red cloth cover with the gold elephant's head stamped on it, trunk curled up, the adored *Just So Stories*, and he could hear his mother's voice reading, reading about the elephant's child, a child of insatiable curiosity, the two of them waiting for the chanted refrain:

The great, grey, greasy Limpopo River all set about with fever trees.

On his last visit back to England he'd found his mother more stooped, slower. Her flat, though, was just the same. She had insisted on making him a cup of tea, no, no, he didn't know where things were, and from the sitting room he heard her in the tiny kitchen talking to herself, nothing he could understand, a whispery drizzle of words. On the wall, the souvenir plate from Bavaria. On the occasional table, audio cassettes of James Herriot's *All Creatures Great and Small*. A ghastly Alpine scene on the wall above the mahogany bureau, a more than decent piece from the old house. He noticed she had knitted, in turquoise wool, a cover that fitted over the Kleenex box.

She brought the tea to him on a doily-covered tray on which stood a floral cup and saucer, a small cut-glass milk jug, a matching floral bowl of sugar cubes with silver tongs beside.

As the afternoon wore on she suggested they watch on television a programme for children, one of her favourites, none of the violence and goings-on and the things they showed these days. The programme was called *Blue Peter*. The presenter was a particularly nice young man. The co-presenter was a young woman who showed a group of little girls how to make a doll out of the cardboard core of a toilet-paper roll.

Following this they watched a programme involving school teams answering general knowledge questions.

Following this they watched a programme about the rescue of animals in distress and their subsequent treatment and recovery in what looked like a greenhouse.

He had suggested to her that to save them both trouble he would stroll down to the High Street and bring back some fish and chips for dinner. He suggested this not only to forestall efforts on her part to cook, but also to escape from the flat for half an hour. It was not only the children's television that weighed on him. It was her unceasing rehearsal of events in the lives of people he'd never heard of, members of her church, the man who ran the charity shop, the sister of her friend in Eastbourne, who had a little white dog called Penny that rode in a pram, the woman who came to the flat to do her hair, the husband of the woman who came to the flat to do her hair, who, until the accident to his arm in Sainsbury's had had a garden, well, you could scarcely *imagine* the red runner beans...

These unending stories oppressed him with a kind of mental pain, the same kind of pain—he cast about—the closest he could come to comparing the pain with any other kind of pain was possibly the pain felt if he were subjected to Lieder or folkfuckery by Benjamin Britten sung by (Oh, poignant Christ!) Peter fucking Pears.

When he came back with the hot package, he heard her in the kitchen, cupboards closing, drawers opening, that same whisper of words. She came out into the sitting room and opened the bureau.

She was looking, she said, for the cutlery canteen. It was a dark leather box. What cutlery, he had wanted to know. There was cutlery in the kitchen drawer. The fish knives and forks, she had said. He said they should use the ordinary forks.

She ignored him and went back into the kitchen. Cupboards again. After a minute or two, an exclamation.

The silver knives and forks were tarnished black and gold. Her eyesight too poor to notice. He rubbed the knife surreptitiously to see if the black came off. He employed the fork gingerly.

"No fish forks, indeed!" she said. "Whatever is the world coming to!"

*

Photocopy
Buy stamps
LCBO—Sancerre
Bank

The man in front of him in the line looked to be about sixty years old but was wearing gaudy, unlaced shoes, which swirled in black, white, orange, and blue. Ruby reflectors twinkled on the heels. Forde no longer knew what to call such shoes. They seemed to be moulded, one-piece things made of rubber and canvas, or, for all he knew, of extruded protein, two words he'd once read in a magazine. At school in England, a simpler version of such things had been called tennis shoes or running shoes or sneakers. They had been worn only for sports. Mothers condemned them for daily wear as harmful to the growing foot. The times, thought Forde, condemned one to be cautious in the use of the word "mother."

At *his* school they'd always been called plimsolls. Though, come to think of it, he didn't know why. The Plimsoll Line man? He recalled the almost military inspection of the plimsolls before each gym class, the canvas blancoed to chalky perfection. Gould had been his name. Sergeant Gould. Now, in England, they called such things "trainers."

Forde disliked the technicolour vulgarity of the man's shoes intensely and especially so on a man well past middle age. They were a part of what he thought of as an increasing infantilism, shoes with Velcro tabs instead of laces as though laces had become too complicated to tie, T-shirts with writing and pictures on them. Nursery clothes. Obesity. Saggy sweat-pants with elasticized waistbands. No ties, T-shirts, tattooed tits. He deplored this flight from formality. On irritable days, half the people he saw on the streets suggested to him the populations of clinics, mental hospitals, and sheltered workshops.

Forde knew that something had broken. He felt that the world he'd inherited was disappearing. This shift in the world, this slide, had been slow, unremarkable, almost invisible at first, and he, like the frog in cold water brought to the boil, motionless, unaware. He lived now, he often felt, in wreckage, treading water, straining for the feeble cries of other survivors.

Forde was aware of his crankiness. He put it on a bit to amuse himself and to irritate and amuse Sheila but, even if exaggerated, caricatured, at base it represented the way he really felt.

The woman at the teller facing him was conducting an endless transaction; he could tell by the bend of her leg, by the relaxation of her body against the counter, that she was settling in for aeons more of it; probably, thought Forde, cashing in 1945 Victory Bonds.

His attention drifted away. The sentence was wrong; *definitely* wrong. "Beer" had to come out. It weakened the sentence, fudging, blunting. It defeated delivery of the right sound.

"In the elevator a bottle rolled."

His eye lighted on a large poster high on the wall behind the tellers. The poster was red and white and looked professionally printed rather than stencilled or hand-lettered. This suggested that the posters were probably on display in other branches all over Ottawa and possibly in branches of the Bank of Nova Scotia all across Canada.

TRANSFER YOUR MORTGAGE
THE 5% ADVANTAGE

And diagonally across the top left-hand corner:

NO FEE'S

When his turn at last arrived, he said, pointing at the poster, "Why the apostrophe?"

"Apostrophe?" she echoed.

"Where it says 'No Fee's.'"

"I'm sorry?"

Pointing, he said, "Look! Top left."

One of the supervisors seated some way behind her at a desk got up and came to the counter.

"What seems to be the problem?"

"Oh, there's no problem," he said. "I'm just pointing out that the apostrophe in 'No Fee's' is incorrect."

She looked up at the poster.

"Incorrect how do you mean?"

"An apostrophe," he said, "indicates either possession or omission. But 'Fee's', you see, *doesn't*. Doesn't fit either of those uses."

She considered this.

"Perhaps," she said, "this is a financial meaning."

Forde pursed his lips, shaking his head slightly.

A hectic flush started up her neck.

"The only thing to do," she said, "you'll have to see a Personal Banking Officer."

She opened the wicket and clacked across the marble to a doorless cubicle, in which sat a Personal Banking Officer.

"This gentleman," said the supervisor, "has a complaint."

"More of an observation, really."

The Personal Banking Officer was short and had a ginger crew cut. A little, bulbous nose. He looked just like Josef Lada's line drawings of the Good Soldier Švejk.

The three of them stood in front of his cubicle.

"You see? The top left corner. Says 'No Fee's.'"

The Officer nodded slowly and, after a long pause, said, "So what's your problem?"

Forde launched into it again.

"... and therefore it's simply incorrect."

The Officer frowned.

"That poster," said Forde, "must have been seen by *dozens* of people before it was actually printed."

He shook his head to convey sorrowful amazement at this state of affairs.

The Officer seemed to inflate himself and said, "I have no idea what you're telling me here. Why don't you cut to the chase, fella?"

"I am attempting," said Forde slowly, and with insulting pantomimed patience—deep breaths, slow hand movements—"to explain to you why your poster is illiterate."

Again the Officer frowned.

"... a very bad impression," Forde concluded.

And because he resented being addressed as "fella" by a little ginger prick, added, "You're one of the country's major banks. People—not I, of course—but some might think that if you can't punctuate you might not be able to add and subtract either."

"Listen, fella," said the Officer, turning back into his cubicle, "I go with what I'm given."

Forde rejoined the line. The Victory Bonds woman was still slumped against the counter. At the next wicket another woman was exchanging rolled coins for notes and paying some complex bills. An old man had forgotten his PIN number and lost his bank card and kept opening and closing his wallet in a distraught manner. The man with a business deposit had a cell phone that chirruped *The Bonnie Banks of Loch Lomond.*

Forde did not feel like working—Sheila in her bathrobe, the radio, Pogo seeping, the dailyness of his ugly desk, the draining effort that had gone into *Chamber Music*. He decided on a stroll. He stopped at the corner of Waverly Street to read the densely printed poster in the window of the Nutri-Chem Pharmacy. The store had recently changed hands. Previously it had been an ordinary pharmacy stocking aspirin and Contac-C and toothpaste but now it had been made over into a Centre for Holistic Medicine. They sold elixirs, tinctures, infusions, extracts, and laxatives all derived from leaves and twigs and bulbs and bark.

The poster's headline asked:

WHERE HAS ALL THE GOOD BACTERIA GONE?

Forde considered all the little bottles and boxes and the bundles of twigs and a saucer of cocoa seeds and some leaves gone brown and a big pod. He wondered who would be rash enough to swallow something called Slippery Elm on the advice of people unable to distinguish singular from plural. He thought of going in and trying to make this point to the girl behind the counter, but the ochre hair and the cluster of stainless-steel surgical clamps climbing the cartilage of her right ear dissuaded him.

He paged through some magazines in Magazines International.

He browsed in the bookstore.

He strolled on up Elgin towards Sparks Street. Outside the restaurants the chalkboards advertising daily specials offered the customary mangling of the words Omelette, Spaghetti, and Caesar. The chalkboards were also spattered with quotation marks, dishes being described as "famous," "delicious," "hot," and "juicy," daily examples of the conviction of the semi-literate that inverted commas act as intensifiers.

At the entrance to the Sparks Street Mall reared some fifteen feet high a sheet-metal grizzly bear, its mouth agape, just about to crunch the fish, presumably a salmon, held in its left paw. This travesty of sculpture always caused Forde both anger and cringing embarrassment.

Behind the sheet-metal grizzly bear hung an elaborately framed sign which read:

SPARKS STREET MALL
Great Shops—Services—Parking
ON CANADA'S MOST UNIQUE STREET

Forde thought, with great weariness of spirit, of trying to explain to urban planners, to representatives of community associations, to aldermen, to city councillors, to streetscape specialists, urban renewal specialists, Heritage specialists, specialists in acceptable and non-conforming signage, that the word "Unique" cannot be used with comparatives, that the word means that there is only one of something, that there cannot be more or less of singleness, that "Unique" comes via French from the Latin "unicus," single, akin to "unus" meaning "one."

Overcome by the need for a beer, Forde seated himself in the small outdoor café situated between the sheet-metal grizzly on one side and another monstrosity on the other, a naked and seemingly anorexic family group capering in welded copper and entitled *Joy*.

The waitress offered him the Sandwich of the Day. Forde shrugged and then nodded. The sandwiches, he noted, were kept in a cooler. He read its packaging. It was a Chicken Tikha sandwich and contained, among many other things, gum arabic, sundry citrates, and Stabilizers E 412, E 415, and E 410. It was soggy and tasted faintly of chutney.

To one side of the sheet-metal bear stood W.E. Noffke's main Post Office, its entrances flanked by elegant pairs of heraldic lions supporting shields. The crisp and vigorous carving always pleased Forde. One of the lions had been defaced some years before by a man with a hammer protesting something... Forde forgot what. The Royal Family, perhaps. English Canada's domination of Quebec? Canada's colonial status?

As he passed by on his way to the Hill, he glanced at the Second Empire façade of the Langevin Building, the decorative string courses dividing the floors, that horizontal emphasis invigorated by the vertical movements of the windows, large and rectangular on the ground floor but, pulling the eye upwards, smaller and arched on the second and third floors, the arches recessed and set off by flanking columns and capitals, charming little confections of polished pink granite.

On the gates across the tunnel leading into the building's black bowels, an enamel sign presumably directed at chauffeurs waiting to pick up politicians or bureaucrats:

PLEASE SHUT OFF MOTOR'S

*

Adrift on the Hill. His mind churning. Wandering past the West Block. Stood regarding the black-and-white enamel sign:

RESERVED PARKING
FOR
MINISTER'S VEHICLES

Past the Info-Tent, where someone had dropped on the path *Discover the Hill: Outdoor Self-Guiding Booklet*. Forde stood staring at the seated statue of Lester B. Pearson. He was portrayed as sitting casually in an office chair with his left leg crossed over his right. It was—Forde struggled with what he was thinking about—it was, it had no life, it was not a sculpture but *an illustration*.

He consulted the *Self-Guiding Booklet.*

Originator of the concept of UN Peacekeeping forces, our 14th prime minister did much to foster the image of Canada as a peaceful nation on the world stage. Thank you, Mr. Pearson!

Pearson's left shoe shone yellow.

In the *Booklet* he read:

People rub Lester B. Pearson's left shoe for good luck.

Like rubbing the left breast of the statue of Juliet in that squalid courtyard in Verona or kissing the exposed brown toe of St. Ignatius in the cathedral in Goa. Though rubbing the left wingtip of a statue of Lester B. Pearson seemed to Forde *desperately* Canadian.

He pottered about the Hill from statue to statue. Those made in more recent years, Diefenbaker, Pearson, Mackenzie King, George Brown, Sir Robert Borden, were stiff, awkward, lacked fluidity. The best statues were all by Louis-Philippe Hébert from Montreal and had been unveiled, Forde noted, either actually in the nineteenth century or within a year of it.

According to the *Booklet,* the young lady on the base of the statue of Queen Victoria is "an allegorical figure of Canada"; the young lady on the statue of Alexander Mackenzie "an allegorical figure of Probity"; on the statue of Sir John A. Macdonald the young lady represents "Confederation."

Allegorical figures! thought Forde. Probity! It was obvious, simply, that Louis-Philippe Hébert had a liking for titty wenches and good for Louis-Philippe thought Forde.

But the more modern statues. It was the same thing he'd been thinking about all morning. The motionless frog in the slowly heating water. When had it become impossible to cast statues of public figures? And why exactly? The dates seemed to suggest the Great War. Those four years seemed to mark...

Louis-Philippe's statues had all been cast in the great bronze foundries of Paris. International sculpture radiated from Paris. Hébert himself had trained and worked there. Most sculptors at this period studied under the same masters at the École des Beaux Arts. And later, in the world of contracts and commissions, sculptors worked as artisans for each other and shared their workmen.

All this was much in Forde's mind because his reading lately had been almost exclusively in the art history and biography of this period. This international language, as it were, of sculpture was silenced by World War I. But the tradition was under attack, too, by the dominance of photography, by surrealism, Dada, Deco, movements away from realism, Rodin, Jacob Epstein, Maillol, the beginnings of modernism, Ossip Zadkine, new ways of looking. And at this time, too, sculpture had split into two camps, monumental sculpture and studio or gallery sculpture, and it was studio sculpture that proved more vital.

Forde was contemplating a novel involving dubious authentications, a corrupting art-dealer based on Lord Duveen, and a scholar based on Berenson. All in a brooding villa like Berenson's *I Tatti*, replete with wife and mistress, secretary, and a sexually ambivalent protégé, the whole seraglio indirectly prompted years earlier by his reading Malamud's *Pictures of Fidelman.*

It was the Berenson-figure he was relishing, patriarchal yet petted, cosseted, food fads, enemas, pompous with precepts and prejudice, a *ridiculous* little man but at the same time something of a genius being lured onto the perilous lee shore of Duveen's dark intentions. The Berenson-man had an ebony cane with a silver pommel in the shape of a skull. He was rarely parted from it. Two half-turns of the pommel released a two-foot blade. The cane was called The Blogue. Forde could hardly wait to get his hands on him.

The cane had transported itself from a biography of Sir Arthur Evans, an imperious and theatrical little man, who all his life carried a walking stick called Prodger.

But *The Blogue*?

He turned away from it. It was a perfect detail, a gift. He did not want to pick at it. He luxuriated in this welling up, the swimming in of detail.

The Blogue. Unexplained. Inexplicable.

Perfect.

But these figures, these statues, his mind worrying at the matter, these neoclassical figures of Louis-Philippe Hébert—he glanced up at the dominating figure of Queen Victoria—they were at the end of the tradition, which had flowered in France in the seventeenth century. He thought almost with anguish of the loveliness of the radiant figures in the sculpture courts of the Louvre, bronze, marble, *terre cuite*, nymphs, warriors, satyrs, bacchantes. Louis-Philippe's work was at home inside that tradition. The rest of the statues were not.

Degenerate—no, that wasn't the word he was looking for—*debased*, that was more what he wanted. The more modern statues were debased – as coinage becomes debased by lowering its gold or silver content. As tribal sculpture becomes debased when it is separated from its people and purpose.

*

Forde stood behind the cannon's cascabel, running his fingertip over the Broad Arrow cut into the metal. He patted the sun-warmed metal and walked around the cannon, looking at the touchhole, trunnions, quoins, and tompion, revelling in this antique terminology. This was the kind of thing he had been taught.

This gun, a nine-pound muzzle-loading ship's cannon, had been cast, the *Booklet* said, in Wales in 1807 and had been used in the Crimean War in the siege of Sevastopol. The British Army presented the cannon to their garrison in Canada as a trophy and commemoration of the Crimean battles.

Far below on an outcropping of bare rocks in the middle of the river, a white myriad of gulls ceaselessly screeched and fluttered. Across in Hull, federal office buildings now dominated the view, sterile hives looking as if they had been stuck together by an unlikeable child. Forde could remember the vast hoarding belonging to the E. B. Eddy Company pulp and paper mills, which from Hull, had faced the Parliament Buildings—a hoarding advertising White Swan Toilet Paper.

In 1698 a law was passed imposing harsh penalties on anyone found in possession of naval stores or other goods marked with the Broad Arrow. Government rope was marked by a coloured strand woven in, a strand called the Rogue's Yarn. In the main dockyard roperies, a yellow strand denoted Chatham cordage, a blue strand, Portsmouth, and a red strand, Devonport. This was the kind of thing he had been taught.

The cannon with its Broad Arrow, the statues of Louis-Philippe Hébert, the Gothic Revival buildings behind him, all spoke the same cultural language, all belonged to the same world, a world for which his education had groomed him, a world now as relevant as potsherds and shell-middens.

His hand on the warm bronze, he stood gazing up the river towards the Chaudière Falls. He remembered standing in the gun embrasures on the parapets of Malakhov Hill and looking down into the harbour of Sevastopol, the sea a strange, almost turquoise green with dark-brown patches further offshore. He remembered the Two-Headed Romanov Eagle on the cannon barrels, the tumbledown revetments, the glacis overgrown with scrub and bushes. Behind the cannon, black painted garlands of shot. Sevastopol had withstood siege for eleven months, during which a hundred thousand Russian soldiers and residents died. Malakhov Hill fell to the French in 1855. It seemed to Forde not long ago.

He remembered, too, the battlefield at Balaclava. The valley was planted now with vines, the leaves limp and yellowing along their wires, fall mists wisping. He had walked along the Causeway Heights to Redoubt No. 4, overlooking the North and South Valleys. The guns Lord Cardigan was supposed to capture were some British-made cannons captured by the Russians from the Turkish redoubts further down the Causeway. They were being hurried away by Russian troops in the South Valley. Lord Lucan, misunderstanding Lord Raglan's orders, instructed Lord Cardigan to ride, not against those skirmishers and stragglers, but against the dug-in positions of the Russians at the head of the North Valley.

After receiving the orders, Lord Cardigan rode out some yards ahead of the first line of cavalry and said, at conversational volume, *The Brigade will advance.*

Later, up on the Sapouné Heights where Lord Raglan had dithered, Forde had overlooked both Valleys. The advance down the North Valley looked to be about a mile, maybe more. What an eternity it must have seemed as the Brigade walked their horses, bits jingling, then trotted into the increasing barrage of nine-pound shot savaging the thinning lines, the crackle of musketry, the bruise-yellow banks of gunpowder smoke, acrid and blinding.

As the pace of the charge picked up, an excited officer rode up alongside Lord Cardigan and Cardigan barred the flat of his sword across the man's chest and called,

Steady! Steady! The 17th Lancers.

Behind him, as the men and horses fell, the squadron commanders, preserving the mass and weight of the charge, shouted repeatedly against the roar of the guns,

Close to your centre!

Look to your dressing on the left!

Close in!

Close in!

Up on the Sapouné Heights, high above the battle, General Bosquet watching the slaughter, murmured

C'est magnifique, mais ce n'est pas la guerre.

Riderless horses bolted out of the smoke, the whites of their eyes wide in terror. Troopers forced forward with knees and rowels as horses baulked at bodies on the ground.

Close in!

Close in to the centre!

Lowering his sword in the signal to charge, Lord Cardigan unleashed into the Russian gun emplacements a thunder of red uniforms, the charge subsiding into individual actions as the horsemen worked their mounts around guns, carts, water butts, fascines fallen from the breastworks. The Russian gunners struck at the cavalry with ramrods or tried to hide or run but were quickly sabred.

Some three or four hundred yards distant, the Russian army was drawn up, but the ranks watched in silence and made no move to engage.

The Light Brigade had suffered some two hundred and twenty killed or wounded. Lord Lucan, Lord Cardigan, and Lord Raglan were all variously incompetent, arrogant, petulantly vicious, or doddering, but no one, thought Forde, could deny the magnificent, imperturbable courage.

He glanced down at the *Booklet*.

From 1869-1994, the cannon was fired at noon to allow all postal employees to synchronize their watches, thereby regulating and ensuring the quality of the postal service.

Christ! thought Forde as he gave the bronze a farewell pat.

*

For some time Forde had been aware of a voice behind him. The speaker was French Canadian, his English heavily accented. Forde turned from the gun to look at the old man, who was talking to some obvious tourists.

"Me, I've been here coming on fourteen year. The Catman, they call me. Every day I'm here. Never missed a day. That's a long time."

"Kitty, kitty, kitty," called one of the little girls.

Forde moved closer and looked over the ornamental iron railings at the patch of bare earth spread with squares of filthy old carpet, the wooden hutches raised on bricks, the paper Maple Leaf flags and Stars and Stripes stapled to little sticks—tongue depressors, possibly, or popsicle sticks—and tied to branches and bushes. Two ginger cats were sleeping on the roof of one of the wooden boxes. Their faces were so fat their tongues stuck out. Pictures of cats hung from branches and wires strung overhead. The biggest pictures were of the cartoon cat, Garfield, and looked as if they'd been trimmed from the covers of comics.

"I have thirty now. Two weeks ago there were twenty-five. Too many cats, that's not too good. The houses, it's good for twenty-four. They go in there to the straw, two by two. When I have more they can go four or five in each one. You can't kill a cat with the bad weather. They get close together and they sleep good."

Forde looked at the Outdoor *Self-Guiding Booklet* and read:

Parliament Hill has been home to stray cats for decades. However, it is only since the 1970s that volunteers have paid special care and attention to these animals: creating the "cat sanctuary," maintaining its infrastructure and ensuring that the animals (cats, raccoons, groundhogs, squirrels, pigeons, chickadees and sparrows) are fed on a daily basis.

Maintaining its infrastructure! thought Forde.

Bizarre punctuation to boot, courtesy of the National Capital Commission.

The juxtaposition of the formality, pomp and ceremony of the Parliament Buildings and the modest cat sanctuary reflects the important Canadian values of tolerance and compassion.

The old man fell silent as families, groups, or couples walked on but started up again in a sort of soliloquy with each new passer-by.

"Maybe it's time for me to retire. I put an ad in the paper once and nobody showed up. It's volunteer, that's why. When Irene Desormeaux, she died, I've been the Catman since that day. The government they don't give me any money at all. But you know when you like something? Do it well or don't do it at all. The cats they keep me young. Two weeks ago there were twenty-five. I have thirty now. People, they drop their cats. They're not supposed to drop their cats. But they do it. If they get caught, they're gonna pay a fine. But it's hard to catch them. There's a squirrel. If I put a peanut in my ear they jump out of the tree onto my shoulder here and they take it out. I call them all Charlie because they look the same. I know all these cats. Her—that one sleeping underneath the house—that's Lapout. Lapout and Lulu, that's two sisters. Their mother is Brunette. When I see them, I know right away their name. Fluffy now, Fluffy was here a minute ago. Fluffy, now that's a nice cat. Fluffy's got a long robe. His fur, it's long. Big Mama—her sleeping under that bush—she's big. And Cocoa and Brownie. That one just went in the house. That's Princess. I had four grey but I see only two… Timin and Tigris. Here I have Bon Bon. I tell you! That Bon Bon! I bet you every day he's in the bushes."

He started working something bulky out of one of the plastic bags hanging from the railings. He set off with a plastic jerrycan to get water.

Forde drifted closer to the railings and stood regarding the scruffy cats, the squalid squares of carpet weighted at the corners with rocks. A plastic windmill on a stick. Among the paper flags, larger cloth flags on sticks were stuck into cans and toilet-paper cores, which had been worked onto branches as holders. Dozen upon dozen small pictures of cats were tacked to trunks and dangled from bushes, pictures cut from magazines or labels from cans or entire empty packages with cat pictures on them, *Whiskers, Finicky Cat, Nutrition First, Iams, Fancy Feast, Friskies, Meow Mix, Pounce Minouche, No Name Beef and Chicken Dinner*.

A raccoon toiled into the tiny clearing. Cats fled. It was hugely pregnant, its distended dugs leaking on the ground, staining the dust. Its fur was dull. It began eating from the nearest aluminum-foil dish. His presence did not deter it. From time to time it looked up at him with bleak eyes.

Forde stood staring.

On the tops of tree stumps, in rusted cans, wilting posies of flowering weeds. Scattered lids of opened cans. A plastic sunflower on a stick. Copulating flies dizzed on the crusting food and on the beaten earth.

LIVES OF THE POETS

Not beguiled by fluorescent hum, not beguiled by the weepy whinging of country and western *artistes*, Forde stood in the Australia aisle. Bottles clinked as a wire cart clanked, font wheel baulking. Loose from their nightmare shacks in the dripping woods, scrawny men strutted, feral, seemingly without buttocks, their wallets somehow attached by long, looping chains. When they grinned their dangerous grins, black gaps, caries. In their wake toiled their obese and waddling women yanking impetigo toddlers.

Pastel elasticized pants.

Guts like growths.

Drifting into his mind the notion

Figgy duff

The thought of their gruesome matings, the wallowings, the squelch... His averted gaze played over Australian labels—*Koala, Blue Gum, Shearers Shout Cabernet*—cheery egalitarianism which depressed him. The vintners of Southeastern Australia, he thought, had another think coming if they imagined he was going to spend his pitiful mite on a shiraz called *Hairy Belly*.

*

He pushed the balding tennis ball onto the plughole in the bath, weighted it with the half-brick, and turned on the taps. He stirred through the garbage bag for the least soiled white shirt.

The three-month writer-in-residency paid $20,000, on which he had to pay tax, with which he had to pay rent and, as the application forms had put it, "alimentation," and for which he had to teach two classes, make himself available to students and the general public, reach out to high schools, and give readings and talks in surrounding retirement residences, hospitals, palliative care hospices…

Compère spelling bees, bugger the dean

He was sworn to taking home much more than half what the application forms had termed "all or any emoluments." He wanted to be able to give money to Sheila. With financial conscience thereby a fraction eased, he wanted to buy time to explore oddly congruent images that were besieging him. He wanted to get the images down before they stopped insisting, before they faded. And then—delicious, *delicious*—he wanted to smooth them down, push them around, shape them, sculpt them like ice cream with a spatula, like the manufacture of ice-cream sandwiches—"wafers" were they called?—from the Italian carts of his childhood, the spatula scraping the excess along the edges, mounding it back on top, tamping it down into corners…

He had investigated a recommended long-term bed-and-breakfast deal, a late-nineteenth-century gingerbread, but was stifled by toy bears, flounced dolls, wicker hoop-handled baskets of soaps, the notice on an easel in the foyer:

Cherished Guest, please remove your Shoes to Join us in Preserving the Beauty of our Floors.

He sprinkled the shirt with *Tide*, squelched the big bubble under, sloshed the shirt about. It and the water felt slimy. He left it to… marinate? steep? macerate?

Desperate to save, he had settled for this furnished living room with a swayback bed, and kitchen-cum-bathroom, in what had turned out to be a building not simply grungy but a refuge for alcoholics, people "on the pension," dubious women, and single men furtive as fugitives, silent in undershirts.

He broke the seal on the screw-top wine, filling the apartment's tumbler.

Switched on the TV; a screen of buzzing snow; thumped the top, turning the blizzard into bars of upward-scrolling opalescence.

Wandered into the kitchen/bathroom. Sprayed *Lysol* onto the warped backsplash.

"Eat *that,* you fuckers!"

Back into the living room/bedroom. Looked at the Fredericton *Daily Gleaner*. Under a photograph of a swamp or pond, from which stuck out a stump, a caption reading:

Moments before this study, a family of mallards had taken wing.

Consulted his watch.

"Sheila. It's me."

"Hello, you."

"Everything OK?"

"I know it's you. One of those days. That Cloutier… the *putz!*"

"Sheila! Hello out there? I'm lonely. I miss you."

"Have you been drinking?"

He paused.

"The implications of your question are both insulting and—"

"Oh, don't be silly, Rob. *Pogo* misses you. He goes up to your room and whiffles about. Poor beast can't figure it out."

"Pogo! Pogo is a *dog!* Don't *you?*"

"What?"

"Miss me."

"Oh, yes, *I* know—don't forget it's Ben's birthday. Don't send him CDs. You'd choose Miles or Robert Johnson or something and it'd just lead to, I mean, what he listens to we've never heard of. Oh, and no books. Definitely no books. Just send him a cheque. No, a money order. That'd be safer after that contretemps at the—"

"I was not likely to forget my own son's—"

"Oh, don't do huffy, Rob. Not after today."

"*Tomorrow*," said Forde. "Tomorrow's *another* stretch of horror. I have to squire the granddaughter of a poet about all day."

"Granddaughter?"

"Don't you raise your eyebrows at *me*."

"What do you mean 'granddaughter'?"

"She's bringing his ashes to Fredericton. Well, already *brought*, I suppose you could say."

There was a silence.

"Or *sent*, rather."

"*Whose* ashes?"

"Her grandfather's."

Another silence.

"She's coming on the train," added Forde.

He knelt down in the kitchen beside the bathtub and scrubbed at the collar and cuffs with his toothbrush. Even hanging the shirt from the string dripping wet didn't get all the wrinkles out, so he was relieved that the temperature had been dropping all afternoon, with snow threatened overnight. That would give him reason to wear a sweater covering up most of the shirt, and the sweater mostly covered by his rather dark-coloured sports jacket. As for the "business attire" called for in the *Bulletin*, he had neither attire nor business.

Tresillian, that was it. This granddaughter. Mrs. Tresillian.

So far as he could untangle matters, this ashes person—and reading even potted biogs of these poetasters had been scarcely endurable—this Childe Chauncy, the ashes person, had been termed a "Confederation Poet" because he'd been born in Fredericton in 1864 and had been an acolyte of the ineffable Bliss Carman. And had also been somehow related to *the* Confederation biggie, Sir Charles G.D. Roberts.

What sort of weird, wondered Forde, were parents who would name a child Childe? Assuming they weren't nineteenth-century Fredericton fans of Lord Byron or students of medieval titular address. Which seemed a safe assumption.

What sort of weird named a child "Bliss"?

On leaving the Fredericton Collegiate School, Childe joined his mentors Carman and Roberts in Boston and Connecticut, variously, where they scrabbled with hack journalism and editing while emitting skim-milk bleatings claiming mystic kinship etc. with Mother etc. Nature.

According to the *UNB Bulletin*, Childe Chauncy's slim vols were entitled, after a phrase of Emerson's,

The Vernal Ides

Followed by:

April's Benediction

Anthem of the Hermit Thrush

Open Road

and culminating in:

A Pealing Cadence Thrills

Childe!

Christ! thought Forde.

The Early Canadian Texts Society, conversationally referred to as "Etcetera," was preparing a Variorum Edition.

Rinsing was vital.

Several rinses.

He was worried particularly about granules of detergent possibly trapped in the slots for stays.

This drivelling Chauncy had died in 1935. His ashes had been sitting on the President's desk when Forde had been summoned to receive his marching orders. They were in a small ebony casket set off with silver fittings. The ashes had been handed to Childe Chauncy's daughter and on her death had descended to *her* daughter, this Mrs. Tresillian, and were now to be interred in Poets' Corner in Forest Hill Cemetery beside the ashes of Bliss, Childe's stupefying mentor. The casket had arrived in advance of Mrs. Tresillian by UPS.

He ran clean water and gave the shirt a final swish and slosh. He felt apprehensive of becoming tense, weary, harassed, and sweating therefore, the hot sweat interacting with insufficiently rinsed residue of *Tide* causing him at cuffs and collar to become sticky or, possibly to even publically foam.

For dinner, he made himself baked beans on toast.

The apartment's toaster, an authentic "collectible," opened downwards on each side like an upside-down-gull-wing-car, glinty mica in its insides. It smoked when the toast was done.

With the beans he finished off the Chilean *ordinaire.*

He watched the thick flakes in the street lamp glow. The silence in the apartment was deepening, that unnatural quiet of the world being blurred, muffled.

Lay on the bed.

Read further into R.S. Thomas' *Tares,* but couldn't tether his attention to the poems.

On the plus side, of course, the advent of Mrs. Tresillian would save him from morning's Creative Writing One. He flicked through his mental file cards of those bovines. The obese boy with the laceless high-tops... God! He couldn't have cared less if they'd all contracted ebola fever and dropped in hemorrhagic heaps. He found the pretence of humility, modesty, warmth, concern and caring, the projection of benevolent charm, left him desperate for numbing quantities of Famous Grouse and Bombay Sapphire London Dry Gin. Or any London Dry Gin, come to that, with or without Botanicals...Vince, Vince Somebody; Middle Earthite; laceless high-tops; grey, pissy drawstring sweatpants; particular interest: Trolls. Jane Parkin. Denim jacket cluttered with buttons and badges, army-surplus bag hung with miniature pink teddies and Garfields, sparkly thing in nose, carabiners. No apparent particular interests. The impenetrable Mrs. Williams, *Laetitia* as she insisted, forty, forty-five, somewhere in there. Face like that on the porcelain head of an antique doll. A woman effaced. Coloured-advertisement woman in a coloured advertisement for a washing machine, *Saturday Evening Post*, the Eisenhower era, joyfully smiling upon washing-machine installer in peaked cap like chauffeur smiling back at Laetitia. Also joyful.

He did not, did *not* understand—and it was by now a time-worn puzzle—*why* they wanted to write and talk about writing when they did not and *would* not read. Scarcely *could*. He always asked them to write down titles and authors he might mention when in spate, but the request was merely part of his "benevolence" act. His pearls were never noted, his "spate" a device to fill an hour. Literary history was for them a blank. *History* was a blank. They stared at him with heifer eyes as if he were a source of danger.

He always failed to interest them in words or sentences. What they *did* want to know was how to secure the services of an agent. Or how to copyright stories or works-in-progress; would the letter "c" inside a circle be sufficient protection against the predations of an editor or the mailman?

Should one insist on a sliding scale of royalties?

When negotiating subsidiary rights, was a separate agent for film rights the best way to go?

Would he recommend self-publication?

When he reminded them that self-publication used to be called "vanity publishing," they stared uncomprehendingly, reminding *him* one couldn't "remind" them of something they'd never known.

He always politely sidestepped their delusions. Summoning the "bluff commonsensical" aspect of his persona, he always recommended getting the *Shorter Oxford* and a good American dictionary, *Webster's New World Dictionary: College Edition*, say. And passing on years of wisdom, he'd advise them to buy hardcover copies because perfect-bound paperbacks would fall to pieces with constant use.

"Constant use" was one of his dry comic conceits.

And then the crazies.

Women, oddly nearly always women, placid, impervious, who had written one story or Chapter One and offered it up for discussion, unchanged, year after year, to courses and workshops from coast to coast.

One who wept because all the artists the professors said were important were all elitist and many also sexist and racist and how could writers be good who did not care about the people? Her problems and the problems of others like her were, Forde suspected, other.

Other troubled women phoning his hotel room at night saying they'd just been passing and were now in the lobby…

Men who wished to share with him Polaroid evidence of their wives' infidelities.

Strange young men whose writing ambitions veered towards obsequious aggression who, after courses were over, phoned him from "group" or "the facility," saying they saw exactly what he'd been saying, very good, absolutely agreed with every word, everything he'd said about words and sentences, yes, no contest, all that, they absolutely agreed with all that, no question, but had he thought that what he was saying was because he was of an older generation?

Perhaps he wasn't into Urban Fantasy, Alternative Worlds, Heroes, The Knights Templar, Genghis Khan.

He thought it was all probably something to do with dominance.

They offered to lend him Vampire books.

Forde switched off the light and lay on the bed, staring towards the glimmer of the street lamp and the steadily falling snow and the unhappiness of his life.

He laced his fingers behind his head.

Mapped the shadowed ceiling.

Wandered.

"I'm forced to ask, Mrs. Williams."

"Laetitia."

"Laetitia. I'm forced to ask if you've ever *been* to New York."

"Well, to Radio City Music Hall."

"Ah, the Rockettes?"

Jocular / avuncular.

Mrs. Williams responding with tight, minimal smile.

Blouse.

Collar frilly.

Buttons pearlescent.

Floral brooch.

"Because, you see, Mrs.... You see, Laetitia, I wondered why you had set your story in New York."

The heifer stare.

"Because that's where they are."

"Who are?"

"The gangsters."

The "one-on-one," strongly suggested by the English Department head, Professor Sinclair—*got to leave them feeling they've had their moneysworth*—the one-on-one dragged on its weary length. His unravelling briefcase might be stitchable by a shoe-repair man. Thinking about lunch occupied him; the day felt chopped-eggish; with a half-sour; wondered if Fredericton could rise to a half-sour. Professor Thing on sabbatical; titles on his shelves immediately to the right of the desk: *Homilies of Aelfric, The Poems of Cynewulf, Awntyrs of Arthure at the Terne Wathelyne…*

Christ!

"No, you see, it's the words themselves—when you write "going to" the reader can't escape the idea of *going*, leaving the room. Right? But she isn't, is she?"

The cornered stare.

He glanced down again at the pristine typescript.

"Bananas" often commanded her to go to the bathroom on his head.

"*Think*, Laetitia. By using a euphemism… and would a woman who would *do* that *use* a euphemism? I mean, you describe her as a 'moll,' don't you?"

Pretending to consult the crisp pages.

"'A gunsel's moll.' Now. *What* is she doing? She's naked and she's crouched over his face with her legs apart. *See* her, Laetitia. Do the words 'go to the bathroom' capture what we're looking at? Would *she* think those words? What words would *she* use to describe to another—er—'moll'—what Bananas liked her to do?"

Head lowered in the heifer stare.

Forelegs braced.
Silence.
"What is this woman *doing*, Laetitia?"
"She's…"
"Mmm?"
"Doing…"
"Pardon?"
"Doing Number One."

*

As he settled towards sleep he summoned up again the picture. Or, as he had come to think of it, The Picture. The sequences, the silent, cathedral-high barn, the rumbling collapse of the drystone wall, the feed shed with its strong, brown smell, the leveret in the hedgerow and the wavering weight of the old double-barrelled twelve-bore, partridges rocketing low out of the dew-drenched rows of kale… these pictures flowed from The Picture. It was all about something that had not yet come together, something he hadn't yet got a grip on.

What was going on started with The Picture. He was with his father in Cumberland, staying on his Uncle Joseph's farm. He was—couldn't quite figure this out—ten? Ten or eleven. It must have been on a summer holiday. All the sequences were sunlit. In The Picture, he and his father had been setting nightlines in the beck. The hooks, No. 12 on 4-lb. leaders, were baited with worms, thin red worms they'd dug out of a manure pile behind the barn. This particular kind of worm was the very best for fishing, his father had said, they were called *brandlings*. He silently rehearsed the word.

The beck dropped down through the fields from the tarn in the fells above. The water level was low in the summer, only inches deep through the stones and boulders except where it pooled, widening, deeper, silent, until the slow current chattered on again through stones and eased down towards the next little pool, flowing eventually into the river at the valley bottom.

The water rilled into the little pool down a big slab of rock. In the wet gloom of that end of the pool under the hazel trees, maidenhair and hart's tongue ferns grew out of the cracks and he half-caught the flit of wrens. The pool was perhaps two feet deep, boulders dry and grey above the water. *Somewhere* in the shallow water lay small, speckled trout and eels that rather frightened him. The green-and-pink stipples on the trout faded so quickly.

Hazelnuts, his father told him, were called *cobs*.

One morning, as they checked the nightlines, his father showed him how to still the writhing knots of an eel so that he could get the hook out. It seemed almost magical how immediately motionless the eel became on sheets of newspaper. His father nailed the eels to the barn door with a nail through the head, cut around the neck until he'd loosed a flap of skin, stuck a tine of an old fork into the skin and pulled down, skinning the eel like turning a sock inside out or unzipping a boot. The collie waited in the nettles for the guts and skin. When they'd cleaned the trout and eels, his father fried them in bacon fat and they ate them with hunks of dry bread for breakfast. His mother refused to stay in the kitchen, calling them "disgusting" and "barbarous," her revulsion a piquant sauce to the rich, white flesh.

In The Picture, his father was balanced across two boulders, face an inch or so above the water, moving his hand very slowly along the underside of the stone. This, he told Rob, was called "tickling" trout. The fish held their position against the current—no one knew why—until the caressing fingers reached the gills and hoisted the fish into air. There had been no fish that day and his father had not used the word "tickling"; he had used a word that Rob had never heard before.

When The Picture first started he could not remember that word, knew it ended in "ing"—*grappling, cuddling,* something like that, but it would not come. The Picture was incomplete, without it, *powerless*. For several weeks he had tried—out walking, sticking on a stamp, while reading—to conjure that word. He thought eventually it *might* be "guddling," that was the word that kept coming back, but such a word wasn't in the SOED or *Brewer's* or any dictionary he tried. He mentioned this to a dinner guest who had grown up in Scotland and who said, yes, of course it was "guddling," a common enough word in Scotland, a dialect word. Scottish words and usages would have been common in Cumberland their lands being so close together.

So. His father *guddling* trout.

His father balanced precariously across two boulders. He was not wearing his usual black suit and white plastic dog collar attached to the black dickey, but a blue shirt with a red tie and a dark-blue blazer. To see his father not in a black suit and clerical collar, not in black gown, not wearing starched Geneva bands, this was a Red Letter Day, this *guddling* with his father, rapturous festival.

Having put off black garb, free of vestments, his father was a different father from his everyday father who rarely spoke. *This* father was lavish with the gift of secret words, gems from a hoard, precious stones gleaming from the jumbled, black-tarnished hack-silver…

Elver, caddis larvae, tercel, jesses, drey

Screaming wrenched him from sleep.

Red round and round, washing the ceiling. He pulled himself up in the bed until his head was propped against the wall. He lay, stunned, until the thudding in his throat calmed. The scream of metal on concrete. The snowplow lowering the blade into roaring acceleration. The bellowing, the screams of steel, yellow lights now pulsing, the throbbing continuo of the attendant trucks piling with spewed snow, sounded like a battle, sounded like battling dinosaurs, sounded like the bounding raptors in *Jurassic Park* savaging smaller beasts, blood, rending and ripping, blood running on their serried teeth.

*

Kate scrunched up her shoulder to hold the phone in place and gestured at the pigeonholes.

A Guaranteed Acceptance offer of a MasterCard and a letter from The Arts Council of Ontario, known conversationally as TACO. He had applied to these pustular bureaucrats for a grant not much longer ago it seemed, than a week. He reread the letter with growing astonishment and rage.

Dear Mr. Forde,

We received your application to the Works-in-Progress Program. However, your application has been deemed ineligible because the manuscript material you submitted as a sample of your project, at 45 pages, is over the 40 pages stipulated in the Program Guidelines.

I have enclosed a copy of the Program Guidelines. Please refer to page 6 of the Program Guidelines for detailed information on how to submit an application.

Sincerely,

John Degstra

Literature Officer

"You *cunt!*" said Forde to his filing cabinet.

Piffler. Pencil-pusher, Prisspot. Pencil dick.

"You fucking *merkin!*"

Literature Officer.

Officer!

OFFICER

Christ!

You and whose army, Degstra?

Poor, posturing sod. Degstra was an officious fool, a footler, yes, a pettifogger, yes.

But no bigger fool than he, Forde, had been in applying to TACO and opening himself, and his work, to humiliation.

"A jury of his peers."

Peers!

He felt—the best way of putting it, he felt—*soiled.*

The faculty lounge for a last coffee before heading to the Cathedral.

Checked his watch.

Crockery, cutlery noises as he went in. Oh, God! Beasley! Too late. *That* Brylcreemed bastard, the bugger's hand already waving.

"Do come and join us. And how is our Itinerant Mountebank this merry morn?"

Forde nodded.

"Us" being the sniggering Beasley and some rheumy-eyed Emeritus of the History Department and a rather pongy old man who looked like a couple of settee cushions stuffed into a waistcoat, to whom Beasley said, "Have you met our Charlatan-in-Residence, Vicar?"

Beasley had arrived at UNB from some British bucket shop of a university—Bournemouth, that sort of place—having earned kudos by scouring foot-of-fines and manorial rolls and such for the amounts and frequency of scutage in the area roughly corresponding to present-day Hampshire, contributing information thusly towards a sociological portrait of lesser nobility in the fourteenth century.

Forde loathed him.

"So, old boy," said Beasley, "you drew the short straw."

"Straw?"

"The widow."

"The *only* straw," said Forde.

"What?" said the Vicar. "What?"

The Emeritus tilted onto one buttock and emitted a long, keening fart.

"Well-played, Sir!" said Beasley.

Sniggered.

"And it's not his widow. His *granddaughter.*"

"But ancient," said Beasley.

"Seventy-five?" said Forde.

The Vicar's chin dropped to his chest.

Odd place, UNB.

The trophy wife of the History Department head, ferried about by her husband, apparently went trick-or-treating naked save for a fur coat and high heels.

"Spanish," his informant had confided.

An ex-member of the English Department, now a fugitive, was wanted by the FBI for cross-border trafficking in stolen Rolls-Royces.

The Northrop Frye Poetry Chair was regularly sighted in the Lord Beaverbrook Hotel's River Room *en travesti.*

"… in the library," bore on Beasley. "I go over there to read *Time* magazine. Too cheap to buy one. And it started raining so I was rummaging around until it stopped, reading about this Bliss Carman person and Childe Chauncy and this Sir Charles D.G. Roberts…"

"G.D." said the Emeritus.

"Pardon?"

"What?"

"Anyway," said Beasley. "I discovered that this Bliss person had written a verse in a poem—

Let me have a scarlet maple
For the grave-tree at my head,
With the quiet sun behind it,
In the years when I am dead.

Exquisite, isn't it? A sort of Canadian William McGonagall. Anyway, an old chap I met in here one evening told me that a chap called Pacey, Desmond Pacey—used to be here—organized just such a tree with some graduate students in an act of—"

"They *used* to give you little cookies with the coffee," said the Emeritus. "Coconut. With sugar sprinkles. I was particularly partial to them."

"IN AN ACT," said Beasley, "of—can one say?—'Parnassian Homage.' And *then,*" said Beasley. "And this is the funny bit, tickled my funny bone. Do you know what happened? The tree, the scarlet maple with the quiet sun behind it, the grave-tree, *died.*"

"Who did?" said the Vicar. "Who did you say?"

"*Particularly* partial," said the Emeritus.

"But the most interesting of these sorry chaps, apparently quite well known in his day, was this Roberts fellow."

"G.D." said the Emeritus.

"Quite," said Beasley. "By all accounts, quite the swordsman. A real alpha male. Rogered his way from coast to coast."

He stuck up his forefingers above his ears, indicating horns.

"Monarch of the Glans."

Again did his snigger.

Forde recalled a photograph of Sir Charles G.D. and remembered thinking that Sir Charles had put him in mind of W.C. Fields, the famous photograph of Fields from—was it, *Never Give a Sucker an Even Break*—Fields holding a spread poker hand to his chest.

Both men *exuded* fraudulence.

"When these lady audiences were suitably *moistened by metre*, mmm? Mmmm?" said Beasley. "When they were suitably *lubricated by lyrics*, he was noted for slipping selected *belles* a length of the old *Parnassian pancetta.*"

"The cathedral," said Forde, getting up and glancing at his watch.

Nodding to the Vicar, *Gentlemen*, and the Emeritus.

As he started across the expanse of floral carpeting, Beasley's voice at his back.

"After the bestowal of his knighthood he was everywhere…"

He was through the doorway.

Beasley baying in horrible triumph…

"… treated with *vas deferens.*"

*

Forde walked through the great West Door, accepted an Order of Service from a Boy Scout and stole from the Tract Rack *A Guide to Christ Church Cathedral.*

"What party, sir?" said another busy Scout.

"Party? Ah, yes, UNB."

He followed the boy.

He sniffed. Most peculiar. He seemed to be smelling mothballs.

The pew ends bore printed signs: Fredericton Fire Services, Fredericton High School, Beaverbrook Art Gallery,

Parks Canada, St. Thomas University, Mount Allison University, The Maritime Forest Ranger School, Mayoral Party and City Council, Scouts Canada, Fredericton Police Services, RCMP.

The smell of mothballs was becoming both acrid and cloying. Simultaneously, if that were possible.

Royal Canadian Legion, Micmac and Maliseet Nations, Canadian Forces Base (Gagetown), University of New Brunswick.

Around the brass-eagle lectern with its widespread wings, CBC and CTV were taping down cables and messing with blinding lights.

He took a seat at the rear of the UNB contingent so that he could look around. Academic hoods colourful against the black academic gowns, some tasselled mortar boards, a few puffy, velvety, Muffin Man caps. Mothballs, much stronger, yes *gusts*. The gowns' annual airing, he realized.

Priests progressing about in unctuous robes and chasubles and albs and gold-thread-glinty stoles, hands folded over tummies. The white stoles were lesser stoles, Very Reverends, but the alpha stole, the *Right* Reverend, was purple.

CFB (Gagetown) had sent a Lieutenant General, a Brigadier General, two Colonels, and two Majors.

As he looked at the rings and loops and curlicues on their cuffs, he resolved for the umpteenth time to find out what it meant in *New York Times* bestsellers when an officer was described as a "bird colonel."

The Scouts were apparently no longer The Boy Scouts but rather Scouts Canada. The seated Scout brass were wearing neckerchiefs gathered at the throat through little leather napkin-ring-things, and lanyards and patches and badges. The Chief Beaver, or whatever they called him, wore glasses that hung down his chest on a cord decorated with seashells.

On an elaborately carved oak chair up near the Choir, more *throne* actually, sat the Premier of New Brunswick in conversation with three what Forde supposed one would call aides, young men with razor-cut hair and shaved napes.

The peaked caps, the gold braid, the insignia, the medals, the glitter and deportment, it was all, thought Forde, all more entertaining than television.

Certainly, *his* television.

He returned to glancing through the stolen *Guide.*

"... completed in 1853... new edifice was the first entirely new Cathedral foundation on British soil since the Norman Conquest... 'Decorated Gothic'... the whole modelled on the Parish Church of Snettisham in Norfolk... stonework executed by a former mason of Exeter Cathedral."

Over the Credence niche beside the altar "a beautifully carved head of Christ... the only surviving fragment of an ancient stone reredos brought from England but reduced to rubble in transit."

To the left of the altar, Bishop Medley's crozier, "believed carved from an oak beam from Christ Church Monastery in Canterbury."

The World War I memorial "made in the shape of a cross of stones taken from the Cathedrals of Arras and Ypres."

On the opposite pier "a replica of an eighth century cross, discovered beneath the streets of Canterbury in 1918, set in stone taken from the walls of Canterbury Cathedral."

He was becoming bored, irritated even, by these orts and scraps of another time and place. 1853 seemed to him like yesterday, a great-great grandmother away, a blink. The only thing in the Cathedral that had engaged him were the colours, the regimental flags hanging out from poles high above the aisles, faded wisps, flags as transparent now and fragile as the skeletal ribs in dead leaves.

Aha!

Purple Stole ascending into the massive pulpit. The organ stopped its doleful stooging about. Chatter slowed, ceased.

Order of Service

O God, our help in ages past
our hope for years to come,
our shelter from the stormy blast,
and our eternal home.

Under the shadow of Thy Throne,
Thy saints have dwelt secure;
sufficient is Thine Arm alone,
and our defense is sure.

The congregation sat again.

Silence extended.

A scout brass rose and stood in the aisle looking anxious; Purple Stole inclined his head towards him; the scout signalled to someone Forde couldn't see. Two little boys appeared from the left transept carrying the remains of Childe Chauncy by the fore and aft silver handles of the ebony box. Cubs or kits or whatever they called them now. Knee socks, those little green tabs below the knees, khaki shirts with two pockets, badges. They were bumping the ebony box into the back of the front cub's thighs, back into the front of the rear cub's thighs. Forde imagined a comic cloud of mortal ash rising from the accident and dusting over the assembled academics, sifting onto the Gagetown spit-and-polish, ash and bone-particles insinuating their way between Mayoral shirt and waistcoat.

The scout brass helped the little boys settle the ebony box onto a small table beside the eagle lectern; a White Stole spread over it a shiny purple cloth emblazoned with a yellow cross.

Order of Service

From the West Door a bugle sounded the Last Post, leaving behind a solemn silence. Into that silence, the sound of boots on the stone flags. Six soldiers from The Royal Canadian Regiment followed, at an interval, by six soldiers from The Royal Canadian Dragoons in the ceremonial slow march down the nave towards the Choir, the rear brought up by two kilted pipers of The Nova Scotia Highlanders.

Eyes Right at the purple-draped box.

At the Choir the crash of boots, crash again, choreographed turns, The Royal Canadian Regiment disappearing into the left transept, the Royal Canadian Dragoons into the right, leaving the two pipers at Parade Rest facing the congregation.

Order of Service

I am the resurrection and the life, saith the Lord: he that believeth in me, though he were dead, yet shall he live: and whosoever liveth and believeth in me shall never die.

Man that is born of a woman hath but a short time to live, and is full of misery. He cometh up, and is cut down, like a flower; he fleeth as it were a shadow and never continueth in one stay.

In the midst of life we are in death: of whom may we seek for succour, but of thee, O Lord, who for our sins art justly displeased?

Yet, O Lord God most holy, O Lord most mighty, O holy and most merciful Saviour, deliver us not into the bitter pains of eternal death.

Thou knowest, Lord, the secrets of our hearts; shut not thy merciful ears to our prayer; but spare us, O Lord most holy, O God most mighty, O holy and merciful Saviour, thou most worthy judge eternal, suffer us not, at our last hour for any pains of death, to fall from thee.

For as much as it hath pleased Almighty God of his great mercy to take unto himself the soul of our dear brother here departed: we therefore commit...ah, *his ashes to the ground; in sure and certain hope of the Resurrection to eternal life, through our Lord Jesus Christ...*

O death, where is thy sting? O grave, where is thy victory?

The Cathedral's Dean, white stole, crossed to the eagle lectern.

The Very Reverend Herbert A. Butterfield.

Order of Service

"Childe Chauncy and his beloved friend Bliss Carman were famous poets. We are gathered here this morning less in grief than in celebration. A native son returns.

"The ashes of Bliss Carman, as most of you will know, are buried in Poets' Corner in Forest Hill Cemetery. As are those of Sir Charles G.D. Roberts, that slightly older poet, friend, and relative of both Bliss and Childe.

"Some of you will be familiar with Bliss Carman's poem "The Grave Tree."

Let me have a scarlet maple
For the grave-tree at my head,
With the quiet sun behind it,
In the years when I am dead.

"Tomorrow, Childe Chauncy's ashes will be buried beside those of Bliss Carman, two luminous spirits reunited.

"Childe Chauncy and Bliss Carman were famous poets. But before they became famous they were simply... boys. New Brunswick boys. Fredericton boys. They attended Fredericton Collegiate Grammar School—and we are especially pleased to welcome students this morning from that school's evolution in excellence, Fredericton High School."

"Boys! High-spirited boys! Boys whose love of Nature, what Bliss always referred to as their *kinship* with Nature, was nurtured by their adventurous expeditions on the St. John River and the Nashwaak by canoe.

"This was no placid paddling. In the spring on the St. John, when the water is at freshet level, the paddler has to stand to battle the current and the waves. They would cross the St. John, navigate the Nashwaak and reach its tributary, Kane's Creek, in the upper hills. This was the Adventure Heroic!

"Bliss' first canoe he named *Cheemaun* after the canoe that had carried Hiawatha to the great Gitchi Manitou, the Giver of Life. Some years later, Childe named *his* canoe *Mishe-Nahma* which means 'Sturgeon' and refers to that section of Longfellow's mighty poem where Hiawatha subdues Mishe-Nahma and tells the people to bring all their pots and kettles and make oil for winter.

"I like to imagine that the forests through which Childe and Bliss paddled were not unlike the arboreal landscape Longfellow so memorably describes as surrounding the wigwam of Nokomis, Daughter of the Moon.

Dark behind it rose the forest,
Rose the black and gloomy pine-trees,
Rose the firs with cones upon them;
Bright before it beat the water,
Beat the clear and sunny water
Beat the shining Big-Sea-Water."

The congregation was becoming audibly restive. Legs were crossed and recrossed. Shoes scraped. Umbrellas fell. Coughing here and there erupted.

Boredom and mothballs, thought Forde.

Bollocks, too.

The Very Reverend paused, made an ushering gesture towards the lectern. From the front UNB row rose an old man wearing a fringed buckskin jacket and a lumberjack shirt secured by a turquoise-tipped four-in-hand.

"I would like to welcome Chief Alcide Simon of the Nashwaak Maliseet. What, you might ask, is the connection between Childe Chauncy and the Maliseet Nation?"

He paused again and surveyed the congregation as if actually expecting an answer.

Leaning forward, clasping the edges of the eagle, he said, "Canoes."

He straightened.

"*Cheemaun* and *Mishe-Nahma* were fifteen-foot birchbark canoes built for the boys by the braves in the village at the mouth of the Nashwaak. These famous canoes were of a type called 'St. John River' birchbarks, the... the *apogee* of First Nations craftwork.

"Chief Simon is going to honour us by reciting a traditional prayer and blessing in the Maliseet-Passamaquoddy dialect of the Algonquian language to welcome home Childe Chauncy's soul."

And recite it the bugger did.

Forde thought it would never end.

This entire performance, he was coming to think, was the most peculiar event he'd ever attended in a church.

Order of Service

The pipers advanced down the nave upon the congregation, halted, threw their sticks and cords and ribbons up on their shoulders, girded up the bags, squawked into a dirgeful pilbroch.

They then played *Will Ye No Come Back Again?*

Forde sang the words inside his head.

Bonnie Charlie's noo awa
Safely oer the friendly main
...

English bribes were a' in vain
The puir and puirer we mun be;
Siller canna buy the heart
That aye beats warm for thine and thee.

Splendid sentiments, thought Forde.

Though a warm, beating heart cut out at Culloden.

And even bagpipes preferable to chanting in the Maliseet-Passamaquoddy dialect of Algonquian.

But what connected bagpipes and the Forty-Five to Childe Chauncy?

Order of Service

Forde had to admit that the President's suit was *built:* very dark blue, exquisitely cut, a suit shouting four thousand dollars. Everything about the President looked like a glossy, standout advertisement in a magazine heavy with sybaritic advertisements, perfect hair, perfect tan, dentrifice, shirt dazzling, cufflinks onyx and gold. Had he smoked, he would have carried a slim James Bond cigarette case in bluish-grey machined gunmetal.

He drew his words of wisdom, a single sheet, from a thin leather folder.

... an occasion sombre yet joyous...
the cultural fabric of our nation...

"Who among us"—he looked about him and smiled his smile—"of a certain age cannot recall the thrill of being introduced in high school to the verse of Childe Chauncy? It is serendipitous that..."

His eyes flicked to his page.

"...that the Very Reverend Butterfield has reminded us this morning of Childe Chauncy's canoeing exploits in *Mishe-Nahma*, for I had chosen to refresh your memories of Childe's lyric mastery by reading just the first stanza—for time presses upon us and our Premier yet has words for us—" bowing his head slightly towards Premier Toomer, half-reclined on the throne-thing—"reading the opening stanza of the poem, which so immediately proclaims itself as having only one possible author."

He paused and again surveyed the congregation.

Paean of the Birchbark Men

From the paddle
Shards of silver,
Water-boatman
Malecite!
Drive the birchbark
'Neath dark willow,
On balsam boughs
Embrace the night.

"This," he looked down at the purple-draped box and allowed the lid to receive the slow, descending benediction of his palm, "this *casket* will tomorrow be interred beside the mortal remains of his friends and mentors, Sir Charles G.D. Roberts and Bliss Carman, in Poets' Corner."

Forde wondered at the President assuming this portentuous tone, these sacerdotal mannerisms; he had, after all, only been CEO of Trinidad Asphalt and Bitumen Company and, before that, Bauxite in South America.

"In his poem 'The Grave Tree' Bliss had wished for

...a scarlet maple"

Forde flinched.

"For the grave-tree at my head,
With the quiet sun behind it...

Tomorrow the University of New Brunswick will pay the same tribute to Childe Chauncy by planting at his grave a hardy maple hybrid called Autumn Blaze."

Order of Service

A mighty fortress is our God, a bulwark never failing;
Our helper He, amid the flood of mortal ills prevailing:
For still our ancient foe doth seek to work us woe:
His craft and power are great, and, armed with cruel hate,
On earth is not his equal.

Did we in our own strength confide, our striving would be losing;
Were not the right Man on our side, the Man of God's own choosing:
Dost ask who that may be? Christ Jesus, it is He;
Lord Sabaoth, His Name, from age to age the same.
And he must win the battle.

Order of Service

The Premier's address was rambling, disjointed, mildly aggressive. Forde wondered if he could be drunk. Certainly, rumours swirled. He had been noted in the River Room of the Lord Beaverbrook Hotel in the late-night company of the Northrop Frye Poetry Chair.

The main thread of his argument seemed to be that the graves of Sir Charles G.D. Roberts, Bliss Carman, and Childe Chauncy in Poets' Corner should be publicized as a National Shrine. *Were* a National Shrine. In their own way, they were just as important as the Fathers of Confederation. Indeed, they themselves *were* Fathers of Confederation. Fathers of Cultural Federation. And were undoubtedly genuine and authentic.

He was not averse to gathering-in other dead poets from other provinces so the entire nation of Canada could come to New Brunswick to pay homage to Canada's cultural Titans. So that Forest Hill Cemetery would become a kind of Cultural Arlington.

Forde, something of an expert in these matters, estimated that the Premier had ingested an eye-opener, followed over the course of the morning by three or four stiffeners, and was now at about what Forde thought of as the mid-Fink-Nottle stage.

The Premier imagined that in the future small, tasteful mini-buses or little trains, perhaps Hop-On, Hop-Off, could carry visitors and tourists from the city's major hotels to the Forest Hill Cemetery. That, at each grave, tourists could select the poem they wished to listen to and hear it over the headphones which would have been factored into the price of the bus-ticket.

The central *point,* of course, *being,* the Premier continued, that there could be no question as to authenticity. As there *was,* of course, about Charlottetown. He would wager that not many among them knew that the painting of the Fathers of Confederation in the Confederation Centre of the Arts in Charlottetown, famous painting, right? Wrong! It was a copy. Which we know because the original painting was destroyed when Parliament burned down in 1916.

You could not expect tourists to pay money to see, say, a suit of armour hundreds of years old if it had been made recently in China.

This was an incontestable point.

But with Forest Hill there would be no question of authenticity.

Nor need the vision end there. *Anne of Green Gables* he dismissed with a wave of his hand. Theatre New Brunswick could put on poetry evenings where an actor performed the life and works of Childe Chauncy or Sir Charles G.D. Roberts like that American actor what was his name did with Mark Twain. And as had been done with Dickens. A ticket to the evening performance could be combined with an All-Day Hop-On Hop-Off ticket. Hotels could integrate with a Childe Chauncy Menu or a Bliss Carmen Buffet....

He could envision an All-Day Bus, Cemetery, Theatre, Dinner Ticket....

Forde revised upwards his estimate of the number of stiffeners.

Premier Toomer's inchoate vision soared, capricious, catachrestic, swelling, slipping finally the surly bonds of earth.

Order of Service

Rock of Ages, cleft for me,
let me hide myself in thee;
let the water and the blood,
from thy wounded side which flowed,
be of sin the double cure;
save from wrath and make me pure.

Not the labours of my hands
can fulfill thy law's commands;
could my zeal no respite know,
could my tears forever flow,
all for sin could not atone;
thou must save, and thou alone.

The cleft Forde found himself thinking about was the cleft of the gunsel's moll, as seen from the viewpoint of Joe "Bananas" Bonano; he had, he thought, been too long away from home.

He stood on the edge of the small group around the UNB President. *That* was Mrs. Tresillian. She reminded him instantly of a robin. Generous of breast, bright, and a little beady of eye, pretty and pugnacious.

He remembered visiting his mother in England, working in her garden pulling down smothering ivy from the old brick walls, digging out a garden bed run wild. What was that word? *Parterre.* He liked that. Sounded posher than "bed." And he'd driven the fork into the lawn to stand upright and had hunkered down for a rest. A robin, he remembered, red-breasted as a Christmas card, had flitted from the top of the wall, from where it had been overseeing operations, to perch on the handle of the fork, cheerfully overbearing, cocking its head as if to say, "Come on, lad. Get digging! Turn me up those white ones, those lovely grubs with ginger legs."

She looked just like that.

The President noticed him and sketched an inclusionary gesture.

"Mrs. Tresillian, Mr. Forde, our Writer-in-Residence."

"So you're the young man deputed to trot the old bag about."

Forde inclined his head.

"An honour," he said, "and what will doubtless be a pleasure."

"Oooh," she said.

A tiny flick of his middle finger, the President murmured "Taxi."

Forde and Mrs. Tresillian walked up the nave towards the West Door.

"Had that man gone on for *five more seconds*," she said, "I'd have wet myself."

"Which one?"

"The Gitche Gumee man."

Forde let out a strangled snort.

"What?"

She pulled his arm and stopped.

"What?" she said, grinning up at him.

"Gitchee Gumee!"

*

The waiter stood stolid.

"Olives?" said Forde, "Or twist?"

"If it's Childe you're after," she said, "it's Bliss you have to look at."

"*Bombay Sapphire?*"

"Rule Britannia!" said Mrs. Tresillian.

"Not?" said Forde to the waiter. "Then, oh, *Beefeater*."

"With my grandfather," she said, "it was monkey see, monkey do. If Bliss had a new canoe, then..."

"Yes, olives. Thank you."

"If Bliss wore turquoise jewellery, Childe wore turquoise jewellery. *Big* jewellry, Navajo, Ute, you know the kind of thing. If Bliss wore clumpy, homemade sandals, Childe made same. If Bliss wore cravats, Childe ditto."

"*Made* sandals?"

"All part of the wretched health-thing. The feet in closer contact with Mother Earth. Grounded balance. Foot beauty. Greek dancing. Liberating the emotions. Breathing. Deportment. Carriage. Interpretive dance. The Delsartean System. Delcroze Eurhythmics. Isadora Duncan."

Forde made a bafflement face.

Presumably in summation of this farrago, she made a dismissive gesture and said, "It was a load of... *kale*."

"Pardon?"

"All of it," she said, "bountiful, unmitigated *kale*."

"Sorry.. What do you mean, 'kale'?"

"Bung-full," she said, "of Nature's Goodness but tasting like stewed tin cans."

"Well," said Forde, "cheers!"

"And never mention to me," she said with theatrical shudder, "salad."

They touched rims.

"Bung-ho!" she said.

They both savoured the icy advent.

"Sandals," she said. "You wish to hear The Bard on the joys of sandals?"

She struck a schoolmarmish pose.

Great toe, little toe, three toes between,
All in a pointed shoe—
Ne'er was so tiny a fo'castle seen,
Nor so little room for the crew.

"Childe?"

"Bliss."

"How do you *remember* all this stuff?"

"Some children had bedtime stories. I had Bliss Carman. My mother *adored* him. She was always quoting him to me, talking about him, and she had big photo albums with squashy padded covers and brass corners. Hundreds of photographs… 'Blissikins,' Mrs. King called him."

"And what did your father think?"

"Actually, I've sometimes fantasized that Bliss *was* my real father. But he seemed more than a little…"

She waggled a hand from side to side.

"Oh, I see. And *was* he?"

She turned palms up in a "Who knows?" gesture.

"They had long, long hair, did I mention that? And they wore cravats and deerskin boots and Stetsons and they were *encrusted* with turquoise. To our eyes nowadays they'd look like dress-up cowboys, gay gunslingers."

"And your father? The real one? What did *he* think of your mother's adoring Mr. Carman?"

"Oh, he lit out for the Territories when I wasn't much more than an infant."

She dropped an olive pit into the ashtray.

"If I take the long view," she said, "wisely so."

And was silent suddenly.

"This um, this Mrs. King you mentioned. Who called Carman 'Blissikins.' Who was *she*?"

"Oh, Carman lived with her and her husband for years."

"What do you mean 'lived with'?"

"Ah!" said Mrs. Tresillian with renewed sparkle, eyes saucy. "You've put your finger on it. As some think Bliss did too."

Forde realized with some fascination that Mrs. Tresillian was *flirting* with him.

"It's a matter of some speculation, my dear. She was arty and had pretensions. She liked having a tame poet. Carman's 'fame' flattered her. She liked being a patron. She and Bliss wrote a stodge book together called *The Making of the Personality*—what they were doing ostensibly at the camp. But all this went on for, oh, some thirty years."

"The three of them?"

"Her husband, well, difficult to even guess. He was wealthy and bankrolled her every whim. He thought of himself, I gathered, as being a little arty too when he wasn't busy with sterner things. He bound books. A dull man, Dr. King, supremely dull. He was the Medical Examiner for The New York Insurance Company."

"He was complicit...?"

"Who knows? And Bliss?"

She did the hand-waggling thing again.

"But dotty and hysterical though she was, he *did* adore her. He wrote this about her—

> *...a soul more subtle*
> *Than the light of the stars,*
> *Frailer than a moth's wing*
> *To the touch that mars;*
> *Wise with the silence*

Of the waiting hills
When the gracious twilight
Wakes in them and thrills...

What do you think?

Lovelier than morning,
Dearer than the sun.

It's too awful to be anything but sincere."

Forde nodded.

"But he was a moocher, too. Petulant. Years of pampered bed and board. Though if it was board and no bed..."

She shrugged.

Forde raised his martini glass by the stem, thumb and forefinger, made enquiring face.

"Absolutely!" said Mrs. Tesillian.

"But what were they *doing*? Apart from..."

"A camp," said Mrs. Tresillian. "A retreat."

"And when you say 'camp'—...?"

"Childe worked at one called *Lifwynn*, which apparently meant 'Joy of Life'—that's the one I knew—and Mrs. King's camp was called *Hengsthall,* no idea, something to do with horses."

"And 'camp' means...?"

"Though there *was* a donkey," she said.

She frowned.

"*Moke!*" she said. "That was its name! Sorry? Well, at *Lifwynn* there was a hall, quite large, logs, a screened porch. And there were several wooden cabins, and cabinny sort of tents on wooden platforms. I remember that if you petted Moke your hand got covered in a sort of dust that smelled really horrible. There's a word..."

"Dander?" said Forde.

"Oh, *clever!*"

"So who went there?"

"Oh, and a clearing in the birch woods where they lolled about and sunbathed and drew horoscopes and played with Tarot cards and painted *en plein air* and scrootled away on their recorders attempting to play 'Greensleeves.' Of course, when I say 'work,' Bliss and Childe didn't actually *work*. They graced the joint with their ethereal presence. Recited the occasional poem. Added lustre. Stirred the juices."

Only make me over, April,
When the sap begins to stir!
Make me man or make me woman,
Make me oaf or ape or human,
Cup of flower, or cone of fir;
Make me anything but neuter
When the sap begins to stir.

Forde caught the pressed-glass vase and the plastic orchid as they fell under her outflung gesture.

"*Who* went, did you say?"

Forde nodded.

"Rich young women. Boston. Connecticut. New York. *Lifwynn* and *Hengsthall* were in the Catskills. About twenty-five of them, thirty at a time. Endless salad and exercise and brooding about their *severely limited* Personalities."

"No men being Personally Harmonized?"

"Just Bliss, if you can count him. And Childe. My grandmother said they called Childe 'our faun among the nymphs.' They *twinkled* at him."

"That's where he met her?"

"None twinkled brighter than she."

"So they wore toga-things, Greek things, and danced?"

"*Danced!*" Dear Boy! Not dancING. DANCE. We are talking of Plastic Motion, of Motor-Mental Rhythm, The

Expression of Inner Being, Harmonizing of the Personality, *Interpretive* dance!"

"Right," said Forde, "so they draped themselves in toga-things and danced about."

"Yes, and heaved vast medicine balls at each other round the circle. And singing roundelays and part-songs. And Spontaneous Clubs."

"Clubs?"

"Indian."

"Ah," said Forde.

"Not togas. *Tunics*," said Mrs. Tresillian. "Practically starkers."

"Hmmm," said Forde, picturing this.

And sipped at the fresh martini, luxuriating in a vision of scant and gauzy tunics and unrestrained *floppiness.*

"And Miss Bentley—Good God! I've even remembered her name. Miss Bentley wound up the Victrola and played records of Beethoven and Brahms for the interpretive dancing. She wore *enormous* straw hats with streamers and floral clumps on them and screamed at the girls "Let go! *Let go!* LET GO! MELTING. MELTING. Soft, soft, like timid bunnies."

"Shsss," said Forde.

The waiter was eyeing them.

"You see, I remember it all. All that chubby sweating and writhing about and girls staggering and falling under the reception of medicine balls and Indian Clubs whizzing spontaneously through the air and Miss Bentley screaming and the Beethoven record with a scratch going *scritch-scritch* at *great* volume... It was," she said, "like a war zone."

Forde smiled at her, at this vigorous vision.

"I feel so ashamed," she said.

"Of what?"

She shrugged.

"Implicated," she said. "I know it's silly but, I don't know, tarred with the same brush, I suppose."

"Why would you feel that?"

"Well," she said, "I *am* closer to them than you are."

Forde made a dismissing face.

She laid her hand on her heart.

She declaimed.

But there be others, happier few,
The vagabondish sons of God,
Who know the by-ways and the flowers,
And care not how the world may plod.
They idle down the traffic lanes,
And loiter through the woods with spring;
To them the glory of the earth,
Is but to hear a bluebird sing.

She reached across the table and gripped his hand.

"So *humiliatingly* third rate," she said.

He stroked the back of her hand with his forefinger.

"But not you," he said, "not you."

"When I was growing up," she said, "I was pleased to discover that Isadora Duncan had been strangled to death by her own scarf. It was immensely long and she was dramatic with it. Such a tiresome woman. Caught it in the wheels of her car. I imagined her pulled out horizontal, like an Edward Gorey cartoon. I thought it funny. I hope you won't think ill of me."

"Not at all," said Forde, "perfectly reasonable. I've always loathed Jean-Paul Sartre and wished upon him death."

Had he just said 'and wished upon him death'?

Her mode was catching.

"Harold," she said, "put it all rather well."

"Sorry?"

"Harold is my younger brother. Harold… Harold is never seen without a tie and a tiepin in the form of an aeroplane, a blue enamel body with sparkly bits in the enamel. Quite a large tiepin."

"You mean?"

"Exactly."

"Go on."

"A Professor had arranged to visit the house, an Assistant Professor, somewhere in Massachusetts I believe it was. Wanted to ask us our recollections of Bliss and Childe, and Harold wouldn't speak at first but then said 'He was a Kangaroo.'"

And the Professor said, "Bliss Carman, do you mean, Harold, or Childe Chauncy?"

She paused.

Head turned away from the Professor and, staring fiercely at the floor, lips scrunched, she did Harold.

"And the Professor prompted him, 'Harold?' And Harold glared at the floor and said —"

She giggled.

"What? What?"

"And said—"

"*Stop it*! Tell me."

"And said, '*He* was a Kangaroo and *he* was a Kangaroo.'"

*

They ate lunch in the cavernous and nearly deserted hotel dining room.

"Pointless trying to find anywhere better," said Forde. "Sorry. Unless you like Chinese things in red sauce."

Obtrusive French service by a youth not long out of high school, a slatternly girl from the kitchens in pumps mashed down at the heels, dumping plastic buckets of washed cutlery onto the rear service station tables; her feet, Forde noticed, were bare.

With lunch they drank a bottle of *Croze Hermitage*, which Forde found too thin, too acidic, though that might well have been the martinis. Thin or not though, he thought it probably preferable to *Hairy Belly*.

During dessert, *Berries from the Boscage? Feuilleté Drizzled with* what?, the safest bet being *Homemade Apple Pie à la Mode*, they settled on visiting the Beaverbrook Art Gallery.

Forde described to her the immense and *stupendously* awful Salvador Dali in the Gallery's entrance hall, *Santiago El Grande,* Saint James on a bloody great horse giving the Risen Christ a bunk-up into Heaven.

The calvados was pleasantly fortifying and the more pleasant in that the President was paying for it.

"I remember," she said, "a man I knew in London, Brian... Brian *Sewell!* He'd known Dali—Dali lived in one of those Robert Graves-sort-of-places, an island, Spain..." She waved her hand impatiently to fill in the detail. "He was unnecessarily vivid about Dali's homosexual practices. They were, apparently, of an *assembly-line* frequency and involved photography."

The hotel foyer was deserted.

Mrs. Tresillian, passing by the bell on the counter, struck it a flat-palmed *bling,* and continued "... if you remember it on the radio, they were always playing it, a song about suburban houses, *Little Boxes* I think it was called, somesuch name and it had the lines,

and they're all made out of ticky-tacky
and they all look just the same

...and I've been thinking that what my grandfather and Bliss were all made out of was *plinky-plonky.*"

Pulling on his arm to stop him, she acknowledged an audience and, striking a pose, declaimed

Shrilling pipe or fluting whistle,
In the valleys come again;
Fife of frog and call of tree-toad
All my brothers, five- or three-toed,
With their revel no more vetoed
Making music in the rain...

The desk clerk emerged from his cubbyhole, eying Mrs. Tresillian. He wore his black suit with the unease of a costume. His white shirt was uncrisp and his tie a throttled knot, reminding Forde of ties in his youth called Slim Jims. He coughed apologetically into his fist. Smiled. Laid his finger across his lips.

"Don't shsss *me!*" said Mrs. Tresillian in a voice projected to reach the rearmost stalls.

"*Grasp,*" she fluted...

She held out beseeching hands to the clerk almost as if in prayer.

"*Grasp* gaiety."

They emerged from the Lord Beaverbrook Hotel onto Queen Street, sudden daylight, cars honking, a heaving mob of young men milling with a Montreal Canadiens banner and drinking beer from bottles, *whoops,* shouting; it was cold.

"What is it?" said Mrs. Tresillian.

"Hockey probably. No idea. It's usually hockey."

"Oh, look!" she said.

Roped to the top of a car was a moose, one stiff hind leg angled at the sky. Closer, they could see the dopey face masked in dried blood, teeth, coarse hair in stiffened clumps, the matted flank, dung.

"On the radio some mornings," he said "there are moose warnings. They wander up and down Queen Street looking in shop windows."

"But why have they tied it...?"

"There's a wildly popular lottery to win licences to kill them," he said.

"Yes, but why...."

"They parade them around."

She had stopped and was staring at the carcass.

"So it wasn't hockey," she said. "It's..." pointing.

"Think 'tribal,'" he said, thinking of the sweatpants boy in Creative Writing One and the girl with the carabiners and Garfields and the glinty thing in her nose," think *National Geographic.*"

"It *smells,*" she said.

He hurried her towards the Gallery entrance, past the snow-spattered, forgettable statues *after Watteau*. Christ! such pretentious drivel, "after," *after* my arse, he thought, and of all bloody excruciating painters the *fête galante* Watteau, *Christ!* past a statue of a leopard about to leap from a tree WHY past the grotesque *Santiago El Grande* and into the heated hush where Mrs. Tresillian undid her coat and sat heavily on a padded bench and slumped rather, presumably recovering from the *Croze-Hermitage* and the moose.

The room they were in was brown. Forde wandered away. It was a brown room. Windsor soup brown. Nasty mastic. Windsor soup pictures. He peered at informative labels.

George Romney (1734-1802) *Charles Lennox, later 4th Duke of Richmond, Duke of Lennox and of Aubigny.* Particularly nasty brown dog.

Thomas Lawrence (1769-1830) *A Portrait Group of Mrs. John Thomson and her Son Charles Edward Poulet Thomson, later Baron Sydenham etc.* Charles Edward, of indeterminate sexuality, standing on a meticulously rendered brown chair.

John Constable (1776-1837) *Scene of Woods and Water* (c. 1830). Forde glanced at this preposterous brown daub in disbelief. He checked in the paperback guide to the

Gallery he'd lifted from the front desk on the way in. This Constable, and the adjacent Joseph Mallord William Turner (1775-1851) *The Fountain of Indolence*, were both "later proved not to be autograph." Forde took this example of curatorial bafflegab, well-buried in the guide text, not to mean "unsigned," but rather "not by the hand of," which translated as "fakes."

He could imagine the oleaginous Bond Street and West End dealers battening on Lord Beaverbrook's pretensions: Knoedler, Agnew, Leggat Brothers, Spink, Marlborough, Wildenstein, Gimpel Fils, Alex Reid and Lefevre, Arthur Tooth and Sons, Sotheby's, Christie's; the Beaverbrook Art Gallery put him in mind of poor Isabella Gardner and her tatty palazzo on Boston's Fenway. Berenson and Duveen had plucked her in much the same way Bond Street had probably plucked Max Aitkin of Newcastle, New Brunswick, the Lord Beaverbrook.

He wondered why these fraudulent canvases hadn't been relegated to basement storage.

John Constable.

He smiled with sudden affection and pleasure at the thought of Gulley Jimson, the painter in Joyce Cary's *The Horse's Mouth*. How many young hopefuls *that* book must have lured into a life of art and penury.

She asked me twenty pounds for a Constable, two trees, four clouds and a little piece of dog-shit in the foreground.

His mind was full of such sentences lodged completely without effort and lodged exactly. Full, too, of word placements, poniard verbs, punctuation points. Such sentences needed no rehearsal, no learning by heart; the second he read them they registered indelibly. Mined from hundreds of books, they had somehow over the years cohered to become his palette, his signature line.

Gulley, that lovely old visionary, haggling for cheap, crappy canvases to paint over.

Every junk shop in England has two or three Morlands... Ikey had two. Nice brown ones. The first had a horse, stable, dog, man and tree. The second was more important. It had a stable, a dog, a horse, a peasant, a tree and a gate.

"What are *you* smiling at?"

He turned to look at her.

"Farting Annie Laurie through a keyhole."

Raised eyebrows.

"So," he said, "ready for the fray?"

"it's all..." she said, "rather dispiriting, isn't it?"

Trudged on through The Kreighoff Collection (pried by Beaverbrook, according to the Guide, out of mining magnate James Boylen and press baron Roy Thompson and out of the corporate assets of the Canadian International Paper Company and Royal Securities); through an exhibit of Inuit Prints—temporary, Forde could only hope, but probably, he thought, not; through bits and bobs of Pre-Raphaelite flotsam; through distressing canvases described as belonging to The School of Incident:

The Slide by Tomas Webster (1800-1886)

When the Day is Done by Thomas Faed (1826-1900)

CHRIST!

The Crew of HMS 'Terror' Saving the Boats and Provisions on the Night of 15th March 1837 by George Chambers (1803-1840), Purchased with funds from Friends of the Beaverbrook Art Gallery and with a Minister of Communications Cultural Property Grant.

A James Tissot canvas from which he had to look away.

"Shall we?" said Mrs. Tresillian, gesturing.

Emblazoned above the Gallery entrance:

Marion McCain Atlantic Gallery

"Who is that?" said Mrs. Tresillian. "This Marion McCain?"

"Frozen French Fries," said Forde.

"Ah," said Mrs. Tresillian.

"... *blah, blah,*" he read, "and creates the finest collection of Atlantic Canadian art in the world."

Slapped the Guide shut.

"Not just the finest but probably the *only*. No, no, you go ahead. I haven't the stomach for it."

She climbed the steps, disdaining the handrail, and stood within the proscenium entrance, which was panelled in sheets of differing, light-coloured woods, lavender trim, four peculiar and ugly pillars lacking bases, capitals or flutes, a pastel place suggesting to Forde an Ikea catalogue.

He stood watching the small black figure in the flooding light.

He had in fact seen her from the corner of his eye while he'd been looking at the "not autograph" Constable, seen her hesitate at the threshold. Thinking herself unobserved, she'd been looking a little weary and beset and he'd known better than to acknowledge her.

Then her voice teasingly accosting him at his back.

What are you *smiling at?*

This mock-pugnacity, her flirtatiousness, that robin quality, her *will*, reminded him of Marian Petersen in his *Father Would Have Wished,* a book now nearly four years old. Reminded him not of the novel's events, but of the novel's genesis, the unlikely seed of it all, what he had seen for a few moments from his study window.

His next-door neighbour's mother, somewhere near Mrs. Tresillian's age, came into view around a bulging hedge of cedar trees two houses down. She was carrying two plastic shopping bags. She was walking very slowly. She set the two bags down on the pavement and massaged her hands where the plastic handles had been cutting. Then she just stood. Staring at the ground.

She'd put him in mind for those defeated seconds of a winded horse or a bull in the ring, head dropped, weakened by *banderillas* and *pique,* a drool of blood spindling to the sand.

Then, she stooped and picked up the bags, a surge of almost visible will, squared her shoulders, and—what?—as though the band had struck up and she was coming out of the wings into the lights—almost *strutting* to her son's front door.

And from that seed had unfolded imagined lives, Maria Petersen's domination of her middle-aged son and daughter, their emotional and financial dependence, the son's career undermined by money and his life further anaesthetized by a dutiful marriage, the daughter's descent into obese alcoholism, Maria's death by agency of the apartment-size electric kiln in the pretensions of her "studio".

There had been rumblings of disquiet about the theatricality of Maria's death but in the main conventional plaudits by ill-qualified reviewers were pronounced: "... dare one suggest the word 'genius'?" *Globe and Mail;* "... the magic once again of his old mastery" *National Post. Quill and Quire* had awarded him a star.

Lifetime (i.e. three years)

Lifetime Sale: 523 copies.

Copies sold since last Reporting Period: 2

He made a snorty noise in his palate and nose.

"So!" he said. "Are we ready to...?"

"Oh, *pots!*" she said. "British."

"How do you know?"

"Soft-paste porcelain. European's hard. At a glance," she said as they approached, "Worcester Porcelain Works,

Barr, Flight, and Barr, the beginning of the Regency—about 1815, somewhere in there. *Probably* painted by Baxter but I haven't got my glasses on."

Forde stopped and stared at her.

She grinned at him.

"Showing off," she said.

"When he had hoisted his jaw off the floor," said Forde, "how on earth…?"

"They're fruit coolers," she said. "Inside, they'd have had an insert retaining the ice. Some had a fairly deeply recessed lid, too, a sunken lid that you fill with ice. On top of the lid, I mean. When it was on."

"You're right," said Forde, looking up from the Guide, "Thomas Baxter."

On one side of one cooler was a painting of Jupiter and on the other side the fight between Hercules and Hippolyta, Queen of the Amazons.

"And what's this on the other cooler?"

She shrugged.

Forde again consulted the Guide.

"'King Alfred with the neatsherd.' Must be the 'Burning of the Cakes' story. And on *this* side it's 'Queen Margaret and her son Edward being attacked by a robber.' I wonder what story *that* is? *Queen*? If it's *Queen* Margaret it can only be… Margaret of Anjou who was wife to Henry VI, so *Edward* must be…"

"Forde?"

"Mmmm."

"You are failing to grip me."

He looked at the coolers again, the rigid neoclassicism of the shapes, the slathered gilt, the static painting.

"They're sort of horrible, aren't they?" he said. "Pompously inert. *Can* something be inert pompously?"

Mrs. Tresillian laughed.

"No, you're right," she said. "They're dead. Absolutely dead, but very pricey in the auction rooms."

"Gift," read Forde, "of Mrs. Howard W. Pillow... member Board of Governors... related to *blah, blah* Charles Hosmer *blah blah*... inherited *blah*... a fortune derived from Ogilvie Mills Ltd, the Ritz Carlton Hotel, and the Canadian Pacific Railway."

"*Exactly*," said Mrs. Tresillian.

*

The roadways had been plowed black. Away from the scrubby trees and bushes, the white of the snow, thicker than white, a cheesecake sort of colour, the gravestones, the fall of light, suggested to him a fantastic *gateau* studded with stick-up wafers of milk and dark chocolate.

"Forde?"

"Mmmm?"

Here and there, topped by stubby crosses, grander monuments to the presumably illustrious, some leaning now, lichen.

"In confidence?"

"Yes, Anna, of course."

"Well, I didn't come up here to bury my grandfather's ashes, well, I mean I *did*, but I was really hoping to meet someone, talk to someone... You see, I have all Chauncy's stuff and—not to put too fine a point upon it—I need to flog it."

"What sort of stuff?"

"There's packets of his letters to my grandmother, letters to my mother, there's a big box of letters to publishers in Boston—Small, Maynard and Something and

Dodd, Mead, and Company. Contracts. Magazines he had poems in. Letters from Sir Charles G.D. Roberts. He always addressed him as 'Old Man.' Fawning, really. And Roberts' replies in this relentlessly *jocular* style. Cringingly unfunny. God! How they loved themselves! And stuff about his getting an honorary doctorate from here in Fredericton, a Doctor of Laws. I don't know why *Laws*, but anyway tons of manuscripts of poems and rough versions of things and magazines and newspaper articles and there's the complete handwritten manuscripts of the books—they're in big ledgers stamped in gold on the covers *The New York Insurance Company*—Bliss must have got them for him from Dr. King. So I don't have the first one but there's *April's Benediction, Anthem of the Hermit Thrush, The Open Road,* and *A Pealing Cadence Thrills.* Oh, just tons of stuff. There's two steamertrunks full of it."

"Sounds good," said Forde, "but these university buggers are always crying poor. The thing *is*… What?"

She tugged them to a halt.

"It just struck me," she said. "A lot of young people these days wouldn't even know what a steamertrunk *was*."

"My dear Anna," said Forde, "they wouldn't even know what a *steamer* was."

"God Almighty."

Forde nodded.

"Doesn't do to dwell on it," he said.

They were silent for a few moments.

"What I was going to say," he went on, "I imagine it all depends on whether the Americans consider Childe American or Canadian. He lived there most of his life, all his books published there. Don't know. Just don't know. I shouldn't think—no offense—that Austin, Texas would be in the running, but Boston maybe or The Rock at Brown, big manuscript collections there. And then there's the Harriet Irving Library here—oil, lumber, stingy bastards. I believe I heard somewhere....

Was it bloody Beasley who'd been braying on about it?

"... that they've got *acres* of Bliss Carman. And there's the university in Kingston—*Queen's*, it's called, and they're fairly rich and collect this period."

"How do you know all this?"

"I flogged some of my own stuff to the University of Toronto and I did some looking around at the time."

"So who should I talk to?"

"Well, I can tell you straight off, if you talk to librarians or university people, they'll tell you they're broke, but if they're interested they'll offer you a tax credit. Which is bugger-all use to you or me because we don't earn enough to need tax credits, and in your case doubly useless because you live in the States and don't pay tax here."

"Ooh," she groaned, "all things like this *oppress* me."

"What you need to do," said Forde, "is go on the attack. Bypass the bureaucrats and make the matter public."

"How do you mean?"

"Well—for a start—after they've buried the ashes tomorrow you should buttonhole the savant from the *Daily Gleaner*..."

He recalled yesterday's photograph of a swamp from which *moments before this study a family of mallards had taken wing.*

"... and *gush* at this seedy scribe about how you have all these Confederation Heirlooms and precious *blah-blah*."

He told her about the mallards.

"If they run a photograph of non-ducks, they'll go *ape* over Poets' Granddaughter, Confederation, Precious Canadian Manuscripts, precious *New Brunswick* manuscripts… and you'll have done an end run through their tightass obstructions."

Mmmm.

How about *this!*

You go right to the top. A letter to the Premier. You were so impressed by his Vision in the Cathedral. A Childe Chauncey exhibit! On the Hop-On Hop-Off Cultural Trail. Bung in some scraps of Carman and Roberts. Unique Confederation Manuscripts of Unchallengeable Authenticity, the cost for the Province a mere bagatelle."

She nodded her head slightly.

"I *like* this, Forde."

"I'll organize some letters for you."

"A widow," she said, "a poor, old widow woman."

"Yes, good, good."

"Poor but the Guardian of Canada's Treasures."

Forde groaned with mock-relish.

"The *Faithful* Guardian."

"Exquisite!" said Forde.

'*Your* style is not so shabby," she said.

He leered at her.

"Dangerous men," she said. "Always my downfall."

"You little minx, you!"

"A masterful play," she said, nodding vigorously in confirmation. "Plenty of wristy follow-through."

"And a P.G. devotee, too."

"What do you mean 'too'?"

"As well as knowing about—Worcester, was it? We *must* be near there now. I've never been, but there was a photograph in the UNB *Bulletin*. The taller monument is Sir Charles and the other's Bliss."

"I can remember seeing Sir Charles," she said. "When I was small. He was in the kitchen with my mother. And I remember him because he was wearing pince-nez and they were attached to a button on his waistcoat by a flat black silk ribbon that lay down his cheek and I'd never seen that before. And he used to take pellets."

"Pardon?"

"I remembered him because of that, too. 'Pellets.' It was such a peculiar word to use and it stuck in my mind because I thought pellets were what we fed the hens, so I thought he ate hen-pellets. But 'pellets' was what he called pills, tablets. He had angina."

"Angina," said Forde.

"Forde, Forde," she said, "we grow old."

"Let us not repine," he said. "Let us *grasp* gaiety."

"When we were quite young girls, all the *Lifwynn* kids had heard it…"

"Sorry?"

"Sir Charles," she said, "His party trick. It involved a quarter and his *membrum*…"

"Quite, quite," said Forde. "Quite."

"… well, on his *membrum virile*."

"What!" said Forde. "*On?*"

Mittened palms up and out towards him in a gesture of refusal,

"Absolutely," she said…

averting her eyes

"… not."

She was, thought Forde, without doubt, *without doubt,* flirting with him.

He smiled at her.

"Tony left me some money," she said, "but I worry about Harold. I *do* have to make some sort of provision for him."

"Jeeves is not required," he said. "We will give it of our best."

They walked on in silence. A blue jay squawked and fled. A dollop of snow plopped.

"When you talk to the *Gleaner* tomorrow, you refer almost exclusively to the Premier's speech—the cultural benefits to the Province, the unique treasure trove of manuscripts, Native Son *blah-blah*—and stress the Premier's stress on Authenticity. In a way, the Honourable Richard Toomer has sort of trapped himself. You can't get much more authentic than Childe's holograph manuscripts and his mortal remains."

"But do you think he'll read it?"

"His aides with the shaven necks sure as hell will."

"Hmmm."

She walked on.

"What?" said Forde.

"It's getting towards the hour," she said, "for an Old-Fashioned."

"Resolve waning?" said Forde.

"Forde?"

"Mmmm?"

"In confidence?"

"Yes, Anna, of course."

"Coming back to what the Premier was saying."

"Which part...?"

"About authenticity."

"Mmmm."

"Well, you see, they're not."

"Pardon?"

"Well, my mother always referred to the box as her father's ashes, and if you shook the box there was definitely something inside, it made a thumping noise, but the key was lost."

"Go on."

"But when *she* died I was looking through some old photograph albums with puffy covers—you know the sort, they used to have black or brown pages and photographs stuck into four little black triangular corners..."

"Yes, yes."

"And people wrote who people were and dates and so forth in white?"

"Yes."

"Well, in one album there were photos headed 'The Ceremony' and pictures of my mother and her consort of the time and other people I didn't know, with drinks and straw boaters, and there's the black casket on the lawn and a black Labrador with a huge bow around its neck and they each have a spoon. And there was one of them all standing in a semi-circle behind the casket holding their spoons up in the air like d'Artagnan."

"For scooping out..."

"Exactly."

She sighed.

"So I *think*," she said, "they did it around the big horse chestnut tree. It's still there, white candles in the spring, *so* beautiful. My mother exactly—a drinks party with straw boaters to scatter ashes."

"But there was still something left in the casket you said?"

"I got a locksmith to open it up and what it was—I don't know if you have this up here—it was a bag that Chivas Regal *Crown Royal* came in, very plush cloth, very posh, almost like velvet, purple with stitched yellow writing on it and a drawstring."

"Actually," said Forde, "It comes *from* here. Anyway what was it?"

"Earth," she said.

"Earth?"

"Soil."

"With bone in it or anything?"

"No. Just soil."

"So then what?"

"I threw the soil out when I'd arranged to come up here and I put ashes in the box from the fireplace. But they didn't look right. They *smelled* like wood ashes."

"But you locked the box again?"

"No. I didn't have a key. So I went to Home Depot and I bought some of that special glue you mustn't get on your hands."

"Epoxy?"

"That's it. You have to mix two tubes together on a piece of cardboard. The man said it was so strong you'd have to chop the box open with an axe."

"Hmmm," said Forde.

"And I gugged up the keyhole with glue so no smoke-smell can get out."

"No one can open it," said Forde, "and no one can smell it."

"*And,*" she said, "I wanted it to *sound* right. I mean, I'd read somewhere that ashes have bits of bone in them that they didn't completely crunch up so if someone shook it, do you see? So I put a unicorn in there."

Forde stopped and stopped her.

"A unicorn," he said.

She nodded.

"When you say, 'a unicorn'—"

"It was a neighbour's, her toddler had left it, it was white plastic. Solid. Quite heavy and it had a spirally golden horn. So before I did the glue I went down to the basement, there's an old workbench down there with a vice fixed to it, and I cut the unicorn into little bits with a hacksaw and mixed them with the ashes."

"So if you shook it there'd be a sense of bigger bits."

"Exactly."

Forde nodded in a considering way.

"Forde?"

"Well," he said, flipping his left hand, palm-up, "ashes," flipping his right, palm-up, "are ashes."

She nodded.

"No *essential* difference between this lot of ashes and that lot of ashes. Any thought of hugger-muggery is merely in your head alone. Just bury the box with an expression on your face of solemnity and loss."

She took his arm again and they walked on.

Then she stopped again, paused.

The light was thickening.

"I *think* that's why I did that."

She looked puzzled, sounded unsure.

Taller crosses aspired to the sky, black against it.

"Why I put the unicorn in there."

Up ahead of them, Poets' Corner. A parked miniature back-hoe-thing, yellow. A man moving about. On the snow, a bright-green tarpaulin with a small mound of earth on it. The glint of a spade.

"That'll be you," said Forde.

The man was standing now in the square hole. His back was to them. Along the yellow arm of the back-hoe-thing the word BOBCAT.

She brought her hand up across Forde's stomach, halting him.

Her frown smoothed.

He heard her intaken breath.

She seemed to expand.

She called out to the man.

"Hola, gravedigger!"

The stooped donkey jacket and flat cloth cap stiffened but did not turn.

"Hola, gravedigger!" she called again. "How's my hole?"

*

Looking up from the menu, Forde said, "'The Catch of the Day'?"

"Haddock, sir."

Not the lunchtime boy, but a man got up in bistro garb.

"Haddock," repeated Forde. "It is, I take it… frozen?"

"I think we need a few more minutes," said Anna.

The waiter padded away.

Anna had been withdrawn in the taxi, largely silent. As the street lights came on, glints in the taxi's shadows suggested she was a little moist of eye.

Surely, thought Forde, it couldn't have been the cemetery?

"*So,*" he said. "Plymouth. You were starting to say earlier—"

"Torquay."

"Sorry. Torquay."

"Are you sure you want to hear this?"

"Of course," said Forde. "Of course."

She sighed.

"We were to open in the Pavillion, Torquay, with a creaky old farce…"

She flapped impatiently fill-in-the-details.

"The same vintage as *Love in a Mist*. *Norman's Conquest*, it was called. By the second night of the run I'd realized that the only thing in the world I really wanted I could never have. This realization, this bitterness…"

She fell silent.

Aligned her cutlery.

"Does this sound a bit rehearsed? Well, you'd be right. It's been my party-piece for years."

Feeling embarrassed, apprehensive, helpless, Forde sketched a carry-on gesture and said, "Please..."

"This bitterness," she said.

Stopped.

"Just listen to me!" she said. "As though I'm in Gethsemane saying *let this cup pass from me.* But heigh-ho. Bitterness it was. Delivered courtesy of Mary's fever and infected molar. I was understudy. Word perfect, *that* was never a problem, but the whole thing—no other word for it—was a shambles."

"Oh, surely..."

"I'd watched it night after night for weeks, but I couldn't *do* it. I felt like someone given shorts and a jersey and pushed onto a pitch during a soccer match. One group running one way, then another group running about so I'd run one way after this lot and then run after the other lot, and the ball criss-crossing about as if there was some purpose in where they kicked it. And then sometimes it seemed to disappear and then reappear near a net and they'd be hacking about down there and I'd be standing alone near the middle, still wondering how the ball had *got* there."

"But didn't you say," said Forde, "this was the first time you'd had to act a full-length— "

"No," she said. "I knew, *knew* it wasn't something I could practice and learn how to do."

She shrugged again.

"It was something they had and I didn't. I wasn't *in* the play like they were. Their timing, it was like a language I couldn't speak. When the ball was coming my way and they were swarming it towards me, I couldn't do anything, just stupidly watched."

The waiter padded towards them again.

"Oh, I don't know! A steak, I guess."

"The chef recommends his *onglet de boeuf.*"

They both nodded.

"Gigondas, that's OK?"

"*So,*" she said.

"In Fredericton!" said Forde. "*Onglet!*"

"So we now come," she said, "in this gripping narrative to Captain Anthony Tresillian, my very own 'stage door Johnny.' Flowers and his card left at Mr. Anstruther's cubby-hole. He was smitten by my beauty. *Me!* He thought I was a wonderful actress. *That* should have warned me. He took me to dinner. To dinn*ers*. With wine. *Wine!* When Mary and I—if there wasn't a technical rehearsal or a press call *we* could only afford a quart bottle of cider between us on a Sunday afternoon."

She sipped the Gigondas, *hmmm,* looked up, and nodded her approval.

"Truth be told," she said, "some part of me was tired of being cold and poor, tired of packets of crisps and ginger-coloured fishcakes from MacFisheries and baked beans and tea turned orange from *Carnation* condensed milk."

She set the glass down, ran her fingertip and thumb up and down its stem.

"Marrying Tony," she said, "was the one *really* unforgiveable thing I've ever done."

Forde did not know what to say.

"You were young."

She nodded.

After a moment or two, she said, "That cider. It had a bird on the label, one of those birds with red heads."

Forde looked blank.

"They attack trees."

"Woodpeckers?"

"Exactly! *Woodpecker Cider.* Bulmer's, that was what it was called. It made one shudder even as one drank it. *Warm* cider! They didn't *have* fridges."

"Yes," said Forde, nodding. "It all seems so long ago."

"You're making me suddenly remember all sorts of odd things," said Anna. "I remember how much pleasure it gave me—you're going to think I'm *really* silly—but going to an off-licence to buy a bottle of wine and there was always a thick wad of pink or mauve tissue paper on the counter, and the man put the bottle on the wad and rolled it up in the top sheet so tightly and beautifully and a twist at the neck."

"With me," said Forde, "it was ice cream. Watching them make wafers. *Sculpt* wafers."

She reached across the table and squeezed his hand.

"Lovely man," she said

"Not the sort of memory," he said, "to share with one's colleagues of the professorial variety."

"Thinking back," said Anna, "the things that Mary and I put up with. We roomed together in Nottingham and we usually shared when we were on tour. She looked out for me right from the beginning. She was kindness itself. Some meals we were reduced to sugar sandwiches. And those 'boarding houses for theatricals'—one place always gave us curried mince with bloated sultanas in it. The curry powder tasted chemical and turned the stuff bright mustardy-ochre, the exact colour, Mary said, of a newborn's shit."

She smiled at a memory.

"Have you ever eaten a meat," she said, "called 'scrag-end'?"

"Christ, no!" said Forde. "What is it?"

She shrugged.

"Don't know. They served that too."

"What an adventurous life!'

"Those curses of Mary's. We knew what they *meant* but how she got there...? Always effing and blinding, Mary was. If she was searching for something or if she'd broken something, 'Gilbert and fucking *Sullivan!*' she'd say, or if she was in a rage and threatening to quit she'd say, 'If he gives me one more note like that in front of the company it's *Goodnight Vienna!*' So long ago now."

She paused, shaking her head.

"What's that you're writing?"

"A nugget," said Forde, "for future use."

What?"

"'Scrag-end.'"

"And those 'boarding houses for theatricals' are etched in the memory. *Etched.* Rooms half-filled with ancient wardrobes the size of double coffins. Ovaltine and a motor bike under tarpaulin in the front garden. And cold, *cold.* Sometimes, in the north, there'd be no washbasin in the room, just a washstand with a jug of cold water standing in the matching bowl. You'll find them in antique stores now. No such thing as showers, of course. You had to *book* a bath. Appointments for baths in one place we used to stay, they recorded them in a big black ledger held closed by a huge rubber strap like the ones they cinch around your arm for a blood test.

"One place, I remember, Mary and I were having breakfast in 'The Breakfast Room'—red plastic salt-and-pepper shakers, shaped like tomatoes and greasy to the touch—in what would have been the parlour, though sometimes it was in the basement, the breakfast room, I mean, anyway we both felt somehow uneasy as though, I don't know, as though there was another presence there, and then under a side table that was covered with a green sort of cloth hanging down, baize, bobbles along the edges, very Victorian, the *things* one remembers! So vivid. We saw a tartan slipper and *eyes* and there was a small child under there entirely naked—'feral' Mary said—except for these adult-sized tartan slippers like slithery boats on his feet."

"Very unnerving," said Forde.

"And it was that house," she said, "that had a shared toilet for two floors. I used to read a great deal in those days, and I remember a line in a novel about someone finding in a communal toilet 'a turd like a conger eel'...*well*..."

"And Mary?" said Forde. "What happened to her? Are you still in touch?"

"No," she said. "after I married Tony I let things drift. Then cut myself off entirely."

Forde cocked his head in enquiry.

"Don't you understand?" she said, "*Norman's Conquest*. Everything, *everything* I did was on the rebound from Torquay. I'm sorry," she said, "Do stop me if I'm becoming garrulous. It's the wine."

"Not at all!" said Forde. "It's so interesting, so, I mean, all *I* do is sit at a desk and turn sentences around."

"So, then," she said, "Tony."

She set down her knife and fork.

"Does the word 'Dubbin' mean anything to you?"

"For waterproofing—"

She nodded.

"A sponge bag?"

"Yes?"

"Does the name 'Cash' ring a bell? Labels?"

"Yes, of course. With your name on them. They were printed on cloth, sort of—what? Tabs? You sent away for them. My mother sewed them into shirt collars and waistbands, football shorts and such—why are you asking?"

"Just to see if you knew what I'd got myself into."

"With Tony, you mean?"

"How old were you?"

"Cash, you mean, labels? Ten? Eleven?"

"Yes, well *he* was thirty-two."

She fell silent.

"I never loved him. Tolerated him, I suppose. That was what was unforgivable."

"We all made young mistakes, Anna."

"I think he saw me as a 'free spirit,' an 'actress,' an 'artiste,' something outside his experience entirely. Sort of *ethereal*—if you can imagine. He had a lick of floppy hair at the front, like a boy. He was used to girls in jodhpurs, girls who wore pyjamas they kept under their pillows in zip-up pyjama bags that were shaped like horses. The kind of girls who called 'Coming!' to a ringing telephone.

"Turned out he was quite wealthy. His collar stays were made of ivory. From the family elephant I wouldn't have been surprised. His parents lived in a sort of manor-house-y place in the Cotswolds, near Little Rollwright. There was an *enormous* brass naval shell case from World War I in the hall for umbrellas and walking sticks. He had lovely manners, really, but he was overbearing. Not nastily or anything, but overpoweringly *there,* if you know what I mean. And loud. 'Bluff,' they'd have called him in earlier days. The men he led, by report, worshipped him.

When he wanted to exercise his conjugal—"

"Quite," said Forde.

"And 'exercise,'" she said, "is *le mot juste*, he'd always say, 'Fancy a spot of rumpy-pumpy?' Though he *smelled* nice, I have to say that. Sweat a little bit, Wright's Coal-Tar Soap and a bit lemony from his shaving stick. It's funny, isn't it, about smells. There was a general aroma around him, Kiwi-Shoe-Polish smell and a vegetable, flowery sort of tweed smell from his jackets.

"And manly sports! God! Fell running. Rugby. Spelunking. Rock climbing. Off-piste skiing in the French Alps—Val Claret. Mirabelle. He coached rugby, shivering little boys in bright jerseys. Bellowing round the house 'Have you seen my creel?' And hare coursing. They wore little green outfits and caps like jockeys and there was a Master and beagles foaming about and pouring over each other, and those skeletal grey dogs looking terrified and quivering and they made toot noises on little copper bugle-things and it was always soaking wet.

"And his damned car I was supposed to admire. British Racing Green—"

"An MG?" said Forde.

"'A 1930 M-Type,' I was told to say. The hood was held down by a leather strap—"

"Bonnet," said Forde.

She stuck out her tongue.

"And the roof fastened on with studs. 'Poppers,' he called them."

"And 'boot,' said Forde.

She shook her head.

"Yes." she said, "conversation was often a minefield. And the weird class, is it sillobeths? No. Never could remember that word."

"Shibboleths," said Forde.

We use Colman's Mustard, never Keen's.

Cane sugar is always to be preferred.

Other than a signet ring, gentlemen do not wear jewellery.

"And *loud*. He boomed. Took up most of any space. *Boom. Boom.* He was affable enough but boomy, always the first to tap knife on glass to give boomy speeches. He wasn't SAS—I don't know if they *had* that then—but something in that line. *Officially* he was in the Worcestershire Regiment, but he was always being seconded to 'training exercises,' desert places, Oman, Arabs, the Trucial States. I believe they call them now the United Arab Emirates."

She waved a dismissive hand.

"When he was off on these jaunts it was the only time the house was restful. Then it was back to boom, boom, boom, and Mess Nights. Though he was very proud of the Worcestershires. They used to be called the Twenty-Ninth Foot, and in 1770 they shot four rioters in Boston. And because of this the Americans called the regiment *The Vein Openers*—not very catchy, is it?—more like apothecary's assistants—and that's still the official nickname or whatever the word is."

She frowned.

"Nickname doesn't sound dignified enough, does it? 'Sobriquet'?"

"I can't think," said Forde, shrugging.

"'The Boston Massacre,'" she said. "That's what the Americans called this scuffle. *Much* referred to," she said, "in Mess speeches and toasts and so forth. So," she said—holding out both palms—"there I was"—she made a clicking noise, tongue pulled from palate,

"—an army wife."

"What about his parents?" said Forde."How did they take to you?"

"Oh, his mother was warily welcoming. A young girl from the colonies, the *colonies!*, a girl of what antecendents? an actress, a doubtful *hmmm* to *that* one, the bass line there being *no better than she should be,* taking her darling boy away by wicked wiles."

She grinned at him.

"*Me!*" she said. "*Wiles!* Polite smiles at the beginning. But little doubt left as to who was Matron. A household," said Anna, pausing, "a household, you might say, folded and bound into hospital corners. She soon had me marked down as a malingerer, a shirker. A distant politeness," she said, "descended."

"Oh dear, oh dear," said Forde. "I could imagine."

"If she was making coffee in the morning—she actually *did* have an Aga cooking range—she always served it in astonishingly horrible mugs.

'They're thrown locally and one does feel a responsibility to one's local craftspeople.' Thick, squat, but the coffee was stirred with silver apostle spoons. And the sugar! I always remember that. The weight of it. Demerara sugar, not cubes, but sticky in a bowl, sort of a glistening, brown sludge.

"She was a Divisional Commander of Girl Guides, always supervising whatyoucall'ems—in a big field with tents and odourous portables—*jamborees*—making speeches and dragging Girl Guides out of hedgerows from the clutches of 'village oiks.'"

Silently, white, black, the waiter materialized.

"The dessert menu, Madam? Sir?"

"Mmmm?" said Forde to Anna.

"A few more minutes?" Anna said to the waiter.

Forde opened the menu.

"When I went over there—" said Anna.

"Good God!" said Forde. "Sorry. A chapeau! A *chapeau!* Listen to this. 'Baba au rhum served with syrup of rum, vanilla seeds, lemon zest and topped with a chapeau of whipped cream.' Sorry."

"It was when the verse drama revival was starting. I was reading poetry all the time, how to speak it, that was what I wanted to learn. Christopher Fry had just, just written *The Lady's Not for Burning*. Do you remember it?"

"Years and years ago," said Forde. "To be honest, I don't remember much about it at all."

"It once seemed so alive, so *sophisticated*," her out-thrust fingers theatrical in their tension. "It seemed so, you know, so *beaded bubbles winking at the brim.*"

Forde shook his head in slow sympathy.

"It was only Richard Burton's second role. That was in 1948. He was twenty-three then and beautiful. So beautiful. And in 1950 Gielgud took it to New York and played the lead. Do you remember Thomas Mendip's speeches?"

"No, I'm afraid not."

"Or Jennet Jourdemayne's?"

"She was…"

"The Lady," said Anna.

She set down her glass.

Why do they call me a witch?

Forde, recognizing quotation and remembering the plastic orchid in the bar, moved the everlasting flowers to the safety of his side of the table.

Why do they call me a witch?
Remember my father was an alchemist
I live alone, preferring loneliness
To the companionable suffocation of an aunt.
I still amuse myself with simple experiments
In my father's laboratory. Also I speak
French to my poodle. Then you must know
I have a peacock which on Sundays
Dines with me indoors. Not long ago
A new little serving-maid carrying the food
Heard its cry, dropped everything and ran,

Never to come back, and told all she met
That the Devil was dining with me.

Forde stared at her

"That was my audition," she said, "at Nottingham. Well, part of it."

"How do you *remember*..."

"And now," she said, "it's all so faded."

She paused.

"So faded."

With a sigh she fell silent, head down, her finger tips tracing up and down the tablecloth's starched fold.

The silence extended.

To break what he felt to be deepening emotional awkwardness in the silence, Forde reached across the table and took her hand.

"Anna."

Cradled her hand in both of his.

"Anna."

"I know," she said—

"We're *here,"* said Forde, giving her hand a little squeeze.

"I know. I'm sorry."

"Before," said Forde, "tell me. You were telling me about Tony's mother."

"Well," she said, "in a roundabout way I suppose I still am."

She made a grimace.

"*This,"* she said, "might have been written just for her."

Struck a pose, declaimed:

Stern daughter of the voice of God!
O Duty!

She gave him a brave grin.

"I suppose she *must* have worn other things but I always picture her in oatmeal-coloured cardigans, she was a bit dumpy, and oatmeal lisle stockings and a sort of cut-down Robin Hood hat with the eye of a pheasant feather in the band. And a shortie duffle coat that did up with toggles made from the points of deer horns. You know what I mean, eye?"

Forde flick-flicked his fingers.

"But what you couldn't take your eye *off* was the brooch she wore on the cardigans. Always the same one. It was a silver-and-cairngorm mounted grouse claw. Grisly thing. The nails gone yellow."

"A vision! said Forde. "A vision! And his father?"

"I was never *entirely* sure," said Anna, "that he'd quite mastered who I was. He always addressed me as 'little lady.' The Brigadier was, shall we say, *vague*. He usually held out until 11 a.m., but then he'd wander into the kitchen and point at the window and say something-something-*yardarm* and get a gin bottle from the pantry. Then he'd retire to his dovecote."

"His—?"

"Yes. It was a round, tower-thing like a silo, original and untouched, I was told, since the sixteenth century, with a sign over the entrance KEEP OUT. DANGER. FALLING MASONRY, and apparently he sat in there most of the day in a deckchair drinking gin-and-bitters while studying the *Daily Telegraph*. Or 'whilst,' as he would have said, 'whilst studying.'"

"Christ!" said Forde. "You really *did* stumble into the mother lode, didn't you?"

"What light there was," she said, "came from the nesting slots, they were like a wedge of cheese with the thin end going to the outside, two layers of them round the top of the walls, not layers, tiers, I should say, and the light seemed greenish for some reason, sort of thick, almost as if you were underwater, *subaqueous,* that's the word."

"So," said Forde, "there—"

"How strange," she said, "that light. As though you were deep under water and looking up towards the surface and the light from the slots was the sky."

She stared at him for a few seconds from some far distance and then seemed almost to shake herself.

"Pardon?"

"So," he said, "there you were, married…"

"Roast beef," she said, "roast beef with Bisto gravy and roast potatoes, roast pork with apple sauce and roast potatoes, roast lamb with mint sauce and roast potatoes, married life," she said, "progressed."

"Mmmm," said Forde.

"I read a lot, returned the library books on time, went for walks with dog and without dog, shopped, rummage sales at the church marking the seasons, bought the *Observer Book of Trees and Shrubs,* little holidays were pleasant if only to ski places, then there were courses on English pottery in which I was *fairly* interested but—I don't know if you'll understand this—but bored by at the same time. Because it was *there,* historically, if you see what I mean, but it wasn't beautiful. Unlike studio pottery, but studio pottery wouldn't have done at all. Tongues would have wagged. If they'd seen Lucie Rie in my house or Hans Coper. Leach and Shoji Hamada were just getting started up then in St. Ives. Don't you love Bernard Leach, those chargers, that mushroomy-coloured glaze?"

"I'm afraid I'm not up on Leach," said Forde. "*heard* of, but—"

"You see," said Anna, "dinnerware, tea cups and saucers, there was a practicality there, a function they understood, a dinner plate was a dinner plate, and the more hideous the more they liked it. They *loved* the Worcester stuff, floral, florid, gilt, views of Castles and Stately Homes—vulgar beyond description—but Hans Coper would have puzzled them, aroused hostility.

Army wives..."

She paused.

"*Raku,*" she said, "and army wives would have been like—save me from some awful cliché, Forde. Like, oh hell, like oil and water. What? No, no, Mess Nights were obligatory, of course, but beyond that one couldn't escape socializing to a degree. Tony's rank demanded it.

"Anyway, I enjoyed getting out and about, the day trips up to Hanley in Stoke-on-Trent to the Ceramics Museum and the Wedgewood Memorial Institute, you know, the Etruria stuff and the pseud Jasperware, and a decent lunch all on my own sitting in state with a real tablecloth being gracious and pretending not to be me.

"But the real treat was poking about in antique shops and junk shops. I'd started to buy lustreware, the pink or silver mainly. It was all made with a compound called 'Purple of Cassius'—though even as I say that, and it's perfectly clear in my mind, I have no idea—no idea at all *why*. Which has never occurred to me before. *Why* 'Cassius,' I mean, which is what I mean by being interested but bored at the same time."

"Because," said Forde, frowning in concentration, "if you'd really been interested, you'd have found out."

"Exactly!" she said.

"Coffee," said Forde.

"Am I beginning to sound ridiculous?"

"Shall we have coffee in the lounge? It would make a change from this rather," waved his hand about, "caveronorous... caver... cave-like."

Passing through the foyer, Anna gave the bell on the unmanned front desk a *bling*.

"That'll teach him to *sssh* me," she said.

A young woman wearing a tie appeared; Forde wondered, not for the first time, why he found women in ties sexually attractive.

Shrilling pipe or fluting whistle
declaimed Anna
In the valleys come again;
Fife of frog and call of tree-toad—

"Shssh," said Forde, hurrying her elbow, "shssh."

In the lounge, sole occupants, they sank into armchairs.

The waitress fussed with things.

"What are you smiling about?" said Forde.

"Junk shops," she said. "Just remembering. One lovely day. I bought a badger."

"In a glass case?"

"No, he was just standing there. On a plinth. A really handsome fellow! I'll never forget his coat. The hair, when you stroked it, it felt very thick and coarse, brittle, bristly almost, rather like…"

She cast about.

"… rather like a cheap crowd-scene wig."

"Hmmm," said Forde.

She glanced down at her palm.

"It was so, so *unexpected*."

"And how was the advent of the badger received?"

"It caused for some days a certain..." she did one of her actressy little gestures, "... a certain *froideur*."

She shook her head and firmed her lips.

"When I was out one day Tony disposed of it."

She undid the paper wrapping of a sugar cube.

"It did *not* smell!"she said

"*Cane sugar*," said Forde, "*is always to be preferred*."

Holding the cube out as if it were a disdained specimen, she said, "Quite. Irredeemably *infra dig*."

She flashed a grin.

Then her expression settled again and she said, "But you know, my badger was just like everything else. Indulged just so far and no further. Setting limits for the child. It was all pretending. Pretending to be something, more inventing an interest than feeling it, all those years pretending, playing a part. That's what being the wife of an army officer was like for me, like being on an unending invalid's diet, unending blandness and accord, a life-sentence of, oh, *blanquette de veau*, say, and raspberry jello."

Forde nodded in what he thought might look like a judicious manner and poured more coffee.

"So when Tony died, I was sad. Of course I was sad. All those years. But I wasn't *grief-stricken*."

She held Forde's gaze.

"But I'll tell you something."

An 'ummm?' was forced from Forde.

"That fetching white stripe, the feel of him, that stuffed badger, *he* was real."

Forde resorted again to measured nodding.

Anna sipped her coffee.

She stared at him across the table.

"I want very much," she said, " to make you understand."

"Oh," said Forde, "I think I—"

"Take," she said, "say, Mess Nights. Black tie, maroon cummerbunds. The chic drink in those early days was gin with Rose's Lime Cordial. The noise rising fast. Chit. Chat. Chump. *The other half, old chap? Tilt the wrist, pray, on the Tanqueray, hmmm?* Women's plump shoulders. A heated pong seeping up, Johnson's Baby Powder, foul Lily-of-the-Valley Bath Salts on some of the matrons, Chanel, Givenchy, a *miasma*. Dreadful noise, guffaws, *teeth*, it was nearly impossible to hear what people were saying, so you were reduced to smiles and nodding. Then the drift to the dining table. Chairs drawn out with ostentatious gallantry. Everyone stood, of course, for the Colonel's entrance. He in the full—what's that lovely word?—the full *panoply* of dress uniform, in full fig, 'gongs,' as they used to say, not black tie, because, you see, he had to wear the Dettingen Sword."

"The what?"

"It's one of the Commandments of military life," she said, "that no one can take a weapon into the Mess. And very wise, too, given that they're piss-artists to a man. But for the Colonel of the Worcestershires—or were they the 29th Foot then?—never *could* keep these damn things straight. But the colonels of the Worcestershires were granted the honour of wearing into the Mess the Dettingen Sword—an honour bestowed—I can't remember if it was given to a particular colonel or to the regiment—but anyway given by George the—can't remember—but one of the three—for valour on the field of battle at the Battle of Dettingen. The French," she said with a dismissive wave. "1740-ish, I think. So it would be, I guess, the Second.

"Anyway, the Colonel stands at the head of the table and is approached by the youngest Subaltern, who is doing the Slow March. Then when the Subaltern reaches him, the Colonel raises his arms out at his sides and the Subaltern—is there such a word as 'ungirds'?

"The sword's in a silver-gilt frog with tassels and braided cords tied into decorative knots hanging from the hilt, the whole mess of it the size of a small bird's nest. So then—do you know the word 'frog'?"

Ford patted his hip.

"Or 'chape'?"

Ford shook his head.

"Gotcha!" she said. "It's the half-moon metal bit at the bottom of a scabbard. Stops the point. Whenever I'm feeling blue or—I don't know, inadequate or something, I think of words like 'chape,' that my enemies don't know, *and it cheers me up.*"

"So what happened then? In the Mess?"

"I often visit a lovely red leather one in Boston."

"Sorry?"

"Frog. In the Boston Museum of Fine Arts. Harold likes it there. When we go in, he always puts his finger to his lips, *ssh.* Anyway, the second-youngest Subaltern Slow Marches up to them bearing a silver tray—pardon *me*—a *salver*, with a pair of white kid gauntlets on it and they're each embroidered on the backs with the Crown. Then—oh, God!—after much rigid backwards-and-forwarding and glove-donning and foot-stamping and about-turning and general palaver, the sword is borne by the youngest Subaltern at Slow March round the table."

With a wriggle forward, she heaved herself out of the armchair, pulled down her dress, squared shoulders, and proceeded, in stately slow march, in and out of the furniture, arms stretched in front of her, palms up, bearing the sword. The waitress passing through with a bus-pan of crockery for the dishwasher stopped, staring.

Sinking back into her armchair, she said, "Then the Subaltern set the sword in the centre of the table and stood back at attention, set the sword on two gunmetal things—stands? No, what's the word? Two… like the things in a Chinese restaurant—but bigger, of course, the doohickeys you rest chopsticks on.

"And the stewards are filling the glasses and then the Colonel proposes the toast:

The Dettingen Sword.

"The older officers are already bright red and when the service starts they pour—well, you see, they'd have a big sherry when they came into the mess and several Rose's Lime Cordials or whatever their poison, but they'd hold onto their sherry glasses and get a refill and take it in to dinner and tip it into their beef consommé to tide them over until the service of the mess Chambertin or Muscadet, which were imported by the Education Officer whose main job it was—whose *sole* job it was—except for delivering occasional lectures on the regimental history of the Vein Openers and organizing the lottery tickets and showing pox films. It was always beef consommé.

"Dozens of candles in the candelabra spaced down the length of the table, you can feel the heat of it rising. The tide of conversation, the oppression of it, cars, perennials, the plots of films, the cure of bald patches in lawns, the exploits of someone or other at Bisley. The perfume miasma..." She flapped both hands, dispelling it, "and the *boom, boom* like an iron torture device screwed tighter and tighter round your head."

She made some small, elegiac sound within a sigh.

"I just used to sit there and stare at the mess silver. At the candlelight playing on it. The most amazing thing—it was always at centre-table next to the Dettingen Sword—was a huge model of a Juggernaut. Must have been the gift of an officer who'd served at some time in India, I don't think the regiment did. You've heard about this mess silver business?"

"From retiring officers?" said Forde.

She nodded.

"When Tony died..." she said, and broke off. After a pause, she said, "It's a tradition I have some feeling for. I went down to London to the Silver Vaults and scouted out an eighteenth-century tureen, gadrooned... Chancery Lane? Sorry. Boring you... I don't suppose the mess could tell the difference if it had come from Debenham's third-floor Kitchen Wares, but I've always believed in acting *as if*. If we don't, I've always felt, what's left?"

"Anyway," she said, "anyway. Inebriated maundering. But this Juggernaut. It was so bizarre I looked it all up. The actual car, chariot, wagon—whatever you call it, was supposed to have been fifty feet high and have sixteen huge wheels. And sitting in it the mammoth statue of Jagganath. The car lived all the year in one particular temple, but on the feast day it was dragged to a neighbouring temple in a procession. Flowers strewn in the streets, flowers in garlands, drummers, thronged bodies and faces masked with coloured dyes. Pilgrims were supposed to have thrown themselves under the wheels in religious ecstasy, and bystanders to have been crushed to death as it rolled on. Couldn't stop the bloody thing, I suppose.

"Well, this silver monstrosity—dozens upon dozens of devotees heaving on the silver ropes and squished bodies, arms flung upwards as the wheels crushed them, chaps at the back in a great collapsing mound pushing, and a mass of chaps clinging to the sides—like those photos of people in India on trains or Africans clinging to the roofs and window frames of Mama buses. It was so big and busy and so ugly, it should have been in a Ripley's Believe It or Not museum.

"One of mess servants told me the silver wasn't sterling. It was low-grade Indian stuff that tarnished faster.

"Native silver, always polishing the piece, ma'm, a soft tooth brush for the crevices and not Goddard's or Silvo, the only thing to get the job done, Duraglit wadding. With Duraglit there's none of that white stuff left behind.'

"Such a pleasant man.

"Talking of India," she went on, "do you remember those Kipling lines?

For the Colonel's Lady an' Judy O'Grady

Are sisters under their skin.

"They really didn't like me chatting to the mess servants. Any 'same under the skin' business didn't go down at all well, wasn't 'on,' do you see? Simply wasn't how one behaved, do you see? Made the *servants* uncomfortable, m'dear.

"Anyway, they'd all be well-pissed by dessert, and Tony would have told off one of the subalterns to drive me home before the games started."

"Games?"

"A feature," she said.

"Cards, do you mean?"

She laughed.

"Games like what?"

"Oh," she shrugged, "like one chap lying down on the floor and seeing how many chaps at the same time could make a pyramid on him before he passed out."

*

They stood in the foyer of the Lord Beaverbrook waiting for the taxi and looking out into the night.

"The man who wrote the menus," said Forde, gesturing towards the doors and beyond, "would describe that as the *porte cochère*."

She pushed her elbow into his side.

"I'm not convinced," he said, "that this is a good idea, but I simply can't think of anywhere else in Fredericton."

Snow was blowing.

"Anyway," Anna went on, "I just didn't seem at ease in England after Tony died. There was nowhere I really fitted in. And Harold was here, of course, and the housekeeper was getting a bit tottery… So I sold the house and there was money in the bank account and some stocks, my solicitor did all that, and then there was Tony's pension. I *was* rather touched by that. He'd been on a training exercise in the Trucial States, the, um, you know…"

She waved them away.

"He'd only been doing inspections, administrative things for years, the derring-do days were long behind."

"Comes to us all," said Forde.

"He became quite morose," she said, "when he couldn't gallivant about with a Bergen blowing things up."

"*Boom. Boom,*" said Forde.

She slapped his arm.

"Comes to us all," he said.

"What was I talking about?" she said.

"Pension?"

"Right! His death," she said, "was a bit, well, iffy."

"Iffy? What do you mean 'iffy'?"

"A couple of the boys, including his long-time driver, told me it was an accident, that the lorry they were digging out just toppled onto him. Which is what I think *did* happen. The four men who'd been with Tony, you see, no one was wounded. But other lads who expressed condolences said Tony'd been killed when the lorry was attacked by marauders out of the desert raiding for guns and equipment. They'd seen the bullet holes in the truck a couple of days later when it was towed back into camp.

"So what I think happened was that Colonel Raven, he was fond of Tony and a real old sweetie-pie, I think he organized the shooting of the truck so that Tony's death would be 'in the line of duty,' or is it 'on active service'? It's TV confuses you, one's British, one's American. Which meant his pension would be bigger, which I did receive—the 'active service' one. Sounds James Bondish, doesn't it?"'

She shrugged the matter away.

"Anyway, Viyella shirts, cavalry twill trousers, his pairs of brogues, his fishing rods and reels—'centre-something,' I think he'd said they were, old ones and valuable, and the rods were split-cane, which is something special he told me, but it all went to a charity shop. Even the ivory shirt stays. It was all—stuff. I just wanted to be *done* with it.

"The only thing I kept from that life was a small painting I'd bought, of a plate and a knife and a fork by William Scott. It's always been an icon for me, literally, an icon. I love it. Do you know him? Tony used to refer to it as 'What's for Dinner?'"

"Oh, yes," said Forde. "Oh, yes."

He scooped her into his arms and they stood together, he rocking her.

"I've loved them for years," he said, "yes, the presence of them. Icon's *exactly* right."

He stooped and kissed her cheek.

Headlights swept across the windows.

Hanging from the mirror in the taxi, a cardboard pine-tree air freshener filling the car with a raw chemical stench, which also brought to Forde the smell of the yellowed mothballs in the urinals of the Beaverbrook's River Room, a smell that was beginning to make him queasy. Too cold for lowered windows.

"Sorry. Say that again."

"The daily round," she said, "going to the butcher's, returning library books, walking the dog, the newsagent's—the daily round—and underneath it all, this unhappiness. It was always with me, not disabling, but sapping, undermining; no, not even that—I'm being dramatic again—more a slow leaching out of some of the colour of every day."

She snuggled up to him, tucking her arm into his.

"It was being shut out," she said. "It was watching greatness from the gods."

Forde offered sympathy in a sigh.

"Which," she said, "is, I suppose, a round-the-mulberry-bush way of saying The Pavilion, Torquay—"

"And *Norman's Conquest*," said Forde.

"I thought that, maybe, coming home, drawing a line under life there, it would go away."

"And?" he said.

He felt her shrug.

"I shouldn't complain. I have a nice little job three days a week and I really enjoy it. It's in a rather chichi package store. I play oenophile. I've heard in roundabout ways that I'm called 'The Wine Lady.' This is the ultra-rich part of Connecticut, remember: hobby farms, estates, weekend mansions for New Yorkers. More money, as Mary would have said, than sense. I dispense oenophilic wisdom in a slightly snotty manner—'This Australian shiraz is more complex, more *engaging* than—well, the French, as you doubtless know, called the same wine, the same grape, Syrah, or Sirrah, and frankly…'

et cetera

"And I amuse myself antiquing. Pin money, really. Some lustreware, not much, but surprising pieces of transfer-printed ware. People tend to think it's much later than it actually is. And Harold much enjoys these outings. We get him old model aeroplanes. And he takes Jack for walks. Jack's a Jack Russell. I know you're going to think dotty old lady and pampered pet, but Jack isn't that at all. He minds his manners with us but generally he's a case of mindless aggression. He suddenly attacks inanimate objects that affront him, chair legs. He's dainty, a born dandy. Elegant as a fox. No unseemly sniffing for him, no wallowing-sniffing, no slurping-sniffing round lamp-posts. The mildest sniff, a 'so what's the hoi polloi been up to' sniff. Dogs put you in touch with the natural world, don't you think? I've always thought that. If you follow where they lead you. A stag beetle, a caterpillar humping across the sidewalk, fungus—they grow out sideways—dinner-plate things—on the boles of trees—Jack always pauses before he attacks."

"Mine's called Pogo," said Ford. "That was my kids, not me. He's old now and leaks Alpo fumes. Sheila tells me he goes to my study every day to see if I'm there. She pretends to only just tolerate him—his farts really are enough to make you gag—but I know that she buys him Salisbury-steak treats I'm not supposed to see."

"But never mind *dogs* getting old," she said. "I have to think about when *I* go and what's going to happen to Harold. There's the house, of course, and I'm not really impoverished but Harold will have to go into a home, and anywhere humane is grotesquely expensive so my steamer trunks of—what was that odd word? 'CanLit' was it? Do you *really* think they'll…?"

"A good chance," said Forde. "We'll give it the old college try."

"Well," said Anna, "as you said, he did paint himself into rather a public corner. *What* was his name?"

"Toomer," said Forde. "Premier Toomer."

"What a *dreadful* morning!"

"*Gitchee Gumee!*" said Forde.

She slapped his knee.

"Yes," said Forde, "if we get the *Gleaner* onto it. To get the ball rolling. Yes," he said, "I really do think The Toomer, as they call him, painted himself into a corner."

He snorted in amusement, thinking of the Fink-Nottle stiffeners.

"*Rhapsodized* himself into a corner."

Forde drifted off into his habitual mental maze in the formal garden of words. Anna, too, had fallen silent. Found himself thinking of P.G. Wodehouse, Gussie Fink-Nottle, newts, and stiffeners, Bertie's waking words to Jeeves,

'... get me one of those bracers of yours, will you?'

'I have one in readiness, sir, in the ice-box.'

The bracers, the stiffeners, a proprietary brand in a brown glass bottle with a Victorian figure in a striped bathing costume on the label, drooping mournful moustache, reared walrus looking leery, first man to swim the English Channel—Scott? No, *Webb*. Captain Webb! Awarded a medal by the Society for the Recovery of Persons Apparently Drowned. Figured on matchboxes in his long-gone childhood. Could the matches have *possibly* been called, could they have *conceivably* been called... *England's Glory*? He would market the stiffeners—along the lines of Carter's Little Liver Pills—None Genuine Without This Signature ... *Toomer's Matutinal Tots.*

Paths of light, spears, shards, across the water of the Saint John River, ice, changed sound of the taxi's wheels over the bridge.

The pine-tree freshener swaying.

Then darkness, faint light from the dashboard.

The brown bottle from its shoulder to its mid-point ribbed, *a feel somehow medicinal.*

"That Juggernaut—"

The sound of her voice dragged him out of this.

"Pardon? What did you say?"

"That Juggernaut, when I couldn't stand smiling any more or turning my head or inclining to left or right and the noise was smashing inside my head like waves smashing on a breakwater, when I was feeling most desolate and lost, I used to put my reading glasses on—astigmatism, too—and stare at the colours and the shifts in the gleaming. I couldn't really see Jagganath sitting there or the pulling-and-pushing chaps, it was all just a silver shape that shrank or jumped as the candles flared or guttered. And that was what I wanted. Seeing it and not seeing it. And I just sat, just sat lost in it till Tony had me driven home."

*

Above the bar of the Legion Hall was affixed a long, polished wooden aeroplane propeller of World War I vintage, a propeller from one of those tiny planes, the toy-like relics he'd seen hanging from the ceiling in the Imperial War Museum: wood, wire, canvas.

"Evening, Mr. Forde."

"This is one of your haunts, then?" said Anna.

"Darts," said Forde. "My present abode is a place of low, silent corridors and women with brittle hair and men in undershirts. There's noise here, people, drink, and usually I'm co-opted to play for the university against the Legion. Most of the university guys are Brits, ex-pats, immigrants, it's funny, no arts people, no sciences people, engineers mostly, geologists. And even if born-and-bred New Brunswickers, most of the Legion team are anglophiles—spent their horrible youth there in the war—these are Marmite-and-Welsh-Rarebit men, HP Saucers."

He nodded politely to the Ozarks pair at the bar.

The man returned a grudging tilt of his head.

Bright-white dentures, unlaced high-tops, feral sideburns to the angle of his jaw. The woman with him, a grey pigtail. Under the fabric of the T-shirt, fabric thinned from washings, the bra-less mounds swaying, the nipples visible as darknesses the size of prunes.

Anna stood looking about at her.

Military "collectibles" crowded and cluttered the walls, what pickers and pack-ratters now dubbed "militaria." Two further words that caused Forde a twinge. Photographs in crude *passe-partout* frames, pennons, gas masks, displays of medals, cap badges, cloth shoulder flashes on a long, hanging piece of carpet, dog tags, battered Lee-Endfields, a sagging Sam Browne belt and holster. The photographs were fading, yellowing, some sepia, laughing-boy air crews, grinning tommies giving thumbs-up and V-signs, crews standing at attention beside ack-ack guns in—where? a town—a park? *Passe-partout* desert men in shorts, brewing up tea in sand-filled oil drums beside Sherman and Crusader Tanks.

Hammered through its cover and pages to the wall with a fat construction nail a grubby Part One Pay Book.

An ancient—was it water-cooled?—machine gun, bracketed and bolted to the wall, a decal of a wolf's head stuck on top of the barrel shroud, and underneath the head, the letters AW(F)SQN. He stooped to read what was stamped into the hasp that secured the breech block:

J.P. Sauer & Sonn. Suhl. 1917.

He wondered how such an oddity from World War I had ended up in World War II in an RCAF mess in Dartmouth.

Curious.

"Well, I suppose we'd better stake out a table," he said, "before people arrive for the match."

He watched the barman preparing a refill for the pigtail woman. It involved thick pouring from a carton of 18% table cream, grenadine, an egg white, a shot of tequila, a shot of rye, the scooping out from the jar with a long spoon of a maraschino cherry.

As this concoction was set before her, the sideburns man, pointing, said, "Can I have that?"

"You had my cherry years ago," said the pigtail woman.

cackling.

"Ne'mind," said Sideburns, "you've still got the box it came in."

"*Christ!*" said Forde, glanced at his watch, "relatively normal people should be coming—*Christ!*—this beer is *dreadful.*"

Looking at the picture on the label, Anna said, "How sad the moose!"

"How High the Moon," said Forde.

Sideburns barked a belch.

"Silly name," said Forde, "because if you want two, 'Mooses' sounds odd, so you have to say 'Two Moose,' which makes you sound as down-home as—"

He moved his head to indicate the couple at the bar.

"Poor Forde!" said Anna, "*Harrowed* by language."

"Anna?"

She flung back her head and raised surrendering hands like little paws.

"Poor *tortured* Forde!"

"Anna!"

"Mmmm?"

"I've been thinking—not intending to be rude or anything—but a couple of acting classes at the Philadelphia Academy of the Arts when you were, what? Nineteen? Twenty?"

He spread his hands, raised eyebrows.

Evening, squire

A Fair Isle pullover strained over a burgeoning paunch

Forde, raising a finger to his brow, sketched a salute

"How did I get a job," she said in a plonking voice, "with a British rep company?"

"Just curious."

"As well you might be. But I was taken on as an ASM, not an actress. Assistant Stage Manager."

"But you auditioned. The Fry thing—"

"A formality," she said, "a nicety. But you're right. I wouldn't have managed even that had not strings been pulled."

"What were the strings?"

"Sir Charles G.D."

She grinned at his expression.

"When he lived there he'd become friendly with a banker, and his family, a great cultivator of the wealthy, Sir Charles, so I was told, and he'd renewed this contact when he was knighted in 1935—Henry Broadley, this man's name was, though we might well be talking about his son here—even his grandson? I'm hopeless about dates. But anyway my mother had somehow become part of all this, the Broadleys had visited Fredericton and Toronto and gone across Canada by train and there was some connection with Childe—Christmas cards, Childe's effusions, photographs of sundry children and Broadley knew Shaw G.B. and sent newspaper clippings and G.D and Childe and my mother had gone to England together in the early thirties, 1933 I think it was, on some sort of Canadian Authors junket—"

She dismissed detail with imperious hand.

"—and so Childe had met this Broadley at some posh dinner in London, where Shaw apparently trashed all the Canadian poets, bless him, though as a playwright he's a clunker, and my mother wrote a letter to him—Broadley, I mean—or his son—I'm really not sure, but the famed Lewis Normande was indebted to one or the other and—"

Forde held up a hand.

"I really do not like this beer," he said. "As our President is paying, what would you say to a brandy?"

"Probably unwise," said Anna, "as I'm more than a little—but what the hell. They don't call me 'The Wine Lady' for nothing. What was it you said he was?"

"Trinidad Asphalt and Bitumen."

"Well, the hell with him," she said. "We'll ruin him from within."

The bar was filling, the noise was rising, the air already thickening with cigarette smoke. While he waited, Forde watched two young women shrugging off parkas, tank tops cut generously loose and low, tarty.

Voices through the hubbub.

As he was bearing the snifters to the table—

Fordie!

Raised one of the snifters in greeting.

"Only *Stock,* I'm afraid. It's all they had."

"The robust earthiness," said Anna, "of stalk and leaf."

"Aaah!" said Forde.

"Do?" repeated Anna. "Well, being on the book, I suppose, the props table. Book? Sorry. Well, *then*—everything's changed now, of course—but *then* we had a copy of the script that had been taken apart and mounted on large sheets of construction paper, where we noted every actor's movements and every technical cue. Always referred to as 'the bible.'"

"This was prompting?"

She nodded.

"And the props table was my responsibility, too. For each entrance the needed prop would be waiting at the right-hand edge of the table—a book, umbrella, flashlight, bird-cage that kind of thing. And then the theatre duties before the curtain—checking the half, the dressing-room calls—"

"The half of what?"

"Oh, the board at the stage entrance where everyone has to have signed-in half an hour before house lights—and the dressing rooms, 15 minutes, 10 minutes, Beginners, please..."

... so he rips the cord and then all shit breaks loose...

Forde leaned closer the better to hear her.

"And I was usually understudy to the female lead. If disaster struck—and, of course, it didn't until Torquay—I couldn't act but I could have said the words without reading from a script. That was my *real* talent. I could learn a script in three days flat and that's probably why Normande kept me on. That, and slave wages. His rehearsals and notes were *electric*, though. A *gestapo* of a man. Wore a reddish toupée and plus-fours. His critiques were addressed to his spaniel. It had a seat next to him in the stalls. It had sad, bloodshot eyes and it was called Madame Noni."

She sat back in her chair nodding slightly, lost, Forde thought, in memories.

Cigarette smoke was gathering under the ceiling tiles, forming a false ceiling which quivered whenever the door at the top of the stairs opened or closed. Like a layer of fibreglass insulation. Those pink slabs.

Called?

Called?

"Batts!" he said in triumph.

"Who is?" said Anna.

... fucking guy freaked me shitless...

The voice seemed to be coming from one of the two tarty young women, the abyss of cleavage aquiver, nudging into Forde's mind the word 'fecund.'

In a glass case against a painted background of weeds, a monster muskie.

"I was always walking backstreets learning lines or pounding the towpath along the canal. The scripts were mimeographed and clasp-bound. You know what I mean? Two flat, tin spikes—sort of tangs, is that the word? No, *prongs*. They went through holes in the pages and then you bent them over to slide into clasp-things—"

"I think the American is 'bradbound,' but maybe that means a big stud-head thing on a sort of split-pin sort of affair because 'brad' in England—"

"Yes, *yes*," said Anna. "You get the idea. So I was always having to take sheets out as I was walking, and I was nicking or cutting myself on these bloody tin things, fingers, palms, and one Thursday—a matinee—I'd come in with a bad one on my palm. My hanky was soaked and Theodore James, who was *operatic*, took my palms, there was a scar on the other, and did a great catch of breath and everyone turned to look at him and then, still holding my hands, he fell to one knee and bowed his head—and you have to imagine all this as atrocious silent film—and then he lifted his face heavenwards and said—uttered—*declaimed*—'By all that's holy! Doris and June Alison! She bears stigmata!' And they were all amused at his fooling around because I was always teased about being passionate about theatre, about being, well, I suppose reverent, and from then on they fell into calling me Stig, then with that Brit thing, you know, 'biccies,' I became Stiggy."

"Because," said Forde, "they liked you."

> *You playing arrows, Fordie?*
> He tapped the snifter with a fingernail
> Shook his head
> "Near legless, mate"

Pointing to the head mounted on a wooden shield, Anna said, "What *is* that?"

"An eland," said Forde.

"But—"

She gestured about her at the militaria.

"But *why* an eland?"

He shrugged.

"Why a muskie?"

"Eland," she repeated.

... so he goes where's the breadknife and I go what breadknife, I don't know what he's talking about, breadknife, well it turns out it's special for bread, breadknife, so I go...

Anna beckoned him closer.

"You do that awfully well," she said.

"What?"

"That 'mate' stuff."

"It is," he said, "but one of my many accomplishments."

A girl far too young to be in the place, twelve or so, thought Forde, called out to her father, who was threading his way towards the bar, "No, no! Ginger Ale!"

A snarling eructation behind him.

Forde glanced round. Two old men staring in the direction of the ginger-ale girl, who was standing, waving, still trying to get her father's attention.

He turned back to Anna.

> One of their voices said
> *If it's old enough to bleed...*
> The other voice said
> *... it's old enough to slaughter.*

Forde risked another glance. They were nodding sagely. Grizzled dirt-road worthies. They looked like extras in a movie staged in the Middle Ages.

She beckoned him closer again, against the noise.

"That stigmata joke," she said, "and that sense of—"

She shrugged.

"Well, reverence, if you will. Well, I'll tell you a naked thing, Forde. I went to England in the fall of 1948, so really it was 1949 before I was settling into that world. And all the actors I met, at some point or another, in conversations it would come up, at a party, green rooms, in the pub, what Olivier had done in 1946 at the New Theatre with *Oedipus Rex*."

"What was that?" said Forde. "What did he do?"

"Those few seconds," she said, "that was what everyone was still talking about. Well," she said, "all through the play, the hints, the suggestions, the fears about his birth and paternity, all nebulous, swirling"—her hands patterning this—"but with the arrival of the Messenger—he brings the testimony of the Shepherd who saved the infant Oedipus—it all coalesces then into certainty. His sins are beyond forgiveness. His realization ... you remember that speech?"

"Well," said Forde, "it's been some years..."

"He rushes offstage into the Palace to find that his wife who is his mother—Jocasta?"

"Right," said Forde, "OK, yes."

"You do *know* the Theban Plays?"

"In ..." said Forde, "outline."

"Oedipus realizes that he has killed his father and fathered children on his mother. He blinds himself in expiation—what he's meaning in the speech, you see, when he says,

O light—now let me look my last on you!

Forde nodded, held helpless by her intensity.

"What they were talking about was what Olivier did at the *end* of the speech."

Hands clenched into fists, she stared into the tabletop, gathering herself.

Then raised her head.

> *O god—*
> *all comes true, all burst to light!*
> *O light—now let me look my last on you!*
> *I stand revealed at last—*
> *cursed in my birth, cursed in marriage,*
> *cursed in the lives I cut down with these hands!*

"It was then, before he rushes from the stage to find Jocasta hanging, it was *then* at the end of the speech, that Olivier gave this vast cry, this cry of horror at himself, it was torn from him, ripped out of his anguish, and it filled the theatre with obliterating horror. The audiences were smashed down by the sound of it and then swept up and carried on the great wave of it."

Forde stared at her.

Anna stared at him.

He could feel his heart beating.

He fell back against his chair, nodding assent to what she was talking about.

The ceiling was wavering.

"Yes," he said.

Through the noise, bottles clinking on glasses, guffaws, chairs scraping, the low hubbub, Forde heard the girl's voice cutting through.

The tank-top girl.

The titty-girl.

She had just said—*could* she have just said?—he sat staring into his snifter—she had just said,

I don't do anal on a first date

"Think of it this way," said Anna. "It's not ephemeral. Don't you see? It's preserved in a chain, an unbroken chain from actor to actor; a juvenile, if they grow into major roles, they use what they saw and heard from Alec Clunes, Scofield, fill in the blanks—" waving her hand to gallop over details. "Great performances are held in the common memory, passed on to the young, changing, but always preserving something, the essence of past performances, the inheritance.

"The *shape,"* said Forde, "preserving the shape."

"Yes," said Anna, "exactly. The *emotional* shape. Not imitation—"

"No," said Forde, nodding, "exactly, exactly."

They smiled at each other.

"And theatres themselves," said Anna. "I mean, think of a cathedral. All those centuries of prayer soaked into the stone. Theatres are like that. If you're quiet and listen, the voice are there, in layers.

Gielgud, Wolfit, Martita Hunt, Sybil Thorndike, Alex Clunes, Jessica Tandy, Ralph Richardson—just their very names make me think of the disciples—'and they began to speak with other tongues as the spirit gave them utterance'—Peggy Ashcroft, Miles Malleson, Irene Worth, Ustinov, Burton, Scofield... people to whom..."

Her voice wobbled, then regained control, strengthened.

"... people to whom utterance had been given."

She paused.

"Sometimes," she said, "when everyone had left and before Mr. George started the clean-up, I'd look out over the red plush, the little gilt-plaster cherubs blowing their herald trumpets on the box fronts, the swags, the cornucopias, the floral garden panels on the side walls and I felt, well, that this was where everything in my life had been leading me. I felt cradled in the voices. And my voice, if I spoke, the resonance, the bounce..."

Her voice beginning to break again.

"Anna," said Forde. "Don't. Please, don't."

He reached for her hand.

She gulped a noisy breath.

"I could—"

The tears welled.

"That smell…" she said.

Wiped under her eyes with the knuckle of her thumb.

Sniffed a wet sniff.

"Even though the stage lights were off, as I stood there I could feel the heat of them still coming off the stage. What they say about the theatre, the smell of the grease-paint. That's not it at all. As I stood there in the stillness and silence, the warmth rising from the boards, the smell…"

She fell silent for long moments.

Forde, held and anxious, stared into her face.

"… the smell I was breathing, the theatre smell..."

She brought both fists up to her mouth.

"that smell—"

She lifted her face to him and stared at him, yet not at him.

"Sweat," she said, "and hot dust."

Silence.

She dragged her sleeve across her eyes.

His shoulders slumped, softening, surprising him.

"Oh, *God*!" she said. "I'm *disgusting*. I am *so* sorry. It must be the brandy."

Sniffy, she said, "That President! Taking advantage of an old widder-woman. Have you got any Kleenex?"

She rooted in her purse.

"I thought I had a little cellophane packet."

What Americans call a 'clutch,' Forde thought.

In irritation, she dumped all the contents out onto the table.

"What's the expression? 'A watery smile,' 'smiling bravely through the tears'?"

"I'll tell *you* something naked, Anna."

She looked at him and did try to smile.

"I stand on that stage every day, too," he said, "listening to the voices."

He looked down at house keys, a propelling pencil, Polo mints, a small screwdriver, an emery board, a compact, a tube of Preparation-H, car keys, a glasses case, a change purse… She picked, picked at the cellophane wrapper.

Caught the direction of his glance.

"No, no, dear boy! *Eyes.* It's for my eyes. Tightens the skin beneath, the droop of flesh."

She picked up the tube—"Mother's—" wagged it—"Mother's little helper."

She patted his hand.

"Good heavens!" said Forde.

"Shrinks the capacious bags beneath."

She wiped and trumpeted with successive Kleenex.

"These latter days," she said, "I worry less."

"Worry about what?"

"When younger," she said, "at an age when liaisons were yet a possibility…"

"Anna!" scolded Forde. "Were I not a married man…"

"Oh, how gallant! How gallant!"

He took her hands in his across the table and, one after the other, kissed them.

"Stop it, Forde, you fool!"

He turned her hands over and kissed her palms extravagantly.

"When younger," she said, considering the tube, "I used to worry, irrationally, *utterly* irrationally, that it made my face smell like an arse."

*

As Forde made his way back from the bar with the balloons of brandy, the room began to feel different, the shape and density changing, men pushing back from tables, drifting together, drifting into a small mass near the metal strip set into the floor, the strip that marked the regulation distance from the board. The bartender switched on the spotlight, which was trained on the board and the floods, which created a corridor of light towards it.

Forde actually preferred "barkeep" to "bartender" but couldn't use it because it was dedicated, in his mind, to saloons in Westerns or joints in the Bowery. Oh, to rap on a bar with a silver dollar, snarl at the barkeep, grab the whiskey bottle, and pull the cork out *with one's teeth*.

The room lights dimmed.

Though *his* bottle would contain Scotland's whisky, not 'whiskey' with an 'e'. Bourbon, he held, was not merely nasty but viciously dangerous, an abomination among drinks. He remembered awaking one morning in what might have been a hotel. It was the morning following a literary bunfest, an event called Southern Writing South, sponsored by the Jim Beam Company in a vast Nashville multi-level bookstore. After he had brushed his teeth and vomited, he slowly, slowly dressed to discover, in his jacket pocket, a faux-parchment document commissioning him Colonel in a Tennessee militia.

At the empty table next to the metal strip, men were opening plastic cases and lifting out their darts, some screwing together the weighted bodies and the long necks, smoothing and soothing, with a fingertip, flights made of feathers, others setting into slots flights of stiff card.

Peering into her compact's mirror, Anna said, "I look like the wreck of the Hesperus."

"This'll set you to rights," said Forde.

It was the schooner Hesperus,
That sailed the wintry sea;
chanted Anna
And the skipper had taken his little daughter,
To bear him company.

"Childe?" said Forde. "Or Bliss?"

"Longfellow."

She peered again into the mirror.

"We had to learn it in grade school."

Snapped the compact shut.

"Talk about *that sailed the wintry sea,*" said Anna.

"To Bitumen!" said Forde.

"Asphalt!" said Anna.

The university team captain, the Fair-Isle-pullover engineer-man, strands of blond hair over a rosy pate, was looking about him over heads. Progressing towards him, almost as if accidentally, the Legion captain, a small man in grey flannels and a blue blazer with an RCAF badge in wirework on the breast pocket. His glasses had one clear and one opaque yellow lens.

Forde held his snifter at his lower lip, breathing in and out at its mouth.

Stock was regrettably sweet.

The ceiling quivered.

He was feeling pleasantly fuddled.

In the brightly lit arena, beer was raised in greeting and salutation. Beer was quaffed. Lips sucked in the thin, foam heads. Shoulders were clapped. Jesting insults exchanged. It was like watching an *enactment*, a rather inept mime, a playlet mounted by rude mechanicals. Though the week before he himself had been playing. Playing a part. But even so, essentially, *in essence*, there was something suggestive of the rustic. Arboreal. Brunswickian, Even

Hardyesque, somehow. *Mayor of Casterbridge*-ish. "Riding the Skimmington," *a skimmity ride.*

Exactly! He felt ridiculously pleased to have got *that* sorted out.

A space cleared about them and Fair Isle called to Yellow Lens.

"Middle for diddle?"

"They're going to play 301," said Forde. "Do you know—"

"I have sat in enough pubs," said Anna, "over the last forty years or so—"

Thunk

Fair Isle managed a single 20.

Yellow Lens an outer bull.

Fair Isle performed a mock-bow and the Legion's first player stepped up to the mark.

Thunk Thunk

Forde drifted off again.

"That man," said Anna, "that one in the purplish shirt and suspenders. Do you know him?"

Forde shrugged. "Just to say hello."

"There'll be something wrong with him," she said.

"What do you mean—wrong?"

"His trousers are hoicked-up round his ankles. It was Mary taught me that."

"Nottingham Mary?"

"*She* said hitched-up trousers identified mentally disturbed people—infallible, she said—exhibitionists mainly, flashers."

Forde made a *would-you-believe-it!* sort of face.

"Raincoats," confirmed Anna.

"Now *this* guy, it's weird," said Forde. "Watch this! He'll score a double 20 then a triple 20—*bam-bam*—but the third dart's always in the 1 or 7 or some damn thing or winging off the lampshade."

The last dart bounced off wire—*told you*—skittered across the floor.

Yellow Lens stepped up, stood at attention sideways to the board, turned his head to face it, threw like an automaton, threw, impossibly, *across* his body.

A red-headed man, sweat standing on his forehead, bent himself nearly double after each of his darts, pulling himself down by his bush of beard and groaning. Another raised his left leg off the floor in the held stance of a baseball pitcher.

Young men.

Loud.

Shove it up your ass.

Glass breaking.

Ah, shit la merde!

Forde tensed, then at a glance relaxed. He reached across the table and nudged Anna's arm. She gave a start. His head urged her attention to the board.

A man stood at the metal strip, staring down at it with a strange intensity, an intensity that spread around him and stilled the chatter. He somewhat resembled Rasputin.

Forde whispered to Anna, "He can't count."

Slowly the head came up.

He stared at the board until it seemed that it was consuming him.

WHERE AM I?

143

WHAT DO I WANT?

treble 20

treble 17

double 8

Thunk Thunk

Oh, shit!

Tough nuggies, man.

Seeing it, perhaps, through Anna's eyes, the game was beginning to look foreign, eccentric.

She seemed to have dozed off again.

He supposed that he ought really to call a taxi and get her back to the Lord Beaverbrook. This day had been crammed enough, but in the morning there would be the ceremony at the graveside, the recitation, possibly more than once, of:

Let me have a scarlet maple
For the grave-tree at my head,
With the quiet sun behind it
In the years when I am dead.

Plus more Childe Chauncy guff, President guff, canoe guff, Bishop-of-the-Anglican-Cathedral guff, interment of the non-ashes and chopped-up unicorn guff…

Thunk

Anna had mentioned a black hat *with a veil.*

Snow had been forecast.

Thunk

Umbrella spokes jabbing necks, eyes threatened.

Daily Gleaner guff.

Extreme danger of *more* Maliseet-Passamaquoddy-Algonquian guff.

Thunk

Pictured *Tide,* toothbrush, the slimy bubble of the morrow's shirt.

In the midst of life we are in death: of whom may we seek for succour, but of thee, O Lord, who for our sins art justly displeased?

Oh, *Fuck!* thought Forde

And raising his weary head, inhaled, imbibed.

*

They were on the end game and a weariness had set in. Play was sloppy. Banter had died away. The table near the metal mark was crowded with empty pint glasses glinting, glasses lacy with the dried white residue of foam.

Fair Isle paused at their table on his way back from the bar bearing what he always called 'a jar'; Forde had pegged him on first meeting as a 'trad man,' imagined him playing hoary trombone in a traditional jazz band of fellow expats, serving up renditions of "When the Saints Go Marching In" and "The Old Grey Mare She Ain't What She used to be."

"So, Skip," said Forde. "This here's a fine hows-yer-father!"

"Not a manjack of 'em can make the bloody pick off. Still—small mercies—they're getting them on the board as opposed to into the ceiling or wounding bystanders. Henry's pissed as a newt, and Gordie—raised his chin indicating the sweaty, red-haired groaning man—" Gordie's working up a nice little aneurysm and—Oh, God! *Him* again—"

The chatter and complaints died down, stilled.

The Rasputin man stared down at the metal strip.

In the deepening silence, a sudden chair screeched and clattered back.

Got to drain the snake

Heads turned to glare.

Rasputin raised his eyes to the quivering ceiling in a display of violent calm before gathering into himself again, communing with the lit board.

WHERE AM I?

127

WHAT DO I NEED?

174

treble 20

treble 17

double 8

"Oh, Christ!" said Skip. "*Look* at that! What he 'needs' is a boot up his arse. He's been playing like a big girl's blouse all night."

He set his pint down on their table.

He held out three darts on his palm in array.

"How about it, Fordie? Do an honest day's work for a change."

Forde pointed at his snifter and shook his head.

Skip sighed.

"Ah, well..."

Anna made a small snore into her shoulder's plumpness; Forde thought of a dormouse slumbering.

Skip considered her.

A Tenniel dormouse, thought Forde, a pastel Beatrix Potter dormouse.

"And who," said Skip, "if I maybe so bold, is your companion?"

"Why not join us?" said Forde, stirring a chair outwards with his foot "This lady is Anna Tresillian. She is the granddaughter—"

"Aha!" said Skip. "I *thought* she was a bit long in the tooth for you."

"*—the granddaughter,*" said Forde, "of a famous Canadian poet, a famous Fredericton poet, a *Confederation Poet.* Her grandfather was the illustrious Childe Chauncy, a figure revered by many in academe as iconic."

"Blimey!"

"Tomorrow," said Forde, "as an honoured guest of the University of New Brunswick, she will preside over the interment of her grandfather's ashes in Poets' Corner."

"I see, I see," said Skip.

"I have been charged and entrusted with her care until the conclusion of tomorrow's obsequies."

"Obsequies," repeated Skip.

"Yes," said Forde.

"And here was I," said Skip, "thinking you were robbing the cradle."

Forde refused complicity in Skip's tiresome bonhomie.

"Mrs. Tresillian is a substantial figure in her own right, an actress, an ASM, an international connoisseur of lustre and commemorative transferware."

"An ASM?" repeated Skip.

"In more than one venue," said Forde, giving Skip a hard glance, a glance he thought of, and hoped would be received as, "steely."

"And such accomplishments aside, I am much taken with her as a person *and with her person.*"

"Oh, quite!" said Skip. "Quite. No offence intended, old chap. No argument from me. Absolutely *not.*"

They considered her.

"She is a jewel among women. A gem," said Forde, "of the first water. A dowager but a dilly."

"She seems to be asleep," observed Skip.

"Dozing, I venture," said Forde.

"Does she, do you know… no, no."

"What?"

"Play darts."

"No idea."

"I was thinking," said Skip, "what with all her honours and the obsequies and so forth, we could make her an honourary, you-know, just for a hand?"

"An idea that does you credit, Skip."

"Right. Jolly good. I'll ah, just have an explanatory you-know with Cecil and the lads."

Thunk

Thunk

He turned back.

"*What* was that word?"

"Obsequies?"

"Began with C."

"Confederation?"

"Right."

When he returned from these confabulations, Forde shook Anna's arm. She started from her slumber and, putting a palm over the top of her snifter, said, "Thank you, no. I suspect I've had an ample sussficiency."She slowly became aware of Skip's presence, her head lifting to take in his height.

"Who is this person," she said, "*looming*?"

She perked up as Forde explained to her the honour that the University and Legion teams wished to pay her. Leaning on the table, she pushed herself from her chair and, placing her hand across Skip's gallantly proffered forearm, they made a progress through the room towards the lights. Forde couldn't hear what was going on. It was like watching a play again. He deduced from the evident palaver that Skip, a stickler for silliness, was benching Rasputin and bringing Anna formally onto the field, voluble courtesies, beaming and bonhomie. He heard only an occasional word, a shout.

He drifted off into thinking about "steely," the "steely" glance he'd given Skip. In his frequent fallow periods when, sodden with depression at the reception of his novels by what, with gross exaggeration, might be called his "public," he had more than once toyed with the idea of betraying his life and committing a thriller, a genre-giant, a thriller so gorgeously written, so depraved, it would be seen as towering above the ruck of *New York Times Best Sellers*, swift, deft, featuring a suave, fastidious dandy. Of aristocratic background, something along the lines of Lord Peter Whimsey or Albert Campion, but deadly rather than goofy, and with a dash of James Bondish priapism though directed at the lubricated bottoms of boys, *his* monster from MI6 was called Johnny Sterling.

His mother's body had lain in state for three days upon an elaborate Italian catafalque in the Great Hall of Castle Malpas, the ancestral home of the Sterlings, before being borne to the cemetery in a hearse pulled by six black horses, white plumes nodding, to be buried, according to her last wishes, in a harmonium.

Upon his succession, and following his mother's death, Johnny Sterling had emerged.

Johnny Sterling was given to steely glances. A steely glance from Johnny Sterling caused panic scurrying in the demi-monde. A steely glance from Johnny Sterling caused hard men to pale. Johnny's hobby was collecting Victorian mourning jewelry in jet, lockets containing hair of the dear-departed, and death masks. Intimate of Paco Sánchez, reigning darling of Madrid's Las Ventas Plaza, Johnny was a frequent guest at Sánchez's *ganadería* and on more than one occasion had joined Sánchez's *cuadrilla* in Las Ventas, in La Maestranza, to place the *banderillas*.

Johnny's weapon of choice was nothing so plebeian as the American K-bar, but rather, a deliciously balanced Sykes-Fairbairn fighting knife alive to his hand, a knife which had been carried by his perverted father, hero of the SOE and seventeenth in the line of succession, a knife which had often been lingeringly bloodied in repulsively sadistic incursions into Occupied France, incursions his father referred to as "going on my hols."

Johnny Sterling's underwear was bespoke silk.

Oh, fuck it thought Forde.

*

Bowing slightly, Skip was extending to Anna the first dart.

SKIP!

Quarter-after Lady!

No! No!

Leave her be!

SKIP!

Skip put an arresting arm on Anna's and then turned away. Forde could not hear what was being said, couldn't grasp what the kerfuffle was about. Skip turned his head to another red-faced, blustering player as if seeking confirmation of what the player at the other side of the scrum had shouted. He raised both hands in a STOP, WAIT gesture, calming, placatory, and turned to Anna, hands still upraised, but she, bored or indifferent, had already started an ungainly roundhouse swing. At the apogee of her arm's arc she let go of the dart, the momentum of her throw stumbling her away from the board.

Thunk

The dart struck into the double 6 at an extreme angle.

There was a sudden silence that deepened.

Glasses at the bar clinked.

The room looked and felt like a movie stopped mid-action, frame frozen.

Into the silence, a voice.

Fuck me!

Then,

Oh, the Dear Lord!

I don't freakin believe it!

"Gentlemen, gentlemen!" remonstrated Skip.

NO

NO!

Slowly, the dart was beginning to droop. It had not sunk squarely and deeply enough into the cork. It declined. Slowly.

Declined. The room was holding its breath. Declined until the dart was lying almost its full length against the cork, its weight just counterbalanced, its point just holding against the wire. Silence held. The light blazed. The dart held every eye. The dart held.

The room exhaled.

"And, I believe," said Skip into the silence, "match."

Hubbub, swelling hubbub.

Anna made her way back to the table through smiles, clapping, heads nodding, whistles.

Skip clanged his key ring against an empty pint and shouted against the clamour OY! Then launched into a bumbling oompah oompah of a speech, a chunder of cheery verbiage, honours, obsequies, poets, Confederation, Childe Chauncy, sportsmanship, the place that poetry held in all hearts, that lived on in our hearts from school days, golden lads and girls all must as chimney-sweepers come to dust, such remembered glories conferring ... well, *conferring*, and there you have it, to the victor the spoils, and so—Evan, without further ado, Evan, THE ENVELOPE PLEASE.

The bartender approached bearing a package, which drooped across both hands. The wrapping of the package was butcher paper. The butcher paper was secured with bindertwine.

Skip presented the package to Anna with further rhetorical fanfaronade.

"Thank you," she said. "Thank you."

Forde, with minute gesture, prompted a greater show of enthusiasm.

"Moose steaks!" she said. "How *kind!*"

*

"*Oops,*" said Anna.

"Steps," said Forde.

A street light shed a thin, sodium-vapour yellow on the road's windrows, frozen sharp now by the wind, and on a wire-mesh waste bin chained to the street light's pole. They'd left the jostling Legion Hall to a babble of friendly recipes. One man swore by a 24-hour marinade of Worcestershire sauce and vodka. In the fridge, mind. Broke down the fibres, he said, and you can drink it but the drinking it, that's an option. Another had confided that *his* old woman boiled them for about five minutes with plenty of baking soda, took away that strong taste, the game taste, *swamp* she called it, then she fried them in bacon fat and you had yourself a real feed.

The road widened into a small circle in front of the Legion Hall and then ended. Behind the Legion Hall the trees began again. Where the road started to widen into the circle there were yellow No Exit signs scarred with bullet holes.

They stood waiting for the taxi, the yellow vapour light, the waste bin, the blackness of the trees.

In that dark, engines coughed, roared. Headlights and ruby brakelights sprang into the branches and trunks of pines.

"G'night, Rose."

"G'night."

"Now then, girls!"

"In your dreams."

An engine revving.

Ta ta. Goonight. Goonight, said Forde.

To the receding lights declaimed, *Good night, ladies, good night, sweet ladies, good night, good night.*

Black silence sifting down.

Oul' butty o'mine, said Anna. *You're a darlin'man, a daarlin' man.*

"Christ!" he said.

"What?"

"It's running up my sleeve."

"What?"

"Blood."

... *who would have thought* said Anna *the old man to have had so much blood in him?*

"Funny, funny," said Forde, plucking his shirt and pull-over and jacket sleeves away from the wetness.

"It's all sticky," he said. "It's cold and sticky."

Go get some water

said Anna

And wash this filthy witness from your hand.

"Oh, it's The Scottish Play, is it? Well—" gesturing at the concrete-block façade of the Legion Hall—*This castle*—at the rucked coconut matting on its steps, the squat portico, the stubby pillars—

> *hath a pleasant seat; the air*
> *Nimbly and sweetly recommends itself*
> *Unto our gentle senses.*

Anna said,

> *Will all great Neptune's ocean wash this blood*
> *Clean from my hand? No, this my hand will rather*
> *The multitudinous seas incarnadine*

and stopped.

Forde waited.

Making he said *the green one red.*

The breath of their declamations visible on the frigid air.

"That is not a line," she said, "of which I can approve."

Forde stared at her, astonished.

"So I don't say it."

"Really?"

"It's the swoop," she said, "that's hokum."

"What do you mean, 'swoop'?"

"From Latin, from boomy words to everyday words. It's meant to suggest depth of feeling. Pathos, even. But it's hokum."

"When you say, 'hokum'—"

"Don't look at me like that."

"I'm not looking at you like anything, particularly. I merely asked—"

"It's hokum," she said, "because we can *see* the trick being done. We're supposed to be moved by the swoop, but real feeling's destroyed because—*because*—we're *also* meant to be admiring the neatness of the trick. There's a word they used then..."

She paused, struggling.

"No, ah, it's gone. A special word for that *kind* of cleverness."

She dismissed this lapse of memory with one of her throwaway gestures.

"I never did much trust cleverness," she said. "I never thought cleverness had anything much to do with feeling. Do you?"

"*Conceit!*" said Forde, "Was that the—?"

"*Well done!* Exactly! Yes, yes. It's a conceit and we're *supposed* to be aware of it and to admire it. And *that*," she said, "is why it's hokum."

"Hmmm," said Forde.

"Had you ever thought that 'the multitudinous seas incarnadine' is saying *exactly* the same thing as 'making the green one red'?"

Forde made a "considering" face.

"He'd have done much better to end with real feeling, boomy but real, he'd have been much better served to end, as I do, with 'incarnadine.'"

Forde nodded to convey that he was following the argument.

"But the green-red stuff dilutes it all *away* from guilt, *enormous* guilt, ENORMITY, to poor little ultra-contrite, ga-ga-driven woman gliding about in her nightie. Pathetic," she said, *"on all fronts."*

She raised her arm.

"BUT, all you need to do is *stop* the cleverness. All you have to do is—

Will all great Neptune's ocean wash this blood
Clean from my hand? No, this my hand will rather
The multitudinous SEAS incarnadine.

"*Zing* 'seas' and end on 'incarnadine' and there you are, BINGO. I have broached this, this ..."

"interpretation?" suggested Forde.

"Rendering," she said. "This rendition. I have encountered and endured much ... it begins with 'C',"

"Contempt?"

"It's something like 'calamine.'"

"Hmmm," said Forde. "Right, rashes, white stuff."

"What I have had to say has fallen on deaf and hide-bound ears."

"Hmmm," said Forde again. "Well, I hadn't thought of any of this."

"Well," said Anna, "I *had*."

She was impassioned, her words slurred slightly.

She drew away from him.

"Calumny!" she said suddenly.

Stood shivering.

The silence between them was becoming uncomfortable, he felt; she was unaccountably angry.

Hoping to break this tension, Forde said, "Hey, Anna, what about this?"

He put his left arm across his chest and gripped his right shoulder. His head down and slightly turned, he directed the words towards his left elbow, sculpting by this pose, he thought, except for the package, withdrawal, introspection, weary resignation.

I am in blood
Stepped in so far that, should I wade no more,
Returning were as tedious as go o'er
Come ON bloody taxi

But Anna was not watching him or listening.

She had drifted away and seemed to be addressing the ditch. He could hear her voice but not the words. As he came up behind her he heard:

It will have blood, they say: blood will have blood.
Stones have been known to move and trees to speak;
Augures and understood relations have
By maggot-pies and choughs ...

and choughs ...

By maggot-pies and choughs ...

and choughs ...

He put his hand on her shoulder. She shrugged it off. She resisted, rigid for a moment or two, then turned.

There was something in her face.

Had there been tears?

Difficult in this light to make things out.

She made a noise, something between a sigh and a soft cry.

"I can't remember," she said. "I can't remember. It's what I do. And I can't remember."

"My Lady," said Forde, doffing his gallant hat, survivor, reluctant herald, pointing down the road in the direction of Fredericton,

he i'th' blood-sized field lies swollen ...

He lumbered himself down until he was half-kneeling before her, the package balanced across his sticky palm, and beseeched her,

Yet let this not make thee bloody-minded.

"Forde, Forde," she said, "so kind, so very kind."

"Oh, Christ!" he said it. "I can feel it."

She patted his head.

"I think I'm feeling," she said, "somewhat odd."

"It's pooling—"

"*More,*" she said, "possibly, than somewhat."

"Pooling—" said Forde.

"Your knee'll get wet," she said.

"—in the crook of my elbow."

AVAST she suddenly bellowed.

GET RID OF THEM

She pointed dramatic arm.

JETTISON THEM

"Yes, yes," she said, "into the bin! Are we the kind of people—I ask you this—are we the kind of people who pro-morade … who *promenade* with steaks of moose?"

Inside the bin's wire mesh, a bulging garbage bag. Foul black stalactites of frozen deliquescence hung from the mesh of the bin's bottom. Frozen to the sidewalk, black rivulets. The garbage bag bulged with coffee cups, what looked like a pair of underpants, pieces of pizza crust red and virulent orange, a running shoe, dog turds in knotted plastic bags.

He dropped into the bin the bloody package.

She threw out her arm in an unsteady gesture of encompassment.

"This place …"

"What?"

"Where *is* it?"

"What? The Legion, you mean?"

"No, I mean are we in a *forest?*"

She threw up her hands to convey bafflement, gesturing about at Hall, bin, trees, their backdrop blackness.

"Are we lost?"

"We came in a taxi, remember?"

"I was asleep."

"We're waiting for a taxi back to the hotel."

"I'm cold. It's very cold."

"It won't be long."

"Where we are is what I'm asking. This place—where we're at, what is it?"

"You mean, called?"

In her eyes a glint, a glaze of tears.

She shrugged.

"Nashwaaksis."

She regarded him.

She worked off her mitten, concentrated on that, then, looking up at him, wagged an admonishing finger.

"*What?*" he said "*What?*"

"Say again," she said.

"Nashwaaksis."

Slowly, slowly shook her head.

"*Exactly!*"

THE MUSEUM AT THE END OF THE WORLD

In the Pontic Alps high above Trebizond, dug into a sheer cliff face, Sumela Monastery. The last three-quarters of a mile was only possible on foot as the track climbed steep and broken, tree roots crawling out over the plates of rock, in places more scramble than walk. Forde and Sheila were moving at a fair pace to get out of the drizzle.

The quaint pamphlet given out with the tickets—a blurry photo on the second page of a filigreed relic of the True Cross—stated that the last Orthodox monks had left in the Exchange of Populations in 1923, taking with them, to Greece, the icon of the Virgin Mary popularly believed to be one of four painted by St. Luke. Now, after years of neglect, and wanton behaviour by tobacco smugglers, only crumbling Byzantine frescoes remained.

Forde cherished such useless information and relished the English in which it was often written. The "wanton" behaviour of tobacco smugglers expanded in his imagination, scenes of peculiarly Turkish debauchery, tight buttocks and turbans, played out under the gaze of frescoed saints stiff in gold and azure copes.

"Come *on*!" urged Sheila. "I'm getting soaked."

When they reached the tiny forecourt, a ledge cut into the face, one last long flight of steep steps climbed into the building itself. Forde stood leaning against a wall winded and puffing.

"What is it?" said Sheila. "What's wrong?"

Forde shook his head.

"Rob?"

"Just ... a bit winded."

And closed his eyes again.

"Stop being so bloody British."

"Well, it's in my arm..."

"Christ!" said Sheila.

They picked their way back down the broken track and across the scree to the area where the vans were parked. One with its sliding door open, inside Father Keogh and the hulking flannel-mouthed man Forde had come to think of as The Minder.

The Minder proffered his little oval tin of mauve cachous.

Father Keogh was wearing a flat plebeian tweed cap and sat staring straight ahead.

"The monastery didn't attract you?" said Sheila.

He considered her.

"And why," he said, "would I be wishing to visit a nest of schismatics?"

"Mmmm," said Sheila.

The minder started his soothing babble of sound, weaving repeated words and phrases, encompassing the rain, the gloomy foliage, the steepness of the path, the grandeur of that morning's breakfast, his mother and something and soda bread. It was a song almost, an Irish crooning which made little sense. The flow of words did not seem to be directed at the priest personally but seemed rather like oil on generally troubled waters, placatory, a hush-now, hush-now.

Forde tuned out his blather and sat watching, through the van's open doorway the quick picking of a sparrow under a picnic table. He was waiting. He was feeling drawn deep inside himself, cautious, tentative in the world. He was waiting to see if the pain would fill his back teeth, crush his chest, bow and bend him.

He thought back to his last stress test at the Ottawa Heart Institute.

Injection of radioactive material.

Tapping Forde's wedding ring, the technician had said, "The wife'll like this."

"Pardon?"

"It'll make your willie glow in the dark."

Eighteen minutes of scanning photographs.

Injection of Persantine to stress the heart. Five unpleasant minutes later the injection of an antidote. Followed by the injection of more radioactive material. Followed by a chopped-egg sandwich. Followed by eighteen more minutes of photographs.

He fingered through the material of his jacket pocket the shape of the pump-spray of sublingual nitroglycerin.

He sat waiting, breathing shallow.

Father Keogh sat primly in remote silence.

Sheila was frowning as she struggled to understand the Minder's brogue. He was extolling the beauties of County Wexford, the soft, silver sheen of the Slaney's sweet waters, rhapsodizing over the red cows of Leinster, hock-deep in wild flowers—the white in the green—and the gorse, ah, God! the gorse, the scent of the gorse on the noon's heavy heat…

Father Keogh produced a silver flask.

The Minder stopped in mid-sentence.

Father Keogh unscrewed the flask's cap, which served as a little beaker.

"It's not yet five o'clock, Father."

"He knows perfectly well what time it is," said Father Keogh.

"Five o'clock was the hour appointed. Five o'clock was the agreed-upon hour."

Father Keogh carefully filled the cap.

"He is not," said Father Keogh, "to be judged by snivellers."

"But. Father..."

"He will not be badgered."

Forde turned his head completely and openly stared.

*

"*What* was she saying? No. Completely gone. Honestly."

"Not everyone can fit in at the same time so half'll go to the palace first and half to the mosque," said Sheila.

"And then switch over sort of thing?"

"Right."

"Well, let's go to the palace. I've gone off mosques. Taking your shoes off and putting them on again and pottering about with them in dirty plastic bags."

"That one's the palace bus," said Sheila.

"And all those athlete's foot carpets," said Forde.

He soon abandoned the local guide with her insistent "If I may invite you this way here shall you see..." and wandered off into the desolate ruins of the palace of the Grand Comneni. Here, where he stood in what had been the palace library, Cardinal Bessarian, as a youth, had read his Homer. Here, in this library, Forde imagined the exquisite Byzantine bindings, ivory plaques carved in bas-relief let into the covers and surrounded by beaten gold set with cameos and gems.

From the corner of his eye, he caught the flicker of a lizard. Seaward were the ruins of the harbour built by the indefatigable Hadrian in the first century, Hadrian, accomplished poet, learned in Greek. Wind from the sea stirred the nettles. Viciously thorned sprays of blue-green caper plants grew from fissures in the tumbled masonry.

Here, eight hundred years ago during the reign of Alexius II, Byzantine court ceremony and splendour reached its apex. Here, in the imperial court, arts and letters flourished. Here had been the last refuge of Hellenistic civilization.

He remembered having seen some of them, the Greek manuscripts that had belonged in later years to Cardinal Bessarian. In Venice, he'd seen them. In the library of St. Mark's.

He stood staring about him.

capperis spinosa

The clink of rock on rock.

Forde turned, expecting to see Sheila.

It was a woman from the ship stepping over what had been the door sill. Seeing him, she tilted her head and for a second or two hesitated, one foot still in the air. Her held stance suggested a hen. His face half-creased into a polite smile.

Tinny tune cackling rent the silence. She rootled in her purse for the cell phone.

The spell violated, Forde picked his way forward to escape the noise of her.

*

The ship people were milling about in the forecourt of the Sultan Mehmet Mosque. Forde stood on the sidewalk waiting for Sheila, who had gone off in search of aspirin. Neatly uniformed school children stared up as they flowed around him. He surveyed the furniture shops with their swollen settees, the jewellers with gold and silver bangles displayed on poles, the pastry shops with savoury pies and borek in the windows. The shops and houses were utilitarian, seemed modern, concrete block and brick slapped together with mortar oozing out of every course.

Forde read a passing teenager's T-shirt: KEEP IT REAL.

In trays, pans, shallow bins, the fish stores displayed the catch of the day; that day in Trebizond the choice was bonito. In clothes stores, child-mannequins, suits and bow ties for three-year-old boys, puffy sleeved froufrou dresses for tiny girls.

Shouting their presence louder than other shops, narrow storefronts selling film, cameras, cell phones, disks, CD-players, calculators, digital pedometers, their windows a blare of posters and logos: SONY, TOSHIBA, SAMSUNG, OLYMPUS, CANON PANASONIC, FUJI, KODAK, HITACHI, NIKON.

"Got some!" called Sheila. "Bayer. *And* Immodium."

"Why, have you…?"

"Just prophylactic. Wouldn't want to get the squitters on, you know, the Odessa Steps or something."

*

Forde sat on the low stone wall that retained the flower beds in the forecourt of the mosque. On his right rose a high brick wall, scabby, rotted stucco, with a course of stonework along its top. To his left, the elegantly designed octagonal stone ablutions cistern where men washed before going in to pray. In front of each of the eight stone faces sat three stone stools and in each face three modern taps.

He had a sense that the precincts of the mosque had been encroached upon, the road beyond the present arched entrance having eaten up what had once been garden, houses built within what once had been forecourt. He suspected—the run of the hill down towards the placing of the mosque, the high brick wall climbing up—that in some more gracious times the wall had carried an aqueduct which fed the roofed, faceted cistern. He imagined the water constantly rilling down each face, the tinkle and plash of it as it ran and fell into the surrounding trough of inward-sloping flagstones before gurgling off into drains.

As inconspicuously as possible, Forde was watching three men as they performed their ritual ablutions. He could still see Sheila in the line-up. He watched her for a moment or two. Had a sudden memory of her standing in the kitchen, frowning as she phoned the plumber on the TV remote, the dark swirling grain of the oak floor, her bare feet in a wide bar of sunlight. The sun was mellow on the brickwork, warm on his back.

Also watching the three men was a girl in jeans and a lighter blue sweater. She looked to be eighteen or so. She was calling out to the men, remarks which, judging from her sexual gestures, were lewd provocations. One of the men was laughing. The others ignored her. Her body was pertly nubile but her face was coarse, her jaw heavy and slightly prognathous, features suggesting some form of retardation.

A man with grey hair and grey beard was trudging across the forecourt towards the cistern. He was paunchy and was wearing old black suit trousers and a white, collarless flannel shirt. Sandals. Over the shirt, a black vest. Most of the shirts Forde had seen on locals and in shops had been nylon or polyester. The man lowered himself with a loud sigh onto a stone stool. He sat with his hands on his knees, staring at the facing stone.

The girl held up a handful of empty, hinged mussel shells and then clacked them on the coping of the flower-bed wall in announcement. She then skittered them across the flagstones, a crinkle of sound.

She launched into the mime of a barnyard rite. Thrusting with her loins, making a jeering, farting noise with her lips, she imitated a man thrusting into a woman.

Then, taking a step forward, she became a man.

The man she had become caught the passing girl—the farmer's daughter?—a servant girl?—by the upper arm and pulled her back against him. His hands came round and cupped her breasts. He nuzzled her neck, nibbled her ear, then stroked and kneaded her buttocks. Letting go of her, he unbuttoned the four buttons of his fly and unshipped a large but flaccid cock. It lay across his left palm. With his right hand, he hauled up her skirts and bending her down piled the skirts onto her back. He stuck two investigating fingers between her legs.

The man at the cistern, surmounting the mound of his paunch, grunting with the effort, strained down over it to unstrap his sandals.

Umph, he grunted, *Umph.*

The barnyard man brought his two wet fingers out, letting the skirts fall, and began to ease back his foreskin, anointing the head of his cock with her stickiness. Slowly the penis stirred, stiffened, rose.

The grey-haired man turned on the tap.

He lifted the skirts again, piled them on her back, pinned them there, pushed her lower. Then with his left boot he tapped the inside of her left ankle, then with his right boot the inside of her right ankle, forcing her to shuffle her legs wider apart. She tried to straighten up a little but he pushed her down again, slapping the side of her head.

He pushed himself into her.

Ahhhhhh!

Gripped her by the hips, pulling her onto him.

Straining over his paunch, the cistern man was rubbing water between his toes.

Left foot. *Uuuh. Uuuh. Uuuh. Uuuh.*

The barnyard man was thrusting, grunting *Aah! Aah! Aah!*

Right foot. *Uuuh. Uuuh. Uuuh. Uuuh.*

Aah! Aah! Aah!

The face carved in concentration.

arrrggul—arrrggul—arrrggul gargled the cistern man.

Splat onto the flagstones.

Doing something with his nose. Snuffling up water from his cupped palm. Nostrils pinched closed. Then *nnnnnnnm* onto the flags.

Coughed.

Retched.

Arr! Arr! Arr! growled the barnyard man.

The cistern man's forefinger wiggling in his ear.

Faster now, faster, frenetic the thrusting.

Ah-ah-ah-ah-oh!

Sudden stillness.

Then a strained cry, almost falsetto, from the barnyard man.

A groan.

Then. Gouts of it. Four separate spasms gripped him rigid.

A soft sigh ended the performance. She seemed to lose interest entirely. She turned her back on them and, plucking a purple dahlia, wandered off across the forecourt, kicking at mussel shells, and out through the arched entrance and disappeared into the street.

*

It was Sheila's turn to sit by the window. Across the aisle from Forde sat the man with the Woolly Bear-caterpillar-eyebrows, things rank and gross in nature, thought Forde, and positive tufts sprouting from his ears. He always wore a squashy sun bonnet tied under his chin with a string. It looked like something a toddler might wear. He must have been in his late seventies. He was deaf and carried his antique hearing-aid apparatus hanging around his neck in a custom-made leather case whose size reminded Forde of World War II naval binoculars. A side flap unbuttoned, giving access to knobs. Wires connected it to his ears.

The aluminum gangway steps leading up from the quay to the entry port on the third deck were solid with unmoving passengers and more pooling at the foot of the steps as buses arrived. It was Woolly Bear blocking the inward flow.

He stared at the Indonesian purser like an astonished baby.

"He needs your identity-card thing, Edwin," said his wife.

"My dear fellow!" remonstrated Edwin. "What an extraordinary thing to say!"

"Edwin," said his wife, "are you sure you're switched on?"

"Of *course* I didn't swipe it. I was *given* it."

"What he *means*, Edwin," said his wife. "Oh … *God!*" she said, twitching the card from his fingers and handing it to the purser to run through the machine.

As the flow started again, Forde heard Edwin explaining, "One gives them one's passport and they give you this card. One buys things with it. Drinks and so forth. Toiletries."

It was a pleasure to ease off the heavy walking shoes. He washed, enjoyed the starched pleasure of a clean shirt, put on his suit and a pair of black Florsheim dress shoes and, taking his journal, headed for the bar, leaving Sheila to the interminable intricacies of her make-up.

Sitting at the empty bar was the Rt. Revd. Chantry Williams, Chaplain in Ordinary to HM Chapels Royal and Bishop of Bodmin and Exeter. A huge bugger, six foot three, at least. Forde inclined his head a stiff couple of inches in acknowledgement of the man's presence. According to the little bottle's label, the bishop was sipping a glass of Britomart Orange Crush, probably to fortify himself for the lecture he would be giving at six o'clock on Trajan's campaign against the Dacians, a lecture Forde would not be attending.

Forde thought the Bishop a bit of a berk.

For daily excursions he affected a sort of safari outfit, khaki shirt with epaulettes, cargo pants, combat boots, the ensemble topped by a silly Tilley-type hat sporting, on one side of it, a cockade of nylon feathers.

His last two lectures—*Feudal Monarchy in the Latin Kingdom of Jerusalem* and *Christendom and The Barbary Coast*—had ended with pleas for closer community with Islam. We must treat with respect and understanding, he had said, Islamic sacred law, *Shari'ah*. As ardent Christians, he had said, we must reach out to the *ummah,* the world-wide community of Islamic believers.

Just as within the Christian community the forces of ecumenicism ... so in that larger community of People of the Book...

Forde was not an ardent Christian.

Embrace our fellow...

Forde had no desire whatever to reach out to unwashed wahabis and mad, hairy mullahs.

Embrace!

"Feh!" as Sheila would have said.

The Bishop of Bodmin could stuff the *ummah* up his jumper; Anglican clerics should confine themselves, thought Forde, to such essentially Anglican activities as the blessing of marrows.

He glared at the back of the bishop's head.

He began to feel the welcome bite of the Scotch.

From his table he could see directly down into the still water under the bow. Further out, sunlight sparkled on the water. He watched flocks of shearwaters, small groups of birds in brief flights before settling again to ride the waves, spirits, the stories went, of sailors drowned. He found himself thinking about the book he'd been looking at in the ship's library, with its reproductions of seventeenth-century woodcuts of fiendish Turks, ranked Janissaries, effete bejewelled pashas. Led by Sultan Mohammed II, the Turks took Istanbul in 1453. In 1461 Mohammed entered Trebizond in triumph and celebrated his victory by praying in the ransacked church of St. Eugenius, which he turned into the New Friday Mosque. Within two or three years, Mohammed had the deposed Emperor, David Comnenus, put to death together with all the males in the Comnenus line of succession. Forde thought of the ruins they'd visited that afternoon, rubble that once had been known as "The Golden Palace of the Comneni," home now to nettles, *capperis spinosa*, and the chill wind from the sea.

As he gazed down into the water, his thoughts washing over Sultan Mohammed and the Bishop of Bodmin and Exeter and Britomart Orange Crush, he became aware of something white, something white rising.

At first he thought it was probably garbage, a paper bag, perhaps, but as it rose up though the dark water he saw things trailing from it, strings…

He pressed closer to the glass.

He saw that the white thing as it rose was not flat like paper but domed like an inverted bowl. He saw that the strings were… trailing tentacles. A jellyfish. Another one rising up from the depths to touch the surface. And another. All along the side of the ship. He hurried the length of the room craning to look from every window. Suddenly dozen upon dozen of them rising through the dark water to hang for a few moments at the surface before sinking, sinking, and then gone from sight. The rise and fall was like a stately carousel, a slow-motion firework display, an underwater Swan Lake of jellyfish.

If he were writing, what words could describe this dance, this vision? They appeared larger as they rose higher, like flowers blossoming and opening. *Bloom*. He would use the word *bloom*. He had the sense somehow that the ship was being visited. He would use *visitant* and *visitation*, with their connotations of the supernatural, for there *was* something ghostly in the whiteness and the slow materialization of the jellyfish. He found himself in the odd position of not believing such chimerical nonsense but at the same time feeling it. He felt—embarrassedly—that he was being… there was no way round the feeling … blessed.

He caught the barman's eye and raised his empty glass, tapping it with his forefinger.

Or perhaps…

He shrugged.

Perhaps the feeling arose from the beneficent effects of *The Famous Grouse*.

He sat, his mind drifting.

Bar sounds.

Sheila's voice said, "Buy a girl a drink?"

He stood and pulled out a chair for her.

"We're very formal this evening, aren't we?"

"It's because of the suit."

The sparkle had left the waves. The light was fading. They sat in easy silence. Lights started to come on in some of the port buildings. He could just make out the shapes of the boys still fishing off the end of the dock. A tug, its bridge blazing with lights, its sides armoured with tires like a row of shields, thrashed past them out to sea.

"For God's sake take these peanuts away from me," said Sheila.

"Grand Comnenus and Emperor," he said.

"Pardon?"

"That's how the Comneni were referred to."

"Hmmm," said Sheila.

Forde sat in silence for long minutes.

"Sipping Britomart," he burst out, "while Rome burns."

"*What?*"

He sighed.

"Ah, well," said Sheila, always sensitive to his shifting moods, "cheer up! I expect the dining room'll be open now."

*

All was aglow and gleaming. Light from the recessed pot lights blazed down on glasses, cutlery, starched napery, mirrored walls. Banquettes down the room's sides were divided into booths by slabs of thick, minty glass etched with a design of Scottish thistles. Conversation rolled in waves, a surf of sound. As they waited for the steward, Forde watched the girls going round the tables with bottles of red and white wine, filling glasses. Waiters in bistro black and white. At their various stations, decorative silver wine coolers, massed flowers, elaborate ceramic cornucopias of fruit. Forde relaxed into the nightly theatre.

The steward led them up the length of the room to a table for two. They passed the little old lady with the make-up. She was wearing this evening, on her left hand, a gold ring with a bezel that clasped a green stone the size of a small frog.

At the next table over from them, the American couple who always introduced themselves with "We're Alan and Martin from Cincinnati." They were wearing identical Haspel seersucker suits, which put Forde in mind of ice cream. He noticed on the table between them a bottle of wine.

He nodded to them and said, "How did you end up with that?"

"We complained," said Alan.

"We lodged a complaint," said Martin.

"Well, really!" said Alan. "What we had last night."

"We made our views known," said Martin.

"We didn't pay all this money," said Alan, "to drink pooey old Merlot from Chile."

"We felt put upon," said Martin. "So Alan complained to that nice steward—you know, the comfy one? From Austria? Who wears pumps?—and he sent us this *Marqués de Cáceres*."

"Rioja," said Alan.

"Tempranillo," said Martin.

"Gran Reserva," said Alan.

"Two years in oak," said Martin.

"*Yum!*" said Alan.

Forde and Sheila busied themselves with menus and Apollonaris mineral water.

"In the hors-d'oeuvres," said Forde, "what does 'Goujonnette' mean?"

"Fish," said Sheila. "A small piece. It's fried usually."

... what with my knees and all that marble up-and-down...

Forde sipped the wine the nice girl had poured.

He wondered why it was that some voices carried almost brutally through the general hive of sound. It didn't seem that they were speaking particularly loudly. Just a strange, penetrating timbre. Odd. This one was a small lady three tables away. He watched the girls filling wine glasses. Well-filled blouses, too.

"He noted, with approval," said Forde.

"Pardon?"

"No, nothing."

Indicating Alan and Martin with the slightest movement of his head, he said, "How old do you think they are?"

Sheila shrugged. "Difficult to say. Fifty? Fifty-five." He watched them covertly. Their lines were beginning to blur—the beginnings of plumpness, little tummy bulges, the suggestion of jowls. In their identical seersucker suits they might have been, thought Forde, a once-lauded vaudeville act from the Ed Sullivan era, about to glide from table to table on roller skates performing close-up with cards and coins.

All, all, it seemed to Forde, was stories or a play and the passengers character actors. It amused and pleased him to shape them and compose their pasts. Though his creation of Father Keogh's travelling companion as The Minder seemed not far off the mark. He had already decided that Woolly Bear had fought in the Korean War either as regular army or National Service conscript though he had more of a Sandhurst feel about him. Probably the knee socks and sun bonnet. Then there was the rude, loud man on the bus with his brass-bound walking stick. The Baden Powell man, Forde called him. Wore a lemon silk cravat with Viyella shirts and claimed to have been a second lieutenant in the Arab Legion under Glubb Pasha. The cravat did not completely hide the craters of old boils on the back of his neck.

Forde had heard him saying to a man on the bus that he sorely missed "my lovely brave young Bedouin"; *hmmm*. But at the same time, he roared words and phrases in Hindi and the dates seemed possibly dodgy. Though Jordan had not thrown Glubb Pasha out until 1954 and so if the Baden Powell man had joined the Legion after the 1948 war at the age of, say, twenty-one, then … but the mental arithmetic was hurting Forde's head and he fell back into watching people and drifting reverie.

… and then I dropped the soap and those shower stalls are like upended coffins so I couldn't bend down …

"Look!" he said suddenly. *"Look!"*

"What?"

"On your right. That woman!"

"Where? Oh."

"Fanning herself," said Forde with delight, "with a side plate!"

*

Forde sat glaring at the line cook—Filipino, Malaysian, or some other mixture—who stood with folded arms at the near end of the steam table. What could be seen of Sochi was not appealing. The ship had docked just after dawn. Concrete, a few tired palm trees, tall wire mesh fences, a flag drooping in the still heat. The day's promised excursion was to Dagomys in the mountains to see the most northerly tea plantation in Europe, a prospect that was not causing him palpitations.

Sheila was making her way through the breakfast throng towards the table for two he had secured them. She had been to the laundry room while it wasn't busy.

"I met Alan down there—he'd been drying two, well I don't quite know *what* you'd call them—'blousons,' perhaps. And do you know what he said?"

"No," said Forde.

"He said they were sixty percent cotton and forty percent 'the P-word, but strictly, *but strictly,* for travel.'"

"Hmmm."

"'The P-word,'" said Sheila. "And I asked him where Martin was and do you know what he said?"

"Of *course* I don't know what he said."

"He said, 'Oh, he's still tucked up in bed like a great big Gummi Bear.'"

"*Christ!*" said Forde.

"A touch homophobic this morning, are we?"

"No. Homicidal."

"*Now* what's the matter?"

"Nothing."

"But the main thing he told me was that a woman was attacked in the laundry. That nice woman who's a hospital administrator in Sheffield."

"What sort of attacked?"

"Well, sexually."

"Probably a lascar," said Forde.

"A what?"

"Like that one over there who makes himself awkward about fried eggs. I *know* he's got them. I know *where* they are. In that little oven under the counter. But every time I ask, the scrawny little sod goes into his 'No flied egg' routine."

"What *is* a lascar?"

"They run amok, rushing about in a frenzy and committing violent acts. They're noted for it. Conrad's full of them. You have to do something Conrad-ish to them when they're amok, lash them to the mast, hose them into the scuppers, conk them with a coal shovel."

"Is this because of the fried eggs?"

"I once read something Conrad said about the expression 'going great guns.' 'Going' implies movement and guns don't 'go' unless you mean 'go off' so the expression becomes somewhat unclear. It now seems generally and vaguely to mean *successful*. But there's a ghost of meaning in 'going' that we've lost. Now *Conrad* said it referred to a ship under full sail and the wind booming the canvas like great cannons firing. So you see what we've *lost* ..."

"Forde!"

"What?"

"Alan said the man was *hissing*. He grabbed her from behind and put his hand over her mouth and while he was rubbing his thing against her bum he was *hissing* and *hissing* like those men do to horses."

"Ostlers."

"Yes. But he was hurting her too, squeezing, twisting flesh, crushing her breasts. And whoever it was had planned it. He'd somehow got most of the lights off so all she really saw was a shape."

Sheila fell silent.

"I wonder," she said, "if it *was* a crew member."

She set down her coffee cup.

She stared at him.

"Or was it a passenger?"

Then she said hesitantly, "It's ... it's that hissing. That's what frightens me."

"Sorry about the fried eggs," said Forde.

She nodded.

"Something about it," she said, "that noise, that's insane."

*

"First Prize," said Forde, "one week in Sochi. Second Prize, three weeks in Sochi."

The utilitarian bus throbbed and shuddered as it waited for stragglers from the Botanical Gardens making their way back from gawking at the Tree of Friendship.

The wood-slat seats gave little ease. Someone had pasted a festive frill of scissored gold foil round the inside top two inches of the windows obscuring the view. Glued to every fourth or so strip of fringe, a cotton-wool bobble. The long gear shift was dressed in a knitted sheath. The punctilious guide kept testing his mike, peering into papers in his brief-case, counting and re-counting the passengers, fingers questioning the knot of his tie. The Baden Powell man began his daily bellowing and pounding the floor with his walking stick.

"You! Bloody driver! You! The tout with the microphone! Music *off!* Music *off!*"

The bus juddered on its way. The guide resumed his litany. There wasn't much to see. One after another, large white buildings, gardens surrounding. High hedges of dark yew. Sanitaria for apparatchiks.

... what you call in your countries not—hospitals? No. Spa. Just so mmmmm. There are many baths 50 metres by 25 metres that is mmm in the measurements of your countries 164.042 feet by 82.02 feet and these baths are full of water from the hot springs. The water is full of health but the smell is very rude.

The State Winter Theatre. Riviera Park with an opportunity to buy local handicrafts. In the grounds of the Zelyonaya Roscha Sanitorium, Stalin's Dacha.

... and a big surprise are the baths full of mud which is heated to mmmm 41 degrees centigrade or in the measurements of your countries 105.8 Fahrenheit which is 4 degrees higher than your blood ...

Forde squirmed on the unforgiving seat.

...and there are also mud mmm cabinets with just heads ...

"The Cabinets of Doctor Caligari," said Forde.

...and the mud sucks out the poison from the body ... not mmm suck ...

He riffled through some notes.

... leaches mmm leaches poison ....

"Leeches?" said Sheila making a sucking face.

"Well, Mother," said Forde in a stage Yorkshire accent, "exfoliation they may call it but I've always said you've a long way to go to beat an old-fashioned scourging."

"And what would *you* know, you old stick-in-the-mud!"

And this got them launched into riffs on soviets spas, gleaming white resorts from the outside but inside crumbling Gormenghasts with lavatory-tiled rooms staffed by smelly crones and doctors with steel teeth. The Beria Room full of people wrapped in wet sheets and stacked. Skink-Extract Treatment in the Molotov Maceration Room. The Gherkin Diet. The Dry Cupping Room. Korean massage administered by Oddjob aided by his sinister henchman Blowjob. In the Malenkov Room, borscht enemas performed by Enigma Machines. On Thank God It's Fridays, the Siberian Plotz executed turn and turn about by the Smersh Sisters, three ex-KGB houris.

This giddiness possessed them until they reached Dagomys and the bus bumped over the gravel parking area and stopped parallel to rows of small green bushes.

"According to the daily bulletin," said Forde, "there's a lecture in Russian about tea, though excitingly with simultaneous translation into English, followed, the schedule promises, by tea grown *on this very plantation*. During the serving of which we will be further titillated by folkloric entertainment."

"Now don't start being difficult."

"Remember the wisdom," said Forde, "of Sir Arnold Bax."

"Who he?"

"A well-known composer I've never heard *but*, but smart enough to have said, 'you should make a point of trying every experience once, excepting incest and folk-dancing.'"

Alan was studying the writing on the back of the bus.

"Hey!" he said. "This bus is from Korea. *This is a Korean bus.*"

"Get a picture," said Martin.

Sheila was helping, along the aisle of the bus, the woman with the walker.

Forde returned to the bus' front steps and helped down the old lady with the make-up.

"*Dangerously* steep!" he said.

The make-up was so elaborate, so excessive, that the word "make-up" seemed inadequate to convey …

Maquillage, perhaps.

"What a lovely—would one call it a choker?"

She smiled.

"Victorian, isn't it?"

"Clever boy," she said.

"And not jet," said Forde. "Rather too matte for that."

She was watching his face.

"It wouldn't possibly be … coal, would it?"

"*Very* clever boy," she said. "How did you know that?"

"I've seen pieces in museums and at auctions."

"I *love* auctions," she said. "My name's Bronwyn."

"They still do it, you know," he said. "I've seen modern pieces for sale from a barrow on the seafront at Whitby in Yorkshire. Not with *that* refinement, of course. Robert Forde," he added, "though people usually just call me Forde. I don't really know why."

She took his arm.

"Nice sleepy auctions in country towns—*such* a pleasure," she said. "Like boxes of chocolates. Magical boxes, always full and waiting to be opened. I lead a lovely, selfish life going to antique shops and auctions, buying little things of beauty for myself. I *adore* Jermyn Street, don't you? Perfume from *Floris*. The Burlington Arcade for antique jewellery. *Paxton and Whitfield* for those special water biscuits. And then the bliss of afternoon tea at *Fortnum*. Of course," she went on, "I wasn't brought up here entirely..."

"Here?"

"England, I mean. Which rather explains it all. No. I spent my early years in Sarawak. My parents were missionaries, you see."

"Anglican?"

She batted her ancient lashes.

"Do I have a Baptist *look*?"

Forde smiled.

"And then I was shipped off to boarding school in England. Nine at the time. Plenty of love for the dusky indigenes but precious little for me. Anyway, that was the way I felt as a girl. Poor Bronwyn, less loved than a Dyak. So I've always comforted myself ever since with *objets d'art* and positively ruinous *delectabilia* and ..."

"Wait for us!" called Sheila.

"... and remain," continued Bronwyn, "with lingering hostility towards Dyaks."

They paused outside the listing wooden swayback shed, which served as a lavatory. Sheila joined the line. Seconds after entering she shot out again.

"Christ!" she said.

"It's easy to see," said Bronwyn, "*you've* never been to China."

The four of them made their way along the uneven path through the woods towards the shed where the lecture and tea-drinking and folkloric entertainment were to take place.

"No," said Forde at the door, after glancing inside, "I'll go for a stroll in the woods. At least they're not wearing clogs."

"Clogs?"

"Mmm."

"Why should they be? They're not Dutch."

"No, but the hulking bulk of them, and the jolliness and headscarves, and *accordions*. I don't know. Perhaps I was thinking of Lancashire."

It was warm, cloudless, the slow-wheeling shapes of hawks sliding down the sky. The rows of tea bushes were planted on hillsides that looked as though the trees had been bulldozed into wreckage. The soil was black and acidic. Rank bracken had grown back in between the rows.

A flicker of movement on the fringe of dappling oak leaves caught Forde's eye. Familiar brown wings laced by demarcating black lines and dots. Two fritillaries. He was excited and intensely pleased.

When he had first seen Monarch butterflies on coming to Canada he had been reminded of fritillaries, the colouration, the black lines of demarcation like niello jewellery, but Monarchs had seemed burly and muscle-bound in comparison, NCOs of the butterfly world, while fritillaries were officers and aristocrats, the browns and ochres, umbers, burnt siennas of their wings like exquisite marquetry.

He used to wander in the New Forest when he was a child catching butterflies and hunting for grass snakes and adders. The boy he wandered with was four years older, and Forde had existed in a haze of love and hero-worship. The butterflies had been shaken from the net into a killing jar, glass and wide-mouthed with a large cork bung. Onto a pad of folded cotton at the bottom of the jar, a rag of an old shirt perhaps—not cotton wool as insect legs snagged in its wisps—he'd pour a few drops from a bottle of *Thawpit*, a commercial solvent used in dry cleaning and then freely available. It was only years later that he'd learned that *Thawpit* was actually carbon tetrachloride and considered to have near-fatal effects on the liver. He and David used to like the sweetness of its smell.

He could see them now, nosing the air for the faint smell of grass snakes, an unmistakable smell, musk and marsh. He could see the two of them now standing beside the silver glint of small streams, breathing open-mouthed so that their hearts would not pound in their ears and mask the faint slither of sound they were straining for, the pause as the head lifted and the black tongue flicked the air, then again the long whisper of sound resumed.

And into an old pillow case went adders, which they handled with dangerous familiarity. They carried an old tobacco tin containing a razor blade and purple crystals of potassium permanganate as first aid. They had sworn to each other that they'd cut a cross over the two fang marks and suck and spit and let blood flow and then force in the purple crystals. He'd had terrible dreams about the thought of cutting. Doing the cutting. He'd been—what? Twelve?

They'd sold the grass snakes and adders to the Ferndown Zoo for a shilling a foot, money that kept them in cigarettes. They'd smoked a brand called *Park Drive*.

Even then, nearly sixty years ago, fritillaries were seldom seen, very local in their distribution. He'd known only three rides in the New Forest near Ringwood, where they might reliably have been found. On St. Catherine's Hill outside Christchurch he remembered catching a Smooth snake, a species considered locally extinct. Remembered the wonder of it, David's jealousy.

He'd read just a couple of years ago a doom-laden list in the *Daily Telegraph* of creatures now extinct or nearing extinction, creatures common in his childhood, adders themselves, slow worms, cinnabar moths, Smooth snakes, green-throated sand lizards, palmated newts, fritillaries ...

But here in the sunlight, in all their remembered grace and beauty ...

There welled into his mind, along with that special Anglican smell of damp and dust and stone, a line from the psalms.

We bring our years to an end, as it were a tale that is told.

He stood staring, transported.

*

"Sir Charles," said Bronwyn, taking his arm again, "was a nasty old man. Very fierce and rude."

"But to think," said Forde, "that you ... I mean The White Rajah of Sarawak! It seems somehow ..."

"He didn't die until quite recently, you know—well, the sixties I think it was. In Cheltenham. Or Cirencester." She waved a dismissive hand. "He had a horrible glass eye he got from a taxidermist to cover a socket. Hunting fall. Eye on a twig. He got an assortment of eyes—rabbits, sheep, deer, and so forth and he used to wear different ones everyday. But yes, he was there—in Sarawak, I mean—well, until the Japanese soldiers came."

"And when you were a child, you remember..."

"Oh, but it was the Ranee all the stories were about! Sylvia, her name was. Oh, she *was* a baggage! Of course, I never saw any of the goings-on but all the children heard the stories from the servants and the agency men and *their* servants... Not that she was in Sarawak all that often. She much preferred Paris and London. 'Frivolous' was the word my father used—such a *weight* of disapproval. She was Lord

Esher's daughter, you know. Sylvia Brett, she used to be. And a merry dance she led him, by all accounts. Do people use the word 'trollop' nowadays?"

Through the trees the buses in the parking lot came into sight.

"It was the drink," said Bronwyn. "Gin for breakfast rarely ends well. She was a living scandal. She even made the Dyaks nervous, and some of *those* johnnies weren't exactly straitlaced."

"Shrunken heads and such?"

She waved her free hand dismissively again.

"Nasty, smelly things," she said.

She paused to pat his arm.

"She refused, just *refused* to leave the table, and stayed on after dinner for port or brandy. Smoked the cigars and drank the brandy. Utterly foxed. And by then she'd be quite *raucous*. Not, apparently, that the esteemed Sir Charles Vyner Brooke appeared to care! He'd be as fuddled as she was and fumbling in some creature's placket."

Forde tutted.

"Too sordid, my dear," said Bronwyn.

She shook her head.

"It is *said*," said Bronwyn, "it is *said*, that after dinner the men repaired to the billiard room and she used to hoist up her skirt and clamber up onto the table ... I'm not embarrassing you am I, dear?"

"No, no. Fascinating."

"And work herself against a corner pocket and open her legs wide ... and shout ... you're sure I'm not ..."

"Please."

"By this time, of course, she'd be hectic with drink."

"And shout what?" he said.

"And she used to shout ..."

Bronwyn paused and drew herself up.

"Come on, boys!" she cried. "Pot the red!"

*

The pork medallions, please.

Sir?

Blanquette de veau.

"Well, as I was saying, the pottery finds from any given site will be divided into *groups*, do you see, on the basis of different *fabrics*. Now what does *fabrics* mean? Well, pottery fabrics depend on the degree to which the clay was worked before the vessel was formed and the kind of temper that was used.

Certainly, Madam. Gazeuse or still?

Oh, um, fizzy.

Temper? The material used to reinforce and strengthen the clay. Clay is tempered—mixed with, do you see, shell, sand, straw, and ground-up, previously fired pottery—shards—which substance is referred to as *grog*. Haven't the faintest idea *why*.

Anyway, the archaeologists would define the groups, do you see, as handmade or wheel-made wares. As fine, medium, or coarse wares. As wares poorly fired or well-fired. And as wares tempered with ..."

"Dear frantic God! DO SHUT UP, ROGER, and have another drink."

*

The Alupka Palace was designed, read Sheila, *by the Scottish architects Edward Blore and Henry Hunt and was built for Prince Michael Vorontsov between 1828 and 1846*... "Are you listening?"

"No," said Forde, "I'm watching this snail."

He thought the Palace vulgar and ridiculous, a potpourri of clashing styles, less a house than a folly. Sheila went into the Palace to see the bedroom where Sir Winston Churchill slept during the 1945 Yalta Conference; he wandered further into the gardens. They funnelled out to the drive, which led down to what was now a parking lot at the entrance to the estate. The Palace had been set into a ledge cut in the mountainside. The drive up to it was walled on both sides. On the mountain side of the drive was a retaining wall well above head height. The other wall was lower, providing a waist-high barrier against the mountain's fall to the sea, where the sun sparked on water and Raoul Dufy sails stood white on blue.

The mountain was thinly wooded and he noticed an ochre scar carving down through the trees, a shallow gully of erosion. He probably wouldn't have seen them if not for the movement. They seemed to blend into the tumbled stone. A file of dogs.

The leading dog was tall and wiry-haired, greyish with something about it of an Irish wolfhound. The dogs following were mongrels, brown mostly, here and there a flash of white. Where the gully widened into grass and weeds, the dogs stopped and looked about. Then they sank almost out of sight as they worked forward to the coping on the top of the wall. Then nothing.

They gave a strong impression of tenseness, wariness. Forde waited until no one was near and gave a sharp whistle. A greyish ear flicked above the grass.

"What are you doing?" said Sheila. "Watching snails?"

He sensed covert movement along the coping and out of the corner of his eye caught the grey dog appearing at the foot of a flight of steps some twenty yards away. The dog sat. It waited until the drive was clear then led the pack across the drive into deep shadow on the seawall side. They trotted down towards the car park seeming almost to flow.

As Forde and Sheila approached the buses, they saw the last two dogs, back legs splayed, squirming and scrunching themselves under the edge of their bus.

"Why are they getting under there?"

He shrugged.

"What if they get run over?"

"I expect they've done it before."

Sheila bent and banged the side of the bus with her umbrella handle.

A ferocious snarl ripped back.

"Perhaps," said Forde, "he's taken up a *querencia*."

"A what?"

"It's when a bull decides…"

"I'm not having Hemingway," she said, "before lunch."

She reversed her umbrella again.

"If something of that size has taken a fancy to the underneath of the bus, I personally would be somewhat circumspect about challenging it."

"I'm *not* challenging him. I just don't want him to…"

"It's not important whether you're challenging him or not," said Forde. "It's what he *thinks* you're doing."

"This is a ridiculous conversation," said Sheila.

"And especially," added Forde, "if you are armed only with a collapsible umbrella."

"WHY," said Woolly Bear, "IS THAT WOMAN HITTING THE BUS?"

"Snails!" said Sheila.

On the bus once again and driving along the coast road, Forde started reading the daily bulletin. "We're promised 'unique Crimean wines,'" he said. "Followed by lunch on the Naberezhnaya Lenina featuring 'wholesome Ukrainian cuisine.' Want to take bets?"

In the yard surrounding the winery building stood rusting, industrial-looking container tanks. The building itself was surrounded by straggling lilac bushes, under one of which lay two unconscious drunks.

Each visitor was given a tray holding twelve numbered glasses of wine, glasses about twice the size of a shot glass, the glass itself thick. A man in a suit expatiated at great volume through a sort of loud-hailer contraption on the qualities peculiar to each wine. They were all utterly undrinkable, each vilely sweeter than the last.

Forde pushed his tray away and shook his head at Sheila.

Tilting his head back, Father Keogh swilled each glass. Then his head came down again, his tongue searching into the glass, filling it, magnified, raw.

With a small movement of his head and a glance, Forde directed Sheila's attention to the sight of the fat tongue pushing in.

*

"You know," said Forde when they were yet again on the bus and waiting for lavatory-stragglers and wine-purchasers," I think the only wine I can remember being as foul as those came from Bulgaria. It was called *Boyar's Domain*. Unforgettable."

...thirteen, fourteen, fifteen... counted the guide.

"Poor man," said Sheila. "He's so anxious."

Lunch was leisurely and awful.

Everyone was given an entire fish. Grey mullet, said the guide.

They seemed to be deep-fried.

Father Keogh spent the entire lunchtime drinking a brown liquid and gazing with obsessive intensity into Mrs. Cleary's cleavage.

*

The Romanov Apartments in Livadia Palace left them both feeling sad. The walls were hung with framed snapshots of Nicholas II, Tsar of All the Russias, the Tsarina Alexandra, the Grand Duchesses Olga, Tatiana, Maria, and Anastasia and Tsarevich Alexei.

The girls in summer white and wide, flowered hats.

On country walks.

Picking wild flowers.

Sitting at elaborate picnics in the woods, white linen tablecloths.

Paddling at the seaside.

Alexei on his tricycle.

Lessons on the terrace with their tutor.

Anastasia, feet swinging under the piano bench, doggedly working on her baggy knitting.

All murdered on the night of July 16, 1918 in Ekaterinburg in "The House of Special Purpose." And, over the years, to be followed by millions more.

Forde felt both moved and oppressed by the family snapshots, and leaving Sheila reading plaques and notices, wandered out into the gardens hoping the sunshine would lift his spirits.

"Schwibzik," they'd all called Anastasia—*"Little One."*

*

The guide was approaching along the bus' aisle.

... sixteen, seventeen, eighteen, nineteen...

Forde drew breath sharply as Father Keogh's knees, one after the other, slammed into the back of his seat.

"I could definitely use what Baden Powell would call a *chota* peg," said Forde. "No, no, I mean a BURRA peg."

"Well," said Sheila, "you've been looking forward to Chekhov's house all week."

"What's so special about this Chekhov fellah?"

Forde turned towards the voice and saw an eye and nose and part of the mouth of Father Keogh, who seemed to be bent double as he peered up through the armrest gap between the seats.

"I said what's so special."

"Well a lot of people consider him the world's greatest short-story writer."

"And you're one of those, are you?"

"Mmm-mmm, yes."

"I've not encountered him," said Father Keogh.

"Not had the pleasure of his acquaintance," said The Minder's voice.

"And, of course, he's also a great playwright."

"Plays, is it?"

"Yes, like *The Three Sisters* and *The Cherry Orchard*."

The partial face disappeared.

Forde raised an eyebrow at Sheila.

A knee slammed into his right kidney.

"And what is it about? This *Cherry Orchard*?"

"Well, it's about upper-class life in pre-revolutionary Russia and..."

"Upper class, is it."

To the armrest gap Forde said, "But it's more about class paralysis and stagnation. It gives a sense..."

"Sense, is it?"

Again a knee.

Forde rolled his eyes at Sheila.

"How do you do, Mr. Chekhov?" said Father Keogh.

"Well, well, I thank you, Father," said the minder. "In the pink."

"And how is your cherry orchard?"

"Laden, Father, absolutely. Yes, it is," said The Minder. "The branches all bent and weeping with fruit."

The partial face reappeared.

"'And the land shall yield her fruit, and ye shall eat your fill, and dwell therein in safety.'"

"Will you *please* stop banging your knees into my seat!"

"And a blessing it is," said The Minder. "A blessing it is."

*

Chekhov had lived in the White Dacha with his mother, Eugenia, and his sister, Maria, called Masha, and his wife, the actress Olga Knipper. Chekhov had lesions on both lungs and coughed out his life in these rooms while summoning the heroic energy to write the three great final plays.

For years he had suffered from colitis, diarrhoea, and haemorrhoids. For the haemorrhaging from his lungs he took creosote, which destroyed his stomach. To stave off pleurisy he endured compresses of cantharides. To sleep he drank chloral hydrate. As the pain and weakness bit in, he was given injections of camphor, arsenic, morphine, opium, and heroin. As his heart deteriorated, he was treated with digitalis. And through all this horror, he wrote.

But to Forde's disappointment the house gave up nothing of this. It remained resolutely ordinary. The feel was very Victorian and respectable, much more Masha than Anton. Chairs covered in loose slipcovers, every table covered with fringed tablecloths, along the top of the piano, with its brass swing-out candle brackets, a long runner crotcheted like a doily. Pelmets and flouncy valances. Massy, unattractive furniture. Iron bedsteads. Heavily framed photographs.

Forde prowled the house on his own, photographing the rooms hoping for some emanation of the spirit who'd written *Uncle Vanya*, who'd delighted in catching crayfish and picking mushrooms and wild berries, who'd loved a pet mongoose called Sod, which roamed the house at night extracting corks from bottles.

Each room was closed off to visitors by a furry rope across the open doorway. Taking pictures was difficult because of the ropes and because of the reflections off the glass framing the photographs on the walls. Forde leaned into the sitting room trying to take a photograph of a portrait of Chekhov, which stood on top of the piano. The glare of the glass was defeating him. He leaned in further over the rope. There was some sort of bustle and to-do in the hall behind him, shuffling, a sudden uprush of conversation, someone calling out. He glanced round and saw the museum guide rounding up stragglers and ushering people towards the front door.

"We must go now," he called back, "and the door be locked."

"Forde!" called Sheila.

"Coming!" he called back, his eye still at the viewfinder.

He turned to see Sheila alone in the hall. She was laughing.

The guide took Forde by the arm.

"Sorry," said Forde.

"You must be quick!" said the guide.

Unhooked the furry rope, which blocked entrance to Chekhov's study. Gestured Forde in.

"Get in front of the couch," said Sheila unzipping her camera.

Forde stood just to one side of the Isaak Levitan painting of the Istra River.

"Hurry!" said the guide. "Hurry, hurry."

The guide was shifting his agitated weight from foot to foot.

Took Forde's arm again, snapped the furry rope into place, hurried them to the front door and out into the small forecourt where the bus people were milling about.

"Well!" Forde said to Sheila. "What in hell was *that* all about!"

"I told him you were also a writer and how much it would mean to you."

"Good God!" said Forde.

"Very un-British, I know," said Sheila.

"Oh, that was so kind of you, Sheila, really… *And* of him. I mean just to up and chuck everyone out."

"And after I told him how much it would mean to you," said Sheila, "I gave him a bribe."

*

As they waited in a little crowd for the steward to show them to tables, Roger was patiently explaining to his wife and another couple that Bronze Age palaces were bureaucratic centres of economic redistribution, that clay tablets, both cuneiform and Cretan Linear B, were essentially *bookkeeping*, lists of stocks, of oil, wine, arrows, slaves, spokes of wagon wheels, shields, sheep…

"Roger…." said his wife

Forde watched the girls circulating with the wine bottles.

There was something *about* girls wearing ties.

Bronwyn was sitting in solitary and bedizened state at a table for two. Forde smiled at her and gave a mock bow as they walked past. Their waiter presented them with the evening's menu.

Forde looked up from reading it to see Father Keogh approaching with The Minder. His hand and arm rested on The Minder's arm as if he were a woman being escorted at some formal function. His face was rubicund and sweaty. As they passed Bronwyn's table, he pulled free of The Minder and veered towards her almost with a lurch, seeming then to crouch over her tiny figure. Forde could see only his back.

Bronwyn's voice rang out.

"How dare you! How *dare* you!"

Father Keogh straightened up and turned.

"The inhabitants of the earth," he pronounced in prophetic condemnation, *"have been made drunk with the wine of her fornication."*

"Sot!"

Her voice followed after him through the generally subsiding conversation and rising tension.

"Hibernian *sot*!"

His face puce with drink and fury, Father Keogh passed their table, grinding out to The Minder, to the air, "'THE MOTHER OF HARLOTS.'"

He turned back and, arm outstretched, pointed at Bronwyn.

"'AND ABOMINATIONS OF THE EARTH.'"

"Oh, *dear*, oh, dear," said Forde. "*Revelation*. Always a bad sign."

*

Forde and Sheila climbed the Potemkin Steps towards the Primorskiy bulvar, described in the bulletin as Odessa's most graceful boulevard. They were free until ten a.m., when they were to meet at the Archeological Museum for a guided tour of the city. The influences were mainly classical, the buildings three-storey and based on the idea of the interior courtyard, the boulevards themselves tree-shaded. The town, they agreed, was rather like a miniature Paris or Madrid. They strolled to the end of Primorskiy bulvar and then all the way back again, past the Steps, to the Vorontsov Palace. Classical in style, still beautiful, but shabby now and run down, some doors and windows nailed up with sheets of plywood, and sadly still called Palace of the Pioneers.

The Pioneers was a Party organization with compulsory membership to indoctrinate elementary school children in communist thought. Upon completing the curriculum of the Pioneers, the children moved into the organization for teenagers, the Komsomol, before graduating into the full-blown embrace of Soviet life.

"Oh, fortunate Prince Vorontsov," said Forde, "that he died in—what was it?—1854."

Forde had had no great expectations of the Archeological Museum and was pleasantly surprised by the Black Sea Greek finds, some vessel-shapes he'd never seen before. He suddenly wished he had hours to spend. But the highlight turned out to be the Gold Room, coins and jewellery of Black Sea civilizations. And the highlight of all for Forde was a hoard of Scythian silver tetradrachmas.

There must have been about fifty of them spilling out of a broken pot of greyish ware. The heaping coins and the smashed pot were dramatically displayed on rumpled black velvet. The coins were slightly smaller than quarters, but thicker. They were displayed, for some odd reason, just above floor level. Forde knelt the better to see them.

He was gripped by the iconography, fascinated by the way the style had perfected itself. The images were various,

Zeus with an upright sceptre, Poseidon, Pallas, a bull, a lone elephant, Nike, a caduceus, but more common than any other image a horseman with a spear.

"Sheila!" he called. "Come and see how *alive* these horses are."

*

In the precinct of the Ilinsky Cathedral, Alan and Martin pounced on two stalls, rough tables draped with old bits of carpet, the one displaying icons, the other naval memorabilia of the Russian Black Sea Fleet, badges, medals, epaulettes, oddments of uniform.

They bought an icon each, the wood distressed and pitted with precision worm-holes, but were even more overjoyed by the Russian high-peaked officers' caps, the badges worked in gold wire against an oval ground of white felt. They rummaged through the caps until they found snug fits and then fussed around each other tugging and tilting. Martin also bought epaulettes to sew onto his bomber jacket. They begged tour members to take their photos on the cathedral steps.

Alan saluted.

Flash

They mugged.

Flash

Linked arms.

Soyuz Sovetskikh, intoned Martin, *Sotsialistichesskikh Respublik.*

He turned his head to one side, and with a rigid forefinger at the cap's rear edge, tipped it rakishly forward over one eye.

Flash

Forde feared that they might, in tandem, clack into slick dance steps.

*

Outside the Ilinsky Cathedral the lady guide brandished her purple umbrella and cried, "Towards the bus!"

Their destination was the Monument to the Unknown Sailor, a granite obelisk on the cliff edge overlooking Odessa's harbour and wharves. They watched the performance of the Honour Guard. The three boys in the front row carried assault rifles held across their chests, the three girls behind them marched with their arms rigidly at their sides. They were all in ceremonial sailor uniform, white belts with gold buckles, gold lanyards, white gloves. The girls in blue serge skirts. They marched down the ceremonial approach past the flanking red polished granite gravestones of resistance fighters killed in World War II, and took up positions of respect at the monument's cardinal points.

The guide said the ceremony was repeated every hour throughout the day, the cadets drawn in rotation from Odessa's high schools. The goose-step marching was obviously inherited from the Russians. Forde was rather chilled by it, having seen it displayed by the Nazis, the Soviets, Il Duce's Fascists, by the dementedly vigorous North Koreans, and by Hezbollah parading through Beirut. The very youth and attractiveness of the cadets added to his discomposure. Such marching, he thought, proclaimed the suppression of the individual and implied what Yeats had meant by "the blood-dimmed tide."

They made halting conversation with the cadets, the girls in white knee socks and improbable, strapped high heels. Was this, Forde wondered, sanctioned formal attire in the Ukraine? Or were the girls naughty and illicitly changed into such shoes after leaving the house? The girls were so pretty in the morning sun but probably doomed, thought Forde in a sudden descent of gloom, to grow to great bulk and play the accordion.

People dawdled back towards the bus, reminding Forde of a herd of heifers on a country road.

Then the driver switched on the engine, the Baden Powell man shouting about having the radio turned off… *eleven, twelve, thirteen…* the Honour Guard marching *stomp, stomp, stomp* back up the avenue and an old man stood suddenly to photograph them through the window and dropped with a cry, felled into his seat by the overhead storage rack.

"And now," cried the amplified guide lady, "away we go to the Lenin Monument!"

*

"I thought you *liked* churches."

"I tire," said Forde, "of the odour of sanctity."

Sheila glanced at him.

"Watch it, Forde," she said.

The church sat across the top end of the long rectangular park, which sloped downhill to the immense, black Lenin Monument brooding over the harbour. He sat on a bench waiting for her and enjoying the sun on his face. He watched a toddler gathering leaves and filling her push-chair with them, enjoyed the scent of late-blooming roses in the flower beds behind him. Sheila waving to him.

"Let's see the Monument," she said.

"I'm not going to look at bad Soviet art. It only encourages them," said Forde. "And I particularly don't want to look at a statue of *that* venomous bastard! You go. I'll wait for you here."

He watched her as she traipsed off to look at the statue and doubtless to read whatever plaques and notices were on offer. Her dedication to plaques and notices had mildly irritated him all their married life. He sometimes suspected that she preferred reading maps to looking at the landscape they represented. Similarly with attributions in art galleries. He, on the other hand, always wanted urgent, unmediated contact with things. If they appealed, he always told her, he'd find out more.

As she trudged back up the hill, he got up and advanced upon her with both arms out in front of him, his hands clenched into fists.

"What? What?"

He grinned at her.

She backed away from him.

"What is it?"

"Come here."

"Is it alive? Is it something alive?"

"Fresh-firecoal chestnut falls."

"What!"

"Look!"

He turned each fist over and opened his fingers.

Glowing on his palms.

"Conkers!"

*

Stained concrete. Shabby storefronts stuffed with shoddy goods side by side with stores selling international brand names. SONY, NIKON, PANASONIC, TOSHIBA. Abandoned lots strewn with rubble and refuse. Decaying buildings. Broken bottle-glass. Doorways reeking of piss. A used-up place, an old rind, all the juice squeezed out of it. And a miasma over all of a scarcely ousted bureaucracy.

Romania's principal seaport, Constanza, depressed them. According to the daily bulletin, the city had been founded in the seventh century B.C. by Greek colonists from Miletus in Asia Minor. It had then been known as Tomis. In the first century B.C. the Romans annexed the region and in the fourth century A.D. Constantine the Great reconstructed Tomis and renamed it Constantiana.

Tapping the bulletin, Forde said, "Ovid was exiled here in 9 A.D." He waved his arm in an encompassing gesture. "Look at it! Look at this bloody place. *Ovid!*"

They looked down onto the mosaic floor, which was protected from the weather by an open-sided, tin-roofed shed. The mosaic was dirty and the colours dull. Bits were missing, the patches filled with raw concrete.

"What's it depicting?" said Forde.

"Well, flowers," said Sheila. "And there's a bird. Oh, and a wine jar. And isn't that a Double Axe?"

"Yes, it's a *labrys* all right but *why?* What *was* this place?"

She shrugged.

"It's not gripping, is it?" said Forde.

Lunch was served in an echoing cafeteria. Forde ordered *scrumbie la gratar* which turned out to be a herring. Sheila was less happy with *mititei*, which when they arrived, were small, skinless sausages. With coffee Forde drank a couple of shots of a drink called *tuica* that someone at their table had recommended. It was a potent plum brandy and it cheered him up. They were then shepherded onto buses for the hour's drive to the ruins of Histria, Romania's oldest city, also founded by colonists from Miletus in the seventh century B.C.

Forde watched the passing countryside. It was as sad and bleak as the city. His *tuica*-induced cheer ebbed. Single fields stretched seemingly for miles with no trees or hedges in sight. Tractors ploughed six abreast. He began to brood about the destruction wreaked upon these people. The farms and smallholdings must have been collectivized during the Soviet period after 1945. It saddened him to think of homesteads destroyed, families forced out, trees felled, footpaths ploughed up, hedges grubbed out, memories obliterated, history erased. Mile after mile of meaninglessness.

The two villages they passed through were in vibrant contrast to this agricultural Passchendaele. They were squalid, ramshackle, two- or three-room houses patched with corrugated tin, beaten-earth yards with hens, ducks, and geese pecking over the garbage, fly-twitched donkeys and ponies tethered to fruit trees. In the gardens, cabbages and beans and grapes. In some stood stooks of cut rushes drying for bedding.

Pony-drawn carts with motor-tire wheels bowled along, stacked perilously with reeds and rushes. The grimy men driving them and lying across the reeds to steady the loads looked villainous. Children in gardens waved at the bus. A woman in a drab brown apron stared from a kitchen doorway.

"It's a bit Fiddler-on-the-Roofy, isn't it?" said Sheila.

"But muckier," said Forde.

The sky was darkening as they neared Histria, and by the time the buses bumped up onto the museum's parking lot of broken brick mixed with asphalt the sky had become electric with gloom and tinged with yellow and unearthly green, the sort of sky that Forde always thought of as Old Testament sky.

Histria was set at the edge of a vast reed-fringed swamp. The museum was a glass box set on a raised, concrete platform. Mosquitoes whined. No rain had yet fallen. All was unnaturally still. On a tussock of reeds rising above the water some fifty yards out stood a large bird startlingly white in the weird light, a crane perhaps, or an ibis.

The museum was intensely boring. The contents, mainly red Roman-ware, had nearly all been broken, and the missing shards had been reconstituted in white plaster. The two big rooms, at a glance, were a leprosy of red and white. No effort at aesthetics or even selection had been attempted; if it had been uncovered at the site, in it had gone, the rumbled rubble of Greece, Rome, and Byzantium. Shapeless, rusted lumps of iron were identified as "anchors"; the profusion of broken pots was labelled variously as "storage vessels," "wine vessels," "conical vessels," and "vessels with spouts"; a row of pieces of corroded bronze was labelled "mirrors"; scraps and unidentifiable fragments were identified as "decorative elements."

Forde stood in front of a glass case that contained a curved piece of metal.

The card read: "Strigil" [?]

Here and there the accumulated clutter was adorned by a stele, but the inscriptions were so weathered as to leave legible only a few words, such as *est* and *hic*.

The custodian or curator or whatever he was wore a black suit and, curiously, over it, a long black cotton apron.

The books were stacked on a table near the front door. The three main periods of the site were recorded in three massive and profusely illustrated hardcover tomes, which gave off a strong whiff of State Publishing. They had been compiled in the 1920s. The authors all wore pince-nez spectacles and wing collars with loosely knotted silk ties. The books cost twenty-five new *leys* each. This seemed to work out at an impossibly cheap eleven dollars or so.

He groaned as he waited for Sheila to stop inspecting a broken amphora.

Outside the museum, a muddy path led to the site itself through a remaining arch in a tumbling brick wall. It had started to drizzle. Feral dogs scoured the parking lot for crumbs. The path ended. The baulk of turf Forde was negotiating crumbled and his right foot slipped deep into the cold mire. A mosquito *zizzizzed* in his ear.

"I hate this place."

"Oh, stop being childish."

"My foot's wet."

"Oh, look, these must have been houses."

He looked at the jumble of low walls, footprints of buildings. Nothing was recognizably anything. Some of the walls were stone, some brick. Some bits of wall contained pantile so were probably Byzantine.

He slapped at mosquitoes.

Stared down what might have been a street.

Inside the stone squares grew sedge and wind-stunted bushes.

In one such square and behind one such bush, stood the Bishop of Bodmin and Exeter. He was standing completely still and staring out over the swamp. Forde regarded his silly hat with its cockade of nylon feathers.

"What *is* he doing?"

"Having a pee," said Sheila.

Although he was perfectly aware that the salutation was reserved solely for *archbishops*, Forde called out "Good afternoon, Your Grace," which caused a gratifying galvanization of the Bishop culminating in his raised Tilley.

The drizzle turned to a steadier rain.

"And what was this big place over here?" called Sheila.

"Fuck!" said Forde.

"What?"

"Blood!"

"Oh!" she called. "Here's a plaque!"

"I'm going back to the bus!"

"But we haven't seen everything."

"I don't wish to discommode you," said Forde, "but I am swelling rapidly."

"So *this,*" she said, pointing to an expanse of ruin and sodden debris, "was the apse but the dome fell in. *So,*" she said, glancing down at the diagram, "over *here,* this must be..."

"I don't care," called Forde, "if it's the collapsed apse of a fucking Byzantine *whorehouse!* It is raining. My foot is wet. I am getting bitten to death. My body is covered in infected Romanian lumps."

He glared at her back as she bent again over the plaque and diagram.

"Goodbye!"

He negotiated the slippery baulks of mud and turf and regained the pathway to the museum beyond the arch.

Alan and Martin were standing on the top step of the entrance to the museum, a step which extended into a terrace. Behind them the yellow-lit expanse of the museum's first room. They were singing. They were wearing their officers' dress caps of the Russian Black Sea Fleet and holding hands. They were singing to the parking lot as to an audience in a night club. With their free hands they were making corny gestures of desire and longing. They were utterly absorbed.

You are the promised kiss of springtime
That makes the lonely winter seem long.
You are the breathless hush of evening

That trembles on the brink of a lovely song.
You are the angel glow that lights a star,
The dearest things I know are what you are.

The custodian in his long black apron appeared at the front door and stooped over a deformed puppy, which kept trying to get inside. Its belly was swollen huge and one eye was much larger than the other and bulged out from its face, reminding Forde of those grotesquely overbred goldfish, goggle-eyed and trailing white fungus-like growths roundthe sockets. The custodian kept making scooping-water gestures with his cupped hands and shouting what sounded like "Marsh! Marsh! and every time he shouted the puppy whiddled on the step.

Entirely oblivious, Alan and Martin sang on

Some day my happy arms will hold you,
And some day I'll know that moment divine,
When all the things you are, are mine!

Back on the bus and in the seat they'd sat in before, Forde dried his glasses on a paper napkin he'd saved from lunch. Some of the stragglers appearing through the gloom had umbrellas, others wore transparent plastic hoods. Mosquitoes whined on the windows. The crinkle of cellophane, somebody opening a packet. The smell of damp clothes.

Forde watched the feral dogs lying on the asphalt and crusted rubble chawing, chawing at the dulled fur of their flea-bitten flanks and haunches. One showed patches of raw skin the size of saucers and the colour of ham. A female was lying on her side with what could have been the right hind leg broken. There was blood on it and its angle odd. Whenever she tried to get up her two half-grown pups pounced in, biting the dragging leg and toppling her. When she snarled at them, one in particular chop-chopped her mask, his lips drawn back in a way that seemed to Forde not at all like play.

The bus swayed again as Father Keogh and The Minder climbed aboard. They made their way down the aisle and sat in the seats in front of him.

"And your hat, now. Have you lost your hat? Left it somewhere. Did you have it in the museum? Or did you lose it in that horrible old bog? Fall, did you? Slipped and fell. Wandering off like that while I was in the water closet. And these stains on your good jacket. Mud from that bog. That's what it'll be. On your lapel, look. And your shoulder. Tweed's a lovely cloth, so it is. A lovely cloth."

Father Keogh sat in remote silence, staring straight ahead.

The Minder stood and took a plastic bottle of water from his little backpack in the overhead rack. He wet his handkerchief and sat again to dab at the stains.

"Is it mud? Mud, is it?"

Through the gap between the seats, Forde saw The Minder looking at the stains on his handkerchief.

Saw The Minder looking at his fingertips.

Smelling them.

Heard his half-whisper …

… *Holy Mother…*

A breathy exhalation.

Heard the little gluggings as he dribbled more water onto his handkerchief.

"It *is* mud, Father."

Coming into view again as he leaned across the gap to dab.

"On the lovely tweed."

The bus swayed again as Sheila climbed up. She plumped down beside Forde and said, "How are your bites?"

He gave her a cold glance.

"You smell," he said, "like a cloakroom."

"Air conditioning ON!" shouted Baden Powell.

...eighteen, nineteen, twenty...

"Not *another* museum," said the man in the seat behind.

"It's mosaics," said his wife.

"I'd rather an early dinner."

"They're *Roman,*" said his wife.

"Oh!" he said. "Why didn't you say? Roman! Well, if I'd known they were *Roman...*"

"Now Harold!" she said.

... *nine, ten, eleven...* re-counted the guide.

The custodian had retreated into the museum and closed the door. The pack had materialized behind the puppy and sat watching the lighted windows.

In the middle of the bus, the guide was saying, "One is missing. We are missing a passenger. Does anyone recognize who it is?"

People craned about. Some stood.

"Where's Bronwyn?" a woman said. "Is it Bronwyn?"

"Which one is Bronwyn?"

"... with the make-up..."

"... from Borneo."

"... the lady in question," Baden Powell was saying to the guide,"will doubtless have got on one of the other buses—silly old trout."

The guide, now standing beside the driver, spread his hands in a gesture of resignation and helplessness.

"Jaldi!" roared Baden Powell. *"Jaldi jao!"*

The bus bumped across the parking lot and ground up onto the approach road. As it began to pick up speed and the museum receded, the custodian shrank smaller and smaller, a black speck within the lighted cube.

ACKNOWLEDGEMENTS

My thanks and gratitude to Dan Wells—*luftmensch*—who imagined Biblioasis into being and who labours in our mundane world building the New Jerusalem.

Thanks also to my copy editor, Emily Donaldson, for ruthlessly enforcing uniformity on my vagaries.

ABOUT THE AUTHOR

PHOTO: MYRNA METCALF

John Metcalf was Senior Editor at the Porcupine's Quill until 2005, and is now Fiction Editor at Biblioasis. A scintillating writer, a magisterial editor, and a noted anthologist, he is the author of more than a dozen works of fiction and non-fiction, including *Standing Stones: Selected Stories*, *Adult Entertainment*, *Going Down Slow* and *Kicking Against the Pricks*. He lives in Ottawa with his wife, Myrna.